Eternal Huntress

Shadows of Otherside Book 5

Whitney Hill

BENU MEDIA

ETERNAL HUNTRESS
Copyright © 2021 by Whitney Hill

Benu Media
6409 Fayetteville Rd
Ste 120 #155
Durham, NC 27713
(984) 244-0250
benumedia.com

To receive special offers, release updates, and bonus content, sign up for our newsletter: go.benumedia.com/newsletter

ISBN (ebook): 978-1-7376311-0-1
ISBN (pbook): 978-1-7344227-9-5

Library of Congress Control Number: 2021915698

Cover Designer: Pintado (99Designs)
Editor: Jeni Chappelle (Jeni Chappelle Editorial)

For those who care too much not to give their all, even if they really need to keep some back for themselves.

Chapter 1

It was almost a shame I couldn't let the gods end the world. Some days, I wished I could do it myself. At least then I might have a chance of making it down I-40 without some reckless maniac with Texas plates trying to run me off the road as they barreled into a merge. There'd be fewer accidents as well. I could remake the world and have 40 all to myself.

The good news for everyone was that I was only inclined to murder in self-defense. I'd only really enjoyed the two, and both had earned it ten times over. Maybe a hundred.

A girl's gotta do what a girl's gotta do.

I'd taken shit from all of Otherside for the first twenty-five years of my life, and I'd be damned if I took any at all for the rest of it, however long or short that might be given my enemies, the gods, and annoying fucks in oversize pickups with Truck Ballz swinging from the hitch.

"Arden," Troy muttered from the passenger seat.

"I see him."

My elven prince consort gritted his teeth and exhaled heavily.

Grinning, I took a hand off the wheel to lace my fingers between his as I gunned the engine of my zippy Honda Civic hatchback, changed lanes twice, swerved around a semi, and drifted back into the middle lane.

"Arden!"

I just laughed, enjoying the wind in my hair as I sped down the freeway even if it was snarling my curls. Troy was a control freak. Always had been. He reined it in with me—mostly—but I'd found that the road was guaranteed to get his temper up.

That always meant extra fun later.

We were on our way down to Raleigh for an audience with Maria. The months had slipped toward autumn, and we were in second summer, that gorgeous time of year when it was warm without being too hot, the humidity had come down, and breezes tickled both the trees and my control of Air. The leaves hadn't turned yet, though a few of the maple and redbud trees looked like they were thinking about it. There was a hint of cooler air in the mornings, tickling through the windows I kept at least cracked, if not wide open, year-round. My favorite time of year, although I had a feeling this year would be different. Less pleasant.

Remembering the imminent Wild Hunt sobered me a little, and I squeezed Troy's hand before taking it back and easing off the gas pedal.

"We have time," he said softly, knowing where my mind had gone.

"Do we? The fae are still playing games. There's been only vague, passive-aggressive bullshit from Asheville. Evangeline is still on the loose somewhere—"

"We have time," Troy repeated grimly, this time with half a flinch and equal parts smoldering anger and carefully banked fear.

I kicked myself for mentioning Evangeline. Troy's blood sister had joined with their grandmother in first disowning him, then torturing him nearly to death for daring to choose me and a blood debt to House Solari—my murdered father's House—over his birth House, queen, and family. He'd lost everything, considering it worth the price of doing the right thing.

I still hated reminding him of it.

"I'm fine." He shifted to loosen tightened muscles. "You don't have to tiptoe around it."

I shrugged uncomfortably and changed the subject anyway. "I hope Maria's actually found something this time."

A spark of amusement came to me through the Aetheric bond between Troy and me. "You know as well as I do she's been looking for an excuse to see you again."

"I know, but we have to find Iaret. I owe Duke." Finding my djinni guardian's long-lost love to fulfill a prophecy was taking all of my detective skills and requiring me to offer a few favors. Like trading my powerful blood to my vampire allies as a sweetener for access to their precious library. I could have just demanded it, but Maria had been an ally from the start, one of the few who'd never given me cause to question her. Pulling rank on her didn't feel right. "And the damn prophecy makes too much sense, given how Neith reacted to you and Duke working together to help me at Jordan Lake."

Besides, it was in my best interest, given that there'd already been one attack on the Raleigh coterie. I couldn't risk someone toppling Maria and kicking a leg off my power structure.

I glanced at Troy. "Gotta say, I'm always surprised you take the blood thing so well."

"I know where I stand." He sent a playful little sting of Aether my way. "And you know I'm always happy to remind you."

I swore as my hands tightened on the wheel in remembered ecstasy. Heat flushed over me as I realized I wasn't the only one thinking of having fun later.

"Damn elf," I muttered half-heartedly.

Given our history, Troy was the last person I'd thought I'd fall for, but here we were. Having someone put me first was a hell of a drug.

Troy just smirked. I'd resent the cockiness from anyone else, but he had yet to take me for granted or go behind my back to take advantage of the power he'd accumulated as my prince consort. He deferred to me completely in public, well aware of the impact it made for the continent's most powerful elven prince to submit to an elemental—the elves' ancestral scapegoat.

The smirk faded as a shadow weighed on Troy.

"What?" I asked.

"Darius is late coming back from his assignment. Neither Allegra nor I can reach him, and we're worried. Then there's the Captain." He grimaced at the spike of alarm he must have picked up from me at the mention of the latter.

Troy's mentor and adopted father led the Darkwatch. He was also the birth father of the captain of my Ebon Guard, Allegra, and her twin brother, Darius. The former Monteagues now helping me had heard from him exactly once since I'd declared the only elven House in the Triangle would be mine: House Solari.

Omar Monteague had sent a terse message saying, "You go your way. I'll go mine."

I tapped my fingers across the steering wheel. "He contacted you?"

"No. That's the problem. Omar should have made a move by now. His loyalty was always to the matriarchy. If he wasn't going to swear to Evangeline as the single remaining elven queen, he should have attacked or taken leadership of the East Coast Darkwatch to another Conclave."

"But he hasn't done anything at all." I frowned, irritated with the fact that I was still having to play elven games after literally pulling down Keithia Monteague's mansion and burning the pieces with elemental magic.

"He hasn't," Troy agreed. "We're in uncharted territory."

"Allegra hasn't—"

"No. She's not talking about it either. I almost wonder if that's the strategy."

"What, the Captain putting his own kids on edge until one of y'all makes the first move?"

"Exactly." He sighed. "You have to understand, Arden. The matriarchy has grown more extreme in the last few generations. Omar was more of a parent to me than to Alli because he wasn't *allowed* to be a father to her. My mother and my aunt were all we were permitted."

I wrinkled my nose. I'd grown up dreaming of what it would be like having a family. I was occasionally jealous of Troy's closeness with Allegra, the cousin he called sister—not because they had a relationship but because I'd always wondered what it would be like to have one like that myself. But on the rare occasions Troy talked about growing up a royal in House Monteague, I wondered if knowing your birth family was really all it was cracked up to be. Maybe my struggles to build my own little family—my alliance—were better. At least for me.

I sat with that as I exited at Wade Avenue, caught up in the usual traffic going into Raleigh.

Troy kept whatever further thoughts he had to himself, sinking into one of his moods. He still checked the mirrors though, making sure the black Acura MDX that was technically his but on loan to the Ebon Guard for the day was still behind us. Protecting me was always topmost in his mind. I was afraid it'd get him killed, but I couldn't make his choices for him.

When I pulled into the parking garage near Wilmington and Hargett, I made sure to park close to the stairs, with the driver's side door on that side. I'd learned the hard way that some of my enemies were totally willing to risk the wrong kind of attention from the mundanes if it meant taking me out—as had nearly happened in this very garage. It was why I'd reluctantly allowed Troy, Allegra, and Duke to talk me into having one of them plus at least two of the Ebon Guard with me whenever I left Durham. A compromise, really. According to everyone else, an Othersider with my political influence and the magical strength to have a power signature should have stayed laired up somewhere, executing my will via minions.

That wasn't how I did things, so bodyguards it was.

Troy was already on high alert, zeroing into the focused, distant mien that said he was a bodyguard first, everything else a distant second. He left orders for the other two guards to watch the car then preceded me down the stairs, keeping himself between me and the lines of sight from the buildings opposite. His eyes darted from window to rooftop to doorway, never still, even as he took deeper breaths to catch scents and Aether prickled over my skin as he sought aura signatures.

Before being kidnapped, I might have laughed. Or at least teased him a little. Now I was glad my boyfriend was a stubborn badass with a frighteningly strategic mind, especially given the ongoing pro-human, anti-Otherside protests. Those had escalated with the second Reveal of werewolves, elves, and witches a few months ago and had been blown into the Reveal Riots by the elven queens, with those queens now dead at my hands. I hated what I'd done on a moral level, but I couldn't let it stand. They'd put all of Otherside at risk in an attempt to put me in what they thought was my place. Getting rid of them had brought human-Otherside tensions back down to a roiling simmer, but all of us were still on edge, dreading the next clusterfuck.

Noah was waiting for us, lounging in the shadows outside the secret second entrance to the Raleigh coterie's nest. The attractive vampire had been born Black or biracial, and centuries of avoiding the sun had faded his skin to a golden brown. His tight curls were hidden under a black baseball cap, and he was dressed a little more casually than usual in dark-wash jeans and an orange silk dress shirt.

Cap or not, I was surprised to see Maria's second out in the open. Noah had done an interview with one of the braver local news teams as part of a public relations effort, and while it had garnered the vampires—and him in particular—quite a few fans, it had also given the anti-fang crowd a face for one of their enemies.

"Everything okay?" I asked.

He grinned at me, not showing his teeth but still in good humor. "I won't let a few death threats keep me in hiding, Ms. Finch. You know that."

I shook my head but couldn't hide my answering smile. Noah and I had that in common, and while the mercurial vampire wasn't always my biggest fan, we did have an understanding. Troy just sighed—quietly, but we were close enough with Maria and Noah that he let his iron control slip a little.

"How's Maria?" I asked as Noah led us downstairs and through a series of heavy, locked doors.

"Pouring too much into the negotiations with the human legislators, as usual." With a cautious glance at Troy, he added, "I'm glad you're here. She at least pretends to enjoy herself when you visit."

"Is there something I should know?" I asked. Maria was a big girl, and as Troy had once pointed out, she was several times our combined age. That didn't mean I couldn't worry about her as a friend.

Noah paused, toying with the key that unlocked the last door between us and the corridor leading to the throne room.

"Noah?" I prompted as Troy's attention sharpened.

"The world as she knew it is dead," the vampire said bluntly. "In every way. As modern as she is, she still thinks that the Modernist movement is extreme. But what if it's not? What if

7

negotiating with the humans for equal rights isn't the end of change for the *moroi*? She doesn't agree. But I need her to at least consider it."

My eyebrows were ready to fly off my face, and I exchanged a concerned look with Troy. For Maria's loyal-to-the-death second to speak this way, things were worse than I'd realized.

"I'll talk to her," I promised.

"I'd be grateful." Tension eased from Noah as he unlocked the last door. "She saved me from a truly horrific fate, Ms. Finch. She says she was just paying forward what Torsten did for her, but I would do anything to save her in turn. Even from herself."

I got a jolt of deep kinship from the bond and reached behind me to squeeze Troy's hand. Wanting to lighten the mood as we reached Maria's hearing range, I changed the subject. "How are things going with Doc Mike?"

Noah's jump and the guilty expression that flashed across his face before he could hide it made me grin. "Who told you—?"

I laughed. "You just did. I had my suspicions for a while, but I wasn't sure."

"You're too nosy," Noah grumbled.

"I was a private investigator. It's in the job description." I couldn't help smiling despite the pang of mourning that struck me thinking about my abandoned PI agency.

Doc Mike had been one of my few friends for years. Noah had been the one to ease him into Otherside, when the vampire had healed the medical examiner of a bite wound from a vampiric sorcerer. There'd been an obvious attraction on both sides, but I hadn't been sure if Doc Mike's deep Christian faith or his turning out to be a necromancer would have snuffed it. Apparently not.

Firelight danced through the gauzy curtain in front of us.

From behind it, Maria called, "Stop teasing Noah, Arbiter. Come play with someone your own size."

As we pushed through the curtains, I threw the tiny Mistress of Raleigh a cheeky grin. "Guess I should keep looking, seeing as you're not any taller than you were last time I was here."

Maria scoffed and rolled her eyes, but a smile quirked the corners of her lips. She was dressed in an amethyst gown today, cut high in front with a hi-low hem. It should have clashed with her emerald hair, but it just gave the usual effect of a living stained-glass window.

She flowed toward us with the grace that said at least she was feeding, kissing first me then Troy on both cheeks before peering behind us. "No Allegra today?"

Allegra? The flash of amusement from Troy confirmed he knew—no, more like suspected—something. I'd ask him later. "She's busy, I'm afraid."

"Pity." She glanced between Troy and me again. "It's still surreal to see the two of you happy together and not at each other's throats, but I'm glad of it."

I exchanged a glance with Troy. She didn't usually call attention to our relationship, having hoped for one with me herself at one point, which made me wonder again about her asking after Allegra. "Oh?"

"Given the news I've just heard, you're going to need him. Since I need you, that works out for all of us."

Chapter 2

Troy tensed, his hand drifting up to the hilt of the longknife riding in a sheathe along his spine before he caught himself. "What do you know?"

"I don't *know* anything." Maria beckoned us to follow her to the cluster of red jacquard sofas and chairs that made an intimate seating arrangement near the ever-present fire. "But an old vagabond acquaintance seeking to curry favor brought an interesting rumor from the west."

"The west," I said flatly as I sat.

Troy, pushed even deeper into bodyguard mode, took a rigid stance behind my armchair.

I left him to it, having learned in the last few months it was best just to let his instincts and training play themselves out. "The west as in…"

"Asheville," Maria said with a dangerous softness.

I stiffened. Asheville was where the Blood Moon clan—the most powerful werewolf pack in three states—had their seat of power. My ex-boyfriend, Roman Volkov, had returned home with his brother Sergei to reclaim it when I'd passed along news that the Monteagues were plotting to kill their father. Their sister, Vikki, was still here in the Triangle with the fiancée Roman had left me for. Ana had fled to the Triangle when old man Niko had been killed, seeking sanctuary alongside Vikki with our local cat prides so that they could continue the relationship they'd started in secret.

Werewolf politics were complicated and conservative.

That didn't even factor in the part where Roman still wanted me—or at least didn't want anyone else to have me if he couldn't. He'd ignored most of my messages these last three months. The ones he'd responded to had contained biting sarcasm and wolfish posturing.

"What's the rumor?" My voice was hard. I'd shifted into Arbiter mode without thinking.

When Maria looked at Troy, I knew. I let her say it anyway.

"Evangeline Monteague and the remainder of the House Guard are there. On Volkov land."

Alarm flared in the bond, and I glanced up at Troy.

"Allegra had no news as of this morning," he admitted. "We're stretched too thin in the Triangle to spare an expedition to the mountains. The Volkovs know we're looking for the remnants of House Monteague. That we've heard nothing and a wandering vampire brings word…" He grimaced. "Either this is a feint by the Monteagues, or Blood Moon is not as reliable as we'd expected from an alliance member."

If it was anyone else, I'd be looking for jealousy in that statement. But as Troy had said, he knew where he stood with me and had spoken well of Roman in the past despite his own—hidden, at the time—feelings for me. No, this was just stating facts.

I thought fast as Maria watched me with dark eyes gone hard as diamonds. "I can ask Duke to swing over that way." I held up a hand at the argument I could feel coming from Troy. "I know. He's being an ass over how long it's taking us to find Iaret. I'll deal with it."

Maria nodded and rose. "In that case, we'd best get you to the library."

I pulled her into a side-hug as we made our way to the heavy doors of the coterie's treasured library. "Thank you for bringing this to me. You've always been a friend, Maria."

"Oh. Well." Red pinpoints flushed her cheeks. "I did tell you the *moroi* could be more than just takers, didn't I, poppet?"

"You did, and you always honor it."

As I'd hoped, the comment and the friendly touch brought Maria closer to her usual self as she led us through the library—more buoyant, back to using pet names. I didn't love people using nicknames with me, but Maria not doing so bothered me. Like she was too weighed down by everything to prick at me even in jest.

Noah had been right. I resolved to see what I could do to hurry the negotiations with the humans along. Maybe a little extra blood today would help as well.

The Mistress of Raleigh led us down a different row than usual before stopping in front of a table holding an antique Tiffany lamp, two pairs of white archivist's gloves, and a single oversized tome.

"It was mis-shelved," she explained. "Rian found it completely by accident. Knock yourselves out. Just wear gloves, or I'll have to listen to his bitching for the next decade. He's still harping on about everything you touched bare-handed when you were researching the lich. You know where to find me when you're done."

She was off again before I could comment, leaving Troy and me with the book.

I leaned over the text on the page it was open to and frowned. "Umm, that's not English. Or Latin. Or any human language, as far as I can tell."

Troy hovered next to me, his body heat noticeable in the room's chill. "It's elvish. Looks like a criminal record. What the hell are the vampires doing with an elven book?" He slipped on the larger pair of gloves and closed the book to see the cover, then the spine. No title on either. "That's strange," he muttered. "I wonder if…"

He switched to elvish as the scent of burnt marshmallow and a prickle along my arms told me he was working a spell. I frowned as, with a faint shimmer, a title appeared in a looping script.

Troy dropped the book in alarm.

"What?" I took two steps back before he could bodily move me.

"This book was supposed to have been destroyed thirty years ago," he said harshly. "It's the Book of the Damned."

"That sounds more than a little ominous. Especially given that timeframe," I said. Troy had been born around then. Callista was just starting with kidnapping wildborn elementals in her sick project to find a bargaining chip to use with the gods, a project that seemed to have culminated with my birth four years later. "What, pray tell, is the Book of the Damned?"

Troy muttered another spell and waved a hand over the book. Nothing happened this time, and he flipped the pages with visible disgust and reluctance. "It's a record of what really happened to political prisoners, dissidents, and other threats to the matriarchy, both elven and non." He paled and shuddered. "My name would have been entered in it this past summer, had it still been in our keeping."

"They didn't make another book?"

"No. Too dangerous, for exactly this reason—it falling into the hands of a Lost One willing to translate it. The Captain and the Conclave of Queens kept everything oral after this was…well. Not destroyed, apparently. Misplaced or stolen."

A pang clenched my heart to hear Troy refer to himself like that. "Lost One" was what the elves called anyone who fell out of line enough to be cast out. It was what they'd called my parents to justify slaughtering them and throwing in the rest of House Solari just to make the point. Sometimes I wondered if he thought he'd been deserving of the torture that'd nearly killed him, but I didn't have the courage to ask.

I ran a hand up and down his spine, and some of the tension in him eased with the touch, as much for being reminded that he wasn't alone as for the hormones boosted into his system by the secondary bond he'd made with me.

"This is ugly," Troy muttered. "Allegra was right. There were several more Ebon Rebellions over the years. All put down hard." He turned a page and paled again. "I got off easy."

Not wanting to think about that or for him to dwell on what had happened during his torture, I said, "If the book was lost thirty years ago, try skipping to the end? Maybe one of the last entries can give us a clue."

With far more care than I would have bothered with given such a hateful book, Troy flipped to the back, working back toward the front until he found pages with script on them again. Under my palm, the muscles of his back went rock hard.

Dread sent icy tendrils crawling through me. "What?"

"Iaret," he said. "She's listed in the second-to-last entry. A favor to Callista, but one granted with relish from the way the sentence is phrased. The last entry—"

The abruptness with which he cut off made me anxious. "Who else?"

Troy swallowed, hard, and looked like he really wished he didn't have to answer me.

"Who?"

"It's a double-header. Quinlan Solari and the djinni commonly known as Ninlil."

I swayed then let myself squat, pressing the heels of my palms into my eyes. I knew next to nothing of my parents, and the first opportunity I had to learn something it was from a book that disturbed Troy—who was, for all I'd grown close to him, a murderer several times over. I forced myself to take a breath. Then another one and a third before I could rise. "That doesn't make sense. I wasn't born for another four years after this book was lost. Are you telling me the elves gave them four years to conceive? They let it happen? Let *me* happen?"

Troy's arms came around me, and I let him draw me into a hug.

"It looks like yes," he said into my hair. His next words tumbled out in a rush. "Arden, it was a favor for Callista. The Conclave knew. But they accepted the soul of another djinni in exchange for holding off on Quinlan's execution. They have Iaret, but the record doesn't say where or in what form. She could be bottled, or she could be dead. The only thing committed to record is that she was given in trade, a djinni life for another djinni life."

I was trembling, and I couldn't stop.

Any lingering guilt or remorse I'd felt for how I'd handled the elven queens was gone. They'd deserved it. They'd deserved to be hunted like animals and die in pain. They'd done *evil*, made a deal so heinous that they'd been willing to destroy an ancient book full of crimes they'd been proud enough to record for who knew how long to cover it up.

Troy was shaking too, the fine tremor he got when he was on the edge of violence and controlling himself. "That's why they had to 'lose' the book. Your grandmother must not have been present in the session when this was decided. Keithia, Catrionne Sequoyah, and Mireia Luna arranged it between them. It wasn't just a favor for Callista. It was a power grab. Solari's prince took the fall. Keithia pretended not to know it was a setup and used it as an excuse to destroy the House then elevate herself and Mireia." His fists tightened, bunching against my back. "This is beyond wrong. *I* was wrong, for not seeing who they truly were sooner."

I pulled away and fixed him with a fierce glare. "No. Don't you *dare* blame yourself for something that happened before you were born. Whatever you did before this year, you're atoning for it now. Every day. Every breath."

He dropped his eyes and shifted to kneel, one fist to his heart. "My queen."

The title and formal salute reminded me I was here as somebody important, not just as a lost little girl seeking clues about parents she'd never had a chance to know. I took a deep breath, briefly drawing on Air as I gathered myself. The heavy chandeliers creaked overhead as I channeled a breeze upward.

"Is this the clue we needed?" I asked when I'd calmed down some. I didn't recognize my own voice, all emotion stripped from it and tamped down into the mental box where I sent everything I didn't want to deal with.

Troy stayed kneeling, answering me in a carefully neutral voice. "I think so. But we'll need to find someone who knows more. I can have Iago check the archives for the meeting minutes and see who else was there."

"Fine. Duke's afraid Iaret is dead, and his prophecy's call for 'the risen flame' means bringing her back. Have you seen any relics or bottles? Trophies?"

"No. I was never admitted to certain spaces reserved for the queens. But Evangeline might have, as queen-in-waiting."

Shit.

"The House of Jade and the House of Onyx are the keys to Ragnarok." I repeated the words Torsten had spoken to a succubus before she'd killed him. "Looks like that has multiple interpretations. And stand up, will you? Goddess, you take this shit more seriously than I do."

16

Troy caught my hands as he rose and leaned in to kiss my forehead. "If I don't, no one else will. You, least of all. We need you to remember who you are, for all our sakes."

Discomfited by the truth, I glared at the book rather than take my mood out on him. "I want to burn that."

"Leave it with the vampires for now. They won't be able to do anything with it once I set an obfuscation spell. The records I skimmed over implicate several more of the North American Houses, plus half of Europe's."

"Blackmail." I grinned, feeling the savagery in it. "I like it."

"You do?"

I shrugged, flushing at the cautious approval that reached me before Troy muted the bond to give me space to think. "For the sake of getting justice for anyone in that book, I do. Besides, if Duke asks why I need him to chase halfway across the state and spy on the wolves, we'll want to have that shitty thing accessible."

As we left the library, I wondered how much Duke had known about the elven involvement in Iaret's disappearance or how far back Callista's plot had gone. Either way, he was going to be furious.

I just hoped he didn't back out of the alliance because of it.

Chapter 3

Duke took the news of our first solid clue about as badly as I'd thought he would—not that I blamed him, given the circumstances.

"What did you say?" he asked in a sibilant whisper, carnelian eyes sparking.

I leaned on the dining table and rubbed my forehead, still a little woozy from donating blood to Maria after Troy and I had finished in the library. After poking her about her workload, I'd gone ahead and let her take a little more than usual, both for the value of the clue and because I thought we could both use the distraction. She'd gotten blood drunk. I'd gotten glamoured enough that Troy had had to pull me out. My natural resistance to glamour only worked when I wasn't bleeding into someone's mouth. When I was, it hit me like it would an elf—hard.

I'd taken the last of the little homemade pills Janae had given me to boost me after blood donations, but I still wasn't in a state to argue with a furious djinni.

Suck it up, Arden. I took a deep, steadying breath through my nose, letting the copal incense I'd lit on returning home soothe me before expanding on my initial statement. "Iaret, in unknown form, was traded to the Conclave as an incentive to ignore my parents. The trade was registered in a book that was supposed to have been destroyed but somehow fell into Torsten's hands.

Which means *someone* knows something. Possibly Evangeline, as Keithia's heir."

Flame crackled as Duke hovered in his true form, smoke and fire with fangs and carnelian eyes. I was glad Troy had listened to me when I told him to check in with Allegra and the Ebon Guard at his safehouse or something—anything to make sure he wasn't the only elf available for Duke to lash out at. I hadn't seen the djinni this upset since…well, maybe ever.

"This is barbaric." Smoke billowed. "Even for those—"

"Duke," I said in warning. I didn't tolerate slurs from the elves toward the djinn, and I wouldn't tolerate them the other way either. My re-establishing House Solari was meant to bring us all—djinn, elves, and elementals—back together, the way it had been before the elves grew jealous of their elemental offspring's connection to the land and sought to exterminate us.

His cloudy form ballooned until his head brushed my high ceiling. "I will have justice!"

"Yes," I agreed, fighting to keep my voice even, "but you don't need to shout. I'm perfectly capable of hearing you, and while I won't dare to say I'm equally outraged, rest assured that I'm furious."

After staying twelve feet tall long enough to make his point, Duke condensed into a smaller, but no less threatening, murky haze. "So you can be diplomatic."

I closed my eyes, lacing my fingers between my curls to massage my scalp in an attempt to ease the headache. I could regenerate lost blood way faster than a human, but I still needed time and fluids. "I get it, Duke. I do. They had Troy for what, a day? And I burned three elven Houses to the ground when we were still barely anything to each other."

But what are we to each other now?

I shied away from the thought to focus on the matter at hand. "I can only imagine what I would do if we had anything like what

19

you've described with Iaret. So please trust me. I will get her back. We had a deal, remember? I'm making good on it. We finally have a real clue."

We needed a hell of a lot more a hell of a lot faster, but we all knew that. The gods would call the Wild Hunt in their own time, but that could be in a month or a thousand years for me. Well, maybe not a thousand, given they needed me for it and I guessed I'd see a hundred and fifty, maybe one-seventy if I didn't get myself killed first.

We were all on a deadline.

Duke studied me then morphed into the form of a lean, athletic Black man in a thousand-dollar suit, although his eyes stayed djinn carnelian. "Fine. What's your next step?"

"Like I said, someone knows something. The Darkwatch Captain is still alive, as is Troy's blood sister. Which reminds me…" I grimaced.

"Spit it out, little bird."

"Maria had a rumor from a vagabond passing through. Evangeline and the rest of House Monteague's surviving guard might be in Asheville."

"You think she's courting your wolf."

I huffed with exasperation, tired of reminding people. "He's *not* my wolf anymore, but yes, that's a possibility. The other being that the vagabond was paid off and the Monteagues are still here in the Triangle. Maybe even sheltering with the Darkwatch and the Captain."

Duke narrowed his eyes in thought. "A good ploy. The vampires have always given their wanderers special guest privileges. Nobody would bleed him or put him to the question without incontrovertible proof of wrongdoing."

I hadn't known that, but it explained Maria's reluctance to speak on their visitor further. "We don't have enough of the Ebon Guard to send anyone."

"If the little princess might be there, I'll go," Duke said before I could figure out how to phrase a request in such a way that it didn't sound like an order.

I might be the Arbiter, but Duke was more than a hundred times my age, and he'd seen thousands like me rise and fall over the years. He was only impressed when I did primordial magic or something unusually and spectacularly foolish, like having him drop me onto the roof of an elven queen's compound.

Best to take advantage of his good inclination while I could.

"I was hoping you'd say that," I replied. "In the meantime, we'll figure out how to deal with the Captain, and I'll try the fae again. Zanna only said they needed time to consider, not that they'd rejected further communication out of hand."

"Is it wise to push the lords and ladies?"

"Do I have a choice?"

Smoke curled from Duke. "No. I daresay you do not."

My stomach turned, but I shrugged in an effort to seem unbothered and covered my sudden burst of nerves by getting a glass of water from the kitchen sink. "Okay then. When will you head to Asheville?"

"I'm already gone."

Before he'd even finished the sentence, he was, the words twisting as he changed planes with a shimmer.

My house was quiet, with me alone in it, for the first time in weeks. I had a hint of the peace I'd enjoyed before becoming the elven High Queen and the local Arbiter and the Mistress of the Hunt all wrapped up in a single cute—but perpetually tired—package. It was weird not having Troy here though, and I frowned at finding myself oddly okay with him being around more often than not. Both elves and elementals tended to be very social, but I liked my alone time. Usually.

That brought me back to the question of what Troy and I were, what we were doing. We'd started the year quite literally ready to murder each other, and he'd made a good stab at it. I'd threatened him in turn. Now...

My heart beat a little faster. He'd been explicit in what it'd mean for him if I made him prince consort. A chance at a love match.

For me, it was an offer of forever with someone who'd chosen me, willing to fight and die for me, even if I never chose him. He hadn't said the three little words yet, but I had a feeling that it was more because he knew I'd outright panic than because he didn't feel it.

I'd always put myself first because nobody else would. He'd learned always to serve others, sometimes I thought for the same reason. We complemented each other in that way, challenged each other in others, and yet the idea of *forever* terrified me. It was part of why I'd turned down Maria's offer, aside from the whole living underground and away from nature thing. But when Troy's heart had stopped on my bedroom floor, something in me had shifted irrevocably.

Now I was terrified about what that meant. If I was ready for it. If in choosing an elf, I was betraying the djinn side of my heritage.

It was fucking ridiculous, of course. We were bound together until death as it was. Allegra had said she didn't dare try to break the Aetheric bond, given it'd warped beyond untwisting and the potential side effects could be deadly. Troy had further allowed himself to fall into a second bond in a gamble to break the House oath his grandmother had set on him, a hormonal shift that aligned his body chemistry to mine and mine alone. He'd already committed to forever, once on accident, the second time on purpose. He'd be at my side, whether I loved him or not, until one of us died or I ordered him away.

It's only been a few months. Goddess you're dramatic, Arden. Stop getting ahead of yourself.

22

Except that I'd known, deep down, that Roman wasn't forever, even before I'd found out he was moving behind my back on negotiations with his family, using my name and influence to back his power plays, without breathing a word to me until his brother showed up in our woods unannounced.

I scoffed at myself in disgust and sent a gust of Air whirling through the forest of air plants in their little glass bulbs overhead, hanging from my ceiling by fishing line. Ash burst from the tray of incense, leaving a white spray across the table.

There were reports to review and orders to send out, but I spent the next few hours replenishing my fluids and listlessly tidying the house. I'd have had yard work to do, but Troy had taken over the yard and garden. I'd initially thought it was so Zanna wouldn't curse his food like she had the first time she'd found him making breakfast after she got back from a round of negotiations with the fae Chamber of Lords. But he always seemed peaceful when he came in, not looking like a prince at all, with smudges of dirt on his face and caked on his knees. He'd even talked Laurel into helping him, and I now had a damn fig tree growing in the yard, flourishing with the little boost the oread had given it. How he'd known I loved figs I had yet to figure out, but he had.

It should have bugged me, but it didn't. And because I was contrary as hell, *that* bugged me.

"Fuck." I hurled a dirty rag in the general direction of the sink. It hit the outside edge, and I caught it with Air to dump it in properly. I had a tidy house, but my mind was still a mess of denial about the feelings I knew I had and was trying to avoid.

Deal with them later. With the cleaning done, I buried myself in reports, a glass of orange juice at my elbow. Terrence and Ximena had sent an update about their people slowly moving out of the city and into carefully selected communities in the surrounding counties. I worried about that choice—Durham was solidly progressive, but drive forty-five minutes out in a few directions and you were in red country, Confederate flags and all. The mixed Black and Latine cat pride might not be welcome in either of their forms, Southern hospitality be damned. But they were confident in their decision, so I'd shut up and support it until proven wrong.

Vikki and Ana were still treading a careful line with their wolves as they settled into their refugee status in Durham. The one time I'd asked Vikki about Roman, she'd outright snarled at me, so I left the Volkovs to sort out their pack conflicts.

Time for that to end.

I could allow some grace for a friend in a life transition, but she needed to remember that I was the power in the Triangle—and I needed to know what was going on in Asheville.

None of my reports mentioned the Monteagues directly, so I put my detective skills to use trying to puzzle together where they might have gone, if not Asheville. I might have had to quietly retire Hawkeye Investigations, but I still had the skills. I was just lucky Iago had managed to get the majority of the dead elven queens' holdings transferred to me, so I didn't have to worry about money anymore. I pushed aside the guilty thought that it was blood money and kept digging.

The fae were hard bargainers. I might need to beg an unveiling spell from them, but the more I knew, the better the terms would be.

Something wasn't right there to begin with. While the fae were notoriously standoffish to the rest of Otherside, they were usually pretty quick to make some kind of bargain with a rising power. They relied on good relations with influential Othersiders in the mundane world to protect those of their people who'd crossed the Veil, like Zanna and some of the newcomers that occasionally turned up at the bar downtown.

Late afternoon was slanting toward evening when I pulled myself out of what felt like a conspiracy theory exercise and realized I hadn't eaten since breakfast. The only messages I had were from the other elementals, confirming this weekend's joint practice. Everyone else was busy, which I hoped was a good thing.

It made me feel itchy though. Useless. I was accustomed to taking an active hand in things, but with the elves too beaten to cause trouble locally and Callista gone, the only things for me to do were find Iaret, keep working on quelling the mundane anti-Otherside protests, and prep for the Wild Hunt.

Or rather, prep to stop it.

Okay, maybe that was plenty. I grimaced, still having no idea how I was going to do any of it—with or without Troy and Iaret.

Chapter 4

When my phone buzzed as I was finishing a late lunch, I half expected it to be Troy. I frowned to see Janae's number on the caller ID.

"Janae?"

"Arden!" Her tense whisper made me stiffen. "We need help. Now. Mundanes in Durham have decided they have an issue with witches. They're going after Hope's metaphysical shop, Midday Moon."

I wasn't quite recovered from my earlier blood donation, but adrenaline surged at being needed and the idea of facing some action rather than sitting here looking at more reports. "Be there ASAP."

As I left the house, I texted Troy. *Trouble for the witches. Omw to pick you up.*

He was standing outside with Allegra when I pulled up, dressed in all black and looking grim as Allegra talked at him. Troy made a terse reply, his eyes on my car, as I parked in the unassuming house's gravel drive. They both stared at the car.

Then Allegra pulled Troy into a side hug, melting a bit of the chill he'd been carrying. He wrapped an arm around her in return before moving to the passenger-side door, kissing my hand when he got in.

The door of the house slammed, and two more elves hustled down the steps, pausing to take orders from Allegra before piling into the backseat.

"How's things?" I asked as I backed down the driveway.

I glanced in the rearview mirror to find the two elves in the back—one male, one female, neither of whom I knew—staring at the back of my seat with big eyes. The man had a vaguely Monteague cast, only with lighter skin and dark brown eyes. The woman was pale-skinned and auburn-haired with grey eyes, almost but not quite looking Sequoyah.

Low-bloods or vassal Houses.

I was intrigued in spite of myself. I hadn't realized that Allegra had expanded the entry criteria.

"The Guard is growing," Troy said, voice tight with an emotion he was muting. "Meet Haroun Carrel and Etain Bossence."

I eyed them as I hit the gas. "Allegra's recruiting from outside the high Houses?"

"Yes, ma'am," Etain said.

Haroun just looked like he'd swallowed his tongue.

"Good." I glanced at Troy, trying to figure out why he'd relaxed at my approval and wondering if that was why they were all acting like squirrels in a box. Maybe they were just picking up my nerves. I was anxious as hell about what was happening with Hope.

"Really?" the elfess squeaked. She flushed a bright red. "I mean…I'm sorry, I just—we don't have much magic and—"

"Can you fight?" I interrupted.

She straightened, and her voice firmed. "Yes. I'm top ranked in hand-to-hand combat and also skilled at nonviolent crowd control."

I nodded. "Sounds great. And you, Haroun?"

"I'm a crack shot with any firearm and have secondary training in breaking and entry techniques."

"Then welcome to House Solari and the Ebon Guard."

The two newcomers exchanged nervous glances as Troy suppressed a smile but allowed approval to flicker in the bond.

"Why?" Etain flushed again but looked stubborn. "We washed out of Darkwatch training for not having enough strength with Aether."

Haroun stiffened, looking equal parts furious with his counterpart for admitting it and stubbornly defiant. "We swore the House oath. We can serve."

Ah. That's their deal. I glanced at Troy, trying to get more of a cue, but he was busying himself scanning the road. "Troy and I have plenty of magic between us if it's called for, but too many Othersiders lean on magic as a first, last, or only method for dealing with mundanes. It means they think a certain way, react a certain way. It makes them predictable or over-reliant on skills that can be stripped away with a fancy bracelet. I'm glad Allegra is addressing that particular gap."

At that little speech, the tension in the car dropped dramatically.

"I was hoping you'd see it that way," Troy said just loudly enough for me to hear him. "I only found out about it when I got back earlier. These two are the first, but she has more candidates lined up."

"It's smart. It doesn't lessen the Ebon Guard to have a broader range of abilities. Shit, I should know. I spent my first quarter century playing human. Didn't make me any less good at my work." The part I didn't say aloud was maybe by taking in those the traditional elven power structure had cast aside, I could get some loyal security who'd remember how I felt about their involvement when Evangeline or an outside House made a play for the Triangle.

"I trust Allegra to do her job." With another glance in the mirror, I addressed our new recruits. "And I trust you to do yours. Okay?"

"Yes, ma'am," they both said crisply. They'd lost the curled shoulders and tight expressions of people who expected to be told to get out of the car, and I considered that, while I might be an odd queen, I'd made a place for outcasts like me. For people existing on the margins of the supernatural community and all the dangers that came with that status. That mattered to me, given how long I'd been there myself and how much I'd ached to have a place in Otherside. It felt damn good.

We made it downtown without incident, but that changed as we drew closer to the intersection where Hope's successful and growing metaphysical shop had a storefront. A crowd of irate-looking humans with Bible verses on hand-scrawled signs were gathered out front. When I cracked the window enough to hear what they were shouting, it was the expected hate-filled nastiness. Witches had only come out a few months ago, and while the reaction hadn't been as bad as it had been for werewolves, it hadn't been all love and light. Val and Laurel were both making quiet preparations in their work as firefighter and farmer respectively, because it wouldn't be much longer before elementals would be forced out too.

I brought the car around and found street parking a block away. Troy caught my arm when I started to get out.

"Let them scout first," he said in the neutral tones he fell into when he was working.

I sighed and nodded. Letting him do his job, broadly defined as "keep Arden alive and out of trouble" was frustrating but necessary.

He twisted to look at the pair in the back seat. "Go. No more than ten minutes. Establish the situation inside the shop, make contact if you can, and report back."

"If they need help?" Etain asked.

Troy glanced at me, and I pressed my lips together in a firm line, sending a push through the bond to make it clear that witch casualties weren't acceptable.

"Secure them if you can without exposing yourselves," he said. "Otherwise, come back here with recommendations for crowd control and dispersal."

"Sir." Haroun and Etain slipped from the car, already shedding their serious personas and slipping into the lighter gaits and teasing manners of a couple out for a stroll.

"They're good," I murmured, watching them critically.

Troy could try, but he wasn't nearly that subtle, especially not now that the double bond was leveling up both his Aetheric capacity and his personal presence. Sometimes he seemed to grow more elven by the day after he realized I'd meant what I'd said when I told him I could handle it. Allegra had made a joking comment about him getting a little feral, but it looked to me like self-acceptance, which I considered a good thing.

"Alli thought we'd be mad," he said. "She was afraid we'd say no and wanted a chance to prove the idea. That's why she didn't say anything until today."

"Why would we be mad?"

"One of the old queens would have had her head for making a decision like that without consulting her. I told her she was wrong not to trust you to see it for what it was and not a coup attempt."

I rolled my eyes. "The only reason Allegra would move against me is if I got you killed. I don't know shit about building an army. Why would I get in the way of her doing her job?"

Troy eyed me, bemused, and shook his head. "It's still weird to both of us that you trust elves that easily. I accept it. She's still trying to protect me."

"Who said it was easy? I've just gotten used to y'all being very direct in expressing your plans for me, good, bad, or otherwise. Allegra made it clear she's on my side, and if you're happy, she's happy. I'll worry about my head if you ever decide to leave."

That earned me a small smile. "Fair enough."

We waited in companionable silence for the ten minutes to pass. I cracked a window to let some air in, never having done well in close quarters and especially not after pulling the earth down on my and Troy's heads back in the summer.

Which was why I smelled smoke.

"Shit." I twisted in my seat, looking for the source.

It wasn't the good woodsmoke smell of human fireplaces. It was October but still too warm for that. No, it was the acrid electrical scent of manmade materials burning.

As though my noticing it was a cue, the howl-roar of a fire truck's siren cut through the evening.

"I refuse to believe that's not associated with the protest," I said.

Troy didn't argue. He mirrored me in getting out of the car, and our paces matched as we hustled down the block. He had his phone out, but we ran into Etain and Haroun before he could call.

"Report," he said in a clipped tone, looking every inch the dangerous, self-assured prince he'd been when I'd met him. Hell, even I stood straighter before I could catch myself.

Etain grimaced, glancing over her shoulder. "Two witches inside, one mundane. The shop owner and her staff. One of the humans got the bright idea to burn them out. The usual line about not suffering a witch to live. They have no safe exit. Hostiles at front and rear entrances. Fire in the stairwell to the roof exit."

I started to head for the door, jerking to a halt when Troy caught me around the bicep. Before I could open my mouth to snap at him, he pointed to the news vans idling on the corner and the reporters standing with their backs to the riotous scene. More humans, presumably those from adjoining buildings, lined the opposite side of the street, hands over their mouths, tears in their eyes.

A rock smashed through a window, feeding oxygen to whatever fire had been started inside and prompting a celebratory cry from the hateful crowd.

"I know your range," he said. "You can suppress the fire from here."

"But the witches inside—"

"Will be helped out by your Guards as soon as I maze the smaller crowd. Which is…?"

"At the back," Haroun said. "But we need to hurry. Follow me."

Troy's eyes narrowed at the idea of us being separated, but the fire was at the front of the building, spreading fast to the upper levels. It'd block off escape in minutes, and the fire truck was still blocked, surrounded now by rioters.

"Fine," Troy said. "Etain, I think you know what will happen to you if anything happens to our queen."

"Yes, my prince." She paled.

I glared at him, knowing he'd just hobbled me twice since I wouldn't do anything to put my newest bodyguard in danger. He just nodded, as though satisfied I'd keep myself out of immediate trouble, and followed Haroun to an alley. As he rounded the corner, he opened the bond completely, and I did the same. We'd discovered we could boost each other's magic that way. It worked even better if we had a djinni involved, but I'd sent Duke away and we had nobody else.

I started to draw on the elements, pausing when I remembered a key problem. "Dammit, do you have a pair of sunglasses on you?"

My eyes glowed gold when I used my powers, which was why I'd never used them in public. The coming night would make it extra obvious, and in a crowd like this, I didn't dare take the risk that somebody would notice.

Shaking her head, Etain pulled off her cap and handed it to me. "Best I can do, my queen."

"You don't have to call me that," I grumbled as I put it on and pulled the bill low, ducking my head.

"Yes, ma'am."

I let that one go, not wanting to erode their respect for me entirely, and pulled on Fire as carefully as I could. Even doing it gingerly, the power wanted to dance, romping through me like a boisterous fox.

"Goddess," Etain muttered at the same time the humans at the edge of the crowd flinched, looking around for what had suddenly put their teeth on edge and made their hair stand up.

My power signature.

Val had described it as being like a jet engine coming online, but mundanes would only get the sense that something was very much not right. If they attached it to me, the uncanny valley effect would set the crowd off.

I had to act fast.

As the fire truck blared its horn at the rioters, trying to get close enough to a hydrant that the firefighters could help, I reached for the flames inside the building. For a terrifying moment, they flared, excited by my magic, until I could coax them into a slower dance. One that smoldered rather than blazed.

Little by little, they backed away from the life forms I could dimly sense inside, buying a little more time for Troy to work his magic.

Gritting my teeth, I drew on Air and thinned the air molecules over the whole area. The humans would be dizzy with the equivalent of altitude sickness, but it'd be mistaken for smoke inhalation. Maybe they'd sit down and shut the hell up.

The fire wavered. If the elements could feel betrayal, this one did. I kept my hold on it, pulling it down to a dull crackling then nudging Troy in the bond. *Go.*

With a force that staggered me, Troy pulled on more Aether than I'd ever felt him use before. I thought I smelled the ghost of the scent of burnt marshmallow and tasted rosemary and sage on my tongue.

"Are you okay, my queen?" Etain's hand hovered in my peripheral vision.

I sidled away. "Don't touch me. Don't want the fire to find a new home inside you. Or the Chaos."

She pulled away as though I'd burned her, angling to stand in such a way that she'd block the line of sight to me for most of the crowd. Shouting rose from the direction of the fire truck as police arrived to force the crowd back. The truck pulled forward, firefighters spilling from it to hook up the fire hose and spray the building.

With their efforts, I eased off of my control of Air, not wanting the firefighters affected by the thin atmosphere. When I sensed the flames dying under the onslaught of the fire hose, I let go of Fire and shunted more of my energy to Troy in the form of Chaos. He couldn't use Chaos itself, but he'd learned to shear the elven half of it out and add it to his own strength.

We'd had an interesting summer.

I had to use the wall behind me for balance as I suddenly saw double. The scene in front of me was briefly overlaid by what had to be Troy's view.

Confused humans milled in the narrow street, more than I'd expected to be there, given it was supposed to be a smaller crowd. Some wandered through flower beds. One tripped over a low planter. Blood pounded in my ears.

Haroun waved coughing people out of the building. One was Janae's daughter, Hope, and I was glad we'd gotten here in time.

"Hey chill, lady, I know Arden," a familiar voice said nearby.

With a gasp, I snapped back into my own head and shook it to clear the last vestiges of the strange double vision. That'd never happened before.

Blinking, I refocused and grinned when I saw who Etain was trying to fend off. "Val?"

"You know her?" Etain asked without turning her attention from my friend and fellow elemental.

"Yeah." I pushed past Etain to hug Val, stopping short at Val's half shake of her head. *Right. News crews.*

"I figured that had to be you with the power sig. Who's the second one?"

I frowned, just realizing that there was another one in the area. "Uh…"

The question was answered by the silent reappearance of Troy, looking as haggard as I felt and radiating the auratic vibe of an icy wind through the deep forest at midnight on the new moon—cutting, dark, and quietly threatening.

He had a power signature. Small and faint compared to mine. But definitely there.

"Get to Haroun. Next block over. Take them home," he said to a wide-eyed Etain. "I'll have someone pick you up from there."

"Sir." As Etain ran, she must have invoked whatever small Aetheric power she had because my eye tried to slide away from her. Not quite like a high-blood's trick with shadows, but it would probably work on most mundanes.

Troy's eyes flicked over me, and some of the tightness in his shoulders eased to find me tired but okay. Then he frowned to see Val and me staring at him in shock. "What?"

"I'm not the only one who needs to be careful about my power anymore," I said in a low voice, mindful of the growing crowd.

When he frowned harder, Val said, "You're leaking, man. Like Arden is right now."

His eyes flew wide, and he put a hand to the wall as he wavered. "No. I can't."

Val and I exchanged glances. Keithia had had a power signature, so I suspected it wasn't that elves couldn't have one but something to do with him.

"We'll talk about it later," I said. "Val, what's up?"

"Did you sink the fire?"

"Yes. There were witches and a mundane trapped inside. Janae called."

The firefighter sighed and lifted her helmet to ruffle sweat-damp hair. "Got it. For the best, I'm sure, but that means I'll either need to do something about the fire pattern or about the report. Unless you're outing yourself."

I winced. "Um. Not yet, if that's not too much of an imposition. Not while I'm working with Maria on the mundane legal proceedings. Sorry."

"I'll figure it out." She offered a lopsided smile. "They're still stumped by the Mon—by the house fire in Chapel Hill this past summer. Too many more of these and you won't have a choice, but for now it should be okay."

I returned the smile. "Thanks. I owe you."

With a nod, she jogged back to her fellows, leaving me and Troy staring at each other, the bond thrumming with question and Troy's sick fear.

Chapter 5

By the time we got home, the tension had exacerbated my dehydration headache, helped along with the beginnings of a power hangover. I hadn't had one in a while, but I also hadn't been a conduit for that much Chaos to Troy either. The nausea and pounding head put me in a bad mood.

"You wanna tell me why you've got the dreads?" I asked as soon as we walked in the door.

He swallowed hard, eyes darting, then took a deep breath and drew his silver-edged longknife of black meteoric steel, the one I'd rescued along with him.

"What the—"

Before I could finish the words or do more than dance back a step, he'd rolled the blade over his wrist and was offering it to me hilt-first.

"Take it," he said, dully resigned, when I just stared at it.

"And do what with it?" I asked. His mood was reverberating through me, and my heart pounded so hard I was surprised it was still behind my ribs. The only time I'd felt him this full of fear and desperation was the first time he'd woken up after I got him back from Keithia. His next words made it all worse.

"Kill me."

"*What?*"

Troy's pretty sandstone-and-moss eyes ran over me, drinking me in like it was the last time he was going to see me. "Please don't draw it out, Arden."

"What in the nine circles of hell are you talking about? Put that away!"

"I'm a threat to your rule."

"What the fuck are you talking about?"

With a frustrated growl, Troy slammed the blade on the dining table. "When I said being with you was a path to being a king, I meant that one day we might… I didn't mean that I'd usurp your place."

I looked at the ceiling, heart in my throat, mouth dry, head pounding, and tried to use my words rather than thrashing some sense into him. "Troy, I am dehydrated and in the grips of a power hangover so maybe I'm being a little dense. I'm gonna need you to back up and explain to me why the fuck I would think you, of all people, would usurp my place after you helped me pull down your grandmother and two other queens and then declared me the damn High Queen of North Carolina to everyone in Otherside."

When I brought my gaze back down, he was staring at me in consternation. "I have a power signature now."

"Why does that mean killing you?"

He gaped at me. "Elven males, on the rare occasion that we develop enough power to gain a signature, are put down. There have been too many attempts to overthrow the matriarchy to allow it."

"How many times do we have to do this? *I am not an elf*," I snapped. "My father might have been one, but fortunately for the both of us, I didn't absorb whatever fucked-up notions y'all have been running around with for the last however many millennia. Ishtar above."

I needed a drink to deal with this. Keeping it at one should balance out the power hangover and keep me from going maenad on him, although given this foolishness maybe he had it coming. Pointedly turning my back, I grabbed and opened a bottle of Tempranillo.

Something rebellious flared in the bond for a moment before he shoved it aside.

By the time I'd poured two glasses, he'd gotten control of himself and was standing in parade rest. The tight skin around his eyes and the twitching muscle in his cheek gave him away though.

"What point were you considering making just then?" I sipped my wine, savoring the burst of cherry and spice.

Troy kept his eyes firmly on mine. "Picking up my blade and reminding you I'm dangerous."

"Mhmm. See Troy, you're so used to protecting me that I think you're forgetting something."

He lifted his chin and the gold flecks in his eyes sparked. "What's that?"

I drew on Air. "I'm dangerous too."

Before he could do more than frown, I had coils of Air looped around him, pinning his legs together and his arms to his sides. When he opened his mouth, I shoved a wedge of Air in.

"Come on then. We're gonna hash this out like Othersiders, since you insist on holding onto the old ways." I hovered him along after me as I headed for the backyard, grabbing his longknife on the way out and ignoring his frustrated noises.

When we were standing in the grass under the house lights, I stuck the longknife into the ground, turned to face Troy, and sipped my wine. "Get free, get the knife, and make your point."

From the muffled noises, he was trying to say something. I let him.

"Arden, I don't know what you—"

I narrowed my eyes. "I gave you an order. Or am I only your queen when it's convenient for you?"

His eyes blazed. "Fine. My queen."

I might have been tired as hell but I was still ready for the burst of Aether he sent through the bond, slicing through it with a scythe of Chaos. "Not good enough. Try harder."

After another half-hearted attempt, I pushed through the power hangover and turned him upside down, lifting him higher so our faces were level.

Over his bellow of outraged surprise, I said, "If I don't believe you're actually trying to be a threat, I'm going to keep making this worse. So come on, *Prince Consort*. You won't like it if I have to go through all of the elements."

That got his attention.

I circled him, sipping my wine and easily fending off Aetheric attacks as the booze eased the hangover. When I made it back in front of him, I cocked an eyebrow. "Fire, then."

"Arden!"

Carefully, so carefully, I built a lattice of Fire around him. It wouldn't so much as glow, let alone burn him, but it would make the cool October night uncomfortably hot in a matter of minutes.

Finally, he decided to take me seriously enough that he leaned fully into his magical strength. His power signature flared to life again, sending a chill through me. I pulled my shields up and muted the bond completely, denying him the ability to draw on Chaos through me, but it was still there.

"Better," I said. "But still not quite—"

The lemony tang of djinn Aether pulled me around. Duke materialized in the yard, took in the scene, and busted out laughing.

"I wondered how long it'd take you to put him in his place," the djinni said, gasping as tears rolled down his face. "This is—

Ishtar burn me, but this is long overdue. Even if the little masochist is probably enjoying it."

Duke's mocking gave Troy the motivation he'd been lacking. The next attempt to mindmaze me and break free nearly worked. I spun back around, lashing out with Chaos to sting Troy's aura. He howled and dropped Aether.

"Have I made my fucking point?" I asked.

Troy was more stubborn than I was when he had a mind to be, and we'd be out here all night if I didn't give him an out. If Duke was back, there was news from Asheville, something too big to tell me via the callstone. I didn't have time to continue this lesson tonight, although I hoped it'd be the last time one was needed.

"Yes, my queen," Troy rasped. Sweat dripped down his face and made his long, black hair stick together in clumps.

"Then let me make one more." I let go of the chord of Fire and got right up in his face. "Just like I am having to learn to consider the needs of everyone else, *you* need to learn to consider *your personal* needs. Do you need to die?"

He hesitated then said, "No, my queen."

"Are you sure? Because this had better be the last goddamn time we have this conversation."

"I—I'm sure, my queen."

"What do you need then? Tell me. Right now."

He glanced over my shoulder.

"What—" I twisted to find Duke watching the scene with a wide grin and a conjured box of movie popcorn. "Get the hell inside, Duke. Go have a glass of wine or something, there's a bottle open."

"Party pooper," Duke complained.

I raised my eyebrows and the djinni obeyed with a wink. Turning back to Troy, I said, "Well?"

When he didn't answer immediately, I shook him. Then again when he opened his mouth and shut it, looking ornery.

Fury painted his face when I shook him a third time. "I need to *be* someone! I have it in me to be a king in my own right. I could take care of my people. Transform elven society. But my whole life, I have lived in fear of what they did to my father, fear for my own life, having to give up everything or work through other people who—" He cut off, looking horrified as though he was just hearing the words coming out of his mouth. "Arden, I didn't mean…"

"I think you did." I finished my wine then tilted my head to study him. I unmuted the bond enough to get a sense for where his head and heart were at. He was terrified. But deep down, feeling justified. Maybe even relieved that he'd finally said his piece. "Didn't you?"

"Yes." He swallowed. Then blinked a few times as a wave of vertigo hit him.

"Is that why you wanted to be with me? You have an agenda?"

"What?" His panic returned. "No! No, Arden, I've never lied about my feelings for you. Ever. Bad or good."

I believed that. His early distaste had been as clearly and directly communicated as his attraction was now. "But it's why you felt the need to prove yourself dangerous to me. Because it seemed like I wasn't taking you seriously? And it felt like just one more queen using and dismissing you when you've just confirmed you're even stronger than anyone already thought? Especially given all you've done to support me?"

He grimaced, and a slippery feeling came through the bond like he wanted to deny it.

"Yes," he finally whispered, eyes averted.

I sighed then flipped him right-side up and loosed the chord of Air. He sat down, hard, and dragged himself into a kneeling position, head down as he panted.

I dropped down in front of him, sitting cross-legged. "Troy, this relationship isn't gonna work without you telling me things like this before I have to go all primordial on you. Just like you resented me not seeming to take you seriously as a threat, *I* resent the assumption that I'm going to behave like the other queens you've served."

That brought his head up. "I didn't think you—actually, I guess I did. I'm sorry."

"You're used to not being trusted or heard, and I'm used to not being chosen or respected. So we keep surprising each other." I looked off into the dark. "Can we at least agree not to assume the worst of each other while we work through our baggage?"

The light brush of his fingers on my cheek as he tucked a loose strand of hair behind my ear brought my eyes back to him. He studied my face and shook his head. "I promise to try."

"All I can ask." I leaned forward and brushed his lips with mine.

He pulled me closer and deepened it.

I had the fleeting thought that maybe Roman would have taken me seriously enough not to go behind my back if I'd done to him what I'd just done to Troy, but there was no use dwelling on the past. For all the pain that had come with it, I liked the present I had.

Duke looked half-surprised when Troy and I re-entered the house, our fingers laced loosely together.

"So you managed not to kill each other. I suppose that means we can get back to the search for Iaret?"

Troy flushed then squeezed my fingers before veering toward the bathroom. "I need a shower. Catch me up later?"

"Of course." I suspected the shower was as much to escape Duke's mockery as it was to wash off the sweat and dirt coating him. Troy had an immense amount of pride, and I'd already battered it enough for one evening.

Duke topped off his glass of wine and poured another for me. "That was long overdue."

"It's none of your business, is what it is."

"Arden, his danger isn't in his power. He loves you and has committed too much to overthrow you. The danger is in his not having a channel to exercise his power independently."

"What are you saying?"

"Simply that encouraging him to stop falling back on the patterns the old queens beat into him is more likely to preserve both your lives than allowing him to continue playing at Houses. Give him a project. Something to do that isn't just protecting you. Before he starts to resent it."

"Yeah." I scrubbed my face and sighed. "Fine. Point taken. What's going on in Asheville? Why'd you come back in person? You could have used the callstone."

Unfazed by the change in subject, Duke swirled his wine. "You were too busy playing with your boyfriend to notice me trying to reach you, and when I looked your way there was a lot of magic. I had to make sure my little bird was okay, given you're inclined to allow an elven king to live." He cocked an eyebrow in rebuke. "The vagabond was telling the truth. Evangeline is sheltering on Volkov land."

A pain gripped my heart so hard that Troy called my name from the bathroom.

"I'm fine!" I shouted back.

But I wasn't. Things hadn't gone well with Roman and me when he'd been in the Triangle last, but somehow I hadn't dreamed he'd go so far as to shelter my worst living enemy at a time when I needed to focus on how I was going to de-escalate human aggression toward Otherside and stop the Wild Hunt.

I pulled out the nearest chair and sank into it then downed half my wine in a go, despite my earlier thought to just have the one glass. Maybe it wasn't Roman. Maybe it was Sergei?

"Does Roman know?"

"Sergei certainly does. I watched him make a supply run for them. The elves are holed up in a mountain cabin a few miles from the Volkov family home. It looks like a hunting lodge."

So the question was whether Roman knew and was keeping his distance until he decided what he wanted to do or didn't and his little brother was making opportunities for himself again. Either way, I couldn't afford to let Vikki settle into her exile any longer.

I tapped my fingers along the edge of the table in a rippling cadence, trying to decide what to do. "Goddess burn the Volkovs. I don't have time for this."

Duke just flashed his eyebrows and drank his wine, leaning against the half wall that separated the dining table from the front door.

"Fine. Roman and Sergei are unreliable. Vikki's reliable, but possibly as much for the threat from her clan as for her friendship with me and sanctuary with the cats. As long as her brothers are acting the fools, her attention and effectiveness will be split."

"A fair assessment," Duke said.

"I can't spare any elves to manage the Asheville wolves right now. Maria, Janae, Ximena, and Terrence are all in similar positions, trying to secure territory against either the rest of Otherside or the mundanes. The fae are obviously out." I heaved a sigh and took another swallow of wine, and more of my power hangover eased away. "I need to figure out what's going on with the Captain so I can free up the Ebon Guard. That'll let me handle both Evangeline and Iaret."

Duke's eyes flashed carnelian before he could control himself. "How does the Captain help find Iaret?"

"That book in the vampire library. The queens and maybe the Captain would have had access to it. If I can't get the Captain to talk to us…" I trailed off as something awful occurred to me.

"What is it?"

"Callista." I could barely get her name out. "Artemis *took* Callista. She did not, to my knowledge, *kill* her. I assume you'd be crowing about being freed from your remaining geasa if she had." My former guardian had put several of the oddly specific death curses on Duke, and they would only be broken if their stipulations could be circumvented—as had happened with me discovering the truth of my parentage on my own—or if Callista was dead.

Smoke curled from Duke. "Callista. Of course. How clever of you, little bird."

I shuddered. Clever…or terminally foolish?

Chapter 6

That idea turned into one of the few real fights Troy and I had had since we'd gotten together. Fortunately, Duke wasn't around to see it.

"Are you out of your fucking mind?" Troy said. The words were delivered quietly and in a tone as cold as his new power signature. It was the swearing that told me he was pissed as much as the searing heat of the Aetheric bond. "You want to cross the Veil. Alone. Because I sure as shit can't follow you there. To confront *Callista*, who wants you dead if she can't control you and is being held by the *gods of the hunt*. The same ones that want you to destroy the world for them. Do I have that right?"

Arms crossed and brow lowered with righteous anger of my own, I ground my teeth and forced myself to calm down. He wasn't being unreasonable, not really. Not when he put it that way, and not given that his job—hell, his life—revolved around keeping me safe. But I had to do this.

"You have that right," I said.

"Do you have a death wish? Is that it?"

"Troy—"

"Because I really can't see why else—"

"Troy!"

He stopped mid-sentence, eyes sweeping over me, and grimaced as he recognized he'd pushed too far. He settled into a parade rest. "My queen."

The title lashed me more than usual. "Don't. Don't do that."

"It's what you are. You made that clear earlier."

I flinched and looked aside, pissed but feeling like I deserved that.

Troy's heavy sigh accompanied a wave of guilt in the bond as he loosened his posture. "That was uncalled for. I'm sorry."

"Yeah. Me too."

Slowly, hesitantly, Troy reached for my arms. When I didn't tear away, his hands tightened and pulled me in. I went, pressing my face to his chest. His heart pounded much faster than usual, and his herbal scent was off.

Fear. He wasn't really angry. He was terrified. For me. For what might happen if he couldn't be there at my back.

That changed everything.

I wrapped my arms around him, squeezing tight and hoping he could feel what I hadn't had the courage to say yet. Instead of saying those words, I tilted my head to the side so he'd be able to hear me. "I'm the only one who can do this, and you're the only one who can hold the House in my absence."

Troy stiffened and pulled away. "Pardon?"

I met his gaze solidly, remembering what Duke had said. "Let's face it. You're a king in your own right now. Claimed by a queen but with a power signature. You're one of the most powerful full-blooded elves on the continent, male or otherwise. Right? You had connections before I dragged the alliance together. That means I'll need you in charge to come back safely."

Naked shock struck the bond like a lightning bolt as Troy stared down at me. His gaze was the shadowed labradorite shade it became when he was emotional, and the bond was such a riot that I shut down my side of it.

It took him another few seconds to find words. "You'd leave your House in my hands? Not Allegra's?"

"Yes."

"You'd leave me with everything."

I gave him the look that said I was running out of patience. "Am I speaking in tongues?"

"No, I just… This is—"

"You need a damn job other than protecting me," I said. Duke had been right about that and Troy himself had more or less stated it. "So help me lead the House while I handle Otherside and deal with the gods. I deputize you or whatever. But I can't sit here while Evangeline and Roman plot or while the gods hold the key to stopping the Hunt. You want to protect me? Make sure I have a damn home to come back to. Because I'm tied to the land."

I cut off, stiffening as the Sight rolled over me and I realized the truth of what I'd said even as I said it.

Troy reacted to my sudden fear. His pupils dilated, and the points of his secondary set of teeth poked from his gums as he hissed a breath in. "You're tied to the land? What does that mean?"

"I don't know," I whispered. "But it feels right. I mean, feels in the way Duke has the Sight. I can't see things in advance like he does or make prophecies. But I know when I'm right about something. I always have. It's how I found Sybil Sequoyah. The more powerful I get, the stronger the Sight is."

Closing my eyes, I pulled on all four elements.

The wards didn't recognize my powers to stop them. They were built with djinn, witch, and fae magic. Elemental magic tapped into the life of the world, like witch magic did, but on a level too deep for the rest of Otherside to recognize.

As I looked now, really looked, I spotted tendrils of Air, Fire, Earth, and Water, curving from my little house and into the sky, the ground, the river, through Durham to Chapel Hill and Raleigh. Bright spots flared at Jordan Lake, Falls Lake, and where I guessed Keithia's mansion was in Chapel Hill—all places where I'd done heavy workings.

Territory I'd claimed by stirring the elements there.

The tendrils weakened as they reached the edges of the Triangle but pulsed like roots, as though they were still growing and had the potential to strengthen as I did. Feeding me power…but also hobbling me.

"Shit," I whispered. "Laurel said the river I knew would be easier for me to work with. I didn't realize she meant more than because I was familiar with it."

"Okay, but what does that mean?"

Looking up at the man I was afraid to be in love with, I worked spit into my dry mouth and said, "It means that if the gods destroy the Triangle, they might destroy part of me as well. Or I dunno, I might lose myself. I—my magic is buried in the land, Troy. The more I use it, the stronger it gets. It supports me, but I don't know what will happen if the gods force me to remake the world. Maybe it always meant I'd die at the end of it."

He stared at me, dumbfounded and beyond horrified, then looked at the ceiling and pulled me close. "I'll have Iago do some research. And Maria."

"What about the House?"

"I'll hold it in your name. I can't lose you, Arden. I won't. Not after everything we've… I won't."

When I peeked through the bond, the only emotions left from him were steadfast devotion and desperation. He'd keep me safe, at any and all costs.

Power, glory, kingship, none of it was in his head just now. Only me.

I skimmed my hands up his chest and around his neck.

When I went to kiss him though, he tangled his fingers in my hair and gently pulled my head back. "I'm in charge tonight."

My pulse fluttered in my throat. He rarely claimed the dominant role. When he did, it was when he was past needing it. I nodded as much as I could.

Troy kissed me like I was the last thing on Earth that could sustain him then pulled back and frowned. "Wait. You still have a headache?"

"A little," I admitted with a grimace.

"I want to try something. A monarch-level spell. An adapted one, rather. If it works, no more headache. Or anything ache. If it doesn't, pins and needles at worst."

"Pins and needles. Nervous system?"

He nodded, his eyes distant, the way they were when he was thinking hard on Aetheric applications.

"Okay," I said. He'd never suggest anything that'd actually hurt me.

That earned me a giddy flash of joy in the bond. Every time I demonstrated trust in him as an elf, I got it. And I loved it, loved that we could both be our fullest, truest selves with each other.

Troy pulled me close and wrapped his arm around my waist. As he kissed me again, a slip of Aether chased through the bond, and then—

I nearly dropped as not only did the aches of the power hangover wash away, but a wave of pure pleasure seemed to hit everywhere at once.

"Arden?"

"Do that again," I panted. "Please do that again. But more."

The concern on his face flipped to dark satisfaction. I never begged or pleaded. I demanded, no matter how well he pushed my buttons. Fierce delight flared in the bond at this submission from me, and for once he didn't bother trying to bury it.

He skimmed his hands over my body like he was thinking of all the things he wanted to try before tugging me toward the bedroom with unapologetic insistence.

When we got to the bed, his usual lavishing foreplay was more commanding. Rather than teasing and building, taking cues from me, he dominated. Pulled the responses he wanted from me with not just his hands, lips, and tongue, but also this new trick with Aether, a magician of desire.

It worked for me, given where my head was at. For once, I needed someone else to take control.

When I was practically begging for him, I found myself on my belly a moment before he was in me. His body blanketed mine as he moved, as much a claiming as protection. The points of his secondary set of teeth startled me into a higher state of arousal. Not a full bite, just the lightest hint of one, right as his hand snaked between me and the sheets to stimulate me. My climax took me by surprise, and I surrendered to it, gasping his name and moving against him as much as I could.

With a last few powerful movements of his hips, he finished as well. We lay there, the evening's chilly breeze stealing through the cracked windows to dance over us.

I shivered, and he pulled away and rolled out of bed.

I stared at the ceiling while he got rid of the condom in the bathroom and, from the feeling of the bond, brought himself down from whatever headspace he'd been in. When the door swung open again to show his tense outline, I held out a hand.

The stiffness eased, and he came to me.

Our fingers twined together, and I pulled him into bed, his back to my front, one arm wrapped around him as I slid locks of his hair through my fingers, the opposite to our usual.

He gradually let himself ease into my embrace. It broke my heart every time he was so hesitant to accept what he so freely gave, especially when he'd only been being himself.

This time, it broke something else as well: the dam I'd put around my feelings.

"I love you," I whispered, quietly enough that he might miss it.

Of course he didn't. Not with elven senses. A storm surge of emotion came through the bond as he held himself perfectly still. "You—what?"

"You gonna make me say it again?"

With a twist, Troy was facing me. "Arden—"

"Fine. I love you."

"You mean that?"

"You literally have a backdoor into my head. Do you seriously—"

The kiss he cut me off with was one of the better ones. Maybe the best one.

Then he was on top of me again, seeming to drink down my soul as he worshipped me with his lips. Before long we were going at it a second time, me on top this time, riding him with all the passion I was usually afraid to let loose enough to show him.

"I'm sorry for earlier. I'm just afraid to lose you," Troy whispered after we'd both cleaned up and lay side by side.

"I know. Me too."

"I was never allowed to even think about loving someone. But now I do, and it's you. I have to fight everything in me that only wants to keep you alive and mine. Because if I did anything other than find a way to support what you're trying to do in your way, I'd be blocking what made me love you in the first place."

I let him feel what I felt then, the throat-closing blend of gratitude and hell, love. I was tired of the word already, but not how he made me feel, so I snuggled up closer to rest my head on his chest, my skin still tingling from his new trick.

He rubbed his hand along my spine, and we lay there, dealing with our own thoughts, until I fell asleep.

Of course, the gods had to ruin it.

I started to dream of the stormy shore again, but it twisted to become the white blankness of the unframed Crossroads.

"It's been a few moons since you let your guard down enough to bring you here," Neith said from behind me.

I nearly dislocated a knee trying to turn too quickly. Time moved differently here, and the pearly sand underfoot didn't agree with the laws of physics I was used to. My heart thudded in my chest as I wrestled with what that might mean. Had opening myself to Troy opened me to the gods as well? Did I dare take the opportunity to ask about Callista?

Tread carefully. As far as I could guess, Neith's gift—the ivory-hilted dagger with a blade of meteoric iron—had enabled a tighter tie to her. I'd kept it in a lead-lined box ever since using it to kill Mireia Luna at Neith's command, which I'd hoped would limit the gods' spying on me.

"How may I serve my lady?" I asked.

Neith's laughter was the sound of a waterfall pouring over the edge of the world, thundering into unfathomable depths. She studied me as she whirled her ankh on its leather thong. "You truly think we believe you wish to serve?"

I thought fast. "I know better than to think I can outmatch the Old Ones."

Her black eyes bored into me, weighing so heavily I couldn't breathe. "In that case, prepare yourself. We come at the thinning of the Veil. Further instruction will come closer to the time. We expect you to have Riders."

The Crossroads faded, and I jerked awake with a gasp that hurt my lungs. Troy was hollering in my face.

"I'm fine." My voice was raspy, and I could barely shape the words as I put a hand over his heart.

He stopped with the shouting and the shaking. "What happened? You went blank. Just gone in my head even though you were still breathing."

"The Crossroads. Neith. They're coming."

Something savage curled through the bond, vicious and deadly. He'd fight the gods to protect me, and I shut the bond to a bare whisper to stop him from reading that I didn't want him to be a sacrifice of blood and bone. He already knew, and I knew I couldn't make that choice for him.

"When?" he said.

"At the thinning of the Veil."

Troy frowned. "Samhain?"

I dragged myself up into a seated position, squeezed my eyes shut, and rubbed my pounding head. "Makes sense, no?"

"Yes. But that's in a week and a half."

"Then we need to get the hell on with finding Iaret."

Rather than answering, Troy handed me a glass of water from the nightstand. When I gulped it down, he went and refilled the glass, offering it to me as he perched on the edge of the bed.

I shook my head and wrapped my arms around my shins, resting my head on my knees.

Troy backed off, knowing from experience that I needed my space for a minute or ten. "I'll go call Alli."

"Thanks." Only when I heard his voice in the other room did I let myself give in to the shakes. Everything I'd worked for, everything I'd built, all the people looking to me for protection. All of it was at risk of being destroyed by the end of the month, and I didn't have the faintest idea of where to find the one person who could maybe—maybe!—help Troy and me prevent it.

Time to change that. Fast.

Chapter 7

News that big on the heels of an attempt by the humans to burn some witches necessitated a parliament meeting. Too much was coming to a head for me to go it alone.

I summoned everyone to my place at dawn and set out several bottles of locally brewed mead and platters of charcuterie, cheeses, olives, pickled vegetables, and artisan bread from one of the bakeries downtown. I thought it was early for that kind of stuff, but some of them would be ready for bed. Fortunately, Troy did most of the grocery shopping these days. Not only did we have enough refreshments for an emergency meeting, but it was the good shit as well.

Normally we'd have met at The Umstead or one of the state parks, but our original group had expanded in the last few months and not everyone was comfortable with it being so public. In addition to Terrence, Ximena, Vikki, Noah, Janae, Val or Laurel, Duke—absent today—and Troy, we occasionally had their seconds. Doc Mike had started joining us as well, representing human sensitives, psychics, and necromancers and providing information on what was happening with all the death cases now under review. I'd had to bring in the deck table and chairs, but we all fit in my dining area. Barely.

Zanna represented the fae when she wasn't negotiating with the lords and ladies. I thought she had been, but she must have just gotten back because she sauntered in the front door and hopped onto the chair at the head of the table like it was her meeting while I was up greeting the weres and Val.

Troy and I exchanged an amused glance, and I shrugged. A kobold would claim ownership of wherever she was, and I didn't need the hors d'oeuvres cursed for something as petty as a seating arrangement.

Taking the chair at the foot of the table, I made myself a mini-sandwich and waited for everyone else to find a seat. "Full table today. Glad you could all make it. As we come in allyship, let us leave thus."

Everyone around the table echoed me, and we all lifted our glasses to take a sip of mead then ate a little something.

Salt and water, meat and mead, the fruits and ales of the earth were the markers of goodwill and hospitality in cultures the world over. A ceremony, however small, was important for a group as diverse—and as potentially deadly—as this one.

I met everyone's eye as soon as they'd all gotten settled. "Docket's as full as the table, and we have some decisions to make. First up: human aggression against the witches yesterday. Then a status update on mundane police cases, updates from each of the other factions, and news on the Wild Hunt."

They all stiffened when I mentioned the Hunt, and Doc Mike patted Janae's hand comfortingly even as his expression tightened. They'd grown surprisingly close, and a quiet but strong friendship had sprung up between the reluctant necromancer and the experienced witch. On Doc's other side, Noah laced his fingers together, probably an effort not to publicly comfort Doc Mike in turn. Maybe it shouldn't have been a surprise that several of us had developed closer-than-usual cross-faction relationships, but for some it would be.

Janae cleared her throat and straightened, visibly gathering herself before launching into the story of yesterday's mob. "The coven leaders are deciding whether it is time to take a more active hand in the negotiations with the mundanes," she said to finish. "After yesterday's violence, we want specific protections in the bill being debated in the state government."

I held back a wince. North Carolina had had a conservative house and senate and a liberal governor for years now. The state split on everything, being solidly purple in recent election years, partly due to a severe gerrymandering problem. The cities and university towns were a deep blue, the rural areas unwaveringly red. Given the Bible verses on the placards yesterday, in a city that was one of the most progressive in the state, it was fifty-fifty or worse for the witches. Organized religion didn't always play nicely with progress. I didn't envy Doc Mike's situation. Being both a devout Christian and a necromancer had to be eating at him.

Val swallowed a mouthful of olives and raised a hand slightly. "I was able to steer the investigation into that arson away from Otherside involvement. We should be fine for now, but we need to figure out what we're going to do when we can't cover everyone anymore."

Everyone looked at me, and I kept my face blank. "I suppressed the fire long enough for Troy to create an opportunity for the witches to escape, under escort from some of my Guard. I won't say we got lucky, but we can't afford to have to be luckier." I leaned back in my chair and crossed my arms. "As always, we're running out of time. Sooner or later, I'll need to out myself as well. Probably sooner. There's too much power rising in the Triangle to stay hidden much longer."

A few gazes shifted to Troy in the seat to my right. He was trying to mask his new power signature and largely failing. Terrence narrowed his eyes but said nothing, likely expecting that we'd talk about it later.

I focused on Janae. "Let us know what you need and when."

She nodded. "Hope and the other witches in the community are shifting to online orders only for now, and Allegra has spared one of her team to fortify our security. Life and financial impacts should be minimal for now."

Troy sent a confirming pulse through the bond.

I nodded. "Good. Thank you. Doc?"

Doc Mike cleared his throat and adjusted his plain blue tie. His usual Southern drawl was even thicker with nervousness as he said, "Detective Rice at Raleigh PD is still pushing. Arden's refusal to cooperate has him at a dead end for the Umstead case. I've diverted him as much as I can, but he seems to have gotten a bee in his bonnet."

I grimaced. "I might have suggested that he was something like a racist when he questioned me. He'd likely have taken that pretty hard. Probably trying to prove he's not by finding an evidence-backed reason to blame vampires."

Noah sighed and tilted his head back to scowl at the ceiling, beyond exasperated.

"Look, I'm sorry," I said. "If I'd given an inch on the vampires, they would have used known and suspected vamp cases to profile the whole community. For better or worse, the Darkwatch's overstep in Chapel Hill has Detective Chan off our backs, and Durham PD has no reason to suspect Otherside involvement in anything. I'll deal with Rice."

With a hand wave, Noah signaled his agreement. He was in one of his moods then.

I let it go, still too jittery about Neith's visit to say anything. "Fine. The witches will let us know their decision about involvement in the state legislation. I'll work with Doc Mike on Detective Rice. Zanna? News from the fae lords and ladies?"

The kobold straightened, looking unusually embarrassed. "My lords and ladies of the Summerlands continue to ask for time. A Grand Summit has been called. Nothing like it since

Stonehenge was raised. It will take time before they're ready to join this alliance. I have emergency powers to represent the fae, but decisions need to be taken back to the Chamber of Lords."

The usually self-assured kobold looked awed by the power she'd been granted.

I moved the meeting along. "Thank you for the update, Zanna. Hopefully, we'll hear sooner rather than later. Who's next?"

Terrence cleared his throat. "Acacia Thorn, Jade Tooth, and Red Dawn have started our move to new territory. Vikki's people are the vanguard, working with the blended pride to identify safe locations and securing property."

"Red Dawn? You've got a name now?" I asked Vikki.

She nodded. "We have yet to socialize it with the other wolf clans, but Ana and I have agreed that I'm alpha."

"Congratulations." I raised my glass again.

The whole group toasted her with solemn respect. It had been a long time since a new were clan had come into being, and this one was special. It was led by two women, as part of a cross-were agreement between the wolves and the locally allied leopards and jaguars. A brave new world was already here, whether or not the gods kicked off. The werewolves were more conservative than the other were clans, more exclusionary. Those who couldn't shift fully, or who were in any way "different," were exiled or murdered until recently. That included the relationship between Vikki and her lover, Ana Farkas, who was supposed to have married Roman.

Werewolf politics gave me a headache for more reasons than one.

"Anything else from the weres?" I asked.

Terrence exchanged glances with Ximena and Vikki. They all shook their heads.

"Great. Noah?"

"Luz and Giuliano are coming out of their hibernation." Noah glowered, probably remembering how the Miami and New York reps had tried taking over our Raleigh coterie. "They'll be weak for a while yet, and their people are still sleeping. In addition to her work with the mundane state legislature, Maria is in negotiations with the rest of the Masters of the Eastern Seaboard to secure our territory. Perhaps even expand it."

That was news to me. "Expand it?"

Noah's smile was predatory. "We have leverage. Raleigh has always been overlooked, mostly due to the power-sharing agreements with the Chapel Hill Conclave and Callista. For all his faults, Torsten grew the coterie much larger than would be expected for a territory this size and was clever about it. We rival Charlotte in strength now and are catching up with Atlanta. If we can combine the Charlotte coterie with ours..." He flashed his eyebrows, clearly pleased, his earlier mood already forgotten. "So many possibilities open up."

Troy leaned on the table. "That's a shift in the balance of power in the territory."

"It is," Noah agreed. "But with House Solari being the only elven power in the Triangle and the local elven presence significantly reduced, the Charlotte coterie is supportive of making Maria Mistress of the whole state, not just Raleigh. We have a primordial elemental, an alliance, and the seconds of the two most powerful coteries on this coast in custody. They don't. Our Mistress has strong connections with the local community. It's only right that Raleigh becomes the new vampiric power center."

A pulse of approval came through the bond. Troy liked this. Despite the acrimony between him and Maria back in January he'd generally had a good relationship with her, and she'd backed him in a few things before we'd met. He was probably glad for an opportunity to return the favor and secure the vampires as statewide allies.

Personally, I was a little overwhelmed at the idea that I was one of the factors that was enough to shift the center of vampiric power in the state from Charlotte to Raleigh—effectively making the Triangle a cosmopolitan Otherside capital of sorts with the alliance. It was something completely new as far as I was aware. The more I considered it, the more I could see why Troy approved. We'd have collective bargaining power with both the rest of Otherside and the mundanes. Something to look forward to, after the Hunt.

"Good stuff," I said. "Will Charlotte's master be coming this way for a parlay?"

"Yes." Noah looked insufferably pleased. "When we're ready, which is not now."

I nodded, relieved not to have to rush on something for once. "Fine. Val?"

"Same as usual. The Collective is still, um, hesitant, let's call it, to be involved with either the alliance or the mundanes. Especially now that—" She halted and grimaced, glancing at Troy.

He sighed. "The elephant in the room. I now have a power signature."

Terrence pursed his lips. "I wondered when we were going to get to that."

Troy looked at me. I flashed my eyebrows at him. This was his rodeo.

"It manifested yesterday," Troy said. "I drew deeper on Aether than usual to maze and disperse the crowd trapping the witches and…" He shrugged, the stiffness of the movement telegraphing his discomfort with the topic.

"So Miss Arden could help the rest of us level up?" Terrence asked after a long silence.

I shook my head. "Highly unlikely."

They stared at me like I was holding out, and my heart pounded at what I finally had to admit after almost a year of hiding it. "There's an Aetheric bond—an accidental one—between Troy and me. We tried untangling it, as did Allegra and Iago, both of whom have greater skill with auras and auratic residue. It's only deepened over time. Likely because my capacity to tap Chaos has increased with the rest of my powers. In any case, now Troy and I can draw on each other's strength as needed."

"Ah." Noah nodded like I'd finally answered a long-held question or two, and Troy tensed. If anyone called magical trespass he'd be in a heap of shit.

Suspicion twisted a few faces—especially Vikki's—but nobody said the words that would have triggered a trial. Goosebumps rippled over me. Magical trespass carried a death penalty. It was how I'd gotten Troy to pay his debt in lives. And how he'd ended up saving mine twice over when we'd faced the Redcaps for a second time.

To solidly negate any future plans to target either of us for it, I said, "The gods are pleased with the situation and it ensures our ability to secure the territory, so it's in our best interest to leave it at this point."

Under the table, Troy squeezed my thigh in thanks. Doc Mike blanched, as he always did, at the mention of multiple gods. Janae patted his hand in reassurance this time. Val crossed her arms and slid down in her seat, clearly not liking any of this. The weres bristled as their eyes shone with the colors of their beasts, Ximena going so far as to let a low warning growl slide from her, but they didn't push.

Then Terrence said, "There are two halves of Aether, and I don't see the djinn leaving a development like this unchallenged. Where's Duke?"

"Keeping an eye on my sister," Troy said before I could. I nodded for him to continue when he looked at me. "Evangeline is in Asheville."

Vikki stiffened. "What?"

"When Arden destroyed the local elven Houses, Evangeline was the only royal with any influence who survived without swearing to House Solari. She followed up on an existing plan and fled west, or so we surmise. Sergei has been in contact with her for sure. Roman's involvement is unconfirmed."

Vikki shot out of her chair to pace. "You couldn't have said something sooner? That creates complications."

"Trust me, I'm well aware," Troy said.

"She's your sister." Vikki looked between Troy and I with open antagonism. "What are y'all gonna do about it?"

"She *was* my sister." Troy's voice was thunder and ice, and his power signature spiked as he tugged the collar of his shirt down to show the burn scar that was all that remained of his House tattoo. "I'm disowned. Violently. Because my life, body, and soul are pledged to Arden's. Don't go there, Viktoria. I survived my family's wrath. I'm not responsible for your brothers' ambitions."

Silver flashed in Vikki's eyes.

I let it go, used to were posturing.

Until black claws sprouted from her fingers. That was more than posturing. It was an open threat in my home and at a table of allies.

One I couldn't let stand.

I rose, dropping the auratic shields that tamped my power signature down, and let it spill through the room. "Sit, Vikki, and get control of yourself. We have bigger issues."

She bared wolf-like teeth at me in challenge. "Do tell."

I stared her down until she shifted her claws back to fingernails and threw herself into her chair with a bad attitude.

Then I met the eyes of everyone else present.

Terrence and Ximena, Janae, Doc Mike, and Noah. Zanna. Val.

Troy, who gave me a tired, sad little nod.

I leaned on the table, grounding myself in the wood whose grain I could now read as the tree it had been. "The Wild Hunt starts on Samhain."

Chapter 8

The room erupted.

Everyone abandoned their efforts to control their magic, and power crackled and flared.

Instinctively, I extended a hand to Troy. He twined his fingers in mine. Our magic met with a spark. Melded. Crested. Blew through the room with the blinding power of an eclipse and the frosty certainty of the grave.

Silence fell as everyone stared in shock.

I rarely showed my power so openly and had never blended it with Troy's in front of other people. They'd gotten a hint of his new power level with what was leaking from his shields, but he'd been tamping it down to avoid setting someone off.

Now they knew that as strong as I was as Arbiter and a primordial elemental, Troy and I together were unassailable—and our powers were still growing. I watched comprehension slither through their minds, watched the narrowed eyes and weighing looks that told me they understood he was no longer just a prince consort.

He was a full elven king who still deferred to me as the more powerful being.

Light footsteps on the porch sounded a moment before Etain burst in. "My queen?" Her eyes searched my guests. "Everything okay?"

Troy's face was hard as he made a hand signal, his eyes not leaving our allies. Etain bowed and left, although she took a position on the porch where she could keep an eye on things through the window.

Troy released my hand and sat down, setting the example.

I remained standing and waited until everyone was seated again to speak. "We will handle this as Othersiders. United. Not as bickering children or self-interested factions but as an alliance. Is that understood?"

Nobody answered.

Drawing on Air, I let my eyes glow gold and the pressure of a jet engine build in the space. "I said. Is. That. Understood?"

"Understood," Zanna said approvingly.

When I had verbal or nonverbal agreement from the rest of the group, I said, "Good. I expect next time we come together, y'all will be able to act like you're grown."

It was time to wrap this up.

"Doc," I started, "I'll be in touch about Raleigh PD. Vikki, I expect a report about how to deal with your brothers by end of day. Zanna, a report on the objections the lords and ladies have to the alliance, please. Janae, I need your thoughts on protecting the witches against further mundane aggression. Noah, keep me updated on the situation with the Master of Charlotte. Val, let me know what happens with the report on the fire at Midday Moon. Oh, and I'm sorry, but given all this, I'll need to cancel our weekend practice session. I'll be in touch when I have more on the Wild Hunt."

Nobody objected. They didn't look pleased, but I didn't require them to be. After the battles with the queens, all I required was obedience and service to the greater good of Otherside.

"Good. Keep me posted, and I'll do the same. As we came in peace, so may we leave."

"May we leave in peace," everyone echoed.

I made myself stand to the side of the door, solemnly shaking every hand, until they'd all filed out.

"Now what?" Troy asked when the last car had rolled out of my driveway.

"I need to get the hell outta here," I said without hesitation. I needed the woods. I was not going to manage anything else after a meeting like that without time in nature first. The last time things had gotten tetchy, I'd radiated static electricity for hours—not exactly comfortable for an elf. This time had been worse, and I'd had to expose more of myself than I ever had.

Troy didn't question me. He simply nodded and gave me space to burst out the back door and into the woods at a run. I could sense his frustration in the back of my mind, the curtailed wave of protectiveness, but he stayed where he was. My land was secure.

I blew past my usual training and relaxing spot on the river, where I'd overturned a boulder with Air while I was just getting familiar with my powers. The area was rocky, hilly terrain, and I took a steep, root-crossed slope at a dead run, heedless of the risk of tripping. It was easier than it would have been nine months ago. I was fitter, stronger, faster. Deadlier.

I pushed harder.

When the trail sloped back down to the river, I skidded to a stop, finding a protruding rock to perch on and catch my breath. Troy was closer than the house but far enough away that I still felt like I was alone. The woods were quiet otherwise. No human-sized disturbances or even any deer. Fine.

Plunging my hand into the water, I let my shields down just enough to connect with all the elements. Tension left me with a heavy shudder, and my thoughts quieted. I let the breeze and the river flow past me while the sun warmed me and the rock I sat on lulled me into peace.

I breathed. I existed.

Eventually, I'd need to get better at managing myself in high-tension situations. But more often than not, those situations had turned into a fight for my life. I was improving with proportional and appropriate reactions, but it was a process.

Sometimes I just needed the trees and the open air.

When I felt more in control, I sent a pulse to Troy, frowning when I realized he was overhead. I twisted in time to spot him dropping out of the overhanging branch of a huge sycamore tree before climbing over the rocks to where I sat.

"That's new," I said.

"I've always been able to climb trees." He squatted beside me on the rock, dropping to a full seat when I elbowed him.

"Don't tell me y'all have claws as well."

He snorted. "No. But it's a skill that needed practice."

"Note to self: look up next time we spar."

"Exactly. If you can drop onto a roof, you should expect others to drop onto you." His half-smile gave me chills.

"Glad you're on my side."

"Always." He wrapped an arm around me, squeezing briefly and kissing my temple when I leaned into him. "Want to tell me what's on your mind?"

"I can't go to the gods about Callista and Iaret just yet," I said after a few more seconds' thought. "Vikki was too riled about Roman and Sergei. Her position is still too new, and she's under a crap-ton of pressure. Hell, *I'm* too riled about Roman. I knew he had ambitions, but I guess I never thought they involved joining up with someone who outright wants to kill me, even with all his posturing lately. And I don't like this shell game the fae are playing. This should have been a no-brainer to join us. Why are they stalling?"

"Mhm."

"You can tell me you agree, you know. I can feel it."

He shrugged. "You don't like it when you think you're being steered. Especially when Roman's involved. So I'll let you talk it through first."

I tried scowling at him, but he wasn't wrong. I wanted to pick a fight over it, but that was just me being contrary and difficult and mad at Roman. Another thing I was working on—not using Troy as a punching bag just because he'd let me. I sighed, letting the emotion out to flow away with the river.

Troy swayed, and I caught him, not having realized that I'd pulled him into nature's flow again. He liked it and found it soothing, but if we weren't careful, he'd lose himself.

"Sorry," I muttered.

He just squeezed my hand. "So what's your play?"

"I need to deal with whatever's going on in Asheville before trying this thing with Callista." I swatted at the river to send water spraying, partly annoyance but mostly because I liked how the droplets felt passing through the air molecules. "I can't ask you to hold the House and the Triangle while I deal with the gods but leave threats at the back door."

Tension ebbed out of Troy. "I appreciate that."

"Thought you might. The question now is how much does Roman know, and how do I get him to tell us?"

"Could you mimic Evangeline's voice?"

"Of course. Perfectly." I pulled on one of my passive abilities as a sylph to demonstrate.

Troy shuddered and rubbed the burn scar under his collarbone. "That's... Never mind. I can spoof your phone to look like one of her numbers. We wait for Vikki's report to make sure we aren't missing anything. You call Roman and ask what the next steps are then have Duke follow up. Roman's got a short fuse, but he's clever enough to be careful about this. And if he's not, Evangeline is."

I frowned. "That seems too easy."

"Sometimes the simplest plans are the first overlooked."

"Hmm." That was certainly true in my case. I was still avoiding dealing with the back door I'd discovered in Callista's office, the one I'd only discovered by accident because it had been so obvious I'd overlooked it—like everything else to do with her. And, as it happened, to do with the elves. "Okay then. Let's do it."

***

While Troy did whatever he needed to spoof a phone number at the kitchen table, I sat out on the deck and wrestled with how to deal with Detective Rice. Keeping him out of Otherside business had only made him more adamant about digging into the vampire cases, especially the Umstead case. I had a strong suspicion that Raleigh PD in general would not be supportive of Otherside, just based on the fact that our conversation had been recorded and he'd had no problem spewing some bigotry.

But what about Rice as an individual? What might he do— who might he be—if he was separated from his police buddies?

He'd gone thoughtful when I pointed out that a Black man should know and do better than to try persecuting another group who only wanted equal rights. Could I use that to bring him around?

Bigger question: what lengths was I willing to go to for Otherside if he refused to see reason?

That was a question I did not enjoy sitting with, at all. What I was willing to do to protect Otherside in general and myself in particular had escalated quickly since the beginning of the year. I'd gone from hiding and purely defensive measures to killing when attacked, to outright murder. Troy and the rest of the alliance might be comfortable with it, but I wasn't.

Was I willing to give Rice over to the vampires to be turned if I couldn't convince him? Was that better or worse than killing him myself?

Too many questions. I needed to be reasonably sure about this because it would mean exposing Otherside, exposing myself, or another murder. Possibly all three.

Problem was, I didn't have time for certainty. If I didn't have the humans off our backs by Samhain, anything Otherside did to face the Wild Hunt would see us getting attacked by confused or vengeful mundanes.

Frustrated, I channeled some energy into creating and holding a primordial ball. I'd gotten better, much better, at blending the four elements and stabilizing them with Chaos. I could hold it for longer as well, and when I was done, I could separate the elements back out again so they didn't create a minor warping of reality when they collapsed. My power hangovers had lessened dramatically since I'd started practicing with all four elements at once and eating a more elven-style diet. Troy had been right about that one.

Quit stalling, Arden. Make the tough call. I created a second ball and sent it in an infinity loop with the first.

I knew what I had to do. I just didn't like it. Rice needed to be brought into the fold or removed as a threat. Now. No two ways about it. I'd already let the situation go on too long, pretending that I was trying not to step on Maria's toes as she took point on the negotiations with the mundanes.

Sighing, I dissipated the primordial energy and went to the sliding glass door. Troy looked up when I opened it and stuck my head in.

"I need to deal with Detective Rice," I said.

"I thought that might be what you were deciding." He leaned away from the laptop in front of him and crossed his arms. "When?"

"Today."

"How?"

I shrugged. "That depends on him. But I might need Noah on standby."

Troy frowned. "It's that or an arranged accident. The Ebon Guard can manage it if you don't want it to be a weather event. Alli has a couple of ex-Darkwatch agents who specialized in accidents."

Of course he'd already been thinking about it. That would have annoyed me a few months ago, when I was still thinking I had to do and fix and think of everything myself. Now I was just glad that he was around to have my back. I'd spent most of the year floundering from one clusterfuck to the next, barely staying on top of things, scrambling to make plans to react to shit the rest of Otherside threw at me rather than proactively managing them.

Now I had a partner to support me and a whole Ebon Guard sworn to help.

I came the rest of the way into the house and draped myself over his shoulders from behind, hugging him across the chest and kissing his cheek. "Have I mentioned I'm glad you chose me?"

His cheek flexed as he smiled, and he rested his hand on my crossed arms. "You have. But I never get tired of hearing it."

"Call Allegra, please. I assume she already has people on Rice?"

"She does."

My throat thickened, and I squeezed Troy to anchor myself as I worked myself up to giving the order, mourning the woman I'd been before I had blood on my hands.

"Tell her to be ready. If I can't talk him around, I need him taken out."

Chapter 9

Detective Clayton Rice was just as tall and imposing as always, but he looked tired now. Eyes darting, posture tight enough to bunch the starched white business shirt he wore tucked into creased jeans. He looked out over The Umstead's private lake, his back to me, which told me he definitely had backup on site.

He still barely managed not to jump when I sidled up to him and leaned against the guardrail.

"Detective."

"Ms. Finch." Dark brown eyes swept me from head to toe, pausing briefly at the places people usually kept weapons.

I had one, but the godblade at the small of my back wasn't in his line of sight. I didn't like carrying it, but it was the only thing I had small enough to avoid detection by mundanes yet powerful enough to stop an Othersider. "How many men you got placed?"

Rice snorted. "Enough."

I held back a smirk at the fact that he hadn't thought to ask me the same. "Earpiece? Wire?"

"We agreed on not."

"That's not a no."

"Well aren't you Little Miss Suspicious."

When I flashed my eyebrows, he rolled his eyes and turned his head to either side so that I could see his ears then unbuttoned his shirt enough for me to see there was no wire.

Smiling, I leaned in to skim my hands over him to check for one anyway, ending with a kiss on the cheek to turn his pressed lips into a full-blown scowl.

"Relax, *darling*. Just being thorough. Walk with me." I didn't trust him not to have stuck a bug under the railing or have someone on the patio with a directional mic. I had a mini-jammer that one of the Guard's tech experts had cobbled together in my bag, Troy on the patio, and Etain and Haroun watching for obvious cops scattered around the grounds, but acting like I had backup would have Rice and his people looking for it. I was supposed to be a lone private investigator, so I did what I would have done before becoming a force.

"What's all this about, Ms. Finch? After our last conversation, I didn't expect to hear from you again. Especially after Tom Chan fell over himself insisting that there was no reason to think you were anything other than what you claim to be."

I didn't answer for a few steps, both to give myself time to think and to get us a little farther from any listening devices. "I want to talk about the Umstead case."

"I imagined so, given that you chose the hotel for our discussion. Why the change of heart?"

"Because I have larger concerns that have recently escalated and I need you to stop taking up my time and attention with this one," I said bluntly.

That earned me a deep frown. "Excuse me? I haven't—"

"You haven't called me about it again, no. But you're hassling people. People who also have bigger issues. People who look to me to take care of things."

He snorted, looking incredulous. "You some kind of enforcer, Finch?"

I met his gaze and gave him my best dead-eyed stare, the one I'd seen too many times from Troy.

Amusement slipped from his face, and his eyes darted, looking for a threat he knew was there but couldn't see, at least not in me. "What is this?"

"A warning. A chance. A come-to-Jesus chat. The last and only one you'll get."

"Threatening an officer of the law is—"

"Not even the least of my worries. Think about what that might mean."

"It sounds like it means your vampire buddies are a mob. Like maybe you know something more about those bodies at the morgue this past summer as well."

"You're not wrong, although the vamps keep their business restricted to themselves. They're big on consent, actually. More so than most cops I know."

"Finch, if you don't get to the point, I might have to call some of those cops."

"I wouldn't. I really wouldn't." I sighed, careful to keep a lid on my power signature, though I could tell I was leaking by the quick glances at me and the sweat on Rice's brow despite the cool day. I needed to get this sorted. Fast. Before he broke. "Look. I'm sure all your suspects say something like this, but I'm trying to help. The Umstead death was a vampire, but it was handled. He's dead."

"Handled by who?"

"By me. That's my job, Rice. I'm a fixer. If Otherside steps out of line, the community handles it. If they don't, I get involved, and trust me when I say that nobody wants that. The only danger to mundanes—to non-magical humans like yourself—is if you keep pushing on matters that we have already dealt with. We self-police. We always have. Humans are in more danger from each other than they are from us."

Rice stopped dead in the path, looming with his hands on his hips. "What in the name of God and all his angels are you saying? That there's a whole damn conspiracy?"

I just looked up at him, completely unconcerned by his size or his effort to cow me with it.

"You're saying that you've killed people." His eyes darted ahead and behind, checking for people I already knew weren't on the path given the lack of disturbance in the air molecules. "You threatening to kill me?"

"I'd rather not, to be honest."

His eyes narrowed. "What did you do to Tom?"

"Nothing. The people trying to kill me did it. I handled them."

"Trying to kill *you*?"

I offered a cheeky smile, hoping it covered up my fraying nerves. The longer this took, the more tense Troy got in the back of my head. He wouldn't move without orders, but his tension was making *me* more tense. I sent him a little pulse so he'd know I was okay, but it didn't do much. "Well, they kidnapped me first. But yeah, killing me was the idea. Believe it or not, some people really hate me, Rice. I'm hoping that you're not on that list."

"So you're not human."

I shrugged, not able to deny it after everything I'd said, but not really ready to out myself entirely and annoyed that was his big takeaway.

"What are you?"

"Doesn't matter. What does matter is that I am coming to you in peace. I am *asking* you to go back to the station today and say that I, as your last lead, cooperated fully but was unable to corroborate any of your theories and to close the case. I'm also asking you to drop the zombie case because yes, the morgue thing was zombies and no, you really, really do not want to know what that whole deal entailed."

"What if I don't close the cases? What if I bring in Dr. Miller to talk about these so-called zombies?"

Sighing, I rocked into motion, intentionally giving him my back. After a tense few steps, he caught up.

"We'd rather come to a mutually beneficial understanding than the various alternatives," I said. I wanted to threaten him to stay away from Doc Mike, but I couldn't give away my attachment to my friend. "The local Otherside community wants a peaceful relationship with humans. We want to be a model for the rest of the world. The future is here, and we've always lived among you. What difference does it really make that you know now?"

"It means—" Rice started angrily then stopped.

I kept walking, letting him deal with his thoughts.

"Zombies." He muttered. "Vampires. Werewolves. Witches. Whatever that other guy in the second video was. Whatever *you* are. You're not *human*."

"Neither are dogs. They kill fifty people a year, but y'all still keep them in your homes."

"Because most dogs don't—" He cut off as he realized he was about to make my point. "You really expect me to believe that *vampires* and *werewolves* come in peace."

"How many times you been bitten by one?"

He glared at me.

"Okay. And how many times has another human attacked you? Shot at you? Gotten aggressive while you were out on a call?"

"For all I know they were—"

"Stop. They weren't, and you know it." I let my disgust come out in my tone. "If they had been and they were out of control enough to attack, you'd be dead or turned. Come on, Rice, this bigoted shit is beneath you."

He fisted his hands and spluttered, but I didn't let him say anything.

"You're a big, bald, Black man who has to be able to bench two-fifty. How many times have these same arguments been used against you? Half the reason you're at a five-star hotel in pressed business casual with those fancy-ass shoes is because you know that there are people here who'd think you were a thug or a thief if you came wearing anything else. You navigate the world based on the threat *other people* project onto you, and you can't see how you're doing the same to Othersiders?"

"I'm not sure I like your tone, Ms. Finch."

"So you're going to tone police me. Just like I'm sure has been done to you when you raise your voice in a meeting. When you make a point a little too passionately or with too much conviction. When you do anything other than speak in a voice like sweet brown sugar, using small words to hide your intelligence just enough to not be a threat."

Fury tightened his face, the mental gears turning as he tried to deny the experiences we both knew and had had by virtue of what we looked like.

"I don't like this," he finally said.

"I'm not asking you to like it. I'm asking you to help me lead our community—the Triangle, and North Carolina as a whole—forward. Because like I said, we have bigger issues."

"I'll get to those bigger issues in a minute. First, I need to know what you mean by help you lead the community forward. I will *not* betray humanity by covering up non-human crimes."

"I wouldn't ask you to. Only to let us continue policing ourselves. We have zero tolerance for anyone who steps out of line. I mean, hell, I've already admitted to killing people who have, including those who attacked Tom Chan and myself." I studied him, trying to get a read on his mood, and softened my tone. "The mundane police aren't equipped to handle this in a way that's effective or fair. Trying is only going to start a war. I think we both want to avoid that, especially given what's coming. Look at it this way—you save resources, taxpayer money, and lives by letting us do exactly what we've already been doing. Where's the problem?"

"The problem is in a parallel society running on its own laws."

"A parallel society that has *always existed* and abides by mundane laws in addition to our own in an effort to integrate, even with y'all completely unaware."

Rice shook his head, looking more frustrated than anything else now. "I'm gonna need time to think about this."

"Of course. But think fast. And close those cases. Please."

He gave me a warning look that said *Don't push me* as clearly as speech would have, and I just shrugged.

"What's this bigger matter?" he asked.

I carefully kept my face blank. "Otherside isn't all that's out there."

Rice halted in his tracks. "Excuse me?"

"We go bump in the night, but that's just on this plane."

"This plane? I assume you don't mean the kind flying out of RDU."

"No. I mean worlds beyond this one and the beings that inhabit them."

"Worlds. Beings." Rice's voice had dropped an octave. "Beings like…"

"Gods," I said softly. "Among other things."

"Aw hell no. Get the— Gods. *Gods.* Plural."

"Mhm."

He gave me a hard look. "You're not joking."

"Nope. Dead serious."

"Let's say I'm in a mood to humor you. These so-called gods are a problem because?"

"Because for the first time since the last Great Flood, they're coming. Trust me, the apocalypse is small potatoes compared to what they have planned."

"Great Flood." He thought about that for a moment, and then his eyes widened. "As in Noah's Ark?"

"That's the one."

Rice fell into a shocked silence for a few steps. "I don't even know what to do with this load of bull."

We'd almost completed our circuit around the lake.

I needed to wrap this up fast because Troy waited for his cue for what to do next. "I have until the end of the month to find a resolution for that issue, Detective. I would really rather have all my time, energy, and attention freed up to handle it than have to keep worrying about Raleigh PD digging into matters for which there is no further resolution available. I also need someone to take the lead on getting humans in the Triangle to chill the fuck out about Otherside so that we can worry less about protecting ourselves from you and more about protecting y'all from what's coming. Okay? Can we take a step in that direction?"

He studied me again, a hard, weighing look. "Why would you protect us? Why would we trust you to?"

"Because we've lived in symbiosis with humans since beginnings that even we can't remember and if the gods destroy the world in the Wild Hunt, not all of us can cross the Veil to escape it. If you don't trust us, trust our self-interest. It's the only thing that's kept us all alive this long."

We'd reached the end of the loop. Troy was still lounging on a patio chair with the arrogant grace of a big cat, keeping an eye on two nervous-looking men who clearly knew he was there and had an idea who he was. Our obvious plant, to keep the cops from looking too hard for the rest of the Ebon Guard. It meant they'd know he wasn't human, but Troy was willing to take the hit. His new power signature was going to make it hard for him to hide for much longer anyway.

"You brought security?" Rice said once he'd spotted Troy as well. He obviously remembered him as my private security from the first Reveal, even if he didn't recognize Troy as the "other guy" from the second one.

"I did mention that not everyone loves my cute little self, didn't I? It's been a rough year."

The detective crossed his arms, pressing his lips together as he studied me. "Everything you've said sounds ludicrous. I don't like it. I don't like vampires. I don't like *you*." He paused and stood there glaring at me, as though all of his dislikes were somehow my fault. "But I suppose you made some good points."

"Does that mean we have an understanding?"

"What happens to me if we don't?"

I just looked at him.

"Huh. It's like that?"

"I neither confirm nor deny anything. I'm just asking you to ask yourself if your current actions are really what best serves Raleigh."

After another few heartbeats of staring at me, Rice surprised the hell outta me by extending a hand. "I'll think on what you've said, Ms. Finch."

I shook it. "Think fast. And Detective? Don't try following me or getting Durham PD to post up on my house. Or the feds, for that matter. Like I said, it's been a rough year, and I've had to take measures to ensure my safety. Wouldn't want y'all to trip them doing a job that doesn't need doing."

"I'll keep that in mind."

"See that you do." With a last stern look, I jogged up the stairs back to the hotel lobby.

Troy rose and fell in beside me as I passed his table, making no effort whatsoever to hide his elven grace and speed and only a little to contain his power signature from the mundanes. A threat, if the cops needed one and were smart enough to see it.

"So?" he asked.

"He'll think about it," I murmured.

"You trust him?"

I snorted. "Of course not. He's a nosy sonovabitch. And a cop. And he doesn't like me or you or any of the rest of us."

I'd take risks, but I wasn't going to be that foolish. I sighed as I realized that meant I had more plans to make.

Chapter 10

Vikki's report was waiting by the time we got home. I read through it, slouching on the couch with my feet on the coffee table, Troy's head in my lap as he caught a nap. I didn't see how it was comfortable with his feet hanging off the arm like that, but the man was like a cat. He could sleep anywhere. If the sun was high and I was staying outta trouble, sometimes he gave in to his nocturnal nature and crashed.

I sighed as I read the report a second time, then a third. None of this was particularly helpful, and I wanted to think that it was because Vikki honestly didn't know rather than because she was hiding something. She wouldn't protect Sergei. Not after whatever he'd done to Ana to make them all desperate enough to break from the pack.

According to Vikki, Roman was still in touch with Ana, apparently trying to talk her round to the marriage. Ana was stalling, but reading between the lines, it seemed like the pressure had increased in the last few weeks, around the same time that Roman had started answering my alliance-related messages with aggressive non-answers. He was offering Ana assurances of safety, additional concessions for the Farkas pack, the restructuring of power dynamics between men and women in the Volkov pack, and so on. I frowned at that. Roman's previously stated plan had been to let Ana decide for herself what to do if old man Niko was dead and Roman was able to free her from the original marriage contract.

I shouldn't have been surprised. It seemed like he'd approached that whole deal the same way he'd approached things with me—offer a choice he couldn't see wasn't really one. I didn't think it was malicious on his part. He probably genuinely thought it was in everyone's best interest. He was just so narrowly focused on his own ambitions that he couldn't see where they didn't overlap with everyone else's.

Neither Vikki nor Ana had told him yet they were together. Probably a wise move but one that squeezed my heart.

I didn't think Roman would have had a problem with their being in a relationship, if it wasn't for the fact that it denied him Ana—and therefore a solid alliance with the Farkas pack. It sucked when you couldn't tell the people who should have been closest to you what was going on.

Sergei was still…well, Sergei. He'd been an ass when he'd come to the Triangle and tried to wrest the vampires away from me with Callista's help. He was being an even bigger ass now that he was one death away from inheriting leadership of the Volkov pack and the Blood Moon clan. Vikki didn't trust him at Roman's back, but the one time she'd dared to voice her concern about the youngest Volkov sibling, Roman hadn't taken it well. That didn't surprise me at all, given I'd learned the same thing the hard way back in the spring.

Maybe there was a mission for the Guard there. Sow mistrust between Roman and Sergei.

I stared at the ceiling, running my fingers through Troy's hair as I thought. He relaxed completely, contented by the physical attention, and slipped deeper into sleep. I eased a wall up between us in the bond before his sleepiness could pull me under too.

I tried to remember if I'd ever used my passive ability to mimic voices and sounds in front of Roman. I didn't think so. I'd been much more hesitant about using my magical abilities when we'd been together. They slipped out if I was relaxed enough in bed, but I'd still been coming to terms with being known as an elemental after spending my life in hiding. If I could rile him enough, maybe he wouldn't even think about it.

Something nudged at me, the intuitive sense that told me when I was on the right track. I needed to do this.

Dread weighed heavy on me. I needed to know.

But the part of me that had fallen in love with Roman didn't want to confirm that he was knowingly and willingly working with my enemies. I wanted it to be all Sergei. He'd gone off-piste before. Worked with Callista behind his father's back.

I grimaced. I *assumed* it had been behind Niko's back. Or that their mother, Irina, would have stopped it if she'd known about it. But everything in Vikki's report indicated Blood Moon had been rotten for years and getting worse. That Niko had been increasingly paranoid and power hungry. That Irina might have run the pack from behind the scenes, but her efforts were only a stopgap.

Niko wouldn't have sent the only child he saw as his legitimate heir to the Triangle to treat with an upstart like me. Not without a backup plan that involved Callista. And while Sergei certainly was a cocky little shit, he hadn't behaved like someone who was acting without orders.

My heart hurt. I knew, deep down, Roman had either left that part out when he told me about Sergei's confession or that he hadn't considered it worth mentioning because Roman's intentions had been good and therefore canceled out Sergei's. It wasn't logical, but it made sense, given how badly Roman had wanted to reclaim his place with his family.

The Sight pushed at me. Heavy. Insistent. Certain. I knew, and I didn't want to.

"What's wrong?" Troy mumbled.

"Sorry. I thought I'd muted."

"You did. Mostly. But your body locked up."

I grimaced. "Roman knows. About Evangeline."

He was awake and upright faster than anyone who'd been that deeply asleep had a right to be. The gold in his eyes sparked with restrained fury. "Viktoria's report confirms it?"

"No. The Sight. I was mulling over the events of this past spring and moving the pieces around with what Vikki's reported here." I handed him my phone to read for himself.

He scanned it then handed the phone back. "If we were just going on the report, I'd say it was a reach. But you've been right every time you lean on the Sight."

Emotions flickered through the bond as he processed what this meant. Righteous outrage smothered the lingering fear that drove his nightmares. Evangeline had been an active participant in his torture. For my sake, he'd tried to give Roman the benefit of the doubt, knowing it was a bad look to talk shit about my ex-boyfriend and a fellow alliance member. But he wouldn't ever dare doubt his sister or what she was capable of.

I scrubbed my hands over my face and pushed to my feet. "I really want to be wrong."

"Only one way to find out."

"Yeah. Fine, let's get it done."

Troy got up and went to the laptop on the kitchen table, where he'd set up the program to spoof a phone number. "Ready when you are. Just click here to dial."

I stalled, getting a glass of water, then lit some incense and tried to center myself. "Okay."

Troy held out a headset. I took it and dialed.

Roman picked up on the third ring. "Hello?"

"Sergei?" I said in Evangeline's voice, praying he couldn't hear my thundering heart.

"Evie? No, this is Roman. I thought we agreed you weren't going to call me. Sergei's your contact." He sounded pissed.

Evie, huh? Were they that close, or was he just doing what he did with me and talking down?

I pulled out my best eighteen-year-old princess attitude. "It was an accident, okay?"

Roman sighed. In my mind's eye, he was pinching the bridge of his nose, frustrated and trying to be patient. "It's fine. We need to be careful is all. What do you need?"

"An update. How long are we going to wait?"

"Look, I know you're impatient to get back to the Triangle, but I have to finish this agreement with the Farkas pack before we deal with Arden and Troy."

My heart stopped, and I barely remembered to breathe. Fortunately, my mouth was on autopilot with a stab in the dark, pushed by the Sight. "I told you we'd take care of that for you."

"That was before Arden destroyed the elven faction in the Triangle."

"The Darkwatch—"

"Is still sitting on the sidelines despite what you said when you got here. You came to me, Evie. You wanna move on Arden and finish your brother? Clear some of my obstacles with the Farkas pack or get the Darkwatch to move their asses in the Triangle. Now if you'll excuse me, I have a clan to run."

The phone clicked off. I sat down, trying to breathe too fast around a closed throat and unable to see through tears I tried to blink away before they could fall.

I thought I knew what betrayal felt like. I'd been wrong.

Troy's expression and the bond were carefully blank, though whether it was from hiding his reaction to hearing his sister's voice coming out of my mouth or from the open admission of an imminent threat from Roman, I couldn't tell. Probably both.

"They'll figure out that Evangeline wasn't the one who called eventually," he said. "We can't waste time. I'll call Allegra and the rest of the alliance."

Clenching my fists, I swallowed hard. Nodded. "I've got Vikki and Duke."

I stared at the phone in my hand, my thumb hovering over Vikki's number as Troy headed for the deck out back to catch Allegra up on the situation.

I wanted to rage. To go out to the woods and burn something. To scream. Anything other than sit here at my kitchen table, trying to smash my fury about the latest of Roman's betrayals into a mental box in front of my current boyfriend.

Part of my mind was already trying to make excuses. *Roman doesn't mean it. He's just playing Evangeline to get control of his pack and clan. This is some kind of move on his part to prove to me that he's valuable.*

The breath I took came in so hard it hurt.

No. No excuses.

He'd made his choices over and over again, always the reverse of Troy's. He knew the Wild Hunt was coming. Vikki had made a note of it in her report. He knew what I'd gone through with the elves in general and the Monteagues in particular. He knew what Sergei had done.

He was still choosing the path of least resistance to power.

It wasn't even about securing the pack. The alliance would have helped negotiate that. I'd offered in more than one of the many voicemails I'd left, which he'd returned only to bitch about the impropriety of Troy's new status as second of my House.

It was about Roman getting what he thought he was owed and proving to everyone he could get it all on his own after they'd cast him out.

That, and punishing those who'd taken what he'd decided was his.

The worst part was, I'd have forgiven him. I'd forgiven Troy. I wanted to forgive Roman and at least be cordial about everything. Yeah, I'd taken it kind of personally at first when he'd left, but it wasn't personal. It was nothing to do with me.

But it was for him. It had to be.

I'd refused to wait for him to decide to pick me. I'd refused to take him back and give him a fallback for a hesitant Ana when he came back to town over the summer. Possibly worst of all, I'd fallen in love with Troy, practically moved the elf into my house, and declared him my partner in ruling House Solari—all things Roman had wanted for himself, if in slightly different fashion and all within roughly the same amount of time Roman had had with me.

I hadn't realized how much of Roman's complaining was a personal vendetta, rather than just posturing for power between factions. Which made Evangeline the perfect ally for Roman in more ways than one. Jealousy was a hell of a drug.

Bitterness curled through me as I finally dialed Vikki.

She was speechless after I filled her in.

"You still there?" I asked.

"I just… Shit, Arden. I'm sorry. I thought he wasn't speaking to me to punish me for defying him and staying in the Triangle. Or for sheltering Ana. I honestly didn't believe he'd do…this."

"That makes two of us." I debated the wisdom of saying what was on my tongue then said it anyway. "You really didn't know?"

"No, I didn't. I would have told you." Vikki's tone hardened, and her mountain accent thickened at the implication that she wasn't trustworthy. "This whole circus relies on you staying alive. I may not like that from a strategic standpoint, but I would like to think that we're friends as well as allies."

"Fine." I swallowed an apology. I wasn't sorry. This had been her business to sort out, and I'd trusted her to do so. But here I was, fixing everything. Again. "Roman's gonna figure out that he's been had."

"And he's gonna be pissed. Lupa damn it all. I'll talk to Ana. Maybe we can salvage this."

"It's not just about Ana. It's about Troy as well. Think about it. Roman's whole goal has always been to reclaim everything he's ever been denied. His alpha status in the pack, his trophy wife, his tie to me. But in his mind, he'd already given up enough. He was owed. Problem is, people aren't prizes. Ana and I both chose otherwise. Not particularly trying to make it personal, but that's what we did by following our own happiness rather than bending to his."

Vikki made a disgusted sigh. "Yeah. Makes sense. Ugh, I do not want to tell him about me and Ana now. But I guess I'm gonna have to."

"That's up to you."

"He needs to see that whatever perfect vision he had is just not going to happen. Maybe he'll give it up."

"You really think that?"

She snorted. "Not an ice cube's chance in hell but he's still my big brother. I have to give him the benefit of the doubt and try. And—hmm."

"Hmm what?"

"Maybe this turf war with the Farkas pack can be avoided."

I followed that logic. "Ah. They still get a Volkov. If they throw in with Red Dawn, they don't need to fight over leadership of Blood Moon."

"Exactly. Lemme go talk this over with Ana. I'll be in touch."

Troy was still making calls on the deck, so I grasped the djinn callstone hanging around my neck. The polished hematite was warm with my agitation as I focused my thoughts on Duke. "You there?"

"Busy." His thoughts were tinged with bubbly amusement. "Something's kicked your wolf into a tizzy. It's rather entertaining."

"I think I know." I filled him in.

"Tricky little bird. That might indeed explain why the wolf brothers are shouting at each other. Well played."

At least someone was happy with all of this. "Keep me posted. If you find a chance to have a little fun, be my guest."

With a mental chuckle, Duke ended the connection, leaving me to figure out what the hell to do now.

Chapter 11

Given I had confirmation that Evangeline was turning supposed allies against me, I had one more play to make today: reach out to the Captain.

I suspected Omar Monteague's tense truce rested on the fact that I had claimed both his blood daughter and adopted son. I'd yet to meet Allegra's twin, Darius, but she assured me he had also sworn to the Ebon Guard before there was a formal Ebon Guard. I wondered how a man like the Captain, who was so deeply committed to the elven matriarchy, had managed to raise and lose three children to the cause that had torn it down, at least locally.

Part of me wondered if he hadn't had a hand in that and whether it was intentional. I took my thoughts to the yard with me, sending a quick pulse to Troy to let him know where I was going.

I'd meant it when I said I didn't trust Detective Rice not to do anything. At the borders of my property, Laurel and Troy had started a physical boundary to complement the djinn warding stones and the blended witch-fae magic that protected my house: a barrier of briars, bramble, and poison oak, ivy, and sumac. On the side facing the road at the end of my long driveway, they'd coaxed the already thick underbrush to fill in further. Zanna had helped me extend the fence around my house to the rest of the property within the plant line, and I'd gated the entry. Trees had long hidden my house from the road.

Now my property was nearly impenetrable except by the narrow gravel drive in front and the path from the river in back.

I could get Duke to help me escape via the Crossroads if I had to, dragging Troy with me. Zanna could cross the Veil to the Summerlands. But anybody other than us and the djinn would have to drop in from above, as I had at the Monteague mansion—and I could control the air overhead.

That didn't mean I was cocky though. I thought some more about how to approach the Captain as I used a pocketknife to prick my fingers and offer a little blood to the earth. Magic was different for all of Otherside, but one thing in common was that blood ties strengthened it. So I reinforced the warding stones and the witch magic, the briars and other plants, building my relationship with the land and plants and reminding them who it was they were protecting.

As I walked, I kept getting stuck on one question: what would the Captain want?

Everyone wanted something. I'd seen it time and again while working as a private investigator, and it usually boiled down to something far more basic than what was stated. People didn't want money. They wanted security. They wanted connection, not custody. They wanted influence and recognition, not the promotion and the corner office. The things they said they wanted were a means to an end.

So what would a man accustomed to the maximum power and influence afforded to him in a system designed to reduce both want in the absence of that system?

Omar could have left and found other queens to serve if he didn't want to bring the Darkwatch to me. He could have attacked me. He could have followed Evangeline, as the last living embodiment of the old system, to Asheville.

But according to Allegra and Troy, he hadn't done any of that.

Something was keeping him here in the Triangle. That something was the key to winning him to my side, or at least preventing him from siding with Evangeline.

Troy was waiting at the table on the deck with a pitcher of lemonade, a bowl of fresh-picked mint, and two glasses when I made my way back. The day had warmed just enough that the tart drink was welcome. He muddled the mint and poured for both of us when I sat down opposite him and rested my bare feet on his lap.

"I need to talk to the Captain," I said when we'd each had a sip.

Troy grimaced. "I was afraid you were working up to that."

"Why afraid?"

"Because he's acting outside his pattern and Iago wasn't able to find any record of the meeting notes that would have resulted in hiding the Book of the Damned. We think they've been tampered with. It was likely Omar's work."

"I've given him long enough. I can't risk Evangeline swaying him to her camp or having a possible ally sit out the Wild Hunt. Besides, he might be the last person who knows where to find Iaret."

"No disagreement."

I studied him. "So why haven't you advised reaching out before now?"

Troy took a deep breath and blew it out. "Before finding the Book of the Damned, I hadn't realized he might be the key to finding Iaret. Alli has been scrambling to build the Ebon Guard into a force to be reckoned with, breaking thousands of years of tradition to bring in people we can trust. The Guard itself has been busy tamping down on the mundane protests and trying to influence human lawmakers while looking for Evangeline. We

95

don't know where Darius is or what's going on with him or what role Omar has played in that, if any. You've been chasing every possible lead on Iaret. Then there's been the negotiations with Maria and the other East Coast coteries and Zanna's with the Chamber of Lords. Arden, we've had our hands full. The Captain wasn't going anywhere, and he wasn't coming after us."

"Fair."

He looked up into the trees ringing my backyard, as though he was looking for answers or consolation, then back at me. "You want to speak to him now?"

"Yep."

Gritting his teeth, Troy pulled out his phone, unlocked it, and swiped a few times. "Here."

I accepted the phone. Gave him a look that said this was his last chance to change his mind. Then hit the call button.

The phone rang for so long I thought the Captain would ignore it. I almost jumped when it connected and a low voice full of quiet strength answered.

"I wondered when I'd be hearing from you, son. Or is this the Arbiter at last?"

I thought about answering in Troy's voice, but that wasn't who I wanted to be. "Hello, Captain."

"Ah. The legendary Arden Finch."

I wrinkled my nose. "It's a bit early for that."

"Is it? You've claimed my children as your own, destroyed everything I held dear, and put the rest of elvendom on notice. The elementals of old have returned. My people's worst nightmare and everything I've spent my life defending against."

Frowning, I gave myself a moment to really hear what he was saying. How he was saying it. "And yet you don't sound threatened. Or angry."

Troy grimaced.

"That's because I'm impressed," the Captain said. "You thwarted my best efforts to shore up the queens. To advise and guide them. To moderate their excesses. Fifty years of effort after twenty years of training. Undone by a lost, naive, sheltered, twenty-six-year-old girl who should have been dead at my son's hands but survived and dared to dream bigger. Well done, Arbiter."

I shot Troy a confused look. This was not going at all the way I'd expected.

Troy just shrugged, sending a sense that he didn't know either through the bond.

"I'm not sure if I should thank you or hang up and prepare for an attack," I admitted. My skin crawled, and I couldn't help but look up at the unprotected sky as I put my feet back on the deck.

The Captain's rich chuckle gave me chills. "Either response would be appropriate. But tell me, why have you finally decided to use the tool that is my son and reach out?"

"Troy's not a tool," I snapped. "He's—"

I realized what he'd done and stopped, flushing. "Well played, Captain."

"I had to see if he was your captive or your lover. I know my boy, and it had to be one extreme or the other. It sounds like the latter. Which both confirms the reports I've gotten and tells me a whole lot more about you than those reports ever did, given that I also know what Keithia and Evangeline did to him."

I shot out of my chair, trying to hold onto my temper by moving. "Get to the point."

"I want to talk to him first."

"You're talking to me."

"Then the conversation is over."

I stood there, fuming, trying to decide how much I wanted to let this guy run this negotiation. I looked at Troy, read what he was trying to hide, and handed the phone over.

Troy tapped to put it on speaker. "Captain."

"You still call me that, even though you serve her?"

"I can serve her and respect you."

"Don't you mean love her?"

Troy looked exactly like a boy who'd just been caught doing something he shouldn't. "Yes."

"Come on, son. Say it with conviction. Unless you don't really mean it."

Troy's gaze flicked to me, and his expression firmed. "Yes. Yes, I love her."

"Made your father's mistake yet?"

"Yes." Muscles bunched at the corners of Troy's jaw. The color of his eyes shifted from moss on sandstone to shadowed labradorite as he looked at me. "And then some."

"So you *were* lying to me about the tracking tag."

Troy looked sick. He swallowed as the bond roiled with anxiety. "Yes."

Shock hit me in the gut at that. Troy's word was sacred.

Yet he'd lied to his adopted father and military superior. About me. Presumably to protect me, well before we'd come to understand each other.

Well, shit. He'd been doing the right thing longer than I knew.

"Give the phone back to your queen, son."

I took it back and switched it off speaker, knowing Troy could still hear it. His ears were better than mine. "Get what you wanted?"

"Yes, and I know he had me on speaker."

"So the point of all that was what, then?"

98

"I raised that boy after Keithia had his father racked and tortured then exiled. Did he tell you why Cyrus was cast out?"

I hadn't even known Troy's father's name before now. His parents were a topic we never discussed, mostly because of how abjectly miserable it made Troy. I glanced at him. He was slumped in his chair, eyes closed, and pain radiated through the bond. "That's his business, not mine."

"Cyrus made the mistake of falling in love with Troy's mother. He bonded to her, just as Troy has bonded to you. You know what that means in our society?"

"I know it's discouraged and why."

"Discouraged," Omar scoffed. "That's putting it exceedingly mildly. That boy watched Keithia torture his father, every day, for ten days. When she was done, she gave the broken husk that was left of the man to a House in Europe. She gave Troy over to me for re-education. Or execution if I couldn't mold him properly. Troy hasn't heard from Cyrus since. He was a *child* when all of this happened. He knew, viscerally, what awaited him if he followed that path, and he did it anyway, for you. He paid the same price as his father. Or worse. For you."

I looked at Troy in horror.

He was shaking, and I hovered my hand over his, not sure if I should touch him or not.

Troy grabbed my hand like a drowning man and squeezed so hard the bones ground together. He muted the bond as anguish crested.

Biting back the pain, I whispered, "Why are you telling me this?"

"Because I need you to understand exactly what your relationship means not only for him but for all elves. You weren't going to be ready to hear it until you had the stones to pick up the phone and call me for your own damn self."

I had nothing to say to that. "What do you want, Omar?"

"Ah. Now we get to it. What do I want?"

I let him enjoy making me wait, settling in Troy's lap and swallowing a grunt when he held me hard enough to squeeze the breath out of me. The points of his secondary set of teeth pinched in the meat of my shoulder, something that usually only happened when he was really losing it. Always in pleasure, up to now.

This was the real reason why we hadn't spoken to the Captain earlier. Because Troy's past was too painful for him to talk about everything I'd just learned without the sharp end of a stick.

He'd never lie to me. But that didn't mean there weren't things he'd rather not share.

I wondered if even Allegra knew about all this.

"What do I want?" Omar repeated, drawing out the words in a long, slow cadence. "I want you to promise me you'll be different. That the reason you tore down the Houses isn't to rebuild another matriarchy with yourself in place of Keithia. That it's to build something new."

I stiffened, rendered speechless.

This was the man who was dead set on defending and protecting the queens?

"I wasn't permitted to raise my own children. I took in another man's child because he was punished for dreaming of a stable, loving home. I tried my damnedest to make sure Troy would survive Keithia, even if it went against everything I wanted for the future, especially after his mother died and could no longer shield him from her."

My breath shuddered as I tried to hold back my emotion, to be strong for Troy as much as show strength to the Captain.

"For all my work, Troy still followed in his father's footsteps, even as Evangeline followed in Keithia's. What do I want?" Omar growled. "I want better. I want a revolution. I want to know that even though I failed my son in the system our foremothers built, he has a chance to succeed as his full self in the one you'll build together.'"

It took me a minute to answer. I had to choke back a sob.

I was the Arbiter, dammit. I didn't cry. Definitely not while in negotiations with the man who'd commanded the Darkwatch under the Conclave of Queens. Definitely not when there was a chance he was manipulating all of us.

"Then here's what I want." My voice was husky, and I swallowed to clear it. "The Darkwatch, declared for House Solari, and your personal oath that you won't throw in with Evangeline. Because Omar? I just spoke with Roman Volkov, and Evangeline is using him against me, Troy, and the alliance. I can take them both. But not when I also have to think about you on the sidelines and the fact that the Wild Hunt is coming on Samhain."

The Captain's long silence said as much as his words had up until now. "The gods are coming? Already?"

"Yes and my only real chance at stopping them is if you know what happened to a djinni named Iaret."

His breath hissed in. "You found the Book of the Damned."

"We did. If you know why she's in the Book of the Damned, you might be the only person who's willing and able to help me find her."

"Meet me at Occoneechee Mountain. The overlook. Two hours. I'll come alone and have what you need."

"See you there." I hung up, not about to make the same promise about coming alone.

In the back of my mind, Troy was still wrestling with himself.

I twisted around and clasped his face in my hands, resting my forehead against his. "It's okay, Troy. You're okay. I'm here, and I'm not going anywhere."

101

"I wanted to tell you." His voice cracked. My warrior, who'd withstood both culture and torture to be with me, was on the edge. "About my father. About—"

"Troy. You do not owe me every drop of blood and every secret. You know Omar was playing both ends against the middle. He might be a father to you, but that just means he was trying to protect you from me. Even if his methods are fucked in the head. Remember what we said about conditioning?"

He just clung to me and breathed.

I brushed at the itch on my shoulder, finding a trickle of blood from where he'd pricked me. An idea hit. "Hey. Troy?"

I waited for him to meet my eyes. Uncertain. Lost.

"What do you need?"

His gaze flickered to my shoulder, and I slowly pressed my bloody fingers to his mouth. He recoiled, even as his tongue flicked over his lips. "Arden, no. I wouldn't—"

"You wouldn't? Or you don't need? Two different things. If I can offer some blood to Maria, I can give some to you."

His breathing quickened as though he'd run a race. He tilted his head back. Winced. Swallowed. Licked his lips again. "I don't *need* blood."

"But you're a predator under stress, and it would help. No?"

Troy swallowed again. A wave of hunger washed through the bond the moment before he shut his side down again.

"We're about to go face your adopted father to get information. You sure you don't need a little something to anchor you?"

His eyes darted to my shoulder. "I'm sorry. I didn't mean to do that."

"Fuck's sake, Troy." With an effort, I tamped down my exasperation and softened my tone as I willed him to understand I would do what he needed to feel better. "I didn't ask if you meant to do it. I asked if you needed it."

After a hesitation, he said, "If you're offering…"

He nodded, once, tightly.

When I threaded my fingers through the hair at the back of his head and leaned forward, I heard the snick of his secondary teeth sliding down again the moment before pain lanced through my neck and shoulder.

It hurt a hell of a lot more than a vampire bite. No glamour, for one, and he was too distraught to do his new nerve trick.

More pointy teeth, for another.

Flesh probably would have done more good for him than blood, but I wasn't about to let him eat me alive.

He took a lot less blood than Maria would have, resting his forehead against the corner of my jaw when he was done. "I shouldn't have needed that."

"But you did, and I offered it. Don't beat yourself up about it when Omar seems plenty willing to thrash us both, okay?"

"Arden…"

"If you're that bothered, just wait until I go maenad on you. We can have a run in the woods and see who's more in touch with their wild side."

He jerked back and stared at me, eyes wide. "You're a maenad as well?"

I frowned. "You know what a maenad is?"

"Of course. It's a general risk for half-elves, though it doesn't happen to all of you. When elven blood is diluted, Aether can warp and become Chaos under the influence of alcohol. Some become movie stars. Others become serial killers. Is *that* why you don't drink more than a single serving around me?"

"Oh, we have got a *lot* to discuss when we're done with this whole mess."

"Apparently."

I slid off his lap and offered him a hand. "Let's get ready to see the Captain."

Troy looked like he'd rather do anything else but didn't protest. I just hoped my love and blood would be enough to ground him against what we had to do next.

Chapter 12

From the look on Allegra's face as I pulled into the parking lot at Occoneechee Mountain State Natural Area, she hated everything about this plan. Maybe letting Troy and Allegra come along hadn't been wise, but I was hoping it'd throw Omar off. Having my House's king and captain of the guard together in the open at the same time was a massive security risk, but if I couldn't handle a middle-aged elf and whatever backup he might have brought with him, I'd be fucked against the gods. Might as well find out where I stood now.

"What did you tell him?" Allegra hissed at Troy when we got out of the car. The rifle slung over her back wasn't subtle at all, and I wondered if she'd actually use it to protect me from her own father.

Troy shifted in the subtle movement he usually made to resettle the various weapons he typically kept on his person. "He did most of the talking."

I scanned the parking lot, seeing only my car, Allegra's, and a dark grey Audi Q7 under the light of the full moon. That didn't mean Omar really had come alone, but it was a good sign. Of course, he might have just done what I did and have a couple of people posted up nearby.

It was just past sundown and the park was technically closed, but the gate across the entry had been cracked open when we arrived. We'd need to make this quick. Occoneechee Mountain was an odd choice for a meeting because it was situated right near downtown Hillsborough rather than down a long park road in a semi-rural area. There was a house on the gravel drive into the park; the Guard had worked a spell to keep us unnoticed by the inhabitants, but it wouldn't last all night.

Maybe the Captain was just as worried about me as I was about him. That was something I hadn't considered.

As Troy and Allegra bickered in hissed undertones, I sighed and headed for the trail up the mountain at a jog, relying on the moon and my sense of the air currents moving over rocks and roots to keep myself from tripping. The two elves followed at the same pace, not at all hampered by the steep path or the darkness.

"I haven't seen my father in years, and *this* is how you—"

"How was I supposed to know he'd—"

"Because as much as we both tell ourselves otherwise, *you're* his *favorite!* I swear to the Goddess, T—"

I blocked them out as they switched to elvish, focusing on reading the air currents. Despite the chance this was a trap, I'd refused to let more of the Ebon Guard come along to the meet itself. Omar Monteague could have made a move at any point in the last few months. He hadn't, and I was betting my life it wasn't because he'd been licking wounds like Evangeline. He wanted something that I needed to be alive to give him. Troy had uneasily agreed.

Besides, if I didn't get another clue about Iaret from the Captain, we were all dead anyway.

Allegra split off, taking the shorter Chestnut Oak trail up. Troy and I kept going on the Mountain Loop trail to give her time to set up a defensive position.

At the top, a man of average height and solid build stood. I read the air currents as Troy scented, and we nodded when neither of us found anyone other than Allegra nearby.

"I thought I taught you better than to bring your charge out in the open like this, son," the man said without turning around.

Troy extended a hand to stop me about twice as far away as his striking distance was when we sparred. Suspicion radiated from him. "You also taught me to heed my queen. Which is why I'm wondering why you're here and not in Asheville backing Evangeline."

The Captain turned around. I was almost surprised to see how strong the resemblance was between him and Allegra. Even brown skin and eyes, both darker than hers, tight, greying curls, strong features, and a steadiness that said he'd seen it all and had done more than he'd ever wanted. "Where's my daughter?"

The click of a rifle cocking pulled his attention to a cluster of boulders where Allegra had found herself a perch.

"Hey, Dad," she said in a cold voice that meant business. "Long time no see. No funny business, okay?"

I tensed when he laughed, looking genuinely pleased. "Still keeping your brothers out of trouble. I knew you'd be better than me one day. That's my girl."

Allegra didn't answer. Neither did Troy, although the bond practically vibrated with a blend of emotions that set my teeth on edge.

Omar looked between them once more and nodded sadly. "They really are both yours now, Arbiter. Well. At least I got to see them again before the end of the world. Where's Darius?"

Troy stiffened. "You don't know?"

"He was supposed to come home at the same time she did." The Captain nodded at Allegra's rocks. "I assumed he was still mad at me for separating the three of you and giving me the silent treatment."

Tension radiated from Troy as he shook his head, and he couldn't hide the worry that thrummed in the bond.

Omar gritted his teeth. "A matter for another time. Arbiter, you're not quite what I was expecting."

"Nice to meet you in person." I wondered what he'd been expecting but didn't want to look insecure asking. "No tricks? We can do this like normal people?"

"If there were going to be tricks, you'd already be dead."

Ignoring Troy's silent bristling, I took that for what it was and nodded. "Okay then. Why did we need to come all the way up here to talk?"

Omar threw something small and black my way.

Troy's hand flashed out to snag it before I could. "USB drive," he muttered. Louder, he said, "What's on it?"

"Answers," Omar said.

"Iaret's condition and location?" I asked.

Omar shook his head. "Not directly. But it'll get you a step closer. I only know what they did with the djinni, not where they hid her. I don't even think they told Evangeline. Probably for the best. Keithia ruined that girl after her mother died. Now here we are, unable to trust each other when we need to pull everyone together."

I crossed my arms. "Speaking of trust—"

"How do you know you can trust what's on that drive? Trust me not to infect your computer with a virus or turn the Darkwatch against you?"

I nodded.

Omar glanced at where Allegra perched again then at Troy. "Anyone else would have simply killed Troy for what he did to you. You found a way to make it all work to your advantage. Now we have a shot at surviving the Wild Hunt. I told you, Arbiter, I only want one thing: a better world for my children than the one we built for them. They have that chance with you. Better still, they have the chance to build it alongside you, rather than give their lives taking orders from petty queens who think they're disposable toys."

The bitterness in his tone made Troy stiffen as an ugly feeling snapped through the bond.

"Is that why you made me into a murderer?" Troy said in a dangerously soft voice. "I nearly killed her, *Captain*. For a mission *you* sent me on. I did kill Javier Luna and half a dozen others. For the queens. For *you*. Because I was *following orders* and nothing mattered but those orders and the law. Just like you taught me."

Omar huffed a sigh and looked at the ground. "You needed to be beyond reproach for Keithia not to have me execute you when you came of age, and every month thereafter. I won't apologize for ensuring that."

"I couldn't look at myself in the mirror after this winter!" Troy quivered, his voice harsh with rage.

I'd never seen him like this. The same betrayal I'd felt at learning about Roman was burning through him now. I wanted to say something, but this wasn't for me to speak on, so I kept my eye on our surroundings and let Troy have his time.

"But you're still alive," Omar said, his tone hard. "Not just alive. Look at you. You're thriving. That's what matters."

"No. I needed more than that. I deserved more than that. All this talk about wanting better? Where the hell was that in February? I confessed to you after the Redcap mission, and you had me punished. Told me to *refocus myself* on what really mattered."

Goddess, this sucked. Family drama had always been the worst when I was a private investigator. It was a million times worse when it was someone I cared about.

Gravel crunched, and I glanced to find Omar had taken a step forward. He paused at a throat clear from Allegra, and I put my eyes back on the trail behind us.

"Son…"

"No." Troy's voice was accompanied by the dark, icy wind of his power signature. The scent of burnt marshmallow filled my nose.

I shivered. Not sure what was going to happen, I reached for Air as well.

"No," Troy said again. "You don't get to call me that anymore. You may have wanted better for me. But I reached out and claimed it for myself, my way, in spite of everything you raised me to believe. I paid the price for it in blood. Nearly with my life. Because *she* had the vision and strength to offer me a way out. A way to be the man I *wanted* to be."

When the Captain didn't answer, I glanced back for another quick look. The older elf was staring at Troy.

"I didn't believe the reports," Omar said, all other emotion vanished under astonishment. "You really did gain a power signature. You always had the potential, but this is twenty years earlier than even Keithia had hers."

"Then it's a good thing my queen killed her before my grandmother could kill me," Troy said fiercely. "And that Arden refused to do what *you* taught me had to be done in that case. Have you ever handed a knife to the woman you love and asked her to kill you while praying with every fiber of your being that she wouldn't? Do you know what that does to a man? What it did to *me?*"

I swallowed a dismayed sound, but my breath came into my nostrils so hard I was sure everyone could hear it. That was beyond fucked up. I didn't want to be here, on a damn mountaintop, listening to my boyfriend's broken heart. I wanted to be at home, in bed, showing him every way I knew how that he was worth it. That his efforts—his choices—on my behalf meant something.

After a long, fraught silence, Omar said, "I did what I had to do to keep you safe. To keep all my children safe. If it means you all hate me now, so be it. At least you'll be alive for it. Arbiter?"

I brought my attention back to the Captain, squeezing Troy's arm and sending a small, comforting pulse through the bond. He took a shuddering breath and pulled himself together.

The pain in Omar's eyes almost made me feel bad for him. Almost.

He might have been doing his best, but he'd given Troy such a warped sense of self, of right and wrong, of duty and justice, that I couldn't find much sympathy in my heart for him. It had nearly gotten me and Troy both killed. Allegra seemed to have her head on straight, but that seemed to be in spite of him, or maybe because she'd been sent away.

I hardened my voice. "Yes, Captain?"

"You have your deal. I will pledge the East Coast Darkwatch to House Solari. But this werewolf civil war and the situation with Evangeline is not our business. I'll have enough on my hands dealing with the immediate threats from the Conclaves of Richmond and Charleston and any Darkwatch deserters who won't follow orders to uphold an elemental High Queen."

Omar glanced between Troy and me, looking like he was debating whether to say something else before adding, "The other East Coast Houses have stayed out of the power shifts in the Triangle until now because of your alliance, but I've recently started hearing grumblings about taking the risk to throw down upstart elementals and reclaim elven territory in Chapel Hill. I'll keep them off you, but that means you need to handle the princess."

"Fine." I'd hoped for more help with Evangeline, but if the cost was more enemies unchecked at my back, I'd take Omar's offer and do the rest myself.

He looked once more at Allegra then at Troy. "My children are lost to me. I see that. I don't blame any of you for it. But I will hold you responsible for any harm that comes to them, Arden Finch Solari, because I will *always* love them."

At my side, Troy stiffened and clenched his fists, likely to stop himself from reaching for his longknife at the threat.

"I understand," I said.

"Do you?"

Now it was my turn to be pissed. I pulled hard on Air to make sure he saw the glow of my eyes. "Your House colluded with Callista to deny me the chance of ever knowing my birth family. So I'm building my own. And yeah, that means claiming two Monteagues. I was fucking owed, and I still didn't force them to choose me. That means nothing and nobody—not Keithia or Evangeline, not the Volkovs, not you, not even the damned *gods*—will take what's mine from me again. Do *you* understand?"

Omar nodded slowly, looking old and broken for a moment before he pulled himself together and reassumed the mantle of the Captain. "I think we understand each other, yes. I wish I could say it's been a pleasure."

"Likewise." Sadness leaked into my voice in spite of myself. "Stay in touch. Especially if it looks like we're going to have problems with any of the other East Coast Houses."

"As you command, my queen. I ask that you do the same if you hear from Darius."

I narrowed my eyes, but the title had been given without a hint of irony or threat. With a slow nod, I backed away.

Allegra slipped down from her boulder perch without a sound, the rifle slung across her back.

"I'll catch you up," she said to Troy and me before turning to Omar.

"Got it. Come on, Troy." I brushed his hand with mine, and he caught it. His palm was warm and damp when he laced our fingers together.

We made our way back down the mountain more slowly this time, not just because it was full dark now, but also because of the weight of what it had cost to get the USB drive Troy still held. At the parking lot, we waited for Allegra. Troy was still in focus-mode, checking the car and then scanning the dark as though he expected his former Darkwatch comrades to spring from it at any moment. He'd seek more comfort eventually but not yet.

When Allegra emerged from the trail head, she looked like she'd been crying.

"All set?" she asked gruffly.

Troy and I nodded, and he said, "Have Etain and Haroun on security at Arden's."

Allegra's eyebrows shot up. "You spending the night at HQ?"

With a quick glance at me, Troy nodded. "We need to talk."

"Yeah. I guess we do." She gave me a quick salute. "Arden."

"Night, Allegra. Thanks for being here." I got into my car.

Troy gave the inside a check as well before sliding into the passenger seat and saying, "Let's go." We were almost home before he spoke again. "You mind me being at HQ tonight?"

"Not at all. I don't own you. Do what you gotta do." I offered my hand, squeezing his when he took it. "You've had a helluva a day, and I'm here for you. However you need me, or don't."

He kissed the back of my hand. "Hell of a day or not, you call me if anything happens, okay? Especially if Roman or Evangeline call. I don't like that we haven't heard from them yet. They have to have figured this out, which means Evangeline is plotting."

"Yeah. I'd expected Roman to call by now. He's not usually one to think things through."

That situation worried me more than everything else I'd dealt with today, but after a dawn parliament meeting, a negotiation with Detective Rice, and a meeting with the Captain on top of Roman's betrayal, I was too tired to stay up thinking about it after Troy confirmed security arrangements and left.

As I fell into bed, I just prayed none of the fires I'd lit today would come to burn my home down while I slept and that the gods would leave me the fuck alone for one night.

Chapter 13

After spending the day before running all over the Triangle and kicking hornet's nests, I let myself sleep in. I'd learned this year that I was shit at saving the world when I didn't do what I needed to do to save myself first.

Unfortunately, that meant my phone had half a dozen unread messages when I finally dragged myself out of bed and made a light breakfast and a cup of tea.

The first text made me smile, given that it was the usual "Good night, stay safe" message Troy sent whenever he didn't spend the night, with an additional "Love you" tacked on as a second text that read like a cautious test. The rest of my messages were less pleasant.

"Aw hell, no," I muttered at reading the fae demands Zanna had sent as their conditions for joining the alliance.

Freedom to work their tricks and magic on humans without consequence? Living wherever they liked, regardless of human inhabitation?

That was a recipe for disaster given that most fae, even the benefic ones, were exceedingly mischievous and had a totally different moral outlook than even the rest of Otherside. These discussions had been going on for months, and they weren't budging on these basic non-starters?

I shook my head. There was something else going on. I'd figure out what soon, but not just now.

Janae's list of action items was more reasonable, and I'd already started working on it by talking to Detective Rice. The question there was whether Rice would help get the humans to calm down. The Ebon Guard working behind the scenes could only do so much. A public statement and laws on the books protecting Othersiders were what they needed most at this point. The rest was ad hoc and already agreed to by the alliance.

With nothing yet from Rice himself, I went ahead and called Doc Mike with an update on my meeting yesterday. The medical examiner muttered, "Praise Jesus," at the possibility of getting Rice off his back and then excused himself.

There were two short updates from Terrence and Noah about their factions. Things were progressing, but neither had anything big to report. Vikki sent a quick update that she and Ana were hammering out what an agreement with the Farkas pack might look like.

Still nothing from Roman.

That felt like Evangeline's handiwork. The princess was almost as short-tempered as him but far more strategic. She'd fuel her temper into something cunning and hateful.

I tapped my fingers on the table, frowning, trying to get ahead of her. The queens were dead, and as long as Omar's kids were with me, I trusted he'd keep the Darkwatch loyal. There'd been too much pain in last night's exchange for him to be playing me. The vampires, werecats, Vikki's wolves, and the witches were solidly with me, especially after destroying the local elven Houses had correlated with an immediate disorganization in the human protests. The djinn largely minded their business but had an agreement with the rest of the alliance—and the current enmity between the djinn and the elves was deep enough that I doubted a djinni would help Evangeline unless she'd found one bottled somewhere and compelled them.

I groaned. That left the fae. Again. *That* was why nothing had moved in three months, it had to be. I'd thought they were just being slow and stubborn, as usual, arguing amongst themselves and trying to carve out favors and fiefdoms before agreeing to talk to the rest of us. The Sight tingled, and I spent a furious half-minute cussing at the fact that it only worked to confirm things to me, not show me what was or what might be as it did for Duke.

My trick yesterday might have gone undiscovered for a few hours, but as soon as Roman and Evangeline figured it out, they'd be pushing hard on those fae negotiations. I was already falling behind.

I finished my food and my tea, dressed quickly in dark-wash jeans, a black T-shirt, and my leather jacket and stomped into my leather ankle boots. After some hesitation, I got the godblade out of its lead-lined box and tucked it behind my belt, knowing Troy wouldn't be happy about it but wanting something more powerful and less obvious than my elf-killer if werewolves and elves attacked the bar. Besides, my soul itched when I went too long without carrying it.

I told Etain and Haroun where I was going and headed out. On my way to the bar, I called Duke via the callstone and filled him in on the conversation with Omar then asked him to see if he could find anything to confirm that I was right about the fae. Even distracted with someone else's voice in my head, I made it there in record time, parking in the back and setting a wall of Air around my car just in case my guards weren't enough deterrence.

When I got inside, I poked my head through the door to the main space and called for Zanna. "You got a minute?"

She nodded and hopped down from her stepladder, leaving the customers in Sarah's hands.

"What's wrong?" she asked as soon as the door to the front shut behind her.

I paced in the hallway, unable to stand still. "When are you due back to speak to the Chamber of Lords?"

She stared through her mane of dark curls. "End of the week. What happened?"

"How much trouble will you be in if you go back early?"

"Not asking again. What is wrong?"

I sighed. "I think the reason the lords and ladies have been so slow in their negotiations is because Evangeline is also working with them. The list of demands they gave you? They know that won't fly. They want something else, and I think Evangeline is promising it to them."

Zanna snarled, showing every one of her sharp teeth. "Betrayal."

"Yeah."

"You're certain?"

"No. But it fits with information I learned yesterday. I've asked Duke to look into it while he's in Asheville. If the lords and ladies are negotiating in bad faith, that means someone else has something they want more. If it's not Evangeline and Roman, I need to know who it is."

"Roman? Why is the wolf involved?"

I closed my eyes in a long blink, trying to wall off the hurt. "I confirmed that not only is Evangeline in Asheville but also that Roman knows about it. Not just Sergei going rogue again. Roman's promised to help Evangeline quote-unquote deal with me and Troy, whatever the fuck that means."

That sent the kobold into a full-on rage. She paced the hallway with even more energy than I had, snarling under her breath. I stared, not having realized how seriously she took her role as protector of my home and me as her tenant.

When she stopped pacing, she glared up at me with fisted hands. "Will curse him. Curse his home. Curse the bones of his ancestors and the seed in his body so his lineage will never know peace backward or forward. Bad enough he was *rude* and *discourteous*. Now also a backstabbing traitor? *Intolerable. Unacceptable.*"

"Uh..."

"I will go to the Summerlands. Tonight, at the next crossing hour. We'll see what the lords and ladies know of this other negotiation." Still muttering to herself, she brushed past me.

I jumped at the arc of fae magic that tingled over me and called a blessing after her, followed by a mental prayer that she didn't curse the beer again in her ire. I might be wealthy now with what I'd inherited from the deaths of the elven queens, but I hated dealing with the complaints when the beer was turned to piss.

A nudge at my mind pulled my attention to the back door. Troy.

The door swung open, and he swept his eyes over me head to toe and back, reassuring himself I was still in one piece before smiling. Allegra followed him in. They both looked like they hadn't been to bed yet, or showered, still dressed in yesterday's wrinkled clothes.

"Everything okay?" Troy and I asked at the same time.

Allegra made a gagging noise. "I swear to the Goddess I will *die* of you two being this disgustingly sweet." She pushed past Troy, elbowing him teasingly. "Arden, the Guard decrypted the USB drive my father gave us. We're fine, just tired. You wanna tell me why Troy drove over here like the bar was on fire?"

I grimaced and nodded to my office. The two elves stepped inside and dropped into the chairs opposite the desk from my bigger chair, both looking intent and far more awake than they had a minute ago.

When I repeated what I'd told Zanna, they exchanged glances, their expressions hard.

"Makes sense," Troy said.

Allegra nodded, her brow furrowed in a scowl, and toyed with her hair. "Complicates things. A lot."

I rested my elbows on the chair's armrests and indulged in getting rid of some of my nerves by bouncing marble-sized balls of fire across my fingertips. That was a newer skill, one I was proud of for the control it took not to burn myself. "I've done what I can to deal with Roman, Evangeline, the fae, and the mundanes for now. I need to do something nobody will expect because nobody else would dare. It's time for me to go to the Crossroads."

Troy stiffened.

Allegra looked between us. "Why?" she asked cautiously. "What's in the Crossroads?"

"Callista," I said.

"Oh hell no," Allegra said. "Are you—"

Troy cut her off with a hand on her arm.

She whirled to face him. "Seriously? You're seriously okay with this. You are the absolute *last* person I expected to be okay with this, T."

"We've had the discussion." Troy's expression was locked down, as was the bond. He was as unreadable as he'd been back in January. "She's going."

"What about the House and the alliance?"

"Mine, held in trust until she returns."

Allegra looked at me, wide-eyed. "Is that why he's going along with it? Because you'd make him the first elven king in centuries? Goddess, you haven't even married him yet. Who else knows about this?"

My eyebrows flew up and I flushed at the m-word. It was way too soon to even think about that. I cleared my throat. "Nobody knows. We need to keep it that way, for all our safety."

The muscles at the corners of Troy's jaw bunched as he ground his teeth. "Believe me, I'd much rather have her here and safe than be a king. Goddess, Alli. I didn't give everything up for her only to turn around and trade her for a damn title."

"Fine. You want me to agree to this foolishness? Give me a good reason why."

I sighed. Of course she was going to be stubborn. "I'm bound to him and the land, Allegra. He's twice-bound to me." Extinguishing the balls of flame, I gathered myself before speaking my biggest fear aloud, the thing I'd worried about ever since Duke had suggested that I might get lost in the In-Between. "Duke said I should be able to handle the journey but that Chaos is unpredictable. I might find one day my elven half wins out. If something happens to me, like I get stuck because I'm only half-djinn and therefore of the golden hour and not of the light, I'll need an anchor."

I let that settle, nodding when Allegra's eyes widened.

"The djinn or the fae could make the journey," I went on, "but we don't have the fae and I won't bargain with a djinni for this. It has to be me. The more that ties me to what's mine—the land, the House, my responsibilities, Troy himself by way of the bonds and his holding those same responsibilities on my behalf—the easier it should be to find my way back."

Troy shuddered, closing his eyes for a moment.

I went to him and rested my hands on his shoulders, knowing he'd need more physical grounding than usual.

Allegra looked between us, her expression serious. "Get stuck? What does that mean?"

"When I carry Troy through the Crossroads—"

"I shatter," Troy said bluntly. "I can't even describe it, except that it feels like my essence is broken into a million tiny pieces by a piercing light and scattered like window glass in an explosion. I can't find myself. I can't find Aether. I can't feel my body. I can't think. There is nothing, until Arden pulls me back together. It's like being dead. No. It's *worse* than being dead because I'm still vaguely aware of my non-existence with no ability to do anything about it."

Allegra paled. "Oh. Shit."

"Yeah," I said. "So I don't just need an anchor. I need a successor. If all the ties between us, everything he's holding for me in my absence, can't pull me back… I need to be sure that what I've built can still shelter the Triangle and the other elementals. He's the only elf strong enough to manage the House now."

"Assuming the power signature sticks if you're—gone." Troy sounded like he was forcing the words out, voicing a few fears of his own.

Allegra pursed her lips as she studied him. "It'll stick," she said after a minute. "Arden might have helped unlock the power early, but it's yours now."

I took a deep breath and exhaled heavily. "Good. What do you two need from me before I go?"

The chair squeaked as Allegra rose and crossed her arms. "What, you're going today?"

Forcing myself to keep my cool, I said, "Assuming whatever's on that drive doesn't give me something better to do."

"Fuck. This is not what I needed on an hour of sleep," Allegra muttered. She dug into her pocket and set the USB on the desk before sliding it over. "It's decrypted, and we made sure there wasn't any malware on it. Looks like the Captain was actually playing it straight for once."

I crossed back to my desk, turned on my laptop, and plugged it in. A folder full of documents popped up. "What're the highlights?"

Allegra grimaced. "All the deals with Callista that the Captain could remember. The first doc also has what he remembers happening with a djinni turned over to the queens by Callista a little more than thirty years ago."

"We're assuming it's Iaret," Troy added. "The timeline matches the Book of the Damned."

My stomach clenched. I'd start there.

As I read the document, silence hung heavy in the room. Troy and Allegra would have read it already, and I didn't like how they were holding themselves. Tense. Heads bowed. Fidgeting. Unusually uncontrolled for two of the most highly trained Darkwatch agents in the area. As I got to the end, I found the reason.

"They—" I had to stop and swallow bile. "This is heinous. They killed her by forcibly separating her aura from her corporeal form?"

Both elves nodded sharply, looking ashamed.

"That's possible?"

They exchanged a look.

"A Luna could do it for sure," Allegra said. "Hell, I might be able to manage it with enough practice. I wouldn't though." She hurried on the last bit, squirming a little in her chair before she could catch herself.

Good to know this really was as disgusting as I thought it was, even for elves.

I thought back to Grimm's death. Djinn condensed into smoky quartz and then shattered when they died. When Troy had killed Grimm to defend me, she'd imploded before she exploded. But if the aura was separated...

"She's in crystal form. A whole crystal, not shattered pieces." I thought furiously. "It's like a bottle but worse because only a handful of people could pull her out again, and who the hell knows what it is to be trapped within your own soul?"

Troy blanched, and Allegra grimaced. I imagined they both had plenty on their souls that they didn't want to be stuck staring at on loop for a fucking eternity.

"Shit." I scrubbed my hands over my face. "It's been thirty-odd years. Is Iaret even going to be sane?"

Neither elf had an answer for me. They just looked nauseous.

Sighing, I slumped in my chair. Every time I thought the elves couldn't possibly make things worse, they did.

And every time, I had to fix it.

Chapter 14

Duke was pissed to be recalled from Asheville—he was more inclined to tear Evangeline's entire retinue limb from limb right then and there—and neither Allegra nor Troy wanted to be in the same room with him.

I couldn't let that deter or delay me. I stood at the microwave in the bar's kitchen, watching a bag of popcorn spin, waiting for the pops to slow down so I could pull it out before it burned. Eshu-Elegba, the orisha who was Master of the Crossroads, had already complained that the gods of the hunt didn't respect him as they once did. If I was going to access the gods of the hunt via the Crossroads, it couldn't hurt to show a little respect with an offering.

Duke boiled as a cloud behind me.

"Despicable," he muttered for perhaps the hundredth time. "You're certain that's what was done? Today's elves are a shadow of who they once were. I would not have thought them capable of auratic separation."

"That's what the file said. Most people who do something that awful try to cover it up, so I don't see why Omar would be lying, unless it was to get me to do something drastic and remove me that way." The microwave dinged. I snagged the bag of popcorn and poured it into the bar's best bowl, sprinkling a little herbal seasoning over it to make it fancy before grabbing a bottle of red wine. "Ready?"

Duke glared at me with carnelian eyes. "You're not saying goodbye to your *elf*?"

I just looked at him. I'd already said my goodbyes before calling Duke, not wanting him to see me in Troy's presence, let alone being affectionate with him. My stomach flipped. I hadn't felt very affectionate after what I'd read, but I kept reminding myself that Troy needed the reassurance given the hormonal bond with me and neither he nor Allegra had even been born when the crime against Iaret was committed.

Not that it made it any easier with them being related to the people who had done it.

"Fine," Duke said.

Crossing the Veil went rougher than usual, and my off stomach went to full-on nausea. I knelt, trying to breathe shallowly and not spill the popcorn. I wasn't usually pulled here in the flesh, and it was always disorienting. Especially when my carrier wasn't bothering to do anything about the all-over white nothingness as I knelt in the ethereal sand.

"Duke," I prompted.

He scowled down at me, looking like he was debating taking his upset out on me.

"I can't find Iaret if I can't get to Callista," I reminded him.

With a sneer for the limitations of my half-elven heritage, he clapped and spread his hands. Light shifted, and the Crossroads rippled, becoming a static copy of the woods behind my house. There was no breeze, no rustle of leaves or purl of the river. No scent. Nothing but a visual illusion. It'd have to do.

"Thank you." I went to the stump that, in real life, I used as a table while I practiced. Kneeling again, I called out, "Eshu-Elegba, Lord of the Crossroads, I salute you. Please accept my humble offering as I pass through your domain."

"Always so respectful."

Duke and I whirled in slow-motion at the resonant voice.

As usual, Elegba stayed in our peripheral vision no matter how much we turned. All I had was the impression of dark skin and white teeth flashing in a smile.

"What brings you here, trickster girl?" Elegba asked.

I swallowed, not sure if it was a good thing to be claimed by the tricksters. Or if it was even possible when I was already claimed by the hunters and neck deep in shit with them. "I need to speak to the gods of the hunt. About Callista."

"The nymph-bear they've been toying with?"

"Yes."

Elegba roared with laughter. "This should be rich. I'll send you to them myself. The entertainment will be worth it."

I didn't even have time to thank him before my entire being was compressed. The fake forest disappeared. Black emptiness studded with sparkling lights, like stars but bigger, closer, replaced the white nothingness of the Crossroads. I hung in the space, feeling drawn forward to…somewhere…but too taken by the peace and the impossibly simple beauty surrounding me to do anything about it until I was yanked by the ankle.

A slap made me gasp, and it was only then that I realized my lungs were burning and I couldn't feel my fingers or toes.

"Stupid child." Duke hauled off and slapped me again, carnelian eyes snapping with anger and…fear? "I warned you about the In-Between. Pay attention next time."

I sat there blinking, face flaming, trying to figure out how my body worked and where we were now. A forest again but one that felt real. Not just real but ancient, with trees soaring overhead to heights that might even dwarf redwoods. Ferns as tall as I was curled in delicate sprays. The ground beneath me was rich with a millennia of undisturbed loam, and Earth tugged at me, urging me to lie down and merge with the element. The crash of waves came from the distance.

More than that, magic hummed, an almost unbearable pressure that buzzed painfully over my skin and arrowed into my brain to leave a headache. In its sheath at the small of my back, Neith's gift seemed to grow hotter, responding to the power swirling around us and dizzying me all over again.

I frowned. It seemed a lot like the place I'd started dreaming about after the first time I'd been pulled into the Crossroads. Only real.

"Stop trying to figure it out."

I leaned back as Duke raised his hand again.

"Stop hitting me." I pulled on Air and snarled at him.

The djinni's mouth curved in a sharp-toothed smile. "I hope you meant to do that."

Before I could ask why, an arrow whizzed past my face. It crackled with lightning, making my right shoulder ache with remembered pain.

As I scrambled to my feet, Duke went misty and disappeared.

Mixcoatl strode out of the greenery ringing the small clearing, grinning. The red and white paint striping him contrasted with the forest. "You come to us, Huntress? How unexpected."

My mouth dried, and it took me a moment to find words. "My lord."

With a series of shimmers, more gods appeared in the clearing. Neith gave me an inscrutable look, her onyx-dark eyes hard as she leaned on her *was* staff and whirled her ankh in an infinity loop. Ogun pursed his lips as he ran a whetstone over his machete. Odin's ravens cast shadows as they circled overhead.

Artemis gave her usual annoying, braying laugh. "What's this one doing here?"

"She wants your nymph," Neith said. "What else?"

My guts froze solid. I forced myself to push past the growing headache and the fear to answer. "I have some questions for her." I extended the bottle of wine that I had, somehow, managed to keep hold of. "I bring tribute."

Neith swiped the wine with a pleased chuckle.

But Artemis narrowed her eyes at me. "You can't have her. I'm not finished with her, and we didn't summon you here. The Hunt is on your plane."

"I know that, but I—" I swallowed then rushed on. "Forgive me, my lords and ladies. I believe she knows something about a plot to stop your Wild Hunt."

Entirely true. None of them needed to know I was the one trying to stop it.

"Who would dare?" Ogun said.

My ears rang with the boom of his voice. Everything they said and did here was too loud, too fast, too big, too much. I sniffled as a tickle in my nose hinted at a nosebleed. I had to wrap this up and get the fuck out. This had been a mistake.

It was your only option.

I shook the thought away. Tried to gather the ones I needed.

"There are many who might wish to thwart your grand designs," I said. Being this careful was turning the headache into a harpoon stabbing my brow. "I beg you to let me speak to her and find out what she knows."

The blood moons behind Artemis's eyes shone with a raging crimson light. "You will uncover this plot for us. You will resolve it."

Pressure made me sway. "I beg you to allow me to speak with her privately. She may not tell me what she knows if y'all are listening."

Neith and Ogun exchanged glances, like they knew I was playing some kind of game but didn't really care, since Callista wasn't their prey. Mixcoatl chuckled.

Artemis scowled. "You will tell us what happens?"

"You got it. Where is she?"

With a motion like swatting a fly, Artemis tossed me from the clearing, through the starry In-Between, and into a cave.

I landed hard on hands and knees. The scent of blood rose from fresh scrapes, and I coughed on dust and the overbearing scent of musk—then scrambled back to avoid the swipe of claws longer than steak knives.

A chain rattled, pulling a bear up short with a jerk.

From my back, I gaped at the massive creature in front of me, easily double the size of a grizzly. Callista had been tiny when I knew her. Apparently her celestial form didn't follow the laws of physics.

My astonishment redoubled when she spoke, the words mangled in a bear's snout.

"You were never this bold before, brat," Callista said in the same voice I'd know anywhere. "Nor this powerful. Yet here you are, beyond the Veil. Alone. What's changed?"

The bear that was Callista paced from one side of the dim cave to the other, chains clinking. I started to speak and she roared, sending me scrambling back before embarrassment stopped me. I would not be humiliated by her again. Not when I'd kicked her ass once already.

But I had Troy with me before.

I shook my head to clear the doubt. I was a full primordial elemental. I was greater than the sum of my parentage or my allies. I was more than any single being on the earthly plane had been in tens of millennia.

I would not cower before this bitch.

Slowly, I rose. Dusted my hands off, taking my time even if all I wanted to do was hurry up and get the hell out. "How's life as a circus bear?"

Callista charged to the end of her chain and roared. Her hot breath stank of rotting meat as it blew past me.

I waved a hand in front of my face to make my disgust obvious. "Fuck off with that. Where's Iaret?"

Her furious tension culminated and tightened as she froze in place. "Where did you hear that name, Arden dear?"

"I'm asking the questions. I want Iaret. I know her purpose, and I know you know what happened to her. I found the book."

"And an elf to read it for you, apparently. Troy? Of course it was. I should have let Keithia kill him. She wanted to, you know. Grimm said he had a part to play in the Wild Hunt though, so I talked her out of it. Shame our Grimmy-girl never mentioned which side of the Hunt he'd fall on." Her beady eyes focused on me so intently that I knew this was meant to throw me off.

Even if it was true, I couldn't allow myself to be distracted. "Iaret. I won't ask again."

I never thought I'd hear laughter coming from a bear, but Callista sat back on her haunches and roared with it. "You think to bargain with me? Here?"

"I think you want something or you'd be sulking in the corner ignoring me rather than taunting me."

The laughter cut off with a chilling suddenness. "What are you carrying that hums with so much power?"

I pressed my lips together, not wanting to answer. Not wanting to play her game. But I needed leverage, and there was more than one way to play. "Your way out. If you want it."

"You'd free me?"

"Sure. You know how practical I can be. I've only made more compromises since you've been gone."

"Gone." Callista's lips pulled back in a snarl to show yellowed teeth the length of my hand. "*Gone.* As though you had nothing to do with it."

"Oh trust me, I'm proud of having gotten rid of you. That's one choice I don't lose a wink of sleep over. You gonna make a deal? Or you wanna sit here and rot, wondering when Artemis is going to get around to unchaining you so she can hunt you down like the animal you are? I know what that's like, by the way. Running in fear. The moment they catch you. The despair of the end closing in." Remembering Jordan Lake made my voice harsh, and I let the emotion color my words. I needed her to feel what I'd felt.

I stiffened as the bear rose and paced, jerking irritably at the chain every time she reached the end of it. The cave weighed heavy on my mind as I tried to focus on the fact that it was open at one end and a breeze tickled in, one I wasn't going to be foolish enough to reach for.

"You're going to kill me," Callista said finally. "You're desperate, or you wouldn't be here. You'd still be letting your alliance of pissants call the shots. I know it. I know you. Which is why I'm going to allow it. You've always shied away from killing, and if I have to die, it pleases me to go as a weight on your conscience rather than as sport for that bitch Artemis."

You knew *me*. I might not have been rushing for the kill, but I'd take the guilt in exchange for the security. I'd had to make too many hard choices this year. I had too many people counting on me. Then there was the oath I had to keep to Duke.

I drew the godblade. "So. Iaret."

Callista whuffed a laugh. "I thought so. Fine. When the elves separated her aura from her body, it crystallized. The body burnt to ash, but no matter. She can make a new one. If you can get the crystal that contains her soul."

So far, that matched with what I already knew. I narrowed my eyes at her, looking for any telltale signs of untruth. Shock chilled me when all I saw was defeat. She truly believed she was at the end of the line. All this posturing and bravado was the last stand of a bear with its leg in a trap and hunters closing in.

My heart leapt, but I forced myself to mimic Troy's stoic neutrality despite how hard my heart pounded. "Go on."

"There's a vault in the elven archives. Off the records. Anything too dangerous for even the Captain of the Darkwatch to know went there."

"How do you know about it if Omar didn't?"

"Because I told Keithia to build it before I set her up to kill your parents."

Nausea tingled in my belly and up under my jaw then burned away in fury. I wanted to know what else might be hidden there, but I wouldn't let Callista have the pleasure of my curiosity. "Only the Monteagues know about it?"

"Only the queens and mature heirs. They mazed or killed anyone else. The builders, the archivists who transferred materials, everyone who might have heard a whisper of it."

Which explained why none of the Ebon Guard had mentioned it. I'd killed all the queens and likely all their seconds except Evangeline, who was still seven years short of her majority.

Still, it was a convenient story. "That'll be difficult to verify."

The bear's eyes shifted behind my shoulder, and I spun to find Duke hovering in his natural form.

"Good of you to show up," I said. "You wanna go take a look?"

With something that looked oddly like fear in his eyes, the djinni said, "A moment," and vanished.

I backed up a step to lean against the cave's wall, hoping to look nonchalant while we waited. Callista's toothy grin said she didn't buy it, but I didn't care.

With a crackle, Duke was back. "There is no vault."

Callista shook her head. "Always the idiot. It's warded against djinn. Don't look for a vault. Look for an absence."

Carnelian eyes flared before Duke disappeared again. The wait this time was longer.

Then he was back in a burst of flame that sent heat scalding over me. "There's a blank space, on a level below the last I can see. Lower than should be possible given the local soil composition and topography. Arden could probably discover it using Earth."

"Like I said." Callista tilted her head and gave another toothy grin, like she'd won. "Good luck getting in. The spell hiding it is monarch-level."

I kept my face blank as destiny and fate slapped me. *Troy just became the only elven monarch who'd be willing to help me, and he can work monarch-level spells.*

Duke's prophecy, and Torsten's, kept twisting.

When I didn't react, Callista added, "If Iaret isn't there, then she was moved and I don't know where she is. Either way, I'm of no further use to you, my dear. Our bargain?"

I gripped the godblade.

"No," Duke said. "Give it to me. This vengeance is mine."

Neith's voice was as soft as a wind carrying an arrow behind us, sending my stomach plummeting. "If you expect me to intervene on your behalf with Artemis, Arden will wield the blade."

Chapter 15

Fuck. I should have known that at least one of the gods wouldn't abide by my request to speak to Callista alone. That Neith was so insistent on me being the one to kill Callista worried me, but I wasn't on my plane. I was on theirs. My head was splitting, my mouth was dry, my stomach cramped as though I hadn't eaten in days, and the Sight was screaming that something about this wasn't right. But I was out of time and options.

I did my best to embody Troy's dedication to duty as I stabbed the blade into Callista's throat. The shaggy hair, thick fat, and heavy muscle of her bearish neck didn't resist the knife as it slid deep, severing the arteries and veins. Sticky redness coated my arms to the elbows. She laughed as she dropped and kept laughing until she passed out from blood loss. The malicious growling amusement felt like a death knell, but I couldn't move as red washed over my vision.

I dropped to my knees, heaving as though I'd run a hundred miles, trying and failing to fight off the knife's compulsion. I was too far away for the bond with Troy to help me, and Duke wouldn't dare, not here. My headache faded behind a fuzzy haze.

When Artemis materialized in the cave, all I could do was watch as she took in the scene, howled with rage, and lifted her bow. The point of an arrow was aimed at my chest.

"You will not touch her." Neith swung her *was* staff to knock Artemis's bow off target, and the arrow that should have found my heart shattered stone on the cave's far wall.

Artemis drew up in a fury. "You dare! Why should this one be spared when she defied my will?"

Neith smiled, and it sent chills down my spine. "Because not only is she the first and only living primordial elemental since your fuck-up—she has also used my gift to draw blood four times now. That means she's mine. Her bonded Hunter can no longer save her."

Horror washed through me like the red haze that had fallen over me every time I'd used the knife after the quick cut I'd given the succubus. Once when I'd been kidnapped and had sliced Troy's ear when he tried to get me to drop it. Once to kill an elven queen. Then now.

I should have known. All gifts came with a price in Otherside, and no goddess would simply give me a weapon this powerful. I tried to drop it, but it might as well have been superglued to my palm.

"She will lead our Wild Hunt as Mistress," Neith continued. "Whether she wants to or not. Whatever she came here for, it matters not. The primordial is mine."

Artemis smiled this time, a cruel split of her face mimicking the knife wound in Callista's throat. "I see." She turned to me. "In that case, go, Mistress of the Hunt. Enjoy what time you have left until the Veil thins enough for us to ride through it and stay."

She made the same swatting motion as before.

I screamed like I was being turned inside out, and my mind flashed to black then white then to nothing at all.

The next time I was aware of my body, my lungs didn't want to work. Every breath was irregular. My heart stuttered. I couldn't tell if my eyes were open or not, or what time of day it was, or even where I was.

The crunch of dirt off to my side sounded like footsteps.

"Iago!"

I knew that voice. I knew the touch that danced over the pulse points in my neck, recognized the swordsman's callouses on the fingers that lifted my eyelids open ever so carefully. I knew the brush of the mind that suddenly blossomed in the back of mine.

Night. Had to be. The red-tinged light was artificial.

Magic pushed at me. I panicked. Reached for Air.

"No, Arden, it's me! Iago, get down!"

I loosed an uncontrolled burst of Air, laced with Fire.

As soon as it dissipated, the hands were back, clasping both sides of my face. "Arden, look at me!"

It was Troy, looking scared as fuck. A power signature washed over me and was pulled back as the scent of burnt marshmallow crested and was smothered.

I reached up to cup his cheek with a shaky hand, already sad for him. Neith had claimed me as much as he had, although his claiming had been enough to pull me home when Artemis threw me to the In-Between. "You can't save me."

Horror washed over his face before he locked himself down. "I don't know what you're talking about, but I can. That's what we do for each other. I will never give up on you. Never."

More dirt crunching. Another man knelt on my other side. "Priority?"

"Auratic signature. Something's wrong. She's her but not. And that's not her blood."

The new elf hissed as his hands skimmed an inch over my body, hovering over my outstretched hand. "Cursed object. Storage container?"

Troy swore viciously at the sight of the bloody knife still clenched in my grip and was gone before I could drag my eyes into a blink.

"Arden?"

I knew this voice too, if only because it was the only one that was always gentle. Even now. "Iago."

"Good. That's good. What's the last thing you remember?"

I blinked again, searching my memory. Tensed as I couldn't find anything. Then sighed in relief. I could answer this question. "Callista. I killed Callista. With Neith's gift."

Iago grimaced, his eyes darting to the blade. "That was...probably not wise."

The scent of lemon zest bit at my nostrils as carnelian eyes buried in smoke and flame whirled onto this plane. "It certainly fucking was not. I'm sorry, Arden. If I'd known the price—"

"What price?" Troy dropped to the dirt again and started prying my fingers from the godblade. Or trying to. They were clamped tight. "Arden, let me in. Please let me in. We need to get this away from you."

"Too late," I whispered. The gods were coming. There was nothing he could do about it. They'd said so. Who knew better than the gods?

"It's never too late. Remember the house in Chapel Hill? When you were kidnapped? You let go then, right?"

My mind swam, trying to figure out what he was talking about. Then I found it. "Caelan."

"That's right. He was there. On three, okay? One...two...let go."

A stab of Aether accompanied the count in my mind, and my back arched as pain ricocheted through me. Finger by finger, I involuntarily released the knife. Both elves chanted in elvish, the unknown words weaving together and over top of each other as

Duke rested a hand on the callstone on my chest and sang in djinnistani.

As my pinky finger left the blade, I screamed again and reached for any element that would come to me.

"Arden, no!"

The ground beneath me trembled, and the trees whipped overhead as I made the split-second choice to heed the voice I trusted and channeled all the energy into the earth and sky. The sound of bodies hitting the dirt accompanied a metal box snapping shut.

And then I was back to myself. Aching, exhausted, empty, trying to catch a breath that felt like it'd been lost for eons, but I had my mind back.

The crushing doubt fled with the red haze over my vision.

I dragged a breath in. Then another. A third. Focused on the stars and the branches overhead. Definitely nighttime. Definitely the yard behind my house. I was home. Troy, Iago, and Duke crouched nearby. Shaking my head, I groaned but couldn't quite reconnect with myself.

Troy repeated the earlier checks. Pulse. Pupils. Temp. A quick burst of Aether through the bond. He peeled the bloody jacket off me before strong arms scooped me up, and I dangled bonelessly even as I started trembling.

"You're not taking her inside?" Iago asked as Troy carried me toward the gate in the back fence.

"No. She's been gone too long. She needs the elements. All of them. Before she goes into shock."

I bounced in Troy's arms as he jogged down the rocky trail to the Eno.

"Goddess, let this work," he whispered.

Then I gasped as cold river water washed around me. Air kissed me, and after a minute, Fire flickered in the pit nearby. My body settled into the rock beneath me. All of the elements curled through me, revitalizing me. I reached through the link at the back of my mind to find Aether, ready and waiting, to bolster the Chaos that lived within me naturally.

When I opened my eyes, I could count every one of Troy's eyelashes in the dark. The scents of the forest at night bombarded me.

"Arden?"

"Hi."

Water splashed as Troy sat down hard in the river. "Thank the Goddess."

"Or don't, given it was one of them that did this to her," Duke said.

I tilted my head and found him hovering over the flames in the fire pit like a hawk riding thermals on a summer's day.

Troy kept his eyes on me as he answered Duke. "What do you mean?"

"The cost of finding the risen flame was binding Arden to the gods."

I'd never heard Duke sound so bitter. Everything was a game to him, a joke, an amusement. Until now. He wasn't even celebrating being freed from all the geasa Callista had set on him.

Searing fury and despair blended in the bond as Troy spoke coldly. "What the fuck does that mean?"

Shifting air molecules warned me of another presence. Iago. "Binding how? Can it be broken?"

"Arden made a trade with Callista. Information for a clean death. I tried to be the one to complete it, but Neith insisted it be Arden."

The river splashed as Troy turned. "And you let her?"

"She is one of the oldest and most dangerous faces of the *Goddess*! Besides, would you rather I hadn't and Artemis had slaughtered her for the audacity of stealing a kill?"

Troy snarled to show his secondary teeth. "This 'risen flame' of yours had better be worth it."

Duke didn't even bother to answer, and that scared me.

I pushed myself to a seated position, shocked from asking my original question by the pit in my stomach. "Why am I starving?"

Troy looked pained. "Arden, you were gone for three days."

That's impossible. I looked at Duke.

He grimaced and nodded. "You lost a day in the In-Between. It took me two more to find you in Callista's prison. I'm sorry."

Cold gripped me as I shook my head. "No, I was gone an hour. Tops. There's no way…"

But time moved differently for the gods. I'd been on their plane, not mine.

"Shit." I reached for Troy's cheek, and he leaned into my palm. "You're okay?"

"It's been a rough few days," he said, almost as gently as Iago would have. "But we had some good news. I handled everything. The alliance is holding. Detective Rice was a little suspicious when he couldn't reach you, but I think I got him sorted out." He offered an uncertain half-smile. "I didn't even maze him. Didn't think you'd want to do it that way."

I pulled my knees up and scrubbed my hands over my face. Three days gone in what had felt like an hour or less. Three days less to plan for the Wild Hunt. "Evangeline? Roman?"

"The Ebon Guard hasn't found evidence that they're here yet, but there's a text on your phone. It's up in the yard. Fell out of your pocket when you popped through the Veil. I didn't read it."

"Fan-fucking-tastic." The fire died down to a low smolder, and the river purled as I tried to figure out what the hell to do now.

Iaret. We had to find Iaret. That'd been the point of the whole expedition.

"What do you know about a secret sublevel of the archives?"
I asked.

Troy frowned and looked at Iago, who shrugged.

"As far as I know, there isn't one. Javier told me everything
he knew," Iago said.

Duke morphed into his favorite corporeal shape, the lithe
young Black man, and dropped onto a log next to the fire. His
eyes weren't laughing now. "It's there. There's a blank space in
the ground under the lowest level. I missed it at first, but there's
definitely an absence where there should be dirt. A space warded
against djinn or those carrying their blood."

"Whatever there is and whatever Neith did with the knife, it
can all wait until Arden's had something to eat and time to sleep.
She can't help anyone if she's dead of exhaustion or starvation."
Troy rose, signaled for Iago to put out the fire, and aborted a
movement to scoop me up. "Are you ready?"

I nodded and reached for him, allowing him to gather me into
his arms. I needed it, because I was too damn tired to make it
back up the hill, and he needed it, both to feel useful and because
holding me would resettle him after our separation. He was
doing well on the boundaries, but I could feel him fraying on the
edges through the bond. I slumped against his shoulder, and the
blend of contentment and anxiety dizzied me. I rocked as Troy
made his way back up to the house.

When we got inside, Troy let me down at the kitchen table.
"Iago, if you don't mind staying the night, I'd like you around to
keep an eye on her aura. Duke, I'd appreciate a full report to
Allegra on what happened or what you know of it."

I slid into a chair, dog-tired. "We need to make an extraction
plan as well. Iaret is somewhere on the secret level of the
archives, assuming she wasn't moved. Crystalline, a whole
crystal, not shards. They've bottled her using her own soul."

Duke swirled around the living room, having reverted back to being an agitated cloud of smoke. "Did Callista say how to bring her back?"

I shook my head. "I'm sorry. But it sounds like everything that was done had to do with Aether and her aura." I glanced at Troy. "Callista said it'd take a monarch-level spell to unveil the secret level as well."

As Troy started clattering around in the kitchen, Iago sat down across from me. "Whatever I can do to help, I will. I'm sure Allegra will as well."

"Thank you," I said. "And for…" I waved in the direction of the back yard.

"I'm just glad I was here."

After offering him a tired smile, I twisted to watch Troy. The bond had the tattered feeling it had after we'd attacked Callista at the bar, like a rope stretched too far and used too roughly, and fraying with it. He was settling now, but echoes of bone-deep fear and loss still came through. He might be willing to lead my House in my absence, but he truly didn't want there to be an absence. That eased a worry I'd had deep down, one I wasn't proud of having but was only reasonable, given our past history and his newly stated ambitions.

Duke was still swirling and crackling. His magic was giving me a headache.

"Hey Duke? You wanna go fill Allegra in? The sooner she can get to planning, the sooner we can get Iaret."

He dematerialized without a word.

With the prickly magic gone, I took a moment to look at myself. I had a minor magical contact burn from the hilt of the godblade. It itched, as did the nape of my neck. Whatever the elves and Duke had done to get the knife away from me muted its call, but I still wanted it. Grimacing, I rubbed my palm and tried to set it out of my mind. Callista's blood had washed off in the river, but that meant I was sitting at my kitchen table wet, muddy, and completely bedraggled.

"I'm gonna take a quick shower." I dragged myself to my feet, glad that Troy kept himself busy with the food instead of babying me. *Good man.*

I stayed under the spray until Troy hollered about food being ready. Dressed in my favorite pajamas. Shuffled out like a zombie. After shoveling as much of the pan-seared pork chop and salad into myself as I could, I headed for the bedroom and crashed.

***

When I woke the next morning, Troy was stretched out buck naked beside me, dead asleep with shaggy black hair falling over his morning-scruffy face and one big hand resting on my hip. For him to be passed out like this meant Iago wouldn't be the only elf at the house. There'd be at least two more patrolling the grounds. Somehow it was reassuring that the king I'd crowned was still—well, not human, but mortal. More importantly, that he was mine to the bone and to death.

I edged closer, hoping not to wake him, but his eyes snapped open and focused on me with a hint of the fear I remembered from when he'd been healing after Keithia's punishment.

"I'm fine," I whispered, running my fingers along his jaw. "Tired but fine."

Troy drew me closer. "I'd say don't do that to me again, but…"

"Yeah. No promises."

We stayed curled together for a bit until the weight of my responsibilities dragged at me.

"What all happened while I was gone?" I asked. "You said something about Detective Rice and good news?"

"The detective wants to speak with you and only you. Something about making a deal. Vikki made some headway with the Farkas pack. Hope is working on the insurance claims for the shop, but someone is blocking them. I had Allegra put one of the Guard on it to figure out if it's an anti-Otherside thing or simple incompetence." A tired smile cracked through his worry, accompanied by a flicker of relieved joy in the bond. "We finally heard from Darius as well. He's coming home soon." He leaned away, twisting for the nightstand, and came back with my phone. "Your phone lit up when you were in the yard last night. I saw Roman's name but didn't read the message."

My heart stopped. Roman. Breath held, I took the phone and opened the text.

i know it was u, the message said, with Roman's usual inattention to punctuation or grammar. As I stared at it, the phone buzzed with a second message: *c u soon.*

Chapter 16

As much as I'd wanted a leisurely morning with Troy, neither of us were in the mood anymore. A dark cloud seemed to hover over Troy as he dressed and then went to the living room to update Iago. I was in a similar headspace, wondering what the hell Roman was playing at. I called Duke once I'd gotten dressed in jeans, a black T-shirt, and a cobalt blue hoodie.

"Roman might be on the move," I said aloud, clutching my callstone as I paced the bedroom. "I'm assuming Evangeline will be with him. Can you see if you can locate them? Asheville's only a four-hour drive. They could be here already."

"Do I get to eat the little bitch's retinue?"

"Will that make you feel better?"

"Immeasurably."

I hesitated, still not liking the part of my job that involved playing judge, jury, and executioner. I reminded myself that Evangeline and her remaining House Guard wouldn't have the same concern and that trying to play nice had put me into a corner and endangered the people I cared about more than once. I couldn't afford mercy anymore. "Then be my guest. But leave Evangeline. We might need her to bring Iaret back."

"Fine."

With a jolt, Duke wrenched his mind free of the callstone and was gone. I turned to leave the bedroom and jumped to find

Troy behind me, arms crossed and eyes distant. *I'm going to put a bell on the man.*

"That is the strangest sensation," he said. "I can't quite hear what he's saying, but I get an echo of him in my head."

I frowned. Callstones were supposed to be private conversations. "Has it always been like that?"

"No. As the bond tightens, everything gets...more." He shrugged, looking apologetic at being unable to explain it.

"At this rate, we'll be doing that telepathy thing Maria and Noah have going on."

Troy looked thoughtful, and his mood lightened. "Could be useful."

"Yeah." I went on tiptoe and brushed his lips with a kiss then frowned when his mood sank again. "What's wrong?"

"Arden, what did Duke mean last night about you being tied to Neith now?"

I grimaced and shook my head. "The knife had a price. I drew blood with it three times. According to her, that means I have to serve as Mistress of the Hunt whether I want to or not, but fuck that shit."

Troy looked like a cornered puma, pissed and determined, the gold in his eyes sparking. "She can't have you. I don't care what it takes, we're breaking the tie with that damn knife." The unstated *you're mine* came through loud and clear in the emotions I picked up from him, but for once, I felt loved rather than owned.

"Duke's visions have never been wrong." I rubbed my hands along his arms then kissed the sensitive spot under his ear to ground him. I had to lead here. He was too focused on the possibility of losing me. "You and Duke helped me fight off the effects before. We'll find Iaret. The key has to be there."

"It had better be."

"It will." I had to believe it. I couldn't let myself spiral into despair at the idea that I was permanently a goddess's plaything. "In the meantime, I need to sort out Rice, and then I want to hear the plan for finding this secret level of the archives. If Roman's finally left Asheville, then we don't have much time, and I'd rather not leave thwarting the Wild Hunt 'til the last minute. In fact…" I thought about what Duke had said about Troy needing a job. "Why don't you take point on that while I handle Rice and prep the weres."

He offered a lopsided smile, finally letting go of his frustration and refocusing on what he could control. "Trying to keep me busy?"

"Trying to use my assets to their best advantage." I winced at how that sounded then warmed as Troy ran his eyes slowly down my figure, clearly giving my statement another twist.

"You always do." Taking a step closer, he pulled me to him and whispered in my ear, "Don't worry, my queen. You can count on me."

I shivered at the tingle that went over me as he stepped away. He grinned to see me flustered, and I reflected, not for the first time, that he was a very different person than he'd been at the beginning of the year. In a good way.

With a wink, he went to the back door and hollered for Haroun and Etain to come on in.

I shut the bedroom door to call Detective Rice back, wondering if it was time to build an extension onto the house so that I wasn't using my bedroom or my open-plan kitchen-dining-living area as an office.

"Ms. Finch. You're a hard person to find," Rice said in lieu of hello.

I decided to test him. "Had some interplanar business to attend to, but I'm back now. You wanted to talk?"

"Interplanar business. What the hell does that mean?"

"You first, Detective."

Rice held his tongue for long enough that I was sure he was playing a game. "I gave some thought to our conversation."

I played the same game, waiting him out.

"Everything I'm about to say is off the record."

"Of course."

Another long pause. "I thought long and hard about what you said. I don't like it. I don't like vampires. I don't like werewolves or whatever the hell you and your security are. Y'all're ungodly, and you personally give me the creeps."

I gritted my teeth and pushed down a flicker of Fire.

"That being said, I became an officer of the law to protect my community. Be the change." He said that last part half-mockingly, as though he was looking back at a younger, less cynical version of himself. "You weren't wrong talking about being a Black man in this country. In general, let alone in uniform. So I'm thinking…maybe we can have a conversation."

"We're doing that now."

"I mean, about what you're really asking for. You want an ally among the police."

"What I want is for my people to have equal protection under the law, Detective. Law isn't justice, and legality isn't morality. You know that as well as I do. I won't be so bold as to ask you to love thy neighbor, but I am asking for equal rights. And when I say asking, know that I really mean demanding—we've just been too busy holding off the end of the world to get around to being forceful about it just yet."

Detective Rice harrumphed. "End of the world."

"You really want to focus on that?"

"No," he said grudgingly. "I got enough to worry about with Raleigh."

Exasperated, I bit my tongue and forced myself to breathe.

"Fine. I will close the investigations into the Umstead and morgue cases. Trail's cold anyway, and my captain is busting my balls over it. But I want something in return."

"You want something in return for saving your department resources on cases where there's nothing left to solve?"

"I want something for cooperating with...*y'all*."

The ceiling fan spun overhead as I let a gust of Air out and bit back a response about y'all meaning all. Bigoted ass.

"What's that, Detective?" I asked in an icily polite tone.

"Intel. Like I said, I joined the force to protect my community. I can't do that if I don't know what's going on. I've compared notes with Chan over in Chapel Hill, and you seem to be at the epicenter of a whole lot of weird shit. So if something's going down, I wanna know about it."

"An information exchange then."

"Now, I didn't say—"

"You didn't say, but I am. This isn't gonna be a one-sided arrangement, Detective. I'm happy to share information that protects all of the Triangle, but that means I need help protecting *my* community, since you've made it quite clear that Otherside isn't part of yours."

A weighty silence. "I won't tell you anything that compromises human safety."

"I expected as much, just like I'm sure you understand that I won't compromise the safety of Otherside. Just so we're clear, that means no species write-ups, dossiers, surveillance, or anything other than what I choose to give you in the interest of the Triangle as a whole. Me, my property, and my security detail are off limits as well."

Rice started to interrupt.

I spoke over him. "If I find myself under surveillance, the deal is off, and I'm not responsible for what happens to the people spying on me. My security is very thorough and even more dedicated, and please believe I have learned the hard way not to get in their way. I will assist you in determining whether any odd cases have supernatural factors, but if we find that they do, those cases will be handed over to me to investigate. For public safety, of course."

I was pushing him hard, but I was not about to put Otherside in danger asking for anything less.

"Public safety?"

"You ever faced an angry supernatural?"

"I—"

"Call us ungodly all you like, but praying real hard and showing the cross won't save you. Not even against a demon. You need salt for demons, by the way. I'll give you that one for free. We have a deal?"

"How the hell do you think I'm gonna get cleared for this?"

Scrubbing my hand over my face, I took a minute to breathe and find patience. A comforting pulse came through the bond from Troy, and I let it curl through me and ease my shoulders down from my ears. "You hire me as a PI or a consultant. I make it go away. Just like I did with the morgue case. Just like I've been doing for the last five years. It's what I keep telling you, Rice. Nothing is really changing. You're just aware of what's always been going on in the world now. You've been invited to peek behind the proverbial curtain. Trust me when I say that invitation doesn't come often or lightly."

I waited for him to threaten me with arrest, but I thought he was just scared enough of me to not want to find out what would happen if he tried. More than that, I hoped he saw everything I was asking really was in his best interest, even if he didn't like it.

"You better not screw me, Finch. This could end my career if it goes south."

"Yeah, well, you screwing me will cost lives. Believe me, I have no interest in fucking with you, your career, your department, or your species. I just need to get through this damn year."

Another long pause. "Fine," he said, harsh and reluctant. "But if humans are hurt, the deal is off."

"Likewise for Otherside. If there's one of your so-called officer-involved incidents and an Othersider ends up dead, I'll hold you personally accountable, especially if the bodycam footage disappears or is blocked."

Rice spluttered. "You can't hold me accountable for all cops."

"You seemed ready enough to hold any given Othersider accountable for the rest. Two-way street, my dude, and from what I've seen working mundane cases as a private investigator, humans are way more likely to spill blood for no reason and with less control than we do."

"We'll see how this goes then," Rice said after yet another long pause.

I wondered if his brain was overheating from all the mental gymnastics he was having to do today. "Fair enough. Anything else you wanna say?"

"No."

"Great. Then here's my first recommendation: get the riots under control before Halloween. I know the police have been letting things slide and not following up on leads. You've got a local demagogue or two you can bring in for something. Handle it."

"What happens on Halloween?"

"Worst case, the Wild Hunt. The less I have to worry about protecting my people from yours and putting out literal fires started by human rioters, the more resources I can spare toward keeping all of us safe."

"You mentioned that before. End of the world type shit?"

"Yeah. The gods ride, and unless I can stop it, we are in for holy hell. So please. Help me help all of us, okay?"

"Not sure I believe this. But I didn't believe in vampires a few months ago either." He paused so long I wanted to scream. "Fine, Ms. Finch. I will play ball. For now."

"Fantastic. Lemme know your plan for containing the rioters, and I'll be in touch when we have more on the Wild Hunt."

I hung up and slumped against the bed, drained. It wasn't even midmorning, and I felt like I'd moved a mountain. I really, really hoped I hadn't just made a huge mistake, either in trusting Detective Rice to hold to a deal or in making myself the focal point of it. The wards protecting my house—and my privacy— had held so far, and a kobold curse would follow anyone who survived an incursion. But that wouldn't help me if I was captured or dead.

One worry at a time.

I pulled myself together and slipped out of the bedroom, going to Troy and leaning on his shoulders while he talked to the other elves. Haroun's eyes widened at the casual display and then again when Troy squeezed my hands without missing a beat in what he was saying. I'd stopped caring what the elves thought of my indecorous way of ruling a while back, when I kept fucking up with rules I'd never been taught. I was setting up a new order. Might as well go whole hog.

"—then once we have Iaret, we evac to the warehouse," Troy finished.

Iago, Etain, and Haroun nodded, the certain movements of people familiar and in agreement with an already-decided plan.

I frowned and bumped his shoulders for attention. "Warehouse? What warehouse?"

Troy twisted to look up at me. "An abandoned building halfway between here and Hillsborough. It's held by a shell company you own now. Remote enough for us to work freely and should be untraceable if anything goes wrong. Or at least far enough from mundanes to contain the problem."

"I own a shell company?"

Iago smiled. "You own several. House Solari now holds a considerable war chest of assets of various types."

"Huh. Okay. Thanks." I'd signed off on Iago being my Chancellor to thank him for all his work getting assets formerly owned by Callista and the queens transferred to me after Troy had said it would be an appropriate honor. I probably should have been paying more attention to what he was actually doing, but Iago had been the first elf after Troy and Allegra to side with me. He'd defended me against the rabisu, so I trusted him. Seemed like it was paying off. Literally.

"All set?" Troy asked. "Good. Haroun and Etain, you're with Arden while she deals with the weres."

Thus removing himself as a point of contention with Vikki. Clever.

The werewolf occasionally got touchy about my relationship with Troy. We both thought it was insecurity, given her own precarious position, but there was no need to set her off if we had alternatives. Without knowing what kind of protections were on this hidden vault, Troy was the best option to send there as well, given he was now the only elf in the Triangle strong enough to have a power signature—and given that the elven archives were warded against anyone with djinn blood. Duke might know where they were, but he wouldn't be able to gain entry. Neither would I.

"Sounds like a plan," I said. "Detective Rice is on board too."

Iago's eyebrows shot up and Troy shifted in his chair to look at me again. The bond tightened as Troy rapped his fingers against the table, a habit of mine he'd picked up. "Solidly?"

I tilted my head side to side. "Not as solid as I'd like. He's not hiding his biases, that's for damn sure. But he's got an image of himself as one of the 'good cops' and seems to think I'm the lesser evil. Or at least the evil with a face that hasn't chewed his off yet."

"I'll let Alli know."

"She's still got someone on him?"

"Yes, and we still have Estrella inside the station."

I nodded, relieved. At least I'd have a warning if Rice did try sending someone to my house. Dealing with all of this was so much easier now that I had a team, and I sent a satisfied little pulse to Troy. I don't know how he kept up a neutral demeanor when the bond gave me the sense of a well-pleased cat, but I guessed that was part of why the Captain had chosen him as his second. He'd been impossible for me to read for the longest time, even in the early days of the bond.

"Final orders, my queen?"

I flushed, as I always did when Troy called me that in front of other people. "Get Iaret's crystal. I'll deal with the weres as best I can then be on standby for y'all. When you have Iaret, I'll summon Duke to the warehouse, assuming we can spare someone to pick up Roman and Evangeline's trail."

I wasn't about to let them wander around unwatched.

The elves saluted, fists to hearts, while I tried to figure out what the hell I was gonna say to Vikki about the fact that Roman was coming back to town again.

Chapter 17

The weres always reacted oddly to the scents or power signatures of the gods, so I had Vikki, Terrence, and Ximena meet me at the bar. They still shuddered when they caught my scent in the closed space of the back office, even after my taking a shower and spending a night with Troy.

"What'd you get up to this time, Miss Arden?" Terrence asked from where he slouched against the wall. "Nobody's seen you for a few days and Troy's acting cagey. Now you come back smelling of godpower and Aether."

I leaned back in my chair and laced my fingers together over my stomach. "I paid Callista a visit."

That got me snarls and shining eyes.

"Come again?" Terrence said, his tone dangerously soft. "Callista?"

Nodding slowly, I met each of their eyes in turn. Terrence looked wary. Ximena looked equal parts nervous and ready to fight someone. She'd always been the most sensitive to anything related to the gods. Vikki looked unsure and pissed about it.

"We got the elves' Captain of the East Coast Darkwatch on board," I said. "He handed over a USB drive with information pertaining to an oath I'm bound to fulfill. With the queens dead, Callista was the last living person who'd be able to give us the next clue."

Ximena sat up sharply. "Was?"

"I killed her in exchange for the information."

All three weres paled.

"Damn," Terrence said after a tense silence. "She's been around since my daddy's daddy's daddy was here and longer still. She's really dead?"

"No coming back." I dragged my brain away from the memory of scalding hot blood and a bear's dying laughter. "Troy is moving on the intel. Which brings me to why I called y'all here." I looked at Vikki. "I have reason to believe Roman is on his way back. Possibly *is* back or will be here within hours."

She shot out of her chair. "What the hell? And you're just now saying something?"

I gave her a level look until she sat her ass back down. "I lost three days on the gods' plane, Vikki. Nearly died. Again. Then had to deal with Detective Rice when I got back. Forgive me if I was a little too busy to keep tabs on *your* brother."

The werewolf blushed. It should have been her job, really, like Allegra and the Ebon Guard kept tabs on the Darkwatch and Troy had been looking for Evangeline in between everything else I had him doing. Or like Maria was handling the other East Coast coteries while politicking with the mundanes. Vikki was fun to drink with and a good one to have one your side, but she was still unlearning a few bad habits. Like this.

I let that set for a minute. "We know that both Roman and Sergei are collaborating with Evangeline Monteague. I've had Duke keeping an eye on them. Sometime while I was gone, Roman sent a message letting me know that he'd caught on to the subterfuge I used to flush him out. Dunno when exactly, it's not like there's cell service beyond the Veil. This morning he sent a follow-up that just said, 'see you soon.' I have to assume that whatever Evangeline is plotting, she has an inkling that Samhain will be when the gods make their play."

Ximena's face was as hard as her voice. "Is he coming in force?"

"Likely. I know Evangeline has the remainder of the Monteague House Guard, who were good enough to assassinate Niko Volkov in the first place and send Irina into hiding." I paused to give Vikki a moment. These were her parents I was discussing. Brat or not, I could offer some sensitivity. "Duke will try to delay them and reduce their numbers while Troy takes a team to deal with our other concern. Which leaves me with the Farkas pack."

We all looked at Vikki.

She straightened, seeming to pull her pain together into armor. "Ana spoke with her family." She paused, gritted her teeth, and snarled. "Spoke. If it'd been in person, there woulda been blood in someone's mouth. They're furious that their pack's only ranking female has taken up with another woman. But they're taking it better than Pops would have. If we can get Roman to back down, they'll throw in with Red Dawn."

Terrence whistled long and low. "Never thought I'd see the day when the wolves would join the twenty-first century."

Vikki whirled on him. "Fuck off, Little."

He raised his hands but held her gaze with the shining peridot eyes of his cat until she settled down.

I leaned forward to pull her attention and drew on Air to make my eyes glow as a reminder. "We gonna have a problem, Vikki?"

"No. I just—I'm sorry, it's been a shitshow."

Nodding, I leaned back again. "Lots of that going around. We're all on the same side though, and everyone here supports you as you are and what you're trying to do. Right?"

She jerked her head up and down, fighting the raw expression pinching her face.

"Okay then. We need to make a decision about Roman and Sergei. Vikki, they're your brothers—"

"And Roman's your ex."

"Yeah, he is. But if he's thrown in with Evangeline, I can't trust in his good intentions or the innocence of his ambitions anymore. That has bitten me in the ass too many times as it is, and Evangeline definitely wants me dead."

"You probably knew him better'n I did." Vikki slumped in her chair and looked at her hands. Dirt crusted her fingernails, and she picked at it. "I think I just believed in the memory of Roman, ya know? My big brother, unfairly sent into exile for something I never thought was an issue. Certainly nothing that was his fault. I tried coming to find him once and got run outta town. I guess I still feel like I owe him."

I looked at Terrence and Ximena, reading in their hard expressions their unwillingness to let this slide. I shoved aside memories of running in the woods with Roman, of steak dinners by moonlight and sheets perfumed with cedar and musk. The scent of bourbon as he laughed. I loved Troy, but I couldn't delete the visceral remembrance of the first man who'd stolen my heart.

That didn't mean I had a choice when it came to the path he'd chosen for himself.

"Roman and Sergei are censured," I said softly. "Alongside Evangeline and everyone traveling with them. I'm sorry, Vikki."

Her eyes were wolf silver when she looked up. I'd just declared open season on Blood Moon in the Triangle. Terrence and Ximena tensed in anticipation.

"If either of them want to recant and re-swear to the alliance, I'll allow the full parliament to judge their sincerity and set the forfeit. I'll also recuse myself from the proceedings, given the nature of my prior involvement with Roman and my personal prejudice against Sergei. But I can't assume that anyone who'd join up with Evangeline Monteague is on our side anymore. Not after she set up the attempted coup on Maria's coterie or what she did to Troy for choosing me."

Vikki heard the threat in my double meaning and swallowed hard enough for it to be audible. "That's fair. Thank you, Arbiter."

I drew on my years as a private investigator to keep my face neutral. "Terrence, Ximena, your people are free to do what you need to do to defend yourselves against rival incursion." I gave them my best no-bullshit look. "That does not mean you can turn this into a civil war. I just told Raleigh PD that we contain our own messes and punish our own troublemakers. That means no blood in the streets. No injured, turned, or dead humans. As far as anyone is concerned, the Détente is still in force. Got it?"

"Yes, Arbiter," they said in unison.

The scent of musk grew in the office. A little excitement, a little fear, maybe.

I rose, signaling that we were done. "Keep me posted and let me know if you need help."

When they were gone, I sat back down, slumped forward and rested my forehead on my arms atop the desk, just trying to breathe.

Once again, nothing was going as I'd hoped it would go. I couldn't own Roman's choices, as much as I wished he'd made different ones. People had to be responsible for their own shit— and the fallout. I certainly had been. More than once. I hated everything about this, but it was not my job to bend over backwards and get fucked by everyone else's petty problems. I couldn't even worry about my own anymore. I was too busy thinking of all of Otherside.

Speaking of, there was another reason I'd come to the bar: I was looking for news from Zanna about the fae. Surely in the time I'd been gone, she would have been able to get to the Summerlands, get some kind of answer, and come back.

When I stuck my head out the door to the main bar though, Sarah was the only one there. I took a breath to calm down before ambling out and slipping behind the bar to serve myself a glass of sparkling water.

The redheaded witch preempted my question. "Haven't seen Zanna in a few days. She said she was going to the Summerlands but not when she expected to be back."

"Got it. You good managing everything by yourself?"

"Sure thing, boss. Business is quieter with all the protests. Fewer newcomers trickling in, although the valkyries keep coming. People are scared I guess."

"Anything I need to worry about?" I asked. Bartenders heard things even Watchers wouldn't.

Sarah twirled a long lock of hair around her finger as she thought, green eyes going to the TV in one corner. "Hard to say. Been hearing grumbles about how long it's taking to get a bill of rights or something for Otherside. Some of the coven leaders had to discipline a few initiates—they were talking a big game about breaking with the Way."

I grimaced. "That bad?"

"They're bringing the burnings back." Sarah's gaze went hard as bloodstone. "Keeping to the Way is important. But how long can we face violence like that with nonviolence? Nobody has ever claimed what's theirs peacefully."

"I hear you. It's the same for elementals."

She deflated a little. "Yeah. I guess you'd get it. Still."

"Hey." I squeezed her arm. "I'm getting a contact at Raleigh PD on board, to drop the open Otherside cases and get the riots under control. That should give the Ebon Guard and the vampires room to push the state legislators. But I've promised my guy that we police ourselves. Can you let the coven leaders know that I appreciate their efforts? And that I'm working on a solution?"

"Yeah. I can do that." She straightened at being given information and a job.

"Thanks." I smiled and grabbed my water, heading back to my office before she could see my smile slip. I felt like a hypocrite, asking her and the witches for patience when I'd had to destroy three elven Houses to get what was mine. It was what people in power seemed to do: tell those looking to them for change to just wait a little longer, it's not quite time yet, just hang in there, we'll get to you.

Meanwhile, harm kept coming.

Etain and Haroun gave me worried looks from where they waited outside my office door, but I gave them a nod and shut the door behind me. I needed to be alone. My stomach sloshed as I sat back down at my desk. I managed to work on some reports and other small tasks for a few hours, but my mind kept slipping.

I hated this. Feeling justified in the ask didn't make it right. But I was one person, leading an alliance headed by a parliament of a dozen, trying to play the dangerous role of model minority so the far more numerous humans wouldn't come for all of Otherside with silver and fire before we'd even had a chance to find our footing after thousands of years in their shadow.

That some of us could literally eat a human wasn't the point—for one, we weren't and for another, they were at least as likely to pre-emptively kill us.

I didn't know what the right answer was or the right path. Those plates could only be spun for so long before one of them shot off and broke irreparably. A sick feeling crept up on me every time I wondered whether Otherside showing our powers in full force would just make the mundanes' fear of us even worse. People hated what they didn't understand or what made them feel small in their difference.

I didn't have the answers. For someone who found answers for a living, it was terrifying.

One thing at a time.

Find Iaret.

Deal with Roman and Evangeline.

Figure out what the fae were doing.

Stop the Wild Hunt.

Secure equal rights.

Probably not in that order. Shit never seemed to go quite the way I wanted or needed it to, but at least—

The bond flared to life, yanking at my mind, heart, and soul so hard I gasped as it pulled me out of my chair.

An icy midnight wind dragged frost-rimed nails down my spine. Troy.

As had happened when we saved the witches, a weird double vision overlaid on top of mine. A cavernous space. A huge metal door. Flickering fluorescent lights. Cobwebs. I even thought I could smell dust, burning marshmallow, and stale, subterranean air, hear echoes of voices shouting in elvish drowned out by an unearthly roar.

I went to sit and missed my chair, landing hard on my ass as I threw open the magical gates. If Troy was pulling this hard, something had gone very wrong.

Chapter 18

The office door crashed open when my chair rolled away and thunked into the wall. I threw up a hand to stop Etain and Haroun, not able to spare enough attention to speak as I tried to figure out what I was seeing. It was like one of those films made on a hand camera: shaky, too fast, too close to the action.

Backwashed power crawled into me as Troy finished his spell and cast it at what looked like a gigantic, pewter-scaled snake with bat wings, a rooster's spurred feet, a barbed tail, and way too many sharp fangs. I gritted my teeth, channeling the extra power into a crackle of lightning that danced over my skin.

The creature shuddered and tripped as Troy's spell hit it, catching itself on the point of one wing.

My breath caught as Troy lunged forward and swung his longknife. The meteoric blade might work against anything in Otherside, but it seemed way too fucking small to use against something that size. It was already shaking free of the spell as Troy found a soft spot under the jaw, thrust upward, and darted away from a spray of indigo blood that smoked when it landed on the concrete floor.

He'd barely reset his feet before he was drawing on more Aether and dancing away from snapping jaws that could have swallowed him whole. I gasped again at the close call.

Distantly, Etain and Haroun argued.

"What's happening? Why does she smell like—"

"Don't touch her! Just watch the damn door!"

Smart choice.

When Troy's next spell landed, other elves pounced, their secondary teeth bared in snarls almost as sharp as that of the monster they were fighting. He dashed forward as well, finding the same soft spot on the other side of the jaw and disabling it.

I shook sweat out of my eyes and focused on keeping my walls and shields down.

I wasn't the one fighting, but channeling this much Chaos and getting echoes of Troy's exertion was draining all the same.

More spells. More slashing blades that looked like they weren't doing much more than making papercuts but must have been doing something. The creature slowed, each cut taking a toll even as it took its due in turn, spitting acid and slicing flesh.

Then it was over.

The mental handcam image flickered as Troy breathed hard, bent over his knees.

"Shit. Arden," he said aloud, his voice sounding off when I was hearing it through his ears. Then he was gone, and I was alone in my head.

I flopped onto my back, squeezing my eyes shut. "Can someone turn off the damn lights?" My voice rasped. "And get me some flat water please?"

"Yes, my queen," Haroun said.

The overhead light went off as the door creaked open and shut firmly with the smallest scuff of a foot. Apparently the completely silent movement was a high-blood thing.

Another small scuff told me Etain was still nearby. "Are you okay, ma'am?"

"I will be as soon as I find out what the hell Troy was fighting just now."

Silence met me, and when I cracked one eye, she looked pale and shocked. "You can sense him like that? Share magic? Is that why you smelled like him just now?"

Exhaustion loosened my tongue more than usual. I scrubbed my hands through my curls, not even caring if it snarled them further. "I just watched him fight off some kind of monster I've never seen before, like I was watching a movie while he used me as a battery."

Etain's jaw dropped this time. "That shouldn't be possible."

I snorted. "Welcome to my life."

She frowned. "That's a security risk, ma'am. If someone gets to him, if they kill him, who knows what would happen to you? What if you were driving just now? If it's this debilitating, you need more of the Guard on hand."

"You're more worried about me than him?"

"You're the High Queen, and your word gave me a chance to do what I love. What I'm good at. I'm yours to the death." She looked embarrassed, either at her declaration, telling me what to do, or both.

I blinked, wondering how the hell I'd gone from being elemental scum for the queens to personal savior for the elves of the Ebon Guard.

It had been a wild year.

The door opening again saved me from having to find an answer, and the sweet-sharp scent of spiced rum hit my nose as well.

"Oooh. Good man. Thanks, Haroun." I sat up to accept the glass of dark amber spirits, downed the double in one burning gulp, then gulped the bottle of water he handed me next.

"Fuck," I muttered as a wave of dizziness hit me.

Pulling my knees up, I dropped my head between them. That hadn't happened last time, but last time had been more like two minutes, not however long it took a half dozen elves to kill an oversized Komodo dragon with chicken feet and acid spit. Would adding Iaret to the mix stabilize the power draw? Or make it worse?

I almost dreaded finding out, but I'd take it over being dead.

Haroun cleared his throat. "Can I get you anything else, my queen?"

"Protein would be good." I was still getting used to the idea that I didn't have to suffer power hangovers if I took care of myself. Booze still helped. Eating enough protein helped more.

Haroun slipped out again.

On the desk, my phone vibrated. Etain snagged it and passed it down to where I sat.

"Finch," I said, answering without looking at the caller ID.

"I'm so sorry, Arden." Troy sounded drained and shaken. "There was a stone wyvern protecting the vault."

"What the hell? I thought you said wyverns were extinct."

"I thought they were."

"Are you okay? Are you hurt?" Everything in the bond felt raw, but I didn't know if it was because he'd been injured or because we'd pushed it to the breaking point.

"I'll live. Are you okay? I couldn't tell how much I was pulling from you."

With a growl for his stoicism, I pushed to my feet and leaned against my desk. "I'll live. What happened?"

"The Captain's people let us into the archives. I was able to use a monarch-level spell to locate the door to the hidden sublevel. We found and disarmed a lot of traps and then came to a set of big doors. I tried another spell to open it. Triggered the guardian that none of us had thought to look for because we'd all been told there were no more wyverns. We killed it and broke in. Secured everything crystalline in the room and got out."

"Where are you now?"

"On our way to the warehouse."

"Okay. I'll meet you there."

"Any word on Roman?"

"Not yet. I'm not finna sit around waiting for him either."

Troy snorted. "Arms race."

"I'd rather it wasn't. But Evangeline doesn't fuck around."

"No. She doesn't." He sounded equal parts furious and pensive.

I changed the subject before he could dwell too much on his homicidal baby sister. "I'll be there ASAP, okay?"

Etain said loudly, "I'm driving. Ma'am."

I gave her a steady look then sighed when she looked nervous but clenched her jaw defiantly. "Etain's driving."

Troy hissed. "I pulled that much?"

"Enough. Don't worry about it. Better you're alive. We'll figure it out."

"See you soon then. I love you."

He hung up before I could answer, and I almost burst into flame at Etain and Haroun's knowing looks.

I cleared my throat. "Let's go."

Etain held out her hand, and I glowered as I dropped my car keys into her palm.

***

The warehouse was down a dirt service road that gave me the creeps because it reminded me of the one leading to the abandoned cemetery the lich had used for his lair. It didn't have the same lingering sense of evil. It was just overgrown and creepy as fuck in the fog that had rolled in as night deepened. Etain took it slow, as careful with my car as she was with me. Scored herself some points with that.

"Wait here," Haroun said as Etain parked just short of the clearing surrounding the warehouse.

I sighed quietly, knowing Troy was here already. I could sense him inside the building and knew it was clear because he was calm, but I wasn't gonna undermine my security. Not when their positions meant so much to them.

Resting my head against the cool window, I peered out into the darkness and wondered what this place had been in its heyday. A furniture manufacturer, maybe? Lots of those around with the state's reputation for fine, handcrafted wood furniture, and unfortunately, more of them had gone out of business in recent years.

Etain gave me a cautious sideways look when the door shut softly behind Haroun. "You're good at this, ma'am."

"Good at what?"

"Being queen but letting people play their parts. We all know you're strong enough to take anything that might be hiding in the dark, and every elf and half-elf in the Ebon Guard knows you hate relying on people. But you let us work."

I flushed, feeling grouchy because I couldn't deny it. "Allegra's briefings sound real thorough."

"They are. Sorry, ma'am. Nothing meant by it. We can't protect someone if we don't know how they're likely to feel about it or how they might react under pressure."

"Fair enough."

A rectangle of faint light, like that given off by the LED lanterns the elves favored, angled into the night as a door opened. I caught the flicker of a shadow slipping out a window though and the hint of something predatory in the bond. "Troy's going hunting," I murmured. "Probably for Haroun."

"Or for you, to make a point to Haroun."

I laughed. "That's more likely, actually."

Sure enough, Troy dropped his shadows when he was leaning soundlessly against the car just in front of the passenger-side door. Etain jumped and snarled. I just got out and studied him in the glow of the car's interior lights. Etain got out as well and went to find her partner.

"You look like hell." I wasn't able to keep the catch out of my voice.

Troy gave me a half-smile, the one he made when he was pleased and relaxed, despite the bruise on his jaw, the split cheekbone, the blood I smelled on the night air, and something else that smelled like a chemical burn. "I feel like it. But I've survived worse. Got five witnesses to my using a spell only the queens should be able to use and the death blow on a stone wyvern."

Ah. That's what he was pleased about. He'd proven his own strength without having to be in conflict with me—or better yet, while staying in support of me. Two or three birds with one stone.

"Nice one," I said.

Wincing, he deflated a little and curled an arm over my shoulder to steer me toward the warehouse. "You're okay? I meant it when I said I didn't mean to draw that hard on the bond." Sheepishness came through, and he lowered his voice. "I might have panicked a little."

"Given what I saw, that seems fair."

"What you saw?"

I described the wyvern, the room, and the fight. "It was like when you mazed the crowd at the witch shop fire but more intense. I guess because you needed more Chaos."

Troy stopped dead in his tracks and stared at me before continuing on again. "You keep making me have to go back to do more research."

"You actually do it yourself?"

He slanted a look at me. "For something like this, I'm not going to trust intel that valuable to anyone else."

I gave him a sideways hug, enjoying the warmth of his body in the chilly evening. "You said 'everything crystalline' before. What's the haul?"

"You'll see," he said grimly. "Are you calling Duke?"

"Lemme see what we're dealing with first."

We passed Etain and Haroun on our way into the warehouse. I expected Haroun to look sullen, but the look he gave Troy was calculating and admiring instead. Troy's little nod was an acknowledgement, something that seemed respectful rather than mocking. Seemed like the boys were bonding. Maybe it was a mentorship thing? That'd be nice. People did better when their partner wasn't the only person they relied on for socialization.

Three elves I didn't recognize waited inside a huge, open, largely empty space smelling of wood shavings with five more of the Ebon Guard—not that I recognized them either, but they'd taken to wearing something gold to break up the black semi-uniform they still wore. A bandana, a wristband, something to mimic the onyx-and-gold pendant around my neck. The thought that I should get armbands or something formal for them popped into my head, and I set it aside for another time.

A careful space separated the two groups. They all smelled of sweat, Aether, blood, and the same chemical-burn smell clinging to Troy.

"Darkwatch?" I asked softly.

He nodded and leaned closer even as his hand slipped away from my waist, speaking almost inaudibly despite his nearness. "They'll carry word of anything that happens here back to Omar, so watch yourself."

"Understood," I said. Omar might be willing to play ball with us, but if Troy wasn't offering complete trust, I wouldn't either.

As we approached the group, Troy slipped ever so slightly ahead of me, positioning himself for defense. Everyone seemed edgy now that I was present.

I gritted my teeth and decided to address the biggest issue. "Thank you all for being here and for your efforts to breach the hidden vault. Elves aiding an elemental queen isn't exactly what I'd imagined for myself this year, so I imagine y'all are in a similar situation. Sorry not sorry."

As I'd hoped, the tension in the room cracked.

One of Omar's men ducked his head and rubbed the back of his neck, like he was trying to hide a smile. The other two looked somewhere between bemused and surprised, but their postures eased. As they relaxed, so did my Ebon Guard.

"Seriously though, I appreciate this. You put yourselves at risk, not just in the fight against the wyvern, but in choosing to stay loyal to your Captain and your king. To me." I offered a wry smile at their reactions to my casual acknowledgement of Troy as a king. "I stood against Callista. I know it takes courage to go against what your people want or expect you to do. So in case nobody's said it yet, thank you."

Omar's men looked at me like that was completely unexpected. Troy's smug approval in the bond told me I'd judged right. The queens had treated all of the Darkwatch like they were disposable, not just Troy.

Maybe I really was better at this than I'd thought. No time to get cocky though. I still had to figure out how to save a djinni whose soul had been stripped from her body and imprisoned— and how I was going to stop Duke from plowing through these elves like he had the ones who'd kidnapped me this past summer when he got here.

Chapter 19

When Troy had killed Grimm to save my life, back when we were just starting to understand each other, she'd crystallized into smoky quartz as all djinn did when they died. Then that crystal exploded outward in glass-sharp fragments that made it impossible to judge how big a crystal a djinni made.

As it turned out, the only smoky quartz in the lot of crystals the elves had carried out and arrayed on a rickety table was a pillar the length of my arm from elbow to fingertips, a full hand thick and a rich brown at the base, tapering to a blunt point and fading to clear crystal at the top.

The stone was, unexpectedly, an enhydro. Bubbles of liquid were trapped within, which shifted under the hard surface as I tilted it, trying to figure out how to reconstitute Iaret.

I found hope in that, even as my skin crawled to touch the crystal. There'd been no liquid in the spray of shards that'd been Grimm. Only dead stone. I knew because I still had the ghost of a scar in my eyebrow from where one of them had sliced through my face, and there hadn't been any kind of splash. Raw pain screamed through the crystal, and I shuddered as dismay and revulsion shoved bile up to the back of my throat.

Carefully, I replaced the stone on the table and pulled my hand away. "This is her. Has to be."

If I was unsettled, Duke would be nuclear. For all that he'd hidden knowledge of Iaret until a couple of months ago, it was obvious he loved her deeply. I'd pulled down three elven houses for what the queens had done to me and Troy, on the hint of the idea that I might actually care about him. I didn't want to imagine what Duke's reaction would be, knowing how he felt about being bottled and about Iaret.

This was worse, far worse. This'd been spiritual and auratic rape.

"Get them out," I muttered harshly to Troy. Duke had been right, and even I'd underestimated it. This was beyond despicable.

Troy obeyed without question, making a hand gesture that I missed with how focused I was on Iaret's crystal. The Ebon Guard backed away immediately, but one of Omar's people started to protest. Troy growled audibly, and icy Aether flared.

I glanced at him, not having expected the severe reaction. His secondary teeth were out, and his hand was on the hilt of the longknife sheathed on his back. The elves of the Ebon Guard paused and mirrored him.

Nope. Not having this. Not today, not with Duke coming. Not for me either.

Every elf except Troy flinched when I drew on Air and flooded the enclosed space with my power signature.

"Is there a problem?" I asked, pitching my voice much lower and harder than I had before.

Nobody answered me.

"I said, is there a problem?"

Even with the bond strained by its earlier use, Troy's magic blended with mine. Without speaking or touching, we both leaned into it hard enough that humans within a mile or two were probably looking outside and wondering why their ancestral memories warned them of danger in the dark.

Omar's people looked between us, their faces tight with reluctant desperation.

The one who'd ducked his head before, a Luna maybe, said, "We have orders...Majesties."

I didn't let up. "What orders?"

He swallowed hard enough that I could see the bob of his throat. "Our Captain..."

"Wants to know what happens here. I guessed that," I snapped. I tried to reel myself in as the elements thrummed with anticipation that I might use them. Reminded myself that shit had been going well enough up to now. "Look. This crystal? Represents a heinous act. One I thought was bad enough before I fucking touched it. And I haven't even called in the djinni we need to help us break whatever enchantment is keeping another trapped in it. You see what I'm getting at?"

The elves all looked at each other. Looked at me. Hesitated.

Wrong action.

"What she's getting at," Troy snarled, "is to get out. Now. Because I won't step in to save you if our queen or our djinni friend takes exception to *that*." Nobody needed him to gesture at the crystal to know what he was talking about. He wouldn't have been able to sense it himself. The elves had committed the crime, but they couldn't read djinn signatures like I could. "In fact, I'll cut your throats myself for disobeying a direct order."

That's when I cottoned on to Troy's reaction. I could read the magic, and Troy could read me. Even as I was outwardly numbed by yet more elven cruelty, he was incensed on my behalf. He might not know what was wrong, but he'd know I was beyond upset and he was willing to kill everyone in the room for it, based on what I was reading from him. The feedback loop was sending us both somewhere we wouldn't be able to come back from without blood.

Bring it down. Before you kill all your potential allies.

Troy eased down when I took a breath and brushed his hand with mine.

"It's not personal." I forced much more calm and reason into my voice than I felt. "But it's dangerous in a way I have personally seen isn't something y'all can deal with. Go. Now. Wait outside and clean yourselves up, or I'll let Duke have his way with anyone who stays."

I squeezed Troy's wrist when he bristled at their hesitation. The cocky ease he downshifted into felt more dangerous than his overt threat and tipped the scales.

Hell, I was probably echoing him.

Omar's men drew themselves up one last time then exchanged looks. With a last hand sign, they filed stiffly out the door. My Guard followed them.

I let myself relax halfway before clutching the hematite callstone hanging alongside the onyx-and-gold pendant on my chest.

"Duke. We have her."

Whatever the djinni had been doing meant nothing against what I'd just said. He was with us in moments, the sharp lemon-zest scent of his magic chokingly thick.

"Where?" he demanded.

All I could do was point and push Troy behind me as the agitated cloud that was Duke swirled around the smoky quartz tower. Troy might take it as his job to defend me, but I wasn't the one who was going to need it now.

Sure enough, Duke made himself twelve feet tall, looming furiously. "This is an abomination."

"We're going to fix it."

Duke's carnelian gaze focused over my shoulder. "*His* people did this."

"His *people*," I agreed. "Not him. He's the reason we were able to recover Iaret's soul. There were monarch-level spells and a stone wyvern. He disarmed the spells and killed the guardian."

Lightning crackled in the room, not from me, as Duke weighed a few millennia worth of grudges for the elves against the fact that we needed Troy to resurrect Iaret.

"When he breaks your heart, I kill him slowly," Duke said as he condensed into a more human-sized cloud.

"Let's focus on Iaret," I countered.

Troy stiffened behind me. The bond carried his desire to say something, but he blessedly kept his damn mouth shut. Some things—some crimes—weren't for him to speak on. Only to listen and learn from and do what he could to atone for. If he was to be my king and if House Solari was going to survive, I needed him to understand that.

So I stood there, tight as a bowstring, with an elven king at my back and an unbound djinni glaring furiously at us both like Troy was a dead man walking and I was some kind of traitor. But I had the blood of both their people in me. I felt obligated, however unfairly, to bridge the gap. I couldn't turn my back on one half of my parentage to save or condemn the other. So I had to face both.

"Are we ready?" I asked in a firm, even voice.

Duke stared at Troy. "If that elf fucks this up—"

"He won't," I said.

"He—"

"He. Will. Not." I desperately hoped I was right.

Troy squeezed my shoulder. "Duke, we haven't always been on the same side. But I swear to you, I will make this right. You are owed. I will pay the price."

The cloud that was Duke swirled as the carnelian of his eyes flared to lava. Then the djinni morphed slowly into his favorite shape, the youthful Black man with laughing dravite eyes that slanted with rage now, dressed in a thousand-dollar suit. "You certainly will. One way or another."

Resigned dread filtered through to me, but Troy just nodded. "I don't know what spell was used. But I'm hoping that with Arden as a bridge, we can work together to unravel the binding keeping Lady Iaret in her current shape."

Duke stared at him, as though he was trying to find some reason to take offense. Silence stretched. "Fine. Get going."

The hair on the back of my neck stood up as I shivered. Duke could tear apart a roomful of elves. Troy and I together could handle him, or even just me alone at this point, but I didn't want to have to. He was the last person I had left that I was related to by blood, to my knowledge anyway. He'd been abusive and fucked up as a guardian, but I was starting to feel like we were healing together in our own separate, broken ways. It'd hurt to lose him.

I stepped closer to the table where Iaret's crystal rested, opened myself to Chaos, and let down my shields. "Both of you reach for your magic and touch me."

Fire burned one shoulder, ice the other. I bowed my head, eyes squeezed shut as I tried to find the balance. As the polarities raced through me, I forced myself to relax, to lose myself in the swirl of contradiction.

Elf blood mixed with djinn in my veins. Their power raced through me, scalding, freezing, scorching, numbing, until both halves burst into incandescent power.

I was vaguely aware of throwing my head back, spine arching. Of Troy's carefully leashed fear and Duke's grim dread. All that mattered was the smoky quartz tower in front of me. With an effort, I wrestled the two halves of Aether into my own blended Chaos and slowly reached out to the crystal with one finger and magic both.

When my finger rested on the point, all three of us stiffened as a new energy coursed through us, raw and ragged with unending pain.

Iaret.

Both men spoke at once. "Arden—"

I ignored them, focusing on the soul in front of me. My head lolled as I fell into it, drawn in by beguiling meringue-flavored Aether that burned purple trails in my mind. Troy scrambled to push against them, throwing up a wall much as he did when he warded me against vampire glamour. Duke stayed tucked in behind both of us, waiting and watchful.

"There's a lattice." My words slurred like I was drunk.

"Wait. Trap." Troy's words were short, half breathless, and I heard them as much with my ears as echoing in my head.

"Path?"

"Here."

Duke grunted, seeming for the first time in my life to be out of his depth as he fumbled to watch the elven half of Aether, finding the edges of it in the Chaos swirling through me.

I let Troy show me the shape of the crosses in the lattice, each one of them a barbed jumping jack that would snag me and pull me into the crystal alongside Iaret. The pattern looked familiar. Almost like the "be still" spell that had been cast on me a few times.

I knew that spell. I could unhook it when it was fresh.

But this was at least thirty years settled and fed with anguish. Much stronger, like vines that thickened with age until they strangled the tree that provided their frame.

I studied it in my mind's eye, darting from hook to hook like a fish looking for a gap in a net. Doubt crept in, and I shoved it aside. I was tempted to use the same scythe of Chaos that I used to counter elven spells, but something told me that was too broad. I needed a scalpel. Or maybe not an edge at all?

Sweat dripped into my eyes. I shook my head to clear it.

"Can you do this?" Duke growled.

"Shut the fuck up." I leaned back into the net. Thought again about the spells Troy and Allegra had cast on me. Recalled the binding spell Grimm had once put on my mail to make a point. Looked for the common threads of both as Troy wavered and Duke flickered back to his true form.

Both their hands tightened on my shoulders. I had to hurry, even as I didn't dare risk it.

Then I spotted it. The weak point. Almost like a keyhole. I hesitated, certain it couldn't be that easy. Then again, the elves were always more straightforward than I expected.

"Brace yourselves." My voice was raspy with strain.

When they did, I pulled harder on Chaos. A glacial river of lava speared through me as I used both Troy and Duke to stabilize the wild fluctuations of Chaos into predictable oscillations, create an Aetheric key of both halves twined together, and slot it into the gap I'd found.

An unearthly scream echoed through the warehouse as a backwash of blended Aether sent us all flying.

Chapter 20

I recovered first, shaking my head to clear the tinnitus brought on by the physical and magical assault. The floor under my hands was slippery with sawdust and dirt. I wiped them on my jeans as I stood.

On the table, the crystal was gone. There was nothing in its place. No shards, no puddles of water. Nothing.

My stomach dropped. *Shit. What the hell did I do?*

Troy groaned from where he was sprawled on the floor. "Did it work?"

"I don't know. She's gone. Fuck." I looked around. "Where the hell is Duke?"

Grimacing, Troy shook his head. "I don't know. But there was one last trap that triggered when you did whatever the hell you did. I didn't see it until it snared Duke. I'm sorry."

I shook my head as my heart pounded. "Shit."

My next words were cut off by banging on the warehouse door.

"My queen?" Etain's voice. "What happened?"

I nodded toward the door. Troy dragged himself to his feet and went to it, speaking in a low tone to the rest of the elves. I clutched the callstone hanging around my neck and visualized Duke. "Duke? You still with us?"

No answer. Not even a sense of his mind. *No, please no.*

I drew on Chaos, hissing in pain as it burned through me. Handling the amount I just had was too much. I was overly sensitized now, and I swiped at the trickle of blood falling over my lips. It'd been a while since I'd had a nosebleed from overreaching myself. Now it just felt like I deserved it.

"Duke. Come on, asshole. Where—"

A tugging sensation in my chest cut me off, and the scent of lemon zest stung my nose as Duke materialized. "Such a way with words, little bird."

Alongside him, a second form took shape.

Not the smooth interplanar manifestation I was used to seeing but something cracklier. Like there was interference somehow. Power seeped into the room along with the cloud, and behind me, Troy gave a last sharp order before returning to stand at my back.

The cloud slowly coalesced in disjointed fragments, and eyes like fire opals fixed on me.

"This is the one who freed me?" Her voice was deep and feminine but harsh with disuse, coming through like radio static.

Before I could answer, her gaze shifted to Troy.

"Elven scum!" she howled like a sandstorm.

"Iaret, no!" Duke's cloud merged with the new one.

I backed up, pushing Troy with me, as they whirled. Lightning cracked, and heat like the desert at noon sent the temperature in the room spiking.

"Maybe you wanna get out," I said in a low voice. I'd never seen djinn fight like this before. Usually they enjoyed doing it in a more corporeal form.

"I won't run." Troy didn't sound certain of that plan, but he stuck by it. "I said I'd pay for what my people did. That means facing the consequences."

For a man who'd been all about just following orders nine months ago, Troy had come a long way. I reached behind me and squeezed his hand then let it go as the tumult in front of us settled.

Troy and I waited, tension stretched between us, as Duke resumed his usual form.

"Iaret, my love. We will hunt elves. But not this one." He looked at Troy with tears shining in his eyes. "This one is paying a debt."

The cloud that was Iaret buzzed then slowly, almost resentfully, shifted form until a woman of incredible beauty stood before us. Her skin was richly dark with blue undertones. Tiny, tight curls hugged her head. She was average height but seemed taller somehow, statuesque in gauzy linen robes that left her shoulders bare.

Her chin tilted up at an imperious angle as the opaline flashes in her eyes flickered. "Elves locked me away in torment for decades. Why should I trust this one? They all lie. They all manipulate and steal and hurt."

Slowly, with hands spread to his sides and with no hold on Aether whatsoever, Troy eased around me. Then, to my surprise, knelt and bowed his head. "Lady Iaret. I extend my sincerest apologies for the wrongs done to you and my intention to make it right."

She snarled, showing sharp teeth. "Your magic coats this room like scum on a lake, and you taste like a king. A kneeling king with honeyed words? What trickery is this?"

"My love, this is the fallen shadow," Duke said.

Iaret whirled on Duke. "What? Your prophecy? It passes now?"

He nodded. "You are the risen flame."

"I? How can that—" She spun back to me, eyes wide. "The Eternal Huntress."

"Guess that's me?" I forced myself to stay still as she approached with gliding steps. Troy went rock solid with the effort not to rise.

Iaret reached for my face with clawed fingers. Behind her, Duke made a tight shake of his head when I started to pull away. I gritted my teeth and let her catch my chin. She turned my head to either side and inhaled sharply, scenting me. "Ninlil's get?"

"Yes," I said between clenched teeth.

"Her mad plan worked? She seduced Quinlan in the end?"

"She did."

"And the elves didn't find you. Incredible." Iaret half-turned to glare at Troy. "Or perhaps they did but too late. How delicious. Where is she?"

"Dead."

"How?" She released my chin, and I resisted the urge to rub the tingles from it.

"Keithia Monteague and her House Guard slaughtered all of House Solari, including my parents, shortly after my birth. Duke had a human fake a death certificate for the Darkwatch to find and hid me in the mundane foster care system until I was old enough for Callista to bother with."

Iaret shook her head. Pacing to stand at Troy's back, she said, "This one smells like a Monteague. For him to be this powerful..."

She hooked her clawed fingers and raised her hand as though to swipe.

I reached for Air and Troy tensed, steeling himself for a blow.

Duke was there before I could move, catching her and pulling her gently away. "Yes. That's Keithia's grandson. Arden has claimed him as compensation for her loss. Body and soul."

Iaret snorted. "One elf? He's powerful and pretty, but that's not good enough."

I inserted myself between Troy and Iaret, not willing to fuck around with a djinni who'd been locked in the crystal of her own soul for thirty years and had a justifiable rage about it. "That's why I destroyed all three high Houses in the territory, killed their queens, took their incomes, claimed those of their people who would swear, and severed or killed those who would not."

Iaret stared at me. Then glee spread across her features. "Tell me that is the truth."

"It is," Troy said softly but without an ounce of regret. "I helped her do it."

Clapping, Iaret laughed with pure joy and danced around the room. "Then my revenge is already taken. I am truly free." She approached me on light feet. "I like your cousin, Duke. Perhaps we might be friends."

"I'd like that," I said. "But given that I've re-established my father's House and claimed the Ebon Guard to protect it and my fellow elementals, I need to know you can be on board with that."

Sparks lit her eyes, shimmering with rainbows. "You? An elemental, reigning as queen? Over elves?"

I nodded.

Iaret glanced at the ground where Troy still knelt. "This young king takes orders from you?"

"He does."

"I want to hear him say it." She skipped around in front of Troy. "Look at me, little king. Tell me that you serve her."

Troy lifted his head. A fierce light made the gold flecks in his eyes glow in the moonlight. "I serve my queen Arden Finch Solari in all things. Sworn in blood and twice-bonded, body and soul."

Iaret danced from foot to foot, clapped again, and crowed with laughter. "How does Callista like how her machinations have fallen apart?"

It was my turn to offer a savage grin. "She didn't like it at all, not that it matters. I delivered her to Artemis. She traded the knowledge of your location in exchange for a swift death just yesterday."

Iaret froze, eyes wide with disbelief, then burst back into her true shape and whirled around the room as a cloud.

"Up," I said to Troy. To Duke, I said, "Is she…"

"Sane? Maybe not entirely, but she'll recover soon. She's already leaps and bounds better than when we pulled her out. I think the elves' last spell was intended to trap any djinn caught in it in the ethereal realm, but Iaret absorbed it somehow." He glanced at Troy. "I still can't believe *you*, of all people, are the fallen shadow I've been wondering about for the last three thousand years, but fate has always been a clusterfuck."

Troy just sighed, looking tired and rumpled. I laced my fingers between his, and the frazzled edge in the bond eased. He gave me a small half-smile.

I eyed Iaret as she sent clouds of sawdust into the air. "If she's okay, we need to get going. The amount of magic we did here would have broken the Détente, and I can't risk that the local humans won't come out investigating. Then there's Roman and Evangeline to consider. And—" Dread crept into me on feet shod in doubt and fear. "The gods could have stopped us. They can follow me through the planes like Duke does. So why didn't they do anything?"

Troy's expression and the bond both locked down hard, but not before I caught an edge of contained fear. "Maybe they're busy fighting over you killing Callista. Or wanted to see if you could wield as much Chaos as you were."

"Maybe." I thought furiously but couldn't find anything. Who knew the minds or reasons of the gods? "Maybe they're just that confident that the tie from Neith's gift will bind me. Or they're plotting something worse."

Both Duke and Troy just looked at me.

I shook my head. "Either way. We need to go. Now." I wanted my wards and protections. I wanted my home and the security of my land. I was drained as fuck and wanted to be in bed with the blankets over my head and Troy's arms around me.

Duke nodded. "Iaret! We need to go, ḥibtu. Quickly."

She swirled to hover before us. "Then go. I wish to ride the winds a while longer."

I gave her a tight smile. "Fair enough. I hope we can talk tomorrow though."

"I imagine there's much to discuss. I will find you." Iaret shimmered and was gone.

"And I'll make sure she doesn't pop in on you two fucking." Duke's face twisted like he hadn't meant to make himself envision that before he disappeared.

With a tug on Troy's hand, I pulled him after me toward the exit. "Someone's gonna do a cleanup?"

"Etain should have phoned it in to Alli." He took a breath and straightened, seeming to force exhaustion away by pure force of will.

I mimicked him, not wanting to look weak or tired in front of Omar's men. The elves waiting outside would only have been able to sense the elven Aether we'd been channeling, but that had been a staggering amount. Sure enough, as we emerged into the night, the elves watching the door—Haroun, Etain, and two of the Darkwatch—stared at us with wide eyes.

"It's done," I said. "Iaret has been restored. She's gone, for now, but no elves are to go near her under any circumstances. Nobody is to speak to her beyond letting her know, with the utmost respect, that you'll call me. Understood?"

A chorus of "Yes, my queen" echoed around the small clearing.

Troy made a choppy gesture with his free hand, and Etain hustled to my car. Haroun fell in behind us.

"The rest will wait for Alli's team and drop off my car later," Troy murmured.

"Good. I was hoping you'd be coming home."

"After that, with Roman and Evangeline hunting? I'd rather stick close. If that suits you, my queen." He leaned over and kissed the crown of my head.

Warmth curled through me. "Suits me just fine."

I let him open the back door of the car for me, content to be chauffeured for once. He slid in beside me and rested a hand on my knee, more touchy-feely than usual for us being in public. Usually it was me blurring the line of professionalism.

Slouching against his arm, I rested my chin on his shoulder and kept my voice low. "What's wrong?"

He brooded for a few minutes. Long enough for Etain to get the car on the road back to Durham. "She called you the Eternal Huntress," he finally said in a barely audible voice. "I've heard that somewhere. Can't remember where. Or in what context. Must've been as a child."

I waited, schooling myself to patience. Short statements and long pauses usually meant he was containing himself or distracted with something complicated.

Shaking his head, he grimaced. "I know I've heard it. The more I think about it, the more it slips away. I almost wonder if I was mazed."

I frowned. "Keithia?"

"Would have to be. Why, I don't know. But we're missing something. Something important." He shifted uneasily and reached up to rub the burn scar where his House tattoo used to be under his left collarbone. "I think Evangeline knows."

Which meant we couldn't afford to wait for her to find us. We, or the Darkwatch, had to track her down.

Chapter 21

A call to Omar to update him on the situation was the last thing I did before crashing for the night. Nothing more was going to happen until I had gotten a solid eight or ten hours of sleep. I was out before Troy finished tending to his small injuries ahead of his usual peace-of-mind sweep.

I wouldn't have minded a vigorous morning with him, but we both knew there was shit to do that didn't involve staying in bed all day, or even for an hour. After breakfast and catching up on intel reports, we headed for the bar. Iaret wasn't entirely stable, and while I'd gotten used to the idea of having people at my little house by the Eno, I still didn't like it. I especially didn't like it with people I'd just met, so I definitely didn't want her popping up at my home.

When we arrived at the bar, there was still no sign of Zanna.

"What the hell are the fae playing at?" I paced around my small office, keeping balls of fire spinning lazily around my head. "I don't care if they haven't called a Grand Summit since Stonehenge went up, how much could there possibly be to discuss when we all know their objections to the alliance are bullshit and we have four days until Samhain?"

Troy watched me from where he leaned against the wall next to the door, arms crossed. He was used to my temper and my rhetorical questions by now, although he was watching the fire a little more warily than usual.

Grimacing, I let the balls dissipate. He never said anything, but I suspected the bigger Fire workings reminded him of something that'd happened while Keithia and Evangeline had him. With his sister possibly back in town, he was keeping the walls up in the bond a little higher than usual, which usually meant he was trying to spare me the literal upset stomach I got when something bothered him but he didn't think it should. I'd been so caught up in finding the threads of what was going on that I hadn't thought about that.

With the fireballs gone, the pinch around Troy's eyes and the tightness of his jaw eased ever so slightly. "Roman was playing games all summer. He might have sent that text just to put you on edge. Duke hasn't said anything?"

"No, I imagine he's getting reacquainted with Iaret, and after everything… I dunno. It felt shitty to tell him to go look for them again."

"Probably wise to keep him away from them, in any case. But while we're on the topic of Roman and Evangeline…"

I lifted my eyebrows at him.

"I don't like this room having just one way in or out. Not generally. Definitely not with a credible threat."

"It doesn't."

"It does as long as you keep avoiding the back door."

"I'm not—"

"You are."

I scowled at him, annoyance at being caught out making me stubborn. "It hasn't seemed like a good idea to mess with it."

Troy straightened and put his hands on his hips, tilting his head and giving me the look that said I was being childish and he was tired of it. "So instead you went through the Crossroads to the god's realm then came back and used enough Chaos that you might well have tipped them off after Neith claims to have bound you to the Hunt. I'm still upset about that, by the way."

I crossed my arms and looked down as I scuffed a toe. He was right, even if I was reluctant to admit it. I'd put up a wall of Air in front of the back door I'd discovered in this office, telling myself I'd deal with it when things quietened down. Only they hadn't, and I'd kept putting it off.

Then I brightened. "With Callista dead, her enchantments should be wearing off."

Troy just looked at me with the utterly blank expression suggesting he was resisting saying, "I thought so," although the feeling came through strongly enough in the bond that I stuck my tongue out at him.

Upset or not, he snorted a laugh. "So?"

"Okay, fine. I guess I can't have you be a bodyguard and not listen to you when you make a security suggestion."

Amusement and relief tickled through, but Troy kept his face straight. I never knew how he did that—outwardly hid whatever he was feeling. I mean, I was good, but I still gave myself away sometimes, especially to him.

With a sigh, I spun to the section of wall where I'd discovered the back door.

Pulling my wall down was easy as a thought, but I hesitated as I considered the outline I couldn't see visually yet could detect by the faintest air currents passing through. Callista's big silver-edged sword hung on the wall across it, I assumed so it would fall off and make a bunch of noise if anyone managed to discover the other end and come through it.

I'd always assumed the thing was imbued with magic, so I wasn't surprised when it sparked as I sent a pulse of Chaos at it.

"Catch me if I fall?" I asked.

"Until death," Troy said from right behind me. The unexpected intensity of the words had the sound of an oath, and that calmed me somewhat. He kept his word. Always.

Taking a deep breath, I centered myself and lifted the sword from its hooks with Air. No way in hell was I touching the damn thing. Not until we could track down Nils, the tomtar smith who'd made my elf-killer, and get his take. Hell, he'd probably made the sword to begin with, if it wasn't something Callista had brought with her from wherever she'd been before the Americas were invaded and colonized.

Nothing happened as I lifted it away from the wall and hovered it to the top of the filing cabinets I'd had brought in to lock things up for the night. I blew my breath out when it was settled and neither of us exploded into tiny magical pieces.

"One down." I tried shifting my vision to my third eye, the way I did when I was working with unfamiliar elemental magic and needed to see the chords rather than just sense them. Unsurprisingly, I saw nothing. If the door was warded, it wasn't with elemental magic.

I hovered a hand over it, one wood panel at a time, top to bottom and left to right. My jaw was locked so tight I was giving myself a headache. It was *really* not advisable to fuck with unknown magic, but anything set by Callista should be gone. That would leave djinn or elven Aether, which I could easily sense and manipulate with Chaos, or witch magic, which I could sense as a prickle of energy and call someone else to deal with.

When I got to the end, I tried it again in reverse. "Nothing," I said. "You?"

Troy and I swapped places, and the scent of burnt marshmallow rose in the room as he tried whatever new tricks he'd discovered since growing in power. "Nothing."

"So now...how to open it." I studied the outline. "Doors have hinges and clasps. The logical thing is that they'd be metal."

Focusing, I embraced Earth and tentatively rested a hand on the wood. Laurel, an oread, could sense metal if it was shallow enough. She'd saved us from breaking a gas pipe a few months back.

"There." High up on my left. Then again in the middle, then at the bottom. Hinges. I switched to the opposite side, not finding the clasp in the middle as I'd expected, but at the top. "The hell?"

Callista had been tiny. Reaching that would have been a stretch. That meant there had to be a trick to this. I cocked my head and studied it. There was no indication that there was any way to open the door from this side, unless it had been a spell attuned to Callista's magic that had been lost when her death made everything dissipate.

Oh. Duh. There was another possibility. "It wasn't intended for her to get out."

"What?"

I shook my head and squinted at the door. "We've had this wrong the whole time and it was right in front of our faces. Think about it. She was a nymph in service to Artemis, so god-adjacent. And she'd been made a celestial by her time in the stars. Callista could travel the Veil. She did it when we fought her. So this back door isn't meant for her or anyone else in this room to get out. It's meant to let someone else *in*."

Troy stiffened, not liking that at all. "Who?"

I shrugged, trying not to let myself be rattled. "Watchers? Not me. I don't think she ever fully trusted me."

"So other Watchers. Or traitors."

That was the possibility I really didn't want to be true because it meant that someone in the alliance could have been working against us from the beginning and I wouldn't have had the faintest idea. The list was huge too.

Anyone who couldn't travel the Veil was a suspect: witches, weres, elves, vampires. Unassisted elementals. Humans. A damn dog or the trickster hare in the lot next door.

A roiling burn in the bond made me look up at Troy. He was glaring at the door in a grim fury, one that was carefully tamped down but had his mind spinning.

I rested a hand on his shoulder. "Hey."

His eyes alone moved, shifting to look at me. He was holding off his predatory instincts, just barely.

"Let's get it open before we assume we can't trust anyone."

Gritting his teeth, he shook his head. "You're too trusting, Arden. With everything that's been done to you, every betrayal, you still—"

"I know," I said tiredly. "Luckily for you, and Allegra, and the whole Ebon Guard. Right?"

That got me his whole head turned my way, jaw clenched, expression wavering between hard and guilty.

"That's not a dig. I'm just saying…one step at a time."

Troy nodded and moved back to let me work. "After you then."

Part of me wanted to just blow the door off the hinges with Air, but then I'd have a gaping hole in the wall behind me when I was working. There was another option. One I'd never tried but thought I had the skill to manage now.

"I'm going to try corroding the metal on the clasp. A little Fire, a little Earth. Stop me if it starts eating me alive, okay?"

"Okay."

Before either of us could change our minds, I splayed my hand over the wall where I could sense the clasp. With a quick, anonymous prayer, I welcomed Fire to dance in me and twine with Earth. They came easily, no nosebleeds, and I smiled. It finally felt like I was growing into my power. Into myself, even, who and what I really was, all of me.

Gently, coaxingly, I snaked tendrils of blended magic through the hairline slit in the wall and fed them into the clasp I could sense behind it. The metal heated too much, and the scent of scorched wood came through. I winced. I needed acid, not fire. Val might be able to discern the difference, but I hadn't been born to Fire and was still learning the subtleties.

After what seemed like a lifetime of slow, careful manipulation, the smallest *snick* announced my success the moment before the mechanism clattered to the floor. Breath held, I let go of the elements and pressed on the door.

It swung open. The scent of dust, old dirt, and something else, something that raised hairs on the back of my neck, wafted out.

"Well done, my love."

I turned to grin at Troy, equal parts proud and embarrassed, then gave him a look. "If this was a movie, this would be when we found out you were the villain all along."

He flushed and rubbed his neck. "Fortunately, my days of villainy are behind me. As far as you're concerned anyway." His expression hardened. "Not so much for any traitors."

"Let's see what's in here." I sent a burst of Chaos ahead of me. Something flared.

Behind me, Troy hissed. Elven magic.

Wordlessly, we swapped places again.

My office filled with the cloying sweet-burnt scent of Aether as Troy muttered in elvish. A burst of magic washed over me, and I shivered.

"There." Troy spoke a few more words of elvish and gestured as though to tug a rope in half. Pinpricks ripped over me as the spell dissipated.

He eased forward, looking like he didn't trust anything about the bare foot of space that ended in an ominous-looking hole with a ladder downward. With a quick *stay put* look at me, he descended. I was in no mood to let him play hero and followed him down after taking a breath and steeling myself against the inevitable claustrophobia.

It was dark as hell, and I made a ball of flame hover for light. Troy was standing stock still in a dirt tunnel, staring at something small glinting on the ground. His expression was more washed out than I'd ever seen it, scaring me enough that I forgot I was underground.

"What, Troy?"

"I can't—this can't be right."

"What is it?"

He crouched and sent another dart of Aether at the shiny thing then scooped it up. "A ring."

Troy held it in his palm and brushed dirt from it, seeming more distressed as more details were revealed. A raw jade stone, set in a silvery band carved with oak leaves. A man's ring, from the size of it. The color scheme reminded me of the prince's pendant Troy no longer wore.

"You know whose that is?"

He swallowed, hard, and the sense I got in the bond was that he wished it was anything other than what he was seeing. Then, slowly, I felt him wrench himself away from what he wanted and refocus on what he saw. "This belongs to Darius."

I frowned, confused. "What would Callista have wanted with him? Could he have been a Watcher?"

"Maybe. He was the second Monteague knight. He would have risen to prince if I died." His voice was flat. "Allegra and Darius are a few years younger than me, but we're all closer in age than the three of us and Evangeline. We swore oaths to each other. We would always protect and defend the others. We would *always* tell the others what we were doing. Because by the time Evangeline was ten, she was already vicious and clearly Keithia's to the bone. Already hurting people." Something in him crumpled. "But Alli never told me about the Ebon Guard. She couldn't trust me until she was sure I'd bound myself to you. She went to a Luna, to Iago, before coming to me."

His whisper cut through me like a winter wind in a graveyard.

I didn't like the shape of what was unfolding, even as I prayed he was seeing it from the worst light, not the actual fact. "How's Allegra going to take this?"

Troy shook his head and rose. "I don't know, and I don't dare tell her."

"What? Why?"

"Because they were always closer to each other than me. Twins are rare, Arden. Precious beyond measure, to have two assured heirs at the same time. Doubly so when they're royal. Evangeline and I are thirteen years apart. That's thirteen years of waiting for my mother to produce a female heir. Thirteen years of uncertainty and political maneuvering. That's why both Alli and Dari were sworn as knights to defend me. I was marriage bait until Evangeline was born. To be held in trust for the little queen of Keithia's choosing. Until she had an heir-apparent of her own."

A puzzle piece clicked into place. "It's why Evangeline was given so much leeway and why Allegra jumped straight to me marrying you."

Troy nodded. His expression was shuttered, but the bond suggested he was seeing his past in new, painful ways. "Darius was supposed to be out of state. He's been gone for years. This shouldn't be here. It was on his finger when he left. It should be more tarnished if it's been laying here that long. My guess is that it's been here less than a year. That means this homecoming isn't his first one since he left, and it should have been."

I closed my eyes and sighed. If it really was Darius's ring, and if he and Allegra were as close as Troy thought they were, then my entire personal power base was suspect.

I might be in bigger trouble than I'd thought if it came to a fight between me and Evangeline.

Chapter 22

Troy and I followed the tunnel to its end. We didn't bother emerging from the manhole that was the logical entry point. The traffic overhead sounded like normal mundanes, not anything elven, and I didn't sense the telltale signs of electronics that would have made it a Darkwatch fake-out.

Back in my office, I laid my habitual traps of Air and a new one made of a web of Fire over the top of the ladder, shut the door, and blocked it with another wall of Air. Troy and I stared at each other.

"Maybe he dropped it. It could have been planted." I tried to give him something to hold onto, given the anguish he was trying to hide.

He wouldn't take it. "That would mean Allegra. Or someone else close enough to Darius that they could slip a ring from an elven knight's finger and powerful enough to scare him into silence once he'd realized it was missing."

I scrubbed my hands over my face. "Okay. Make inquiries. Carefully."

"Yes, my queen."

For once, I let the title go. I needed to be a queen right now. Step into my own power. Because my options were falling away and I had to believe that a double bond meant Troy would cleave to me despite everything.

The djinn, of course, chose that minute to make an appearance in a burst of zesty Aether.

I sensed it bare moments before they appeared and was already looking for them in the corner Duke usually materialized into. Troy followed my body language and the hint of magic he picked up in the bond.

Duke wrinkled his nose, presumably at the lingering scent of burnt marshmallow. Iaret took it a step further and gagged silently.

"Fuck's sake, enough," I said shortly. "Duke, shame on you. You were happy enough to work with elves if it meant finding and freeing Iaret."

Pinned between my glare and Iaret's, Duke shimmered into half-visibility and said nothing.

Great. The pissed-off djinni was the one calling the shots.

Before Iaret could launch into whatever she was going to say, I stepped forward and seated myself. Troy settled into a parade rest to the right of my chair, face neutral, bond tight.

"Let's start again. Thank you for taking time from riding the winds to join us," I said in my faux-pleasant voice. "I hope you're recovering from your ordeals, Iaret?"

The djinni's chin tilted down, and her eyes flashed dangerously with the rainbows of fire opals. At my side, Troy tensed, until I raised a hand in the signal to hold.

That gave Iaret pause. Her gaze darted between the two of us. "That's right. He belongs to you."

We all just stared at her, waiting for her point.

When she lunged for Troy, I was between them faster than even I'd expected. I forgot sometimes how much quicker I'd gotten in the last few months.

Iaret backed off, nodding as though she expected that. "Or do you belong to him?"

"I belong to Otherside," I said in a hard tone. "I'll be honest, I don't always particularly like it. I want to enjoy my land and mind my own fucking business—"

"And fuck an elf, apparently. Like mother, like daughter."

Duke grimaced, though whether it was for the antagonism in her tone or because he knew this was a losing battle for her, I didn't know.

"Iaret—" he started.

"Fucking elves falls under my. Fucking. Business," I said harshly. People only got patience from me when they weren't being dicks. "Now, I'm not gonna be so low-class as to say you owe me for freeing you from an elven trap. I'm more than happy I could help. But I am gonna say that now that you are free? You can go about *your* business. You can join up with the alliance. You can fuck off and ride the winds. You can go find the Monteague House Guard and have some fun. But what you're not gonna do is come up in *my* office and talk shit to *my* face, about me or *my* king. Not without clear and specific reasons. You got me?"

Dead silence hung in the room. In the bond, Troy wavered between defensiveness, pride, and arousal so intense I had to wall him out.

Duke flickered wildly between his preferred corporeal form and his natural one.

Iaret stayed as she was, the statuesque Nubian queen staring down me, the god's wife of the Triangle. Then she laughed, going from murder to hilarity so quickly that Troy reached for his longknife.

"I like her, Duke," Iaret said.

"Like me or not," I said before Duke could reply, "this can't be the dynamic going forward." I took a breath and intentionally softened my tone. "Iaret, Duke tells me that you're the risen flame. That you're some part of a prophecy where I need you

200

and Troy, as my fallen shadow. We have four days to nail this down before the gods ride. Can I count on you?"

She stared at me, opalescent eyes seeming to spin with color, before she rolled them. "Oh, all right. You take all the fun out of everything."

"So I hear," I said between gritted teeth.

Iaret didn't quite laugh, but her expression spelled out her amusement. "How may I serve, O Great One?"

I started to be annoyed and then went, fuck it. I'd play her game. "A werewolf called Roman Volkov indicated he was on his way here. Likely alongside one Evangeline Monteague and members of the Monteague House Guard. Duke was tailing them and thinning their numbers with a few accidents before we found you. I need them found again and contained."

Iaret went misty with excitement. "Monteague? Not—"

"My blood sister," Troy said in remarkably even tones. "Not that I claim that House anymore."

"Oh! A family stake in the squabble?" Iaret clapped and whirled. "Delicious! Duke, I like her even better now."

Duke gave her an indulgent look, and me and Troy an apologetic one when she went back to dancing. "What if they're already in the Triangle?" he asked.

I slouched in my chair. "I expect they are. Roman doesn't have the patience to send me a text message saying he'll see me soon and then not see me." Especially not with him knowing that I was sleeping with Troy now. I shrugged, hoping it looked more nonchalant than I felt. "That I haven't seen him yet says Evangeline's calling the shots. Do what djinn do best."

Duke's eyes flashed carnelian. "Free rein?"

I stomped on the flash of regret that flared in my heart. "Free rein with any entourage or retainers, but leave Roman and Evangeline alive. We have questions."

Rather, I had questions, and suspicions that Troy's nightmares needed a very specific resolution before they'd start to fade. Resolution driven by choices I couldn't make for him.

Iaret paused in her celebrations. "Just alive?"

Grimly, I nodded. "Alive, contained, and able to answer questions. If you please."

With an enthusiastic if sloppy salute, Iaret was gone and Duke after her. I propped my elbows on the desk and buried my face in my hands. Troy, bless him, said nothing. As tight as both bonds tied him to me, he was unbelievably good at keeping himself to himself—just as I'd demanded he should after the vampire Reveal.

"Let's go see the weres," I said when I'd pulled myself together. "We need to figure out what to do when we catch up with Roman and Evangeline and what to do if the gods take exception."

Troy followed me out, silent and busy in his own head.

Ice settled in my core as I wondered if I was pushing him, and myself, too hard on this. Then it grew as I decided I had no other choice.

***

When we arrived at the garage and body shop that was one of the werecats' fronts, business was slow. A handful of mundanes were scattered around the waiting area or smoking out front. One of the cars had a bad-looking rear bumper, and the rest probably needed state inspections. I had Etain and Haroun wait in the car, wanting to keep this discussion private.

Lola guided us out back, where an informal break area had been set up with string lights and a mesh table. The blueberry scent of a vape pen lingered, and a fan was shoved off to the side, awaiting warmer days to be useful again. Rusting car parts were scattered around the large dirt yard in some order unidentifiable to me.

Troy was still lost in his own thoughts. I left him to it. Either he'd come up with something brilliant, or he'd remember himself and set it aside to wrestle with later. Until then, I could give him space to come to terms with what we'd just discovered about his brother. Lola had taken one look at him and skedaddled, clearly recognizing him as more powerful than he had been and taking his mood as serious.

Ximena and Terrence came out of the main building arguing in Spanish. Terrence had a stripe of grease on his cheek that Ximena swiped off with a sharp comment. They stared at each other for a long moment, eyes flaring to the colors of their cats, before Terrence's mask cracked. They laughed, and he darted in for a quick kiss that Ximena dodged with a scandalized but good-natured exclamation.

The bond eased, and I glanced at Troy to find him watching the pair with a rueful half-smile of recognition.

Terrence was grinning his cat's smile as the wereleopard obong and the werejaguar jefa stopped in front of us. "Miss Arden," he said. "Not often you find your way to us, rather than the other way round."

I barely stopped myself from wincing. "I'm somewhat ashamed to agree that's true."

"So what's the ask?"

Leaning back in my wire-frame chair, I shrugged. "No ask. I've been asking enough of y'all. I'm just here to make sure you're all okay and personally bring word of a few developments."

"Personally." Terrence put emphasis on the word then repeated it as he dragged it out. "Personally. This sounds like the kind of news that's delivered in person because someone's dead, but none of our people are missing. Are they?"

"Not to my knowledge." I accepted the can of Coke that Lola offered me with a grateful smile. She ducked her head in the closest motion to a salute that I'd seen from the weres and hustled back to the main garage.

"Not yet," Troy muttered darkly.

That got the attention of everyone present.

I sighed and poked him through the bond. "We haven't heard anything more from Roman yet. Or Evangeline."

All eyes went to Troy at that.

He stared right back, as dead-eyed as he'd been as a Darkwatch agent ready to kill.

I spoke to break the tension. "However, with Troy leading a team including members of the Darkwatch, we've recovered Iaret. The djinni who should be able to help with the Wild Hunt."

"The other half of your prophecy?" Ximena asked.

Nodding, I took another sip of my Coke before answering, wishing it had rum in it. "She's agreed to help us."

Musk spiked in the clearing with the cats' excitement. Terrence crossed his arms and slouched. "Is that so?"

"It is."

"Seems like there oughta be a catch somewhere."

I shrugged. "She's not entirely sane. Thirty years trapped in your own crystalized soul will do that to ya. I've warned the elves away from her, and I'm telling you the same. I know y'all have good relations with everyone hereabouts, but I can't guarantee her actions or your safety."

Ximena pursed her lips and frowned. "The djinni is that dangerous?"

"I believe so. Aside from being completely unpredictable, I mean. There had to be a reason why Callista wanted her removed but used Duke and Grimm to secure and raise me. I don't buy that it was just to keep Duke in line. If he was the more dangerous one, it woulda been him she traded to the elves. Callista made sure that one way or another, she controlled what she feared. And she feared strength."

Dark consideration crept through the bond. Troy had refocused and was strategizing based on that information. Good. Evangeline's being in town combined with this mystery of Darius's whereabouts had him on edge, for good reason. But there was too much at stake and too little time for either of us to be distracted.

"Fine," Ximena said after a long look at Terrence. "What else? You wouldn't be here just for that."

I sipped some more Coke to give myself a minute. "I've set the djinn on Roman and Evangeline. Their orders are to leave them alive for questioning. Retinue is fair game."

"Well shit," Terrence muttered.

"I meant it when I said they were censured. Only this time, I'm not making the same mistake I made with the elves, censuring them but leaving them to make their own choices."

Terrence smirked. "And you don't know how young miss Volkov is gonna take that."

I flashed my eyebrows.

"I see why you came in person, Miss Arden. That's a heavy thing to say on the phone."

"Yep."

"So what are y'all gonna do about it?" Terrence's glance darted between me and Troy.

Shrugging, I finished my Coke and set it aside. "That depends on Vikki. Y'all have your agreements. I just arbitrate. But I expect if you're the de facto territory holders, you'll be the ones to keep the peace."

Ximena's lip curled, not quite into a sneer. "There's the other reason you came in person."

I sighed. "It's not a stick, Ximena, at least it's not meant to be. We are all doing what we can to make sure you're left alone, as you requested. But you know the saying about those being helped who help themselves. I can't do everything on my lonesome. At least I'm trying to be respectful about it, right?"

The werejaguar studied me with the red-gold eyes of her cat before inclining her head. "Noted."

I supposed that was the best I was going to get. We made small talk for a bit longer. Then I excused Troy and me.

"You didn't tell them about Neith's gift," Troy said softly when we were almost to the car.

I glanced at him. "You didn't tell them about Darius's ring."

His lips pressed into a thin line, and he didn't say anything as he got into the car. This was no way to run an alliance. But until we hunted down Blood Moon and the Monteague House Guard, we had too many enemies to worry about, and our allies were stretched way too thin.

It was time to do something about that.

Chapter 23

I lay in the grass of the fenced back yard at the house Troy had initially bought as a safehouse then given over to the Ebon Guard to serve as a headquarters. The wooded lot was like mine—made private by thick tree and ground cover and a long driveway.

Our unexpected arrival had sent everyone into a tizzy. After an initial comment from me about sending the djinn after Evangeline and wanting a plan to deal with her, Allegra and Troy had started arguing in elvish. I'd taken myself outside to catch a minute or ten grounding myself, thinking that when this was all over I needed to learn the damn language.

Haroun and Etain chilled nearby.

From the feeling of the bond, Troy had settled the initial argument and moved on to a second. Something icky tinged the edges, like he was trying to decide who he could trust, and I figured he was trying to ask after Darius without being obvious about it. Probably why he'd picked whatever fight they'd gotten into, unless it was about the Captain.

Definitely needed to learn elvish.

I pulled a zephyr to me and eased myself by sending it spinning through the fallen leaves. "Y'all have any problem with djinn hunting elves?"

"Not if they deserve it," Etain said darkly. "The Ebon Guard is growing, but there are a lot of threats to cover. The mundanes.

The newcomers. Lots of those lately. Some from some pretty rare corners of Otherside. Too many known and possible threats. So yeah. Put the djinn to work. Besides, high-bloods never did me any favors."

She shut up, blushing—I assumed because she remembered Troy and Allegra were among those high-bloods. Not that she took it back. Haroun grunted, and I took it as agreement.

I tried not to think too hard about the slippery slope of who "deserved" anything, although I was slightly worried about the possibility of an ongoing rift between the high-blood elves and the low-bloods. It was a gorgeous day, and I had a bad feeling—the Sight, maybe—things were going to get ugly before too long. Not in terms of weather but in terms of action.

"What would y'all do about Evangeline and Roman?" I asked instead.

"You want *our* opinion?" Haroun sounded confused.

I tilted my head to look at him. "You're my personal guards now, right? I mean, I see y'all more than the others. I need to know how you'd react as much as you do me."

Etain's mouth twisted to the side as she thought. "Evangeline needs to die."

My stomach clenched as she voiced my fear aloud. "She's a kid. Elves don't even reach their majority until they're twenty-five, right? She's even more a kid than a human would be at her age. Eighteen might be human-legal, but it's still young."

"She's dangerous," Etain said stubbornly. "We've all heard what she did to the king and the rumors about the people before him too."

"You wouldn't sever her?"

Both elves paled. Haroun shifted. "You can really do that? I thought it was a scare-story."

"I can do that." I let them hear the pang of regret in my voice. I didn't like doing it. It was considered a fate worse than death by some. But she'd live, and I couldn't see another way to deal with Evangeline that didn't involve a child's blood on my hands. She deserved some kind of punishment for what she'd done to Troy alone, and I wouldn't get in the way of whatever he decided that should be. But I needed to know what *I* would do if it fell to me. She was too high-profile a target to hesitate.

Etain's smile was nasty. "You know? She's left enough people living with nightmares that it seems just."

Haroun just looked sick, his eyes distant.

I sighed. Troy was one of those people living with nightmares. One of the reasons I'd been reluctant to admit to myself that I loved him was that I'd do anything for the person I loved. I'd forgiven Roman for leaving me. I knew I'd forgive Troy—again—if we put another death on both our consciences. I'd forgive him if it fell to me to order or ensure that death, because I hated the tiny flinch of fear he still made when her name came up. I hated that she'd done that to him. And that she was presumably planning to do it to me too.

I'd spent too many years afraid to go back into that particular box.

"Whatever it takes," I whispered, spinning another breeze to blow the dead leaves littering the yard and rustle a few that were turning to autumn colors overhead. At my throat, the callstone heated. I squeezed it and focused. "What?"

"We found them." In my head, Duke's voice was taut with anticipation. "Apartment complex in Carrboro. The brat couldn't help coming home. It's warded against the djinn-blooded, but Sergei's out for walkies in wolf form with Roman. They're scouting old elf hangouts from the smell of it."

The back door to the house scraped open and shut. Troy approached, probably drawn by the sensation of Duke speaking in my head, and crouched beside me in the grass.

On impulse, I took his hand and shifted mine so that both wrapped around the polished hematite on my chest. "That seems a little too obvious."

"Not if they don't care whether they're found. We thinned the retinue with a road accident, but you were quite clear about not riling the mundanes in public. They still have a good number to their entourage."

Troy grunted in surprise and sat all the way down.

Confusion twined through the stone. "What's wrong with your head, little bird?"

"Troy's here. I think he can hear you too."

Frowning, Troy nodded. "Sort of. It's like listening to a conversation through a wall."

"Well, I can hear him clearly enough. Curious. In any case. If they're being this obvious, they either have more people in the Triangle than we thought, or they've got something they think gives them an edge. Or both."

My stomach clenched. "Let's go with both."

"Wise."

I looked up at Troy, half reading his face, half reading the shape of his thoughts. "Can you abduct anyone? Bring them to us?"

Amusement filtered through the stone. "Can we abduct someone. What do you take us for, fire sprites? Of course we can. They'll shatter if we carry them through the Veil though. I've yet to meet anyone else with your particular gift for reconstructing beings of shadow, and we don't know if it works on anyone you're not bonded to."

"Shit."

"I'll have Alli send a team," Troy said. "We can take them to the boathouse."

I grimaced, not loving the idea of visiting horrors on people in the same place they'd been done to me, but we needed somewhere secure, fast, and Troy and Allegra had quietly maintained the boathouse as a secluded and safe location.

"Do it. Wait." An idea percolated, and I ignored Duke's growing impatience. "Fuck it. We don't have time for shenanigans. Why kidnap one when we could lure them all?"

"What do you have in mind?" Troy asked.

"They want me, right? And you, Troy. Have one of the djinn shapeshift into one of Vikki's people. Ana, even. The other can make a subtly obvious appearance, like they're keeping an eye on her. Bump into one of Roman's people on the street, and our fake Ana can let slip that we're celebrating Red Dawn with a barbeque at Jordan Lake later and suggest they come and reconcile. Roman wants to believe Ana will come round to marrying him. He'll buy it."

"Devious," Duke said. "You've grown up, little bird. I'm proud of you."

I flushed, still not liking who I had to be these days but liking the idea of being dead even less. "I'll call Vikki and tell her to expect one of you to learn Ana. It has to be perfect, Duke."

"Iaret will do it."

I exchanged a nervous look with Troy. "Is she…"

"Up to it? Of course. Besides, they know what I look like. Better that I be the obvious Watcher."

Gritting my teeth, I wrestled with the idea.

"Let her do it," Troy said. "If nothing else, better we know now how well she's recovered than find out when the gods come."

"Fine," I said. "Get it done, Duke. Please."

"As my lady commands." For once, there wasn't a hint of mockery in his tone, only deadly anticipation.

I exhaled as the extra presence in my head melted away like mist at sunrise.

Troy shook his head and rubbed his temples, grimacing. "I don't like that."

"Sorry."

"Don't be. Better that we can do it than not." He glanced over his shoulder. "Etain, Haroun, whatever happens today, do not let Arden out of your sight."

"Except, ya know, to pee or something," I muttered as I sat up, annoyance flaring.

Troy cupped the back of my head and pulled me to him for a kiss. Not a quick one but long and lingering, with all the skill he'd been trained to.

I cleared my throat when he let me go, my face on fire. "Okay, I forgive you for being bossy."

With one of his more roguish smiles, Troy winked and bounced to his feet, heading for the house with the frighteningly silent speed of a high-blood elf on a mission.

Etain shook her head as he disappeared inside, already hollering for Allegra. "He's a completely different man with you."

That made me feel good. "I know."

My good feeling didn't last long though.

Haroun stepped closer, lowering his voice. "What is it, my queen?"

I frowned as I rose and hugged myself, unable to help it. Debated whether to say anything. Whether I could trust them. Decided that if I couldn't trust the two people who credited me with them being able to serve according to their skills and not their birth, then I wouldn't be able to trust anybody. Besides, they were low-bloods. The high-bloods generally considered them not worth scheming with.

"The gods. They still haven't shown up. Not in my dreams, not anywhere. They haven't dragged me into the Crossroads either. Why? The Wild Hunt is four days away." I kept the secret

212

of Neith's gift to myself, but I still couldn't believe the gods would be able to keep from meddling.

Haroun nodded and exchanged a glance with Etain.

She sighed and said, "We've been wondering the same thing."

I frowned. "You have?"

"The king told us to be watchful." She grimaced, sounding reluctant.

"And ordered you not to say anything, right?"

She nodded, looking guilty.

I squeezed her arm. "It's fine. He was doing his job. You're doing yours. I appreciate your honesty."

The guilty look eased from both their faces.

Haroun said, "You won't punish us?"

"No." I wrinkled my nose, annoyed but not enough to be angry. "Part of my arrangement with Troy is that I let him do his job, which, broadly defined, is keeping me alive. He's the king of the House and knows I'm a stubbornly independent ass who hates being looked after, so he finds ways to do his job without directly pissing me off." I shrugged. "If I don't like it, then I can get over myself. Right?"

Both elves stared at me like I'd grown a tail.

"What?"

Etain shook her head. "I've said it before, ma'am, you're not like any queen we've ever heard of."

"Good. They were bitches." I grinned at their wide-eyed looks then gave them a level scowl. "Just don't fuck with me, and I won't have to be one too, okay?"

"Yes, ma'am," they said in unison, with the earnestness of schoolkids.

I led them into the house where Troy and Allegra leaned over a table, pointing at a map and conferring in rapid-fire elvish. Other elves rattled away on keyboards or studied what looked like traffic cam footage from Carrboro. For an operation being run out of a suburban house, Allegra's Ebon Guard seemed pretty sophisticated. I just hoped the power draw didn't get the feds set on us.

Troy switched to English as I joined them at the table. "A team is on its way to scout and set up a barbeque."

I sent an approving dart through the bond. "Good. I'll call Vikki. Then let's be on our way."

***

I almost didn't recognize the boathouse when we got there.

Troy rubbed the back of his neck at my questioning look. "It's a good location for Otherside gatherings, but I figured neither of us needed to relive January again if we needed to use it."

"I see." The boathouse itself had been completely renovated, down to a fresh coat of paint. The rickety old sheds had been demolished. New ones stood closer to the main structure. A parking area had been cleared, with squared logs marking each space and an accessible path leading from the parking to the door. A small motorboat floated at the dock—not the same one that had been here before—and sand had been dumped to create a proper beach. A metal fire kettle stood surrounded by large stones, with chairs set up around it.

Troy was looking at me with as much nervousness as I'd ever seen in him. I slung an arm around his waist and kissed the corner of his jaw. "I like it."

He exhaled heavily. "You do?"

"Yeah. Less grim. More…peaceful." That'd probably change soon enough, but for now, I could appreciate the effort Troy and whoever had been in on it had gone to. I was sure it had used my money, but I had more of it than I could think about now, and I found myself glad that some of it had gone to transforming one of the areas I'd claimed with my elemental power into somewhere I'd actually like to be.

Troy kissed the top of my head. "I'm glad. I wasn't sure, but it felt like the right thing to do."

Vikki's new silver F-150 XL crunched down the gravel behind us, stealing my response. The alpha of Red Dawn and Ana were inside the cab, and three grey wolves rode in the extended bed, tongues lolling. They leapt out and trotted into the woods as the truck slowed and parked.

Troy slipped free of my arm and stood in a parade rest behind my right shoulder as Vikki and Ana stepped out of the truck. It was only the second time I'd actually seen Ana, and the first we were meeting in an official capacity. She was average height and build—a little taller and a little slimmer than Vikki—and pale, with a mop of loose, dark curls that brushed her shoulders. Completely unassuming, until you looked her in the eye. Intelligence and something else, the look of a survivor, shone in her brown gaze. She didn't have the chiseled attractiveness of the Volkovs, but there was something that made you look at her and take note.

"Alpha," I greeted Vikki first as I'd been told was proper.

"Arbiter," she returned solemnly. "You've met my partner."

I turned to Ana and gave her a genuine smile. "I have. It's good to see you again, Ana."

As she had on our first meeting after her arrival, Ana studied me as though looking for the trap before inclining her head. "And you, Arbiter."

"I don't believe you've met my consort, Troy Solari," I said.

They shook hands, and I caught the calculating look, as though she was now understanding why I didn't begrudge Roman leaving me for a chance at her.

"An honor to meet you," Troy said smoothly. "I hope you're settling into the Triangle."

Ana relaxed a tick, as though she was finally starting to believe that she might really be welcome here. "I am. Thank you for your gracious hospitality. It's…well, unexpected, to be honest, to find Othersiders collaborating like this when my own people cannot."

Vikki ducked her head and grimaced as though she wished Ana hadn't said that but didn't say anything.

"It comes at a cost," I said gravely. "I appreciate your willingness to be here today to help us continue to pay it."

Ana nodded, and something sad entered her tone. "I can see why Roman never quite let you go."

That hit me harder than I'd expected. "I'm sorry."

"Don't be. It's nothing to do with me, and I had Vee, in any case." She looked at Vikki and smiled shyly, as though she wasn't used to doing so in public.

Vikki blushed and twined her fingers in Ana's. "I hope there's actually some food, Arden."

I laughed and leaned into Troy again, willing to be as informal as she was. "I think there is. Troy knows better than to let guests go hungry."

"Then let's bait this trap," Vikki said. "And see if my brothers are stupid enough to spring it."

Chapter 24

To nobody's surprise, Roman and Sergei did spring the trap. Not just them, but Evangeline too.

We'd gotten a round of burgers and hot dogs in when a wolf came high-tailing outta the trees like he was on fire. At the same time, Troy tilted his head as someone spoke through the earpiece he wore.

"They're here," he muttered.

"Roman?" Vikki said.

The wolf dipped his head in an exaggerated nod.

"Evangeline?" I asked.

The wolf glanced at me then made the same gesture.

Troy slid down in his chair, obviously trying to act casual. "Three cars. Ten people total, some already shifting into wolf form. Pulling into a game hunting turnoff at the side of 751 so they don't come down the road leading here."

Vikki nodded back toward the woods. "Go. Subdue any who aren't ours. Maximum force authorized."

The wolf dashed away.

"I'm not fucking around," Vikki said in response to my lifted brows. "I tried talking to the boys. They wanted to swing their dicks and act like top dogs. I meant what I said, Arden. You're our best shot, and I won't fuck that up either."

Ana looked concerned but ready. Troy looked to me.

"What she said." I pointed with my chin at Vikki. Adrenaline spiked through me.

Troy nodded and spoke into a mic at his wrist. "Teams two and three, go. Disable the vehicles then circle back to kill any Monteagues who aren't Evangeline. Let the wolves handle their own."

"They can't be this stupid," Vikki muttered. "They're boys, but they really can't."

She had a point. I glanced at Troy.

He casually shifted his chair, putting himself more between me and the line of sight from the trees. "They're not. My bet is that they let Evie and her House Guard out a mile up the road to come in on foot. They'll let the wolves be the vanguard and sneak in after."

That wouldn't do at all. I rested a hand on the back of Troy's neck and held my callstone. "Duke?"

"Busy." A burst of lemon zest came through, alongside pure joy and the metallic taste of blood at the back of my throat. "Evangeline's people are in the woods. Iaret and I are thinning the herd and driving them to you."

Troy nodded when I looked at him.

"Keep at it," I said. "Happy hunting."

Duke didn't bother responding. The sense of him faded from my mind.

I bowed my head, mourning the fact that we couldn't have settled this like friends. But I'd tried. I'd done everything I could.

I will not make myself small again to suit everyone else.

With that commitment to myself in mind, I downed one of the hard ciders from the cooler the Ebon Guard had left.

"Arden?" Vikki said.

"Shit," Troy muttered.

I tossed the empty can back into the cooler and grinned at him. He knew what booze meant, now that he knew I was a maenad on top of using it to ameliorate my power draws. "I'm not gonna have a power hangover for these fools, and I'm not letting your sister have you."

Vikki and Ana frowned.

I rose and grabbed another cider, downing that one too, before rolling my head to crack my neck. The elements clamored, all four of them plus Chaos. I dropped all my shields and any pretense of being anything other than what I was.

At my side, Troy did the same. Our power blended without a conscious thought.

Vikki's expression darkened, and Ana's eyes bugged.

"Don't shift," I said, sensing them on the edge. "We're just having a good time, right?"

"Right." Vikki looked like she was wondering if she'd regret this later.

There wasn't time to reassure her. With a baying howl, wolves spilled out of the woods led by a huge wolfman. Roman, flanked by a wild-eyed Evangeline bearing an honest-to-Goddess sword of black meteoric steel. Snarling, bloodied elves dashed silently out of the trees alongside them as Duke and Iaret barreled into the clearing behind them as massive shedu, hunters driving prey forward and screwing up their initial plan of attack.

Everyone halted as we all came face to face.

"Arden," Roman said, the words mangled in a wolf's snout. "I don't want to hurt you. Surrender and let's do this easy."

"I think the fuck not." I sent a gust of Air at them—only for it to dissipate around Roman and Evangeline. I stared in horror.

Evangeline smirked, superior and ugly. "Told you it'd work."

Soul magic. Had to be. They had an artifact.

My mind flashed back to the item the lich lord and his apprentice had recovered from Mason Farm, the one we'd never found among the items Callista had in her collection. It had to be that. But how'd Evangeline gotten her hands on it?

"Kill the elemental scum." The princess sneered at me. "Secure the rest."

Roman's wolves and Sergei gathered themselves to run at us as he shouted a wordless protest. The Monteague House Guard drew on Aether. Troy was already snarling in elvish, all the fear he'd been carrying around seeing his sister again fueling the fury he poured into his magic. I boosted it, letting Chaos flow. The booze let it spiral higher than usual with my lowered inhibitions.

At the back of the crowd, Iaret tilted her head and grinned then phased out of reality and back in at my side, human-shaped. She slapped a hand over the callstone at my throat. "Let me help."

I staggered, barely keeping my feet as djinn Aether spiked what I was already handling, smoothed by the cider I'd drunk. All of it flowed into Troy as he shouted the last word of his spell before Evangeline could finish hers.

A rifle cracked from the tree line, taking down one of the remaining elves in a spray of blood and brains. The enemy wolves leapt for us.

Cutting, icy-dark Aether exploded outward from Troy. With pained whines, the wolves tumbled, skidding in the dirt. Roman howled as he went to a knee then forced himself back up, shaking his head. Evangeline dropped the sword and clutched the sides of her head, screaming. The other elves dropped to their knees, too pained even to scream, then fell to more rifle fire from the Ebon Guard placed among the trees surrounding the clearing or on the roof of the boathouse.

Before any of us could do anything else, three shadows darted from the woods. The foremost reached Evangeline. Wrenched her head back. And cut her throat.

"No!" I shouted as blood sprayed. "Goddess damn it, we had questions!" When I found out which of the Ebon Guard had disobeyed direct orders, I was gonna have to be the bitch again—and that infuriated me as much as losing the opportunity to question Evangeline.

At my side, Troy tensed as the wind shifted to blow our way. "Darius?"

The shadows around the first figure dropped to reveal Allegra's twin. Same height. Same locs, if shorter. Same face but more masculine. Same honey-brown eyes but deadened, like Troy's used to be. "Hello, brother."

"Stand down!" Troy hollered as Ebon Guard poured into the clearing, weapons drawn and pointed at the remaining enemies. Hope and fear warred in him, and my stomach turned as it hit me through the bond. "Darius, what are you doing here?"

Darius made a hand gesture, and the other two elves flanked him as they dropped their shadows. I didn't recognize them, but they looked like the standard Darkwatch triad: a Monteague leading a Sequoyah and a Luna.

"Helping." He flipped his inner lip to show the same Ebon Guard tattoo Allegra and Iago had there. "Don't you recognize that sword? What it can do?"

Something's not right. The feeling whispered through my mind. Had we missed some of Evangeline's people? What had Darius's ring been doing at Callista's if he really was Ebon Guard? I reached out with my senses, searching for any unusual disturbances of the air.

"Stay put," Troy said suspiciously. "Alli will want to debrief you."

"Alli?"

Something was off about his tone. Confusion. For some reason I couldn't put a finger on it didn't seem like the confusion of why Allegra would do the debriefing but...something else.

Three more wolves limped out of the woods with red-stained mouths. All three bobbed their heads at Vikki, telling me they were hers as much as her relaxing posture.

Roman snarled and tried to break free of the elves holding him. Darius dashed closer and clubbed him from behind with the hilt of the knife he'd used to kill Evangeline, and the wolfman went down with a snarl.

I lunged toward Roman, halted by Troy's grabbing me. "What the fuck, Roman? What the fucking fuck? You want me dead? You want your sister dead? Ana? Fuck you!"

He just knelt there, staring around the bloodied clearing. "It wasn't supposed to go this far. It was... You were supposed to be alone. We were just going to scare you. You and Vikki and Ana and"—he snarled at Troy—"and *you*."

"Misinformation campaign," Troy murmured, for my ears only even as his arms tightened to keep me where I was. "The Captain helped bolster what the djinn started."

Duke rolled his eyes, completely unimpressed with all of this. "You truly are too stupid to lead, Volkov," he said. "The little princess had every intention of killing Arden and leading the Wild Hunt herself. I heard her plotting."

"No! She promised me Arden would live!"

Tone wrapped in iron courtesy, Troy said, "It was me who was supposed to die, wasn't it."

"Just like you tried to kill Arie. Fuck you, Monteague. Evie's business was hers." Roman glanced at her body and slumped. "So yeah. You were going to die. I had to promise Evangeline your life to save Arden's, and I don't regret that at all. I just wanted to keep Arden safe."

"From what?" I shouted. "From who? You and Evangeline are my biggest fucking threats!"

"From the gods!" Roman roared back. "Evie was going to take your place as Mistress of the Hunt."

I shook my head, baffled by the fuckery. "Then what? You and I were going to go live happily ever after somewhere? Once you'd freed me from Troy's elven spells and Vikki's seditious lies? You were gonna send Ana home to be with Cyril as a consolation prize for the Farkas pack?"

I said it in a scornful tone, but from the way Roman snarled and reddened, that was exactly what he'd been telling himself would happen.

Suddenly I was too tired for this. I let go of the elements in a savage burst. Thunder rolled in a clear sky overhead as the earth shook and the lake surged toward our heels. I pulled out of Troy's grasp and turned away, burying my face in my hands. What a fucking mess.

"Secure anyone living," Troy said in a dead-toned voice. "Get rid of the dead. Viktoria, I'd turn your brothers over to you, but you're a guest to Terrence and Ximena."

"That's fine." Vikki's voice promised revenge if she was ever alone with Roman or Sergei again. "They're dead to me anyway. Turn both their asses over to them. I don't fucking care."

"What about me?" Darius said.

I looked up at his question, studying him. The bond raged with Troy's conflicting desires to both hug and violently secure the man, but we had no idea what his deeper play was. There had to be one for him to kill Evangeline, but I didn't know what it might be. He couldn't be one of Callista's. All the geasa and oaths had broken when she'd died. That meant something else. Had he been Callista's, was no longer, and was trying to prove his loyalty? Did Evangeline know something and he needed to shut her up? Or was Darius someone else's, some enemy we hadn't uncovered yet?

"What about you?" I said, stalling.

Darius tilted his head in a movement that exactly echoed one of Allegra's. "I'd like to serve." He bowed. "My queen."

All the right words, but something wasn't right.

I glanced at Troy and found him the dead-eyed Darkwatch agent he'd been in January. Even the bond felt dead, emotionless and empty. He wasn't okay. Not in the slightest.

Sending a little nudge, I said, "Your call."

"Secure him," Troy ordered darkly. "Nobody goes near the queen without being vetted." His tone dropped, growing venomously icy. "Not even family."

My stomach twisted as Darius smiled. "Wrong answer, brother."

Troy shoved me behind him as the scent of Aether flooded the clearing. He darted toward Darius with his longknife drawn.

I pulled harder than I ever had on every element at once, readying a ball of primordial energy—then screamed as an interplanar portal opened just long enough to allow an arrow to shoot through and sink into my thigh. With the sudden pain distracting me, the energy burst outward uncontrolled, flattening everyone in the clearing.

Everyone except Darius, who'd knelt over Evangeline's body then rose with something small hidden in one hand and the meteoric steel sword in another.

I should have known. The gods were always watching.

They'd finally decided their Mistress of the Hunt was a threat, even with the binding of Neith's gift. Or maybe it was Evangeline's death. Maybe, despite everything, the artifact she'd found really would've let her lead the Hunt.

Troy shook himself with a groan and pulled on Aether again as I reached for the elements once more, only for them to slip away.

Darius and the other two members of his triad shouted a single word of elvish, as Darius slashed in my direction with the sword.

My mind shattered into jagged pieces as the Aetheric link to Troy was abruptly severed.

Troy dropped like he'd been shot in the head.

"No!" It was all I could say, and I screamed it over and over even as Iaret fought the two strange elves, one of which held two blue bottles and was chanting. The wolfman that was Roman and the big grey wolf that was Sergei fought a white wolf, a brown, and three smaller grey ones. Duke knelt by Troy, laying fingers alongside his throat then turning to me as he started fading.

All of it was utterly soundless, moving in surreal slow-motion.

As everything went red, Darius knelt in front of me. He held a gem, swirling with every shade of blue and indigo and black. It made my skin itch.

"Don't fight it. As the Eternal Huntress, you could live forever, my queen. A gift from the gods. All you have to do is submit." He put two fingers on my third eye.

And with a push of Aether and a word of elvish, I was lost.

Chapter 25

Blood coated me, weighing down my T-shirt and making everything sticky. The sheets and my arms were dark with it. The stench hung in the air.

I trembled as the front door thudded. Had I been discovered already? I didn't even know what had happened. I'd just woken up like this, mind blank but for the overwhelming sense that something was deadly wrong. That much blood meant something, or someone, had died. How could I explain it?

Whoever was outside kept hammering at the door. My mind raced. Nobody could see me covered in blood like this.

"Arden?"

I knew the voice shouting my name in between the thumping on my door. Troy Monteague. Elf prince. Sort of an ally, I thought, if we ignored the fact that he'd once drowned me. He'd also saved my life. We had a weird dynamic. Maybe dangerous, maybe not.

I blinked. That wasn't right.

We were bonded...weren't we? I mentally dug at the spot at the back of my mind where I thought it lived, like a tongue seeking a dry socket where a tooth had been pulled, finding nothing but sour, pus-filled emptiness. I frowned. That definitely wasn't right. Even when he was muting it, there was something there. A sense of secure superiority, or at least a presence, like someone standing just behind your shoulder, waiting to be noticed.

The pounding intensified. "Arden!"

I curled in over myself and pressed my forehead to my knees. Something was wrong. Something more than being covered in blood. My brain felt broken. What had happened?

Sudden silence made me lift my head. Nobody who was bothered enough to make that much noise would just stop. Was that good or bad? I still had my wards, right? I stared at my palms, trying to get a sense of whether the death signified by the blood etching their lines meant I was safer or in more danger.

The sound of the lock being picked and the door swinging open brought my head up. I patted the bed, looking for the knife I knew I kept under my pillow as rushing footsteps approached. I remembered killing Leith Sequoyah. I'd apparently killed someone else. That meant I could handle whoever was coming, as long as I could find my knife. Even if I couldn't, I was a primordial elemental. I had Air and Fire, which meant I had lightning, and I also had Earth and Water.

I frowned. That hadn't always been the case. I hadn't had Fire or Earth or Water when I'd killed Leith. Only Air because I'd been a sylph then. But I couldn't remember how I'd gained the other elements. I only knew I had them now and could use them.

My memory was shredded. Something was wrong. Very wrong.

"Goddess, Arden. What the hell happened?"

I looked up at the concerned voice, drawing a blank again. A tall silhouette filled my bedroom doorway. The scent of herbs and burnt marshmallow came with it, and I pulled on Air, filling myself with my element until the room seemed like it would blow away to Kansas if I breathed too hard.

The silhouette held up its hands. "Easy. It's me. I came alone." The voice caught. Pain weighed it down. "You know me, right?"

Cocking my head, I let the air molecules wash over me. I knew the voice, knew the patterns it made in the air. Troy. Troy Monteague. That was it.

"Are you here to kill me?" I asked.

That's what he did. He was Darkwatch. I remembered that.

"No. We're past that, remember?" The tone was off. A little horror, a little despair. Troy had never sounded like that. He was cold. Emotionless. Wasn't he?

I frowned, feeling like I really, really should remember more than I did. "No," I admitted. "But I think there's a lot I'm forgetting."

When the silhouette edged closer, I snapped a whip of Air at him. "You stay back," I snarled. "For all I know, this is your fault." I held up my hand, palm out. Othersiders would be able to smell the blood, if not see its darkness in the faint moonlight streaming in my windows.

"I swear on my life and the oaths sworn to you, I'm not here to do you harm in word or deed. We're—" Again, that choked hesitation. "We're allies. You're in need. Let me help." His voice had softened, the note of pain deepening.

I didn't understand, but I supposed I could use the help. If I'd killed someone else, I could always kill this asshole if he betrayed me.

"Okay," I whispered, clutching myself.

With slow, cautious steps, the shadow approached and knelt. Hands rested gently on my arms. "Is any of this blood yours?"

"I don't know," I said, numb and distant. "There's so much of it."

"Can you stand?"

I tried, hissing with pain and staggering as a deep wound in my thigh made itself known.

"I'm going to pick you up, okay? We'll go to the bathroom and look."

Is that okay? I froze, trying to figure out why I would simultaneously think this man might kill me but also save my life. *Can I trust him?*

He hovered, not moving, until the Sight nudged me with an answer.

"Yeah. Okay."

The hands shifted. One arm slid behind my back as the other went under my knees. I let myself collapse into a broad, well-muscled chest.

"You smell good," I said, burrowing closer. A murderer wouldn't smell that good, that right. I was sure of it.

I know this smell. It's not me, but it's mine.

I frowned because that made no sense. I just knew it was true and that the scent was in my room as well, which seemed odd.

He didn't reply, not even a noise to indicate he'd heard me, but his heart pounded faster.

I startled when my ass landed on a hard surface and a light flicked on, blinking to find myself on the bathroom counter. A man stood in front of me, his handsome features etched in concern. Eyes the color of moss on sandstone pinched at the corners as they evaluated me from under an untidy fall of black hair. The well-made clothes and scent of burnt marshmallow and herbs meant an elf. I knew this elf.

"Monteague." It felt like this wasn't the first time I'd come to that conclusion. "Troy Monteague."

"That's me. Or rather, that was me." Hurt sparked and was buried in his pretty eyes as they flicked over me. "Wait here."

Before I could protest, he was gone, returning quickly with a stack of washcloths and towels.

"Those are mine!" I protested, feeling like I'd had an argument about boundaries with this elf before. "You can't go through my house like that!"

"I know. We're going to deal with all this blood then the rest of this mess, okay?"

I looked down at myself and decided that was a good idea. I certainly didn't need incriminating evidence littering the house. "Okay. Sure."

Troy turned on both taps, fiddling a bit before dropping all of the washcloths into the sink. "Do you remember what happened?"

"No," I said in a small voice. "I woke up like this." That I'd become a meme made me laugh, and I doubled over, giggling uncontrollably.

When I sat up again, he was armed with a wet cloth.

"Let me see your face." He gently tipped my chin from side to side with a curled index finger.

I allowed it since it let me study him in return. It was easier to remember who he was now that I could see him.

"I don't see any cuts. What the hell happened? It looks like you literally bathed in elven blood. Your car reeks of it too." He dabbed at my face, starting at my hairline and moving down. The cloth's wet warmth soothed me, as did, oddly, his presence. Like being close enough to smell him was doing something to relax me. Why was that?

"Someone died," I said, sure of it as I closed my eyes and let him work. This was nice. How hadn't I known he could be nice before? Or had I? I was missing something, several somethings, and it was making me frustrated and angry.

"I can see that." He swiped gently over each eyelid before continuing with the rest of my face. "I thought you were the one who'd died. I can't find you anymore."

"The bond is gone," I said sadly, not quite sure what I was talking about but knowing that I'd wanted to be rid of it at some point. Now I was, but it left an ache that felt utterly and completely wrong.

Troy paused. "Yes. Did the gods do it? Or someone else?"

Everything in my body locked up, including my diaphragm, when I tried to remember.

"Hey! Breathe, dammit. Arden!"

Aether crested, pulling back before it touched me.

With an effort, I found my breath. Air came with it, sending the shower curtain to snapping, knocking everything off every surface in the bathroom, and making Troy flinch.

"Shit." He gripped the washcloth until red-tinged drops plunked from it onto the floor.

All I could do was stare into his face. Had he always been this attractive? And this scared? That didn't matter right now. I had to figure out what the fuck was going on. "Help," I whispered. "They...I don't know. Something is wrong." Hair like a red stag's coat and a tooled leather belt flared in my mind. "Artemis...Callista..."

Troy dropped the cloth into the sink and cupped my jaw in his hands, peering into my eyes like he could see my soul. "Callista is dead, remember? You killed her."

"I did? When?"

"A few days ago. You were gone for three days and came back a mess. Scared me half to death."

"Why do I know that I'm a primordial, but I can't remember you or something that happened less than a week ago?"

Troy shook his head. "I have some ideas, but I don't know for sure. Whatever it is, we'll figure it out. I promise."

"How long ago did you lose me?" I lifted a hand to brush the stubble on his cheek and found it softer than I'd expected. He made scruffy look good.

He tensed but didn't pull away. "It's been a day and a half. The bond snapping left me flat on my back for a full twenty-four hours. I can't remember the fight, but Darius is back and he says Evangeline and Roman attacked us. Nobody can find them or the wolves though. Or the djinn. Dari says he followed a burst of magic, found me surrounded by dead wolves and Monteagues and unconscious Ebon Guards, and brought me to Alli." Tentatively, he brushed a thumb over my cheek. "When I came to and found you gone…"

I leaned into his hand, not knowing why but letting my body do what it wanted. A day and a half. Thirty-six hours, give or take. That was recoverable. I was a private investigator. I could investigate a murder, even if I'd committed it myself. "We need to find the murder weapon."

Troy lifted his eyebrows and nodded. "Okay. Then that's what we'll do. First, though, you need to clean up. The last thing we need is mundane police stopping by for an interview and finding you covered in a body's worth of blood. I don't know how you got home, looking like this. One of the gods must have been looking out for you."

"Clean up. Good idea." I slid forward, wincing as my ass went over the edge of the counter. The tile was cool under my bare feet. My left thigh twinged when I put my weight on it, and I hissed as my leg almost gave out. Troy caught me, making sure I was steady before kneeling to take a look.

"Whoever you killed didn't go easy." He carefully fingered a long tear in what I realized were my favorite pair of jeans. "This wound should've healed. It'll need stitching once it's clean." He looked up at me. "Do you trust me to help? Or do you want me to call someone else? Allegra? Maria? Val?"

Those names all sounded vaguely familiar, but they weren't here. I'd have to go through the whole reacquaintance process all over again, when all I wanted was to figure out what the fuck had happened as quickly as possible. Troy's reactions said he was more afraid of—or scared for?—me than I was of him just now.

My reactions said that at one point, I'd trusted him. That'd do well enough. "No. You can help. Please."

"All right. Let's get your clothes off, then."

I got my shirt off as well as could be expected, given it was stiff with blood and my hands were suddenly shaking. He let me fumble with the jeans before gently taking over, undoing the button and peeling them off my hips and down my legs with a familiarity that should have frightened me. His grimace when I swallowed a whimper as they slid over the open wound on my thigh said he hadn't meant to do that, and I wondered why I'd thought he might kill me when he first got here.

"Tub," he said when I was down to bra and panties, keeping his gaze averted. "Throw the rest out when the curtain's closed, and I'll get rid of everything."

I hesitated, wondering again why I trusted him. My whole life had been secrets and obfuscation. I'd lived in fear of elves for more than a quarter century. Why was I so sure that this one would help me?

His eyes flicked to mine and lingered on my face, never dipping lower. "Arden, if I was going to hurt, expose, or kill you, I had plenty of opportunity to do it before now."

The pain that flickered across his features before he could hide it inclined me toward believing him. Still, it was a big ask. I crossed my arms and glared at him, pulling on Air to make the point.

"If you play me, it'll be the last thing you do." I let all my fear and confusion come out in hostility.

"Trust me, I learned the hard way." There was something sad in his voice, like he regretted having to learn like that.

I studied him, taking note of the defensive stance he'd fallen into, the way he kept his attention solidly on my face, and the fact that he hadn't reached for Aether, despite my holding Air. If he'd meant to hurt me, surely he'd have done it now, when I was mostly naked and wounded. He wasn't even checking out my tits.

Rather than answering, I eased back toward the bath, pulling my eyes from his only long enough that I wouldn't trip over the edge as I stepped in and tugged the curtains closed. I turned the shower on, hissing as steaming water hit abrasions and the deep wound on my thigh. I frowned, wondering why that hadn't healed. I knew I had healing powers. Djinn and elves both healed faster than human, and being half of each meant I could too.

"Arden?"

"I'm fine," I snapped. A pulled muscle in my right arm protested as I reached back to undo my bra, and I sat down in the tub to get the panties off before chucking both out.

"Don't go anywhere," Troy said.

"Fat fucking chance," I snarled back, unable to keep the pain out of my voice as water washed over cuts and bruises I hadn't realized were there until just then.

When he returned, I was still sitting there, head between my knees, under water that had gone cold.

I couldn't remember anything. Why? What had happened? Who'd done it to me? There was no way I would just forget a day and a half, let alone months. I wouldn't come home bloody and sit in my bed. I wouldn't be so confused about an elf.

Someone had messed with my mind. When I found out who it was, they were deader than whoever it was they'd had me kill.

"Arden?"

I didn't look up when the shower curtain clinked as it opened.

"Come on, the water's cold. Get out."

I ignored him, watching the little curl of red as a stream of water fled from me toward the drain.

"If you don't get up, I'll pick you up," he said gently. "You can't sit in cold water like that."

I hunched tighter, trying to find the thread of what had happened in my memories.

"Arden…" He sighed and shut off the shower then lifted me just like he had from the bed, making it seem easy as he set me on the closed toilet lid. "Here I thought you could be a pain in the ass before the gods fucked with you."

"Nobody fucks with me," I snarled, bringing my head up. "Nobody."

"Then act like it," he snapped back, thrusting a towel at me. "Here. Get comfortable. I need to stitch your leg. I don't like that it's not healing."

I wrapped myself in the towel and studied him while he stitched. "You're mad but not at me."

He slumped and exhaled heavily.

"No. I'm mad at whoever took—" He cut off and shut his mouth.

"Took what?"

Troy paused to look up at me, and for a breath, there was nothing but heartbreak on his face. Then it was gone. "I don't know if it's better or worse to tell you, if you don't remember."

That scared me more than waking up with a fucked-up memory. "Please," I whispered. "I need to trust someone. I don't know why, but I know in my gut, with the damn Sight even, that you've never lied to me. Hid shit but never lied."

He went very still where he knelt on the floor then reached up to squeeze the hand I'd rested on my stomach. "Yes. I have hidden things from you. But I've never lied. Not to you anyway."

I forced myself to be patient while he finished stitching my leg and wrapped it in a bandage. When he was done, he stayed where he was, kneeling on the floor in front of me.

I tilted his head up. "Who am I to you?"

I thought he'd deflect again.

But the fierceness in his gaze as he met my eyes made my breath catch. "You're my queen, both as ruler of House Solari and as your king consort. You're also the love of my life. I live and die for you. And I am going to figure out who did this and how to kill them, even if it's the gods themselves."

Chapter 26

I sat at the kitchen table with a hot mug of chamomile tea, jiggling my good leg as I stared at the wood grain and listened to Troy talking to Allegra. I couldn't remember who Allegra was yet, but she was important to Troy. He said she was important to me too. Captain of the Ebon Guard.

All just words.

"I already told you, Alli, I don't know what the hell happened or why she can't remember anything. Goddess, *I* don't remember anything. Not from the day it happened. That was one of the side effects we theorized when we were trying to figure out if we could untwist the Aetheric bond, remember?"

My hand rose to my chest, and I frowned when my fingers brushed only my skin. My pendant was gone. That was important for some reason. I reached for the scratchpad and pen I'd pulled out and made a note.

"Look, can you just get here please? Alone? Don't tell anyone where you're going. Don't tell anyone about Arden or me. Just get here. Now."

Another thought occurred to me. The djinn. Duke had been around lately. I could taste his magic on the back of my tongue when I breathed deeply. So where was my callstone? I got up and limped around looking for it then made another note when I found nothing. I did find a box tucked up high though. The closer I got, the more it called to me. Almost hypnotic but itchy. I reached for it.

"Hang on—Arden, leave that please."

I looked at Troy, confused by the sudden fear in his voice.

"Please. I'll explain in a minute."

Okay, so apparently the elf was not only a friend—or lover?—but he'd been to my house often enough to know what I kept in strange boxes on top of cabinets. Interesting. If it made him scared for me and he'd explain, I could be patient. I left it and kept wandering around my house, looking for things to trigger my memory.

"I don't care what you have to tell him, Darius can't come. No. Alli, I do not give a single fuck. He cannot be here. Arden didn't know him before, and she's not—"

Darius. A ring flashed into my mind at the name. Rough jade in silver carved with oak leaves. Something about it had been shocking. I stiffened.

My diaphragm locked up. The chair clattered as I reached for it and missed, going down.

"Dammit. Alli, I have to go. Come alone, or I kill you and whoever's with you. The Aetheric bond is broken. The hormonal one isn't. You know I'll do it. Don't force my hand."

Troy knelt in front of me as I gasped for breath. "Easy, Arden. What's wrong?"

A tunnel flashed in my mind's eye. Stale air. "Ring. Where's the ring?"

"What ring?"

"There was a ring. In a tunnel." I described it.

"You're sure?"

"No? But it feels important."

"That sounds like Darius's House ring." Troy frowned. "But he was wearing it when I left to come find you."

I shook my head, unable to stop until Troy caught my face in both hands. "Something is *wrong*. Not just my memory. My pendant is gone. My callstone."

He frowned, eyes darting to my neck. "Huh. I was so worried about you that I didn't notice."

"Why would someone take them but leave me alive, unless they were important?"

"I don't know. But I think you're right." His hands shifted to my arms. "You're cold, and you're shaking. Have you eaten today?"

"I don't remember." I couldn't help the bitterness that poured out with the words.

"Okay. Let's start there. When Allegra gets here, we'll figure out what she knows. Then we'll make a plan. Sound good, my queen?"

There was that word again. Queen. Whatever I'd been up to in the life I'd forgotten sounded overwhelming, but I'd be damned if anyone thought they were gonna fuck with my head, my people, or my relationships. "Yeah."

Troy had just gotten some steak and fries going when a car pulled up the drive. He waved me back to the bedroom as he got the door and patted down an annoyed-looking elfess I took to be Allegra, tucking a knife behind his belt before he let her in. Something about her face sparked a memory. Her in a tailored suit, standing next to a golden-skinned vampire.

It made my head hurt, and I shook it, distracting myself with deciding that Troy and I must have had a serious thing because I wasn't bothered in the slightest that he knew his way around my kitchen and was using it.

Allegra paced the main room while Troy cooked. "I get why you don't trust Darius, T. The circumstances of his extended absence and sudden return are weird. But that doesn't mean *our brother* wants to hurt Arden."

Troy looked up from the food long enough to give her an annoyed look. "Why not? We certainly couldn't trust Evangeline."

"You gonna tell me why I can't trust my own fucking twin? Why you're making threats?"

He kept his attention on the food and didn't answer her.

"So there is something going on."

"There's always something going on. You know that."

I rubbed my temples, tired of their bickering. "Enough, you two." I softened my tone. "I get he's your twin. But please. Work with me, okay? I can't remember you, and apparently I knew you. I just…I need a damn minute."

Neither elf said anything. I suspected Allegra could sense Troy's distrust, but I had to pretend I didn't notice it or I'd give away that I was in on the secret we were keeping—that neither Troy nor I felt like we could trust anyone but each other. We couldn't be sure what Darius's agenda was, so we needed to go one question at a time.

"Something happened at Jordan Lake. Something more than someone is saying." I waited for Allegra's nod. "What do you think it was?"

Her face went completely blank as something in my tone set her off. I gave her nothing but my neutral private investigator's face, the one I gave sources when I had a theory and didn't want to let on. She shifted her gaze to Troy, who plated the food without taking his eyes off her.

"You two think Darius is covering something up. That he knows something about where the wolves and djinn are, and the memory loss experienced by both of you and the Guards sent with you." Allegra's tone was flat. When neither of us answered her, she leaned back against the half wall between the kitchen-dining area and the front door. "So what's this bullshit then? Why am I here?"

We didn't answer.

"Me? You suspect me?" Allegra leaned on the table, looking furious. "You have got to be fucking kidding me."

"Come on, Alli." Troy put the food on the table, keeping himself between me and Allegra.

She pounded a fist on the wall. "Come on, yourself! I didn't draw down on my own father just to have you two stand there like judge and jury!"

The Sight flickered. "She doesn't know anything."

Troy relaxed, blowing out a relieved sigh.

"Nice, T. Nice. You believe her before me."

"That's how she sounds when the Sight is talking," Troy said. "But yes, I believe her first. Especially when you didn't tell me you were part of the Ebon Guard until I'd already committed high treason."

Shamefaced, Allegra sat down and held her head in her hands. "I wanted to tell you."

"Forget about it. But don't blame me for needing to be just as sure of you where Arden is concerned."

I joined them at the table. I was starving, and the food smelled better than what I usually cooked for myself.

Troy ate with half his focus on Allegra. "Something isn't lining up. Arden's House pendant and callstone are gone. She got a flash of memory when I said Darius's name, of finding what sounds like his House ring in a tunnel. It must have been in the last few days because I don't remember it."

Allegra's head snapped up. "What?"

"Yeah." I shoveled more food in my mouth, starving and tired and grouchy.

"Yet neither of you saw fit to tell me?"

I looked at Troy, finding him looking at me.

He shrugged. "I'm missing the day before the fight. I know we freed Iaret. But I don't remember what happened after. I'm assuming we decided we couldn't trust anyone but each other."

"Thanks, I hate it." The elfess slumped, looking like she'd been kicked in the head. "But that would mean Darius had been here recently. That ring was his majority present. A little over three years ago. We were sent away the next morning. This is the first I've seen him since then."

Troy studied her, and there was a faint whiff of burnt marshmallow.

"You're truth reading me?" she asked.

He shrugged. "I had to be sure." Troy ate a few more bites. "So. We assume he's been back. If you weren't aware or involved, that means he's either being framed or he's someone's agent. It's too convenient for him to re-appear right when Evangeline is killed and the Aetheric bond between Arden and me is severed."

"Shit." Allegra pushed away from the table and went to pace.

I rapped my fingers on the table, invigorated by having a mystery—even if it was a shitty one. "Iaret."

The elves looked at me, and I held up my hand for them to give me a minute. "Troy mentioned Iaret, and djinn, plural. Iaret and Duke. Duke!"

That's it.

I got up and dashed for my bookshelf.

"Arden?" Allegra said. "Nobody has seen—"

"Of course nobody's seen them. If someone is strong enough to break an Aetheric bond and make me forget most of the last—what, six or nine months?—they're strong enough to bottle two djinn." I pulled out the black walnut box and grabbed the iron fire poker from beside the fireplace. "But I bet they aren't strong enough to stop a blood summoning called by kin."

I left the sliding glass door open behind me as I limped out to the backyard. Using the iron poker, I scratched the eight-pointed star of the Goddess in the dirt. My chest tightened oddly as I did so, as though I'd done this recently and shouldn't have, but I pushed past it and placed rune-carved bones at the proper points. "I need a knife!"

"Here."

I jumped, finding Troy closer than I'd expected and holding out one I recognized—the eight-inch lead-and-silver blade I used to kill elves. I darted a look at Allegra, and he nodded. He would have used it on her.

What had I done to deserve someone that loyal?

Grimly, I took the knife and slashed my palm before I could get lost again.

"Nebuchadnezzar, I summon you." Power rose as crimson drops hit the earth, and I smiled savagely. "By the blood we share, I sunder any and all that binds you. I summon you forth from anything that contains you. Come to me here, Nebuchadnezzar, and harm only those preventing you from doing so."

I stepped back out of the star, careful not to scuff the lines. My palm itched as the shallow cut started healing, confirming that something unusual had made the wound in my thigh.

With a swirl of dry, desert wind and the bright scent of lemon zest, Duke materialized at the center of the star.

"As you have summoned me, Arden Finch Solari, so have I come. What the fuck took you so long?"

"Easy, Duke." Troy held up a placating hand when the djinni's fiery carnelian eyes landed on him. "She doesn't remember anything from the last six to nine months. I don't remember what happened two or three days ago. We're just putting the pieces together."

Duke coalesced into his usual form, but the lithe Black man wasn't laughing now. "What?"

I stepped back. "Be free in this place."

With a quick step that made Troy snarl, Duke was in front of me. He grabbed my wrist and licked the blood from my palm then recoiled. "I thought there was something off in your summons. She's been— This is vile."

"What is it?" Allegra called.

Duke's gaze flicked over my shoulder. He took my hand again, setting his thumb across the cut in my palm and pressing hard enough that I winced. In my head, he asked, *Do you trust her? Trust them both?*

I nodded.

"Go inside," the djinni said after studying me for another long moment. "I need to summon Iaret out, and she'll kill anyone who hears her true name."

I handed him the blade I'd used and went without a word, waiting inside with the elves. They were blessedly silent, leaving me to mess with the jigsaw pieces of fragged memory. The more I tried to follow the trail of any one in particular, the more lost I got.

"It'll be okay. We'll get this figured out." Troy hovered behind me. "Can I touch you?"

I hesitated then nodded. I could recall not wanting hugs or casual touch from most people, but I wanted his. The feeling snarled my brain even more than it already was, but I trusted what my body remembered.

His hands landed on my shoulders and gently eased them down then started massaging. His thumbs found exactly the spots that always knotted up when I was stressed. I bit my lip to stop from groaning and swayed on my feet. This was good. It felt like someone who knew me, really knew me, in a way that I would have sworn I'd never allowed anyone to get close enough to learn.

"I need my memory back. I need to remember us." I wanted it more than anything, and something told me that the last time I'd wanted something badly enough, I'd gotten it.

I'd get it again or die trying.

Chapter 27

"Well isn't this cute."

Troy's hands slid from my shoulders as I turned at the bitter snarl of a voice. I didn't recognize the gorgeous djinni in front of me, nor did I know why she was glaring at me, her eyes like sparking fire opals.

"Iaret," Duke said warningly as he came in behind her.

"She really remembers nothing? Neither of them?"

"No," I said. Her tone annoyed the hell outta me. "But I think it's safe to say I never liked your attitude. Don't push me."

The djinni blinked then laughed. "Well, she's still a prickly little thing at least."

I scowled as behind me, both elves sighed. That pulled this Iaret's attention away from me. Her full lips twisted into a sneer, and I stepped to get in her face. "Hey. We don't have time for this. Whoever had you bottled is gonna figure out y'all are gone soon enough. I dunno what any of us did to or for the others, but I need someone to help me figure out why that is and how to fix it. That gonna be you?"

Smoke curled from her. "It seems so. Prophecies are a bitch. I suppose they suit you."

Prophecies. "The House of Jade and the House of Onyx are the keys to Ragnarok." I whispered the words, panting and head spinning as I reached for the pendant no longer hanging around my neck and tried to remember where they'd come from.

"Torsten said that," Troy murmured. "According to the succubus. We always assumed it meant Arden and I were supposed to unite the Houses. Like her parents tried to."

Duke tilted his head. "There's usually more than one way to interpret anything. I have my guesses about this one, given what's happened, but let's see about restoring Arden before wasting time recounting everything, since all of us except our Captain of the Ebon Guard were there anyway. Iaret? Aside from the Aetheric severing, she's been soul poisoned. I suspect Evangeline recovered one of Grimm or Callista's missing trinkets, although where she got that damned sword is anyone's guess. When Darius—"

"Sword?" Allegra paled, before the blood rushed back up to tinge her light brown skin with a flush. "Wait. Darius? You're saying *Darius* did this to them?"

With a none-too-patient look, Duke nodded. "Your height, your face, but a man? Good with Aether? Two friends?"

Allegra shook her head. "He was alone. No sword. No...anything. Just Troy, unconscious, and no answers about Arden. She wasn't here the first time we checked."

Duke pinched the bridge of his nose. "Let's get this sorted. I'm bored of it already. Iaret?"

The other djinni gave Troy an evaluating look. "We'll need him. Any Monteague will do for a mental recovery, but he was her bondmate."

Bondmate? So there *was* something between us. I reached for the sour dry socket of a hole in my aura, shying away when it still felt like something had been ripped free.

"Wait, whoa," Allegra said. "You wanna explain what you're planning to do before you mess with my royals?"

"You won't like it. None of you will." Iaret sounded pleased as punch by the prospect. "You both have the uptight look of

Darkwatch agents. I assume you've been trained in interrogative techniques?"

Troy glanced at me. "I won't do that to Arden."

"One of you will have to if you want a chance for her to recover the memories. I can't affect others with Aether so I can't do it, and as has been pointed out, we don't have time for me to make an artifact attuned to Duke's little bird to channel through. The Thread of Thorns technique will shortcut the process."

I glanced between the two elves. Both had gone sallow. Allegra looked sick to her stomach, and Troy's face was grim.

Duke cleared his throat. "It has to be Troy. I'd recommend reconnecting the Aetheric bond as well. I don't know how loose we can play my prophecy, but Troy's link to Arden made them and whichever djinni worked with them more powerful. Enough that apparently the gods are threatened. Alone, Arden has the power to destroy the world. With allies, she has the power to save it. Maybe even prevent the Wild Hunt."

Looking torn between longing and horror, Troy shook his head. "I won't do that to her again. She didn't want it, and she was stuck with it. I'll fix the memory, but nobody is forcing the Aetheric bond on her again."

"A little late for a crisis of conscience on *that* front, given what we know now." Duke sneered.

"Hey," I said. When nobody paid attention to me, I compressed the air into a thunderclap.

Everyone flinched.

Into the silence, I said, "Do I get a say in what the hell happens with my fucking head? Anyone wanna know how *I* feel about all this?"

That got some interesting reactions. Duke rolled his eyes, obviously finding the discussion tedious. Iaret looked amused. Allegra looked equal parts furious and ashamed.

Troy winced and rubbed the back of his neck. "I'm sorry, Arden."

"Y'all're gonna be a lot sorrier if you don't start treating me like I have a fucking say in this." They all just looked at me. Incensed, I went on. "I'm guessing that I'm *somebody* now in Otherside. Somebody important. Somebody you have certain ideas about. Certain hopes for. But I'm still a *person*. Okay?"

"Yes, my queen," both elves said.

Duke huffed a sigh and spoke as though to a child. "So what do you want to do, little bird?"

Before anyone could do anything, I embraced Air and Fire and sent a bolt of lightning zapping at Duke.

He yelped, going misty until it dissipated in his smoky self.

"You watch your tone with me." I fixed him and everyone else in the room with a hard look. "I dunno what I let y'all push me into before or what I felt like I had to do on anybody's behalf. But I've already had enough of it now. That being said, I want my fucking memories back, and I want to thrash the bloody bejeezus outta whoever thought they were just gonna steal them and use me. 'Cause y'all? Let's not forget that I came back to myself wearing a body's worth of blood. So let's start with the memories and then see what we can do about this fucking hole in my aura. Right now."

If I didn't know any better, I'd say Troy was turned on by my little speech. Allegra looked like a kid set straight after mouthing off. Even the djinn looked evaluating.

With a small incline of her head, Iaret said, "I may have underestimated you, Arden. I...apologize."

From the way Duke's eyes bugged out of his head, those words didn't pass Iaret's lips often.

I inclined my head to the exact degree Iaret had. "Accepted. Now, what do you need from me, and how can I make this an even exchange?"

That set Iaret to smiling again. "I don't know who beat courtesy and sense into you, but I'm glad it stuck." She approached slowly and extended a hand in the direction of the one I'd sliced. "May I?"

I offered my hand to her palm up. As Duke had, she licked the nearly healed slice. Her face twisted. "Faugh. You were right, ḥibu. Nasty bit of soul poisoning." She released me and shifted back to her natural form, her fire opal eyes sparking as she thought. "We'll need to deal with the memory issue first. Then the poisoning. I suspect that was done so that, if an attempt was made to recreate the Aetheric bond, it'd have an adverse effect on our little king here. The Aetheric bond will come last. How long did it take to mutate to where it was?"

I looked at Troy.

"Nine months. It was done—" He pressed his lips together, crossed his arms, and took a breath. "I committed magical trespass against her in January. A tracking tag. Designed to break after a few weeks if it wasn't renewed. I didn't know she was an elemental at the time or that her inborn Chaos would warp the tag. The stronger she got, the worse the tag twisted. By the time Alli got back to evaluate it, it was too late to undo it without" — he waved a hand at me— "this as a possible side effect."

I eyed him. He could have copped out with a passive voice statement, but he'd caught himself and owned up to one of the gravest crimes in Otherside. It was a killing offense, yet he owned it and seemed regretful.

Hot, a good cook, *and* held himself accountable?

"I think I see why I must have fallen for you," I murmured. That got me a look so full of hope and fear that I had to turn away. "How do we start on the memory?"

Iaret didn't answer, looking at Troy.

He cleared his throat. "The Aetheric interrogation technique Iaret mentioned. It's one Monteagues have a natural talent for.

Arden, it's painful. Physically, mentally, and emotionally, by design. I don't know how to do it any other way, and I don't dare modify it. If it twists, I could implant memories or erase more."

"You've done it before?"

He shuddered then took a breath. After a long blink, his eyes were dead, and his voice came out hard. "Yes. Once. One of Omar's tests."

Allegra grimaced and hugged herself. "I only know the theory. Never used it."

I stared at Troy, trying to read those pretty eyes. He'd locked himself down, and they gave me nothing. I stepped closer, fast, pushing for a response. Nothing—until I put a hand on his chest, leaned in, and scented the spot where his jaw met his ear, driven by some instinct I couldn't remember learning.

He caught my chin with a firm hand and turned my head aside.

"Don't. Don't push me. Not now. Not if I have to do this." His voice was still emotionless but for the grim edge to it.

My heart pounded as I rolled my eyes to look at him. Whatever we'd been to each other, he could do this. It'd cost him—cost us both—but time and options were painfully short. I had to trust him. But the most telling thing was that somehow, deep down, I already did.

"Then let's get started," I said softly.

He released me and whirled to pull a chair away from the kitchen table in a single smooth movement. "Sit."

I obeyed. My pulse thundered in my ears, my breath was too short, and a cold sweat broke out over me. After a quick conference in elvish, Allegra backed up to lean against my couch. Iaret stayed misty, buzzing over the room.

Duke approached and brushed a hand over my hair, almost fondly. "Don't fight him. You'll want to. But it will make it harder."

"You sound like you've been through this before." I could barely get the words out around my dry mouth. Trusting Troy to do this didn't mean I wasn't afraid of how much it'd hurt.

Duke's expression twisted before he could hide it. "I have. Trust me when I say this is the desperate path. But I'm proud of you for having the courage to take it because if my suspicions are correct, it's the only way to see us past the Wild Hunt." He looked upward. "We strengthened your wards, enough that the gods' eyes should be turned away. Doesn't mean they won't be nosy, but they used a proxy to attack you at Jordan Lake. They're either preserving their strength for the crossing or blocked from using it further until then. It's now or never."

I frowned at that bit of information then grimaced as my thigh throbbed. Was that why it hadn't quite healed yet, even as my hand was?

"Don't try to recall it. It'll come." He shrugged, all djinn fatalism. "Or it won't, and you'll die, and then so will we all. Always the keenest knife edge with you, little bird. In any case, Iaret and I will run interference against anything else they might send. Be a love and make it fast." He looked over his shoulder. "Eh, Monteague?"

"It's Solari," Troy snarled. "And I'll do my best. Do you have anything bronze?"

Duke frowned. "You don't?"

"We banned the carrying of bronze in the territory last month, with stiff penalties. The state in general and the Triangle in particular are meant to be a safe haven for elementals. We wanted them to know we were serious."

My jaw dropped. Elves *protecting* elementals? What the hell had I been up to in this forgotten life?

With a last flash of carnelian eyes, Duke gestured, pulled a bronze cuff from the ether, pressed it into Troy's waiting hand, and vanished. Iaret followed.

"I hate to do this, Arden," Troy said. "But I watched you stop an elf's heart with a lightning strike more than once, and I know you burned Keithia alive. I don't mind dying for you, but now's maybe not the time."

If I'd been shocked about the bronze, I was flabbergasted now. "I turned into some kind of a badass, huh?"

"You always were one. You just needed time and space."

Well shit. I extended my left arm. Troy gently slipped the bronze cuff over it, and I shuddered as all my magic fled.

"I'm sorry. I'll be as quick as I can."

"Fuck quick. Be thorough. I want to know why I trust you, of all people, to put that on me."

Nodding, Troy stepped closer and cupped the back of my skull in one big hand. "Ready?"

No, I wasn't fucking ready, not if he and Duke were both scared and Allegra was watching from the other side of the room looking shook but trying not to.

"Ready," I whispered, fisting my hands on my thighs and trying to breathe normally.

Troy caressed my cheek with his free hand then set it on my forehead the moment before the burnt marshmallow scent of Aether drowned everything else out and my world spiraled to black.

Spoiler alert: I *definitely* wasn't ready.

Pain was all there was for longer than my brain could comprehend. Tendrils of Aether skittered through me, burning with icy sharp thorns, crawling through cracks and crevices of my mind.

I flashed to a scene from my childhood. Grimm, pushing me hard in mock combat, all savage claws and inky form. I fell back from a blow, tasting blood. "Stupid girl. Do you think a real rabisu would be this gentle?"

Too far. Show me the lake.

The scene wrenched. Snow fell in a forest. I slipped. Found cover behind a stand of American holly.

"No." I knew what happened. I didn't want to be there again. I fought the tendrils then screamed as the hooks dug in deeper.

Dammit, Arden, stop fighting me. Don't make this harder than it already is.

The lake closed in overhead. Water poured down my throat. The world was colder than ice and darker than death. I couldn't breathe. A hard slap to the face brought me back to my house, and I sucked in air so hard my lungs burned then dry heaved at the memory of throwing up water.

"Got her," a feminine voice growled. "Hold steady, T."

I gasped. Was plunged back to darkness and pain.

Keep going, my love. You can do this.

Then the snaking, thorny vines were back, rooting through my brain. Gold-flecked eyes under a streetlight. "You'll be seeing me around."

Duke, furious but drinking wine at my table. "First, necromancy, to defeat death."

Roman's wolf-silver eyes. "He's my brother, Arden. Watch it."

My boulder by the river and the sucking sound it made when I found the strength to topple it. Candles burning the wrong way in the dark, upside down, not extinguishing as I threw all the Air I had at them.

Troy, shoulder-to-shoulder with Val. "Make it fast." Our faces too close as I bullied him away from the door of his car. Then again at the river. "I'm sorry I wasn't wise or brave enough to find another way."

Sharp-toothed elves leering in the dark. A half-drunk Troy looking desperately for options in a bar in Durham. Simmering rage as I fought him in my woods.

His lips on mine at a fancy hotel. The Umstead?

That shocked the hell outta me, and the images spun faster and faster.

Bleeding out at the river's edge, with Neith's power heavy around me. Troy skidding to a stop as he found me. The swaying movement of being in his arms.

"Show me then, hotshot."

Troy, racked and broken. Anguish as I burned Keithia. Desperation as I called on Eshu-Elegba and fled through the Crossroads to my bedroom, clinging to Troy's broken body.

He wasn't breathing, and I couldn't find him in my head. The memories stalled, frozen.

"No! No!" I needed him alive. I needed him with me. I needed...him.

I'd spent more than a quarter century alone, isolated. I'd thought—hoped, more like—that Roman could be there for me. Then he'd gone. I'd just watched it all again. He'd left me, abandoned me. My parents were lost to me. Grimm hadn't wanted anything to do with me, but she'd been the closest thing I'd had to a sister, and she was gone too. Duke had cared in his way but not the way I needed. Callista had raised me to fear her as she'd feared me.

Everyone I'd ever had the faintest chance of loving, everyone I'd ever had the thinnest hope might love me, was gone. Dead. Or they'd hurt me. Abandoned me. There was always somebody more important. Somebody better. They were gone. They were never coming back. I was nothing and nobody and never would be anything or somebody *because nobody would love me* no matter what I did and—

I couldn't take this anymore. I couldn't take this horror reel of my life. Abandonment and death. Fear and disappointment. Over. And over. And over. Never anyone choosing me except for the person I'd just watched die.

I reached for Air. Couldn't find it. Couldn't find any of my magic, couldn't find the bond, couldn't find Troy. He'd been there. I knew it. I'd rescued him. Because he'd paid and paid and paid, and I was certain that meant he loved me. He was helping me find out who I was, and I was helping him accept what he was. But *I couldn't find him.* He wasn't in the back of my head. He wasn't—

The crack of a slap burned my face. A woman shouted my name. "Arden!"

He wasn't *there* anymore, and that meant I must have gotten him killed, another person I cared about gone—

A panicked male voice. "Arden! Come back!"

All I wanted was to be loved and cared for and valued just for me. Just for myself. Not for my power or my—

Pain lanced through me, accompanied by an icy wave of woods-and-marshmallow-scented Aether burnt to ash. Every nerve was on fire. I couldn't breathe. I couldn't think. All I could do was scream.

Then, blessedly, it stopped.

Chapter 28

The rasping harshness of my own breath was the only sound. It stabbed my lungs coming in. I couldn't move. The slightest twitch sent pain lancing through me.

"Get the lights." The voice dragged, past exhaustion. In pain. "The lights, Alli, shut them off. She'll be light sensitive."

I knew that voice.

"Troy?" My voice croaked.

"I'm here." He sounded utterly spent. Broken. "I'm here, my love."

I forced my eyes open to find myself on the floor. He leaned over me, shaking like a young tree in a windstorm, sweat-drenched and wide-eyed in the dark lit only by a last-quarter moon. Half-horrified, half-heartbroken.

"I'm so sorry." His hands hovered over me, fisting and pulling away when I flinched and whimpered involuntarily. "I lost control of it when you thought I was dead."

With those words, the memory triggered again. I was dimly aware of hands on my shoulders holding me down as I arched off the floor. Troy shouting or praying or both. None of it mattered. The rest of my memory pulled tight, looping in what'd been recovered and stitched back together with long, jagged thorns of Aether anchored deep in the recesses of my mind.

The next time I came back to myself, I groaned.

"Thank fuck," Allegra muttered. "Arden?"

"Allegra?"

A stream of blasphemous gratitude flowed from the elfess. "What do you remember?"

"Where's Troy?"

"Right next to you."

Fighting pain, I reached. My searching hand found a body. Bigger than me. Sprawled as though dead. My nose caught a scent I recognized. One that made me feel safe. Loved.

Choking down the bile that rose at my screaming nerves, I turned to my side and wrapped myself around Troy. His heart thudded under my ear, slower than usual. His breathing was as harsh and labored as mine. When I slid my hand under his shirt, his skin was cold and clammy.

"I've never seen anything like that." Allegra sat against the wall, knees up and head hanging. She sounded exhausted and scared. "And honestly I hope I never do again. You damn near killed each other, even with you strapped with bronze. I don't think anyone else would have survived it. On either side. You took everything he had and just kept screaming. Your heart stopped at least twice. I don't even want to know what my father had to do to condition him to keep going. Did it...do you—"

Lemon zest burst into the room as Duke and Iaret reappeared in their human-like forms.

Iaret tilted her head to study me. "The screaming stopped for more than a minute so we figured it was done. Do you remember?"

I shuddered. "Yeah. I remember everything."

It was all there with a sharper crystal clarity than before that hurt as much as everything else, including Troy looking like he hated himself as he slipped a bronze cuff over my arm. I clawed it off and hurled it across the room. Iaret made it vanish in midair with a snap of her fingers.

Troy wasn't waking up, but he wasn't getting worse, so I forced myself to sit up. "Allegra, Darius did this. I'm sorry. But he's working for the gods. There was a gem…"

Something about the gem bothered me. A lot. Much more than just the major fact that it could dispel elemental magic.

"Thank the lamassu," Duke muttered. "That was going to be a ballache to convince you of otherwise."

"My twin is working for the *gods*?" Allegra pushed to her feet, sliding up the wall. "Against Arden? No. No, I don't fucking believe it. How the fuck—"

"Does it matter how?" Iaret interrupted. "He is. But Arden, why don't you tell it, so it doesn't look like djinn bias."

I shook my head. "I need Troy awake first."

Iaret scoffed. "Well then hurry up and kiss him."

"What?"

"You know, true love's kiss. Blah blah boring boring, but all myths and legends and fairytales started somewhere."

I stared at Iaret in disbelief then figured it couldn't hurt.

Ignoring the expectant looks of my waiting audience, I straddled Troy and clasped the sides of his head before leaning down to whisper into his ear. "Hey. Whatever you had to do, I get it. I forgive you."

I kissed him. Without the bond, I couldn't pour love into him as I'd been able to since we started this. But I could put all of me, the physical me, into it. I could pour my hopes and dreams into it. I could put my twisted heart to his and pray it was enough to call him back.

He stiffened beneath me. Gasped.

I hissed in pain as he squeezed my arms and every nerve in them hollered but didn't lift my lips from his.

Eventually we needed air.

"Arden." His eyes searched mine, bleary and fearful.

I rested my forehead against his. "Troy."

With the gentleness of a man trying not to hurt someone, his arms slid around me and held me so tight I thought he might be trying to merge our bodies as our minds had been once. I tucked my face into the crook of his neck and shoulder. A hot wetness made my cheek itch. Tears.

"It worked," he breathed. "You're back?"

"Yeah."

Iaret cleared her throat. "This is cute as hell, but there's more to do now."

I stayed close to Troy for another heartbeat just to irritate her and then sat up. "The soul poisoning then the bond."

"Oh good," Iaret said. "You do remember. A miracle."

At the same time, Troy flinched even as his hands settled on my hips. "You really want to try reconnecting the bond?"

Knowing him, remembering us, I circled his throat with my fingers and lightly squeezed. "You're mine," I snarled as his eyelids fluttered and his body relaxed in submission under mine. "Always and forever. I'm taking you back."

The words should have scared me. I'd been terrified of the idea of forever, enough that I'd pushed away the feeling of loving him as long as I could. I saw now that it'd been tied up in my fears of abandonment, of not being deserving, of not daring to dream or receive what others wanted to give me. I'd thought standing alone was my strength, but in reliving every painful moment of my life, I saw it for what it was: self-sabotage.

My words and the intensity of my stare didn't scare Troy in the slightest. He drank them in like cracked desert soil took in rain and sent cacti to bloom. "Yes, my queen."

He clenched his jaw shut before the "please" could slip out, but I saw it in his face. He wanted it. I wanted it. We knew who we were, come hell or high water, come the gods or their agents—hell, even come severing and near-death.

"Well, thank fuck," Duke said. "We might survive the apocalypse after all."

With a last nip at Troy's bottom lip, I got up and fell into the chair I'd been in when all this started. As keen as I was to clear the soul poisoning and reconnect the bond, there was work to do first. "We need Darius. Now."

"You're sure of the gem you saw him holding?" Iaret looked as tired as I'd ever seen her. "Nobody else saw that."

I nodded. "It felt like a void. Like when I was trying to extinguish the lich's candles. Evangeline had it first, which is why my attacks broke when they reached her. Then Darius took it and used it to get close to me. Evangeline must have used it as her bargaining chip to keep the fae stalling. With that in her possession, I wasn't guaranteed to be the stronger force."

"What about the blood you were drenched in?" Troy looked like he was thinking in overdrive.

I grimaced. "The TLDR is that Darius took me to a safehouse in Briar Creek, along with the wolves and the bottled djinn. His guys had bottles ready, by the way. I was out of it for at least a day, just like Troy. Killed both members of Darius's triad and escaped when I came to, then came back to where I felt the pull of my magic the strongest." I shrugged. "Home."

There was something else missing there, in the shadows. I didn't remember how I'd come to or the fight that'd come after. But I remembered enough to figure it out.

Slowly, and wincing with pain, I forced myself to my feet. "We need to secure Darius and free the wolves. He might be acting willingly, but he might not. Either way, we need to figure out which god is using him as an agent and why he hasn't come after me yet."

"Too late," Allegra snapped. Her eyes were fixed to her phone, her face too blank. "There's an emergency alert for Raleigh. Someone's taken the governor's mansion. Hostage situation. No demands yet. My money's on Darius or someone working with him."

As if on cue, my phone started buzzing. I glanced at the caller ID. "Fuck." For a brief moment I considered ignoring it. Answered anyway. "Detective Rice. I'm aware things have just gone to shit."

"Are you, Finch? Because I don't see you down here, in Raleigh, doing your gotdamn job!"

"You're sure it's not—"

"Not unless humans carry huge motherfucking swords and can make people do whatever the fuck they say! Where the hell are you?"

I scrubbed a hand over my face. Troy had gotten my memory back, but I was drained to the point that I'd either need to sleep immediately or get witch help. "Recovering from an attack by the same party."

"I thought you were some kinda badass."

It was hard not to flinch at that. "The guy with the sword. Looks Black? A little under six feet? Golden-brown eyes? Short locs?"

"Yeah, that's him. So the hell what?"

"He's an agent of the gods of the hunt." I gave Allegra an apologetic look. "When I say 'agent,' I mean the gods gave him some nice toys that even I didn't see coming. Shit that humans can't withstand. Shit I'ma need to pull together multiple factions to stop."

A long pause. "Then what the hell are you gonna do about it, Finch?"

"Stop him." I hoped my voice held more grim and less tired, but damn it if I hadn't hoped for just a night to recover. "We don't have a choice. Halloween is two days away. This is just the pre-game."

"Are you saying this is gonna get *worse*?"

"Much. Send me as much tactical info as you can, and I'll get there ASAP."

"This is not making me like you people any better."

"Just send me the intel, Rice. And get humans off the streets. I don't want to be responsible for collateral damage taking this guy in."

As soon as I hung up, my phone was already buzzing. Doc Mike this time.

"Hey Doc. I know." I tried to keep my tone gentle. "I'm coordinating with Raleigh PD."

To his credit, Doc Mike was steadier than I'd ever heard him. "What can I do?"

I started to say nothing, to tell him to hunker down and stay safe. Doc was a human sensitive. An Othersider, but not like me. Not like Troy or Duke or Maria or Vikki. He was *human*. Not as strong or fast. A necromancer but not like us.

He's still an Othersider. If I didn't value the skills and heart of all my people, I valued none of them.

And they *were* my people. I'd claimed them, intentionally or not, when I'd deposed Callista. They were my responsibility. I wasn't just standing for something. I was standing for someone, for everyone. When there was a risk that the Wild Hunt would spread from the Triangle like an ink stain under spilled wine, I needed everyone. I couldn't handle this myself or even just with the cabal I felt safe with.

Bowing my head, I said, "I need you to be ready to help with any Otherside wounded or dead over the next few days. Can you start organizing a medical corps?"

"Yes, ma'am."

"And you're ready to help? Expose yourself if you have to in order to save lives?"

"Yes, ma'am. As God and his angels are my witness. I'll do my part."

I did flinch this time, to have a long-time friend address me like that. But Troy had called me a general once. I had to act like one. "Okay. Raleigh is the opening front in the Wild Hunt. Is Noah with you?"

A choking sound came over the phone. "You know about Noah?"

"Yes," I said gently. A real smile flickered. "I'm beyond happy that things worked out that way. Is he with you?"

Hesitation. "Yes."

"Put him on, please."

There was the muted sound of an argument. "Ms. Finch?"

"Noah." I swallowed, hard, knowing that what I was going to say would not go down well. "Tell Maria I'll need her people to help me contain Darius, please."

"You know that could cost us," he said, his tone harsh. "Vampires? Against high-blood elves, with the mundanes putting the entire city on lockdown?"

"I know what it will cost the whole damn world if we don't get this situation under control and secure Darius."

"So my people are your cannon fodder?"

"Noah." My hand went to my chest, seeking the pendant that Darius had stolen from me. "You'd only be cannon fodder if I didn't intend on backing you up. I'm coming down personally. Along with the Ebon Guard. We need Darius alive." I shot Allegra and Troy a look. Allegra nodded grimly and got out her phone.

"How long?" Noah said harshly.

I was exhausted and had no fucking clue, so I flipped to anger. "Are you refusing?"

"I only—"

I hardened my tone. "You do it, or you don't. I've spent the last day and a half remembering who the fuck I am and recovering the last year of my life. That's how strong the gods

264

are, and they aren't even here yet. Do you want Raleigh PD on your side or not?"

That wasn't fair at all. But it was the only card I had to play, as much as I hated it.

"Fuck you, Finch."

"Love you too, Noah. I'll be at Claret as soon as I'm physically able." I hung up the phone and threw it on the table with a clatter. Hung my head. "I need Janae. I need some kind of magic to be fighting fit in thirty minutes or less. Then we're going to Raleigh."

Without a question, Troy was on the phone, calling the witch in. After filling her in, he frowned at her response. "I understand there's a lot hitting the fan, but she suppressed the fire that got your daughter out. You're telling me you can't get to Arden's in the next twenty minutes from less than ten minutes away to strengthen the Arbiter and help the alliance contain an agent of the gods?"

I looked up when the conversation ended.

Troy smiled tiredly. "Fifteen minutes."

I was in for a long night, but at least I had allies.

Chapter 29

Janae's homemade pills and some healing magic had me and Troy feeling like new, although she warned the price would be crashing hard when we did finally get a chance to rest. As we prepared to head out for Raleigh after she left, footsteps on the porch announced another visitor.

"Zanna," Troy muttered after glancing out the window. He raised a hand in a respectful greeting.

"Finally!" I went to grab a beer for her. We might have been in a hurry, but being rude could cost us the fae. The Ebon Guard was already on their way to Raleigh to scout out the situation. We could catch up. "Let's hope the lords and ladies have a better answer for us this time."

My kobold friend strolled in like she owned the place, looking frazzled and tired. Her eyes lit up at the can I held out to her.

"Welcome home, Zanna. You well?"

"Well enough." She gave the elves and djinn a dark look but decided they weren't worth the trouble of scolding while there was beer to drink. Hopping onto a chair, she cracked it open and eyed the Ruger riding on one of my hips then the elf-killer balancing it out on the other. "Going somewhere? Lords and ladies have a new demand."

"I thought they might." I grimaced. "But Zanna, I really need them to come round soon. As in, now. The Hunt has begun. We were just heading out to deal with an attack on Raleigh."

Zanna looked up. "Now? Not Samhain?"

"Yeah. Prepping the way or acting out because we sidestepped a play to get me under control." I prodded the empty spot in the back of my mind where the bond should have been, still bugged by it.

"Involved Evangeline?"

"Yes. She's dead."

Zanna scowled. "Hm. That makes the demand easier or harder. They want a gem. One that was stolen from our king centuries ago. Evangeline claimed to have it."

I sighed. "Nice of them to finally come clean. The gem— small enough to fit in a fist? Dark blues, shifts color in the light?"

"You have it?"

"No. But I know who does." I also wondered what the hell the fae were doing with a gem that could block elemental magic.

The kobold chugged her beer and belched. "Coming with you."

Allegra snatched the keys from Troy. "Awesome. I'm driving. The rest of y'all figure out how to capture Darius without killing him."

As we trouped out the door, Duke said, "We'll join the scouts."

He and Iaret vanished with a shimmer of lemony Aether.

***

We were stopped at a police blockade and lost precious time arguing with the officers before Allegra got fed up and mindmazed them. She did the same at each subsequent blockade until we got downtown. The North Carolina Executive Mansion was only a few blocks away from Claret, so that's where we parked. Everything was locked down and the streets were empty, so we just went in the front door this time.

A furious-looking Maria fisted her hands like she wanted to hit me when we got inside. She was dressed for combat, with body armor over a black body stocking, leather boots, and her katanas on her back. "It's about damn time. How dare you give orders to *my* second and levy *my* people. You might be the Arbiter, but *I* am Mistress of Raleigh."

I gave her a steady look as Troy and Allegra flanked me. "Yes, you are. Yet it was Detective Rice and Doc Mike who called me about the situation here. I get that you're pissed, Maria, but we don't have time for it."

For a moment, I thought she was going to tell me to make time. Instead, she said, "We're not finished with this conversation. But I will grant emergency powers, given the situation involves elves and mundanes. Just don't make a habit of it, poppet."

The nickname was dropped harshly, with a flash of fangs. *Aw hell no. Nope. Not today.*

I stepped closer, ignoring Troy's low grunt of warning. "You know I have absolutely no interest in taking Raleigh from you, or I wouldn't have donated so much of my blood. The Wild Hunt is here. Get off your high horse so we can hammer out a plan to get a gods' agent out of your territory, okay?"

Her glare wavered. "Gods' agent?"

"Darius is either working with or under the influence of one of the gods. We assume one of the gods of the hunt and that he's here trying to do something to hamper the ability of the mundanes to muster an emergency response when the real shit starts in three days."

Maria stared up at me long enough to make a point that she wasn't backing down then made a gesture. Her people eased back, taking seats at the scattered tables at the edges of the room.

"Thank you," I said. "Now. We need to get in, secure Darius alive, free the hostages, and get the fuck out. We were hoping the vampires could create some kind of distraction. Maybe do a little community building and take the cops some coffee or something? I'll have Duke take me through the Veil then play like I'm still brainwashed and get as close as I can. The Ebon Guard can slip in while everyone else is distracted, take Darius, and get the hostages out."

"You want us to take coffee to the assholes who've done the bare minimum to defend us this year," Maria said flatly, glancing at the elf-killer on my hip then at Allegra. "Why not just kill Darius? You've done a smashing job of hunting elves so far." She smiled darkly. "Or you could give him to me. We helped with that Sequoyah, didn't we?"

"Because he has information I need right now, plus Vikki, Ana, Roman, and a few of their wolves, as well as an artifact of power that both the fae and I want."

She pursed her lips and considered that. "I suppose I could take one for the team. As long as you're not playing favorites for your captain's sake, baby doll. She's cute, but I have limits."

Allegra snarled. "I'll put him down myself if it comes to it. Don't fool yourself, Maria."

I held up a hand to forestall the angry response flickering behind Maria's eyes. "We don't have time for this. Can your people do something to keep Darius's attention on the mundanes?"

"Why not just maze them? You have two Monteagues."

"I need Darius focused on wondering what the humans and vampires are doing so he doesn't see us coming."

Reluctantly, Maria said, "Fine. I'll have Noah lead a team."

"No mundane deaths? No turnings?"

Silence stretched. "Agreed," she finally said in a hard voice. "But I can't risk my seat of power or my people. You and your Guard had better get in and get the fuck out before any of mine are arrested or killed, or I'll take it out of your skin."

I bit my tongue to stop myself from reminding her that there were bigger issues. She was new to power, still dealing with threats like the attempted coup by the Masters of New York and Miami, and being threatened on her own turf.

"I accept the terms. We'll cut through to the parking garage, if you please, Maria. Duke can carry me through from the throne room, and the elves can continue on foot." Turning to the rest of the group that'd come with me, I said, "Troy, you're leading the Ebon Guard. Iaret and Allegra, I need you to stay here. I can't risk all three of House Solari's ranking people and the other half of our prophecy." And we all knew Troy wasn't going to let me out of his sight if I was going in. "Zanna? Wait here too please. You're my pocket ace. If the police decide to fuck around with the vampires or anyone else, curse them."

Zanna puffed up, proud to have a role to play.

Allegra narrowed her eyes at me, as though looking for an insult, but all she said was, "As you command, my queen."

Iaret just rolled her eyes then stared at the vampires with a predatory look that had a few of them returning it with interest before Maria set them to raiding Claret's bar for coffee and snacks to use in our diversion.

As we made our way downstairs, I steeled myself for the offensive. I'd broken into Keithia Monteague's mansion stronghold. Surely I could sneak into the state governor's mansion.

The difference was that everyone at Keithia's had known what I was. There'd been magic in place to cover mine. This time? The odds were very good that I'd end up exposing myself to the mundanes.

A lightbulb went off in my head as we reached the throne room. "That's why he's doing this," I muttered.

Beside me, Troy tensed. "Who's doing what?"

"Darius. There are half a dozen ways he could have weakened the state's disaster response, none of which would have been nearly so public. It's not just about hampering the response. It's about exposing me. The gods don't give a shit for subtlety or Détentes or secrecy. They want adoration or, barring that, fear. They want attention."

From ahead of us, Noah said, "'Bout time you joined us in the open, *Arbiter.*"

I sighed and didn't bother answering, knowing he was just feeling pissy about what had gone down between me, him, and Maria.

Troy wouldn't let it rest. "Exposing her gains us nothing but more risk to everyone."

"It gains me a measure of satisfaction," Noah sniped back.

I rested a hand on Troy's arm. "Enough. It is what it is."

Neither answered, but I could read the air currents and, to a lesser extent, the frisson of the currents in their bodies. Both of them were on edge. Troy's power signature was leaking, blending with mine to add a jarring note to the tension in the group.

I pulled my power in then nudged Troy. With an annoyed sigh, he relaxed a little and tamped down on his signature.

"We're all friends here," I said in a low voice. "Right?"

"Yes, my queen."

I nodded my thanks to Troy, even as Noah pulled a face, grateful that he'd at least make an effort to play well with others.

"See you in there," I said. "Stay safe, okay?"

Troy studied me like he'd never see me again then saluted, fist to heart. "My queen."

I had the feeling both of us wanted to say goodbye with a kiss, but I was a general and he was my battle leader. We needed to act like it, not like lovers. I watched him go though, praying this time we'd have a better result against Darius, even as my stomach tightened with fear that we might not.

"Ready when you are, little bird," Duke said softly.

"Give them a head start." I prodded my thigh, grateful that the witch magic had sped up the healing even if it was still a little sore. "They've got a couple of blocks to cover."

When the elves and vampires had all filed out, I scrubbed a hand over my face, glad that Maria had stayed upstairs, even if it was likely because she wanted to bait Allegra. Or maybe flirt with her. I wasn't quite sure what was going on there, but there was definitely something. Maybe just Maria's thirst for elven blood.

"Do you know where in the house Darius is?"

"Yes. He's not bothering to hide. I can bring us close through the Crossroads."

"Okay. Let's hope Elegba will accept chaos as payment."

Duke grunted. He didn't care. As a being of light, he had a right to come and go through the Crossroads as he pleased. I, as a being of the golden hour, was better off paying a toll in the form of an offering. But we'd already tarried too long.

"Remind me what your plan is again?" Duke said.

I shrugged and grimaced. "Um. Hope that my leaving the godblade in a lead box at home loosens the tie between the gods and me. Hold Darius off while the Ebon Guard get the hostages out. And—shit, I should call Rice."

The detective sounded irate when he picked up. "You better have a plan for me, Finch."

"I have a team on their way over now. Mixed group, vampire street crew with coffee and snacks for the hostage negotiators to be a distraction and elven commandos to deal with the guy inside."

"Elven. Commandos. What're they gonna do, throw candy canes at this asshole?"

I sighed, mentally cursing the damnable human fairytales of Christmas and Santa's little helpers, and gave him the same rundown I'd once given Doc Mike. "Think Legolas with modern military training."

"Aw hell no. You and I are gonna have a serious talk when all this is over. We can't have—"

"We can, we do, and we will not have any kind of talk about it. The local elves are sworn to me. Any who refused are dead or exiled. Don't fuck with what you don't understand, Rice. Just tell your guys not to shoot the nice vampires bringing them some coffee on a cold night, okay? It's all meant in the name of good faith and community building. Be a shame if someone got trigger happy and created an incident that I'd have to deal with once we got the governor safe."

"Fine," Rice said grudgingly, apparently hearing the threat for what it was. "But we *are* gonna have a discussion later."

"As long as there is a later. Speak soon, Detective."

Rice alerted, I texted Troy and Noah after ending the call. *Cops told to expect friendlies with snacks and armed force for infiltration.*

Acknowledged, Troy replied. *5 minutes out.*

"Go time," I said.

Chapter 30

Duke brought us out of the Crossroads in a closet. I barely choked back a sneeze as dust swirled. It didn't bother him in the slightest, since he was in his true form, and he grinned at me.

My phone buzzed with a text from Noah. *Care package delivered. Minor glamour in play.*

Again with one from Troy. *In position.*

Go, I sent back to both, wondering what the hell the news was making of a contingent of vampires showing up at a hostage negotiation with coffee for police who'd done the bare minimum during a summer and autumn of protests—and that more out of a desire to keep the human businesses safe than the vampires. Funny how the people chanting "All lives matter" gave a hell of a lot more of a shit for businesses, rather than lives.

"Where are they?" I hissed to Duke.

"Down the hall. He has them in a private office, I think. The governor, his wife, a few aides, and a very twitchy security guard."

"Great," I muttered. "Here goes nothing."

I took a deep breath, gave myself a shake, and stuck my head out of the closet wearing my spaciest expression. Halfway down the hall, a pair of elves stood in front of a door. I clubbed them both hard with twin chords of Air, catching them as they went down with another pair of chords, and felt a brief flash of pride at the control that'd taken. For lack of anything better to do with them, I floated them to me down the hallway, bound them with more Air in the closet, and slid what had to be an antique couch in front of the door.

The fancy-yet-fugly old-style furnishings passed in a blur as I forced one foot in front of the other until I reached the door they'd been guarding.

Not wanting to harm the humans inside, I knocked.

"Come in, Arden," Darius called.

Fuck. Had there been surveillance? Had to be. Fighting back rage at the memory of our last encounter, I pushed the door open.

Darius sat behind the governor's desk. He looked like shit, his skin greying and drawn tight over his cheekbones, like he hadn't been eating—or like something was consuming him from the inside out. His eyes burned, though whether it was from madness or fever, I couldn't tell. When I sent a tiny thread of Chaos toward him, I found his aura fragmented in the weirdest way.

The humans were all bound and kneeling against the wall, looking wrung-out and shit-scared. Another elf, probably the third of the triad of the two I'd just dispatched, held a gun on them. With Darius, that meant there'd be another two on the ground somewhere. All things in threes with elves.

Troy and the Guard could handle them.

With a sardonic smile, Darius rose. "Good of you to come back to us, although I'm surprised you came alone. Or did you?"

I followed his eyes to a security feed inside a TV armoire. The screen showed mingling cops and vampires.

"Who are they?" I asked, playing like my memory was still fucked.

Fury twisted Darius's features. "Stop. Don't fuck with me. Not after you killed two of my men to escape."

"I did?"

275

Darius gestured, and the elf with the gun on the humans pointed it at the security guard's head, finger on the trigger.

"Stop with the games, or a human will die for every one of your lies."

"Fine." I choked the words out as my heart hammered. "I sent the vampires. I needed to make sure we could have a discussion. Just you and me. What do you want with these humans anyway?"

He settled back again, looking pleased. "That's more like it. I needed to be sure you'd listen to me. Callista said you were soft for mundanes."

"Callista's dead," I said bluntly. Someone off to the side whimpered, and I kicked myself before plowing on. "Who's running the show now?"

With a shrug as though Callista's death was of no import, Darius replied, "Orion."

I frowned, mind racing as I tried to recall my mythology. "Orion? The huntsman?"

"Yes. He and Callista wanted the same thing. Now you're going to deliver it, in exchange for the lives of these humans."

My mind spun. Some myths said Orion had been Artemis's lover. Keeping my eyes on Darius, I said, "What does he want?"

"Artemis. Dead. Permanently, by way Neith's gift. Silly of her to give you that, but it was her turn to be patroness this time round. She didn't want to risk a primordial with free will."

I glanced at the humans lining the wall, finding them looking even more shocked and confused than before. Troy would have to maze all of them because we couldn't have this getting out.

"Oh," Darius said with a lazy smile as he followed my line of sight. "Before you think of suppressing this conversation, it's going out to the nice law enforcement officials out front via live feed. A little concession to show good faith."

And to trap me. Shit shit shit. I'd guessed that he'd try to expose me, but this was worse than I'd imagined.

A flicker at the window pulled my attention, which pulled that of Darius and his man. As it and the one opposite burst inward, the second elf's gun wavered.

Heart sinking at the inevitable consequences of what I was about to do, I drew on Air and swiped his arm upward. It went off. Plaster fell from the ceiling.

Humans screamed and sobbed.

I didn't bother trying to confront the elf physically as Troy and three of the Ebon Guard spilled into the room. I just pushed with Air—and sent Darius's man straight out the window.

Darius snarled as Troy fell on him. Blades clashed and sparked as Darius pulled Evangeline's sword from behind his chair to block a slash from Troy's smaller longknife, nearly catching Troy across the face as he did.

"Get them out!" I shouted at the Ebon Guard, pointing at the hostages. "All the mundanes, out, right now!"

"No!" Darius turned and threw a hand up, shouting a word of elvish as he did.

I slashed at the dart of Aether with Chaos, severing it before it could reach the humans.

"Move!" I drew on Air and Fire to make lightning crackle over my hands as I slid between Darius and the mundanes.

Troy roared another spell, pulling Darius's attention.

I tried grabbing Darius with Air, only for the chord to melt away before it reached him. He still had the gem on him.

"Fuck!" I drew my elf-killer.

Troy pressed his attack. The sense of an icy midnight wind dragged down my spine, much more threatening now that I wasn't Aetherically bonded to the man to know where his head was at.

Shouting filled the hallway. The thud of heavy boots. The Ebon Guard dragged the mundanes to the door and shoved them out, heedless of any dignity, then slammed the door and dragged a chair in front of it.

"Stay the fuck outta this!" one of them hollered.

With the governor and his people safe, I guessed the cops were willing to let us fuck ourselves because the pounding at the door stopped. I loosed a bolt of lightning at the security feed and then the cameras I'd only just found in the room, half from frustration, half from a hope that that'd give us some kind of breathing room for whatever came next.

The triad of Ebon Guard started chanting in unison. Something in elvish. Aether rose in the room, the scent of burnt marshmallow chokingly thick.

As their voices reached a crescendo, Troy ducked. Was hauled back up in front of Darius, only to spin them both in a move I couldn't follow to put Darius's back to the three of them.

He screamed, back arching, and dropped.

As did Troy.

My heart practically stopped. I ran for them, the Guard fast behind me. While they secured Darius and the sword, I rolled Troy onto his back.

He blinked up at me and groaned.

"I'm fine," he slurred. "Caught the edge of that hibernation spell."

One of the Guard approached, looking nervous as hell, and muttered what I assumed was the counterspell. "Sorry, my king."

Troy pushed himself up to a kneeling position, head hanging. "It's fine. You did right."

"Thank you, sir."

I squeezed Troy's arm to comfort us both, not wanting to make more of a scene than I already had, then went for Darius.

Something zapped me as I searched his pockets, and I pulled back with a hiss.

Immediately Troy went on alert, catching my wrist when I reached for the offending pocket again.

"It's fine," I said. "Soul magic. I wasn't expecting it to react to me."

Looking like he'd rather not, Troy released me.

In one hip pocket was a brilliantly cut gem. It flashed in the light of the one surviving lamp when I withdrew it, all shades of blue, indigo, and black. I gasped, pulling myself out of it, when Troy squeezed my shoulder.

"Definitely soul magic," I murmured. Curious, I reached for Air while I held it.

Nothing happened.

Blood drained from my face, and I immediately wanted to be rid of the thing. I couldn't feel the air currents or the faint rushing of blood in Troy's veins or the electrical currents of the wiring in the room or anything at all. All the background noise to my life was suddenly gone.

It was worse than being cuffed with bronze. It felt like being dead.

"Arden," Troy said.

My hand clenched harder around the gem. I wanted to let it go but was too terrified.

Gentle fingers turned my hand over as another hand cupped my face. "Hey. Do you trust me?"

My gaze met Troy's.

"Yes," I whispered.

"Can I have this?"

I looked back down at my white-knuckled fist. "Only you."

"I'll keep it safe or die trying. I so swear."

With that, I forced my fingers open.

He pocketed the gem then looked at the rest of the Ebon Guard. "Nobody learns about this gem or who has it, or I kill the traitor who so much as speaks of its existence."

"Yes, my king." They all looked nervous as fuck about what the gem might mean and probably about what it meant that Troy had it.

With the gem out of my hands, I could *feel* again. I drew deeply on my power, enough to taste the night for a full mile. It was nowhere near as clean as I liked it, but the open window was better than nothing. Every elf except Troy flinched as my power signature spilled out along with it.

"The elf on the ground is still alive." I could sense the uneven stirrings of his breath. He'd broken a few things when he landed. "There are two more in a closet down the hall."

Troy spoke into a wrist mic. "Secure elven combatant under east windows. Return when clear to secure two more in north wing." Turning to me, he said, "Can you lift Darius and these three down?"

"Easy." I did so, watching via air currents as shadow-cloaked elves carried our targets into the night.

When they made it to the fence, I slumped in relief. With Darius and the gem both, we might have a chance at figuring out how to reverse this soul poisoning and reconnect the bond. Somewhere in the mix, we needed to get the wolves out as well.

Troy squeezed my shoulder. "One thing at a time, my love."

With nobody around to gawk, I went on tip-toes and gave him a quick kiss. "Let's wrap this up and get the hell outta town."

Predictably, a mundane SWAT team had guns pointed at us when Troy pulled the chair out of the way and opened the door. He kept himself positioned in front of me, blocking their shot. "Point those somewhere else."

When they didn't listen, he repeated it slower, harsher, with a push of Aether behind it. Looking confused, the SWAT team obeyed.

"Escort us to whoever's in charge downstairs," Troy said with another lash of Aether.

A cluster of shouting humans filled the parking area out front, along with a couple of ambulances. The shaken governor stared at me with wide eyes. His wife *meep*ed, and I tried not to laugh at the silly sound. They were right to be scared.

"Hey! Arden Finch, stop right there!"

I turned to find Detective Rice approaching. A man in a white shirt with captain's insignia followed him.

"Hands," Rice demanded.

Bemused, I shook my head to stop Troy's move to get in front of me and offered them. Looked like it was time to make a point or two. Rice clapped mundane handcuffs on me.

"Human or not, I have rights," I said. "What'd I do?"

"God *damn* it, Finch. You were reckless as fuck, that's what, and apparently part of some kind of murder conspiracy on top of it! You could have gotten all of the hostages killed for whatever this little vendetta was. You're coming to the station."

Troy eyed the detective balefully as he was cuffed as well. The cops were anxious, wild-eyed, and sweating despite the chill in the night air.

"But I didn't get anyone killed. In fact, all your high-value hostages are alive." I slouched, hoping to exude arrogance. We were in a ball swinging contest, and I had to prove mine were bigger, even if non-existent. "Besides, it was never about killing the governor. It was about forcing me to expose myself and limit my options ahead of the Wild Hunt. That succeeded, doubly so if you think I'm part of a murder conspiracy."

The police captain fisted his hands on his hips. "What. In the fuck. Is the Wild Hunt?"

I gave Detective Rice an annoyed look. "If I don't stop the gods of the hunt, we're on the verge of a second Great Flood, or worse. Biblical shit. Apocalyptic."

No need to mention it'd be my fault.

He stared at me for a minute. "If you're not gonna talk sense, we're just gonna have to lock you up for the night."

"Go head and try, but more importantly, go fuck yourself if you can't see past your tiny fucking worldview for more than a minute," I snapped right back. Troy cleared his throat behind me, and I ignored him, holding up my cuffed wrists. "You think this shit will stop me? *This?*"

"Arden," Troy said warningly.

"No," I shot back. "Not to-fucking-day. Y'all sat with your thumbs up your asses all summer and half the fall, doing jack shit to keep Othersiders safe even as we've been preparing to keep the whole Goddess-damned world safe on your behalf. So you know what? Fuck all of you."

With a focused burst of Fire and Earth, I disintegrated the simple steel handcuffs and shook the crumbling metal from my wrists disdainfully.

Behind me, Troy sighed.

I got in the taller captain's face, my eyes still glowing gold. "I am *done* with hiding so that everyone around me can feel safe when I have done nothing but help everyone. You can get with the fucking program, or you can die when the gods ride. I don't care anymore as long as you stay outta my damn way." With another burst of elemental magic, I freed Troy. "Let's go."

I turned away then back when I heard a gun clear its holster.

Rice and the police captain both looked shit-scared even as they aimed their service weapons at us. "Don't move, Finch."

I smiled at them in genuine amusement, lifted my hands, and made balls of fire dance on all my fingertips. "You really wanna point a gun at me? Remind me how flammable gunpowder is."

They gaped at me.

"I am your one. Fucking. Shot. At surviving the end of the world. I've tried getting things ready without y'all mundanes because you clearly didn't want Otherside around. But it's gonna take all of us, and we are out of time."

Troy shifted, and I extinguished the flames before he got too antsy.

"What's it gonna be, gents? You wanna be the city that saved the world? Or the one that damned it?"

Chapter 31

Fortunately for everyone involved, they decided to save face and back off rather than find out what a primordial elemental could do.

"We still need a statement," Rice said.

I snorted, too fired up to be diplomatic. "I don't have time for it."

"You can't just leave!"

"*You* called *me* in. I committed no crime and saved human lives. You've got nothing to hold me on. In fact, you should be *thanking* me for delivering you a bloodless resolution. If I was human, you'd be recommending me for a damn medal."

"Where's the terrorist?" Rice asked, changing tack.

"In custody." I held up a hand to stop everyone's open mouths from forming words. "And before you ask, no, you can't have him. My people will handle this."

The police captain tried getting in my face but backed off, expression twisting with fear, when I pulled on Air to make my eyes glow again as a small reminder.

"He committed crimes against the state of North Carolina," he said instead, in a smaller voice than I thought he wanted to.

"For which he will answer, you have my word. We're even harder on those of the community who attack humans than we are on those who attack others of us." I tilted my head. "Besides, if he was able to talk through all the security around the governor and take six people hostage, do you think you'll be able to hold him? Really?"

The captain flushed and said nothing.

"Yeah. Exactly. So let me and my people deal with him. And Captain? Tell your people to be nice to the vampires. Start treating them like the people they are, or you and I are gonna have a fucking problem. A *personal* one."

With that, Troy and I left. We were on edge as we walked down Morgan Street, knowing the cops probably had someone following us and not wanting to lead them back to Claret.

Troy reached for his longknife when a car pulled up, letting it go when the window went down to reveal Noah.

"Get in," the vampire said.

As soon as we did, he sped away fast enough that we probably would have gotten a ticket had most of the police in town not been at the governor's mansion. Troy mazed the cops at two blockades, and before long, we were at a tidy townhome on the edge of the city limits.

"Doc Mike's place?" I guessed.

"You're lucky he likes you better than I do," Noah grumbled. "You're not staying. This is just where we took Allegra and Zanna after the news showed the hostages walking out. My mistress said the faster all of you were out of town the better."

Troy slipped out of the car, and I gave him a moment to check the surroundings before following. It stung that Maria was so eager to see us out of her territory, but I had overstepped. I was still finding the balance between getting shit done and not being a dictator.

But hell, sometimes I needed to be a dictator. I couldn't own other people's hurt feelings simply because they were used to being my friend and not my subject.

I set it aside rather than dwell on it on the drive back to Durham. I knew what I'd done wrong, and I'd do better next time, if we had a next time. My immediate thoughts needed to be on freeing the wolves. I said as much and told Allegra to head for Briar Creek.

"What happens with Roman and Sergei?" Allegra asked when Troy didn't, her gaze catching mine in the rearview mirror. Zanna looked between us all, blessedly quiet.

I shrugged. "They can't be tried by the werecats if they're not made available to them. I'm an arbiter, not an assassin, and in either case, I need to know if there are any other plotters left alive."

Allegra grunted and took the exit for Briar Creek. It was a good spot for Darius to have chosen to hide: close to the airport and therefore both on neutral ground and accessible for when he flew in from wherever. The cars with the rest of the Ebon Guard split behind us, two taking Darius and his men to one of the safehouses on the Chapel Hill side of things and two continuing to follow us. We'd have to do this fast and stealthy, especially with the news announcing the hostage situation wrapping up. We couldn't afford to lose them if they moved, and after Janae's warning about how hard Troy and I would crash if we did stop, I didn't want to risk a nap.

My memory of getting home was a little distorted, but fortunately Google Maps had me at a semi-rural residential address east of 70 a few nights ago.

"Here," I said when I spotted the large ranch. It was tucked back from the road, with the gravel driveway looping around back. Allegra stopped long enough to let Troy out then kept going as he jogged back to the other two cars.

"Hey!" I said as the door closed.

"Let him scout. We've got the gem and the sword, but that doesn't mean any little friends Darius is running around with these days don't have more goodies. Like you said, no need to put you, me, and Troy in one place." Under her breath, she muttered, "Mostly I don't wanna watch either of you go through another damn memory reconstruction."

The unexpected roughness of her voice struck me. I hadn't realized how deeply affected she'd been. I mean I had, on some level, but she was always so stoic about everything, even when she was joking about it.

"Good point," I said.

She glanced at me in the mirror and relaxed as we circled the block. "Thank you."

After another loop, her phone rang. She put it on the car's Bluetooth connection. "Talk to me, T."

"One triad guarding Viktoria, Ana, Roman, and five more wolves, one of which smells like Sergei, separated into three bedrooms. All appear sedated. A couple of fresh graves out back smelling like elven blood." He paused, his voice going even more distant. "There's something off about the guards. Can't say what. Area reeks of Aether, multiple heavy workings. Faint scent of Arden and elemental magic, plus something I've smelled before but can't place. Heavier scent of blood, hers and elven, outside a fourth bedroom with a broken window sash. Scent is a few days old."

I blinked at the level of detail. "Your sense of smell is that good?"

"Yes. Give us five minutes to clear the triad." He hung up as Allegra turned back to the house.

By the time we got there, it was all over. Zanna stayed in the car, and Troy was waiting out front, arms crossed, looking deep in thought.

"They've been stripped," he said as soon as we were close.

I frowned and followed him inside. "What's that mean?"

"A mindmaze so thorough there's nothing left. Their only thought is to stop the prisoners from escaping. That has to be why nobody pursued Arden. Darius had his plan—or his orders—and the rest weren't given new instructions. I'm assuming they were told to watch the wolves. Your escape didn't change their orders."

We got to the kitchen, and I shuddered at the utterly blank expressions and lost eyes on all three of the elves. They sat at a round four-seater, unbound and unmoving. Not even blinking. The smell of Troy's Aether was heavy in the room—the usual burnt marshmallow, with more than a hint of the forest.

"The fuck?" I muttered.

"I reprogrammed them." Troy scowled. "New orders. Do nothing at all but sit."

I squeezed his arm, but he didn't relax. I said, "Okay. The wolves?"

"We left them where they are. The bottles on the bathroom counter show they were sedated with a tiletamine-ketamine blend, probably stolen from a local veterinarian."

"Can we move them?"

Allegra hissed between her teeth. "I wouldn't. They might be tripping balls when they wake up—nauseous, disoriented, dizzy, the works. We don't know when they were last dosed, and I don't want a high werewolf in our vehicles, assuming you don't want us to maze them to keep them under until we get back to the bar."

Grimacing, I shook my head. "Got it. Is it safe to look around? Use Chaos? I wanna see if there's anything that explains all this."

Troy and Allegra exchanged a look. Allegra shrugged.

"Stay away from the wolves," Troy said. "Please."

I nodded and started poking around. I found two empty djinn bottles, my pendant, and my callstone shoved in what must have been the house's junk drawer, amidst a clutter of other odds and ends. I shoved the bottles in my bag and put the necklaces on.

As the familiar weights settled around my neck, I shivered. What I had of my parents was mine again.

I vaguely remembered the rest of the house from when I'd been brought here, but I'd been walked to one of the bedrooms and locked in. Darius had been so sure I wouldn't try to go anywhere or do anything—so what had gone wrong? What piece of memory was still missing? The part of me that would always be a private investigator had to know.

I got my answer as soon as I was in the room. "Troy!"

He burst in on silent feet, longknife drawn, eyes darting around the room. "What? What's wrong?"

"There was a god here." My voice shook as I looked for something to confirm it visually, but all I could find in the room was the residue of power. Heavy. Cloying. It felt like when Neith had tested me in the clearing. I rubbed my arms, trying to brush free the feeling that it was clinging to me.

If anything, that wound him tighter. "How can you tell?"

"The…weight. In the air. It was quick, but someone was here." I closed my eyes, willing myself to remember what had happened. I felt drawn to the bed and sat next to a dried bloodstain. "It's like when the witches are doing a working and my skin prickles. Or like the pressure when a djinni is incoming but much, much more."

Troy didn't answer.

I focused on the small gap in my mind. *There. Scent of desert wind and silty, rich river mud. Date palms and sweat. Bronze and stone.*

"Neith," I whispered. Then I gasped as I shifted a little on the bed and the last piece of memory returned when I found where I'd been sitting when she appeared. "She was so angry. Said the gifts of eternity were hers alone to give. That an upstart couldn't usurp the gods. She took off the bronze cuff and cut the ropes then touched my forehead. Right where Darius did. I screamed, and the elven guards came in. I…I killed them."

I shuddered. I hadn't just killed them. I'd torn them limb from limb with Air. Neith had been so pleased with the violence and the destruction, but it'd haunt my nightmares now that I remembered it.

"Then she said I could go home and wait for her. Ordered me to forget this. So I broke the window, got in my car, and left." I opened my eyes, feeling sick to my stomach, with skin too tight for my bones. "It didn't even occur to me to get the wolves. She said 'go home and wait' so I went. I'd probably still be there if you hadn't come looking for me."

Troy sheathed his longknife, took a step closer, and crouched without touching me. "What do you need?"

I started shaking and couldn't stop. I was furious at being so thoroughly used. Furious and dead sick of it. "To finish this. Darius said it himself. He was working with Orion and Callista."

"I missed that part. What does it mean for all this?"

Still shaking, I met his eyes and forced my brain to work on anything other than the memory of the shiny bone head of some elf's upper arm coming free of the shoulder in a spray of blood. "That all of this wasn't for the Wild Hunt and the gods aren't the only celestials we have to worry about. Orion is still out there. He still wants Artemis dead."

Troy's eyes went distant. "Possible ally?"

"No. I think I'm the only one other than him who might be able to kill a god and only with Neith's gift. The knife is bound to me. I have to assume he'll make another attempt."

"I don't like the sound of—"

A howl cut him off. We jumped to our feet, darting to the bedroom across the hall.

"Arie!" Roman's voice was the growl of his wolf. An almighty banging thundered from the behind the door, like a body falling against it, followed by uncoordinated fists. "Arden! Let me see her, you bastards! What did you do to her?" His voice slurred.

Then a dragging sound came against the wood, like someone sliding down the panel. "Let me see her. She didn't deserve that. She didn't deserve what y'all did to her."

I glanced at Troy. His focus was on the door, and he looked grim as hell, bordering on fury. I didn't need our missing bond to tell me he was weighing the pros and cons of killing Roman. But then he took a breath. Steadied himself and settled into a parade rest, face blank.

"Orders, my queen?" His tone wasn't cutting or bitter, resentful or jealous. It was that of a man willing to do whatever duty called for—the core of him, drawn out yet again, regardless of what he wanted.

I cupped his jaw and turned his face to me. "You're all there is. Always. I love you."

From behind the door came a drunk-sounding, "Arden?"

Troy relaxed and offered a half-smile before kissing my palm. "And I you."

Pulling away from him, I said, "Roman?"

"Arie!"

"No." My tone was unyielding as steel. This was going to stop right now. "We've spoken on this."

"Sorry…sorry. I know. You told me and told me, and I never listened. And now it cost me everything." A sniffle. Was he crying?

I rolled my eyes and sighed, too tired of his shit for sympathy. "Roman, the house is mine. The elves who took us are captive or dead. Do you understand?"

"Yes. Good." A low, satisfied growl rumbled, one that didn't make me flush like it used to.

"Okay. I'm going to bring you some water. If you try to bust out or hurt one of my Guard, I'll put you down myself. Got it?"

"Yeah. 'Kay. Deserve it. Evie promised nobody would hurt you, but she lied. Elves are lying liars. They all hurt you."

I sighed again and rubbed my forehead. "Get some water please," I murmured to Troy. "Bowls for the wolves still on four legs. Glasses for the rest."

He went without hesitation, and I leaned against the wall opposite Roman's door. It had already had its new-looking external lock picked. The Guard had had to figure out who was in each room and their status. Roman could have opened the door and walked out, but he didn't, too high or too miserable for it.

The werewolf didn't say anything else in the time it took for Troy and one of the Guard—I really needed to get around to learning all their names—to come back with the water.

"Roman? The water is here."

"Jus' me in here."

"We know. Vikki and Ana are in one bedroom, and the wolfy wolves including Sergei are in another. Everyone is safe, okay? There's no threat." I turned to Troy and extended a hand. He handed me a large, full glass with only a flicker of his cheek muscle. "I'm coming in. Remember what I said?"

"You'll put me down. I'd deserve it."

I looked skyward. I'd never had time for pity parties, and Roman swung heavily toward the morose when he was too far under the influence. Bracing the door with my shoulder, I cracked it, only for it to thump against him. "Move, Roman."

With a grunt, he rolled away from the door enough that I could open it.

I set the glass of water in his reach and shut the door again. "Drink the water."

Gulps so hard they sounded painful came through the door. "Gah. Better. Thanks."

"Can I open this?"

"Yeah."

"No bullshit?"

"Nah."

Troy and the Guardsman moved to get ready, just in case, and I cracked the door again before darting back.

Groaning, Roman dragged himself to his feet and nudged the door wider with a trembling foot, steadying himself against the door jamb. His gaze swept over me, going silver for a moment as he inhaled.

"You're really okay," he said groggily.

"Not quite good as new, but I brought the calvary."

"For me?"

It wasn't hard to harden my voice. "You and Sergei need to stand trial. Y'all and the wolves you brought with Evangeline are censured, and you were part of a direct assault on me and my allies. I can't protect you from that. Nor do I particularly want to. That was beyond fucked up, Roman."

He slumped, looking broken. "I owe you a debt, Arie—Arden. Sorry. I swear that I will pay my debt in life, on my honor as alpha of the Volkov pack and the Blood Moon clan."

That was a surprise, but given he was already sounding steadier than before, I spoke the formal words that would bind him. "So the debt is acknowledged, so is it accepted."

Roman nodded, a lost expression pinching his features. "I also formally submit Blood Moon to Red Dawn. When that's done, I abdicate. I'm done. I never wanted any of this to happen. I just... It was *supposed* to be mine. But maybe it's time to see what the wolves can be if they're led by a woman."

Chills rippled over me as he rambled. Done in that order, Vikki would be the reigning werewolf in the Blue Ridge Mountains, assuming the Farkas pack came around to her partnership with Ana and Sergei could be kept in line.

That would be my werewolf problem resolved in one fell swoop. No more politicking. No more fighting. Just done.

I didn't trust it.

"What's the catch?" I asked.

Roman crossed his arms and shook his head, looking at the floor as the scent of rotted cedar filled the hallway. "No catch. I just can't tell myself I deserve this anymore. Vikki does, or Sergei wouldn't have been so hot for this alliance with Evangeline." He looked up at me, regret and sorrow filling his face. "I'm sorry, Arden. That's not enough. But I wronged you." He looked at Troy. "I wronged you too. I apologize for that."

The words to Troy sounded bitter, choked with what Roman had lost and Troy had gained. But they were spoken, accompanied by commitments that meant something, and Roman had always been too much in his own damn ass for subterfuge.

"Fine," I said softly, if only to end all this. I just wanted it done and behind us.

Troy nodded, though he radiated distrust and didn't shake the hand Roman extended. "She's the gracious one. I need to see those actions done first, Volkov."

"Yeah." Roman dropped his hand, looking pissy and miserable. "Fair enough."

I sighed with relief, even if neither Troy nor I could forgive Roman for his betrayal and the cost it had carried for us. For once, shit was falling into place.

All I could hope was that, with the Wild Hunt two days away, it would be enough.

Chapter 32

I didn't want to take time to crash, but if I didn't do it sooner rather than later, I'd be a liability when it came time to save the damn world. I dropped Zanna at the bar, left orders with Allegra to deliver the wolves to Terrence and Ximena to sort out, told Etain and Haroun to handle shit for the next twelve hours, and overruled Troy when he said some bullshit about taking the couch.

"The fuck are you talking about?" I squared up to him, even if I had to crane my neck back to get in his face, and fisted my hands on my hips.

It was one of the rare occasions I could remember seeing him flustered. "I—you've been through a lot, Arden. I just thought—"

"You guilt-tripping yourself?"

"What?"

"For the reconstruction."

Troy flinched. "I hated doing that to you."

"So you'd rather sleep on a couch that's a foot too small for you instead of sleeping with me?"

"No, but—"

"Seriously?"

His temper finally snapped. "Goddess burn it, Arden, I'm trying to be *sensitive* to what you've *been through*!" He cleared his throat and looked at the floor. "To what I put you through."

"You did what I told you to do, and I don't want sensitive. I want you. Now. In my bed. However you like but with me." I rested a hand on his chest, over his heart. "Please, Troy."

He studied me, the shade of his eyes shifting to shadowed labradorite and the muscle in his cheek twitching. He was in his feels about something, but without the bond, I couldn't tell what feels or which way he was leaning.

"You're infuriatingly stubborn," he muttered, relenting. "But I love you, and I would like to join you tonight."

I smiled. "Good. Come on, shower first. I stink."

"You smell like you." Troy's tone left no doubt that was a good thing, but he made sure our shower was luxurious, turning his frustration into vindictively teasing foreplay that he carried into the bedroom when we were done washing up.

It was weird being with him without the bond, both more and less intense. He seemed to take it as a serious opportunity to remap his understanding of my body, going over every inch of me like he was learning what pleased me for the first time. Maybe he was, since we didn't have a backdoor into each other's heads. I did the same, exploring him, kissing the scars he'd gotten choosing me, discovering new ways to make him feel good. No bond meant no cheat mode, which forced us to really focus on each other. I still came more than once and knocked over a lamp in the process, and he still had trouble controlling his teeth.

"I almost tried the Aetheric bond again," Troy confessed when we'd finished. He kissed the sore spot where he'd almost broken the skin with the sharp teeth. "Just out of reflex. We can't do that again until the soul poisoning is cleared."

"Top of the list for tomorrow." I ached to have the bond back.

It surprised me in a way that maybe it shouldn't have, given how close we'd become, but it was so far from where I'd started with him. I snuggled closer, my back to his front, willing him to embrace me. If the world was ending, I was determined to steal what joy, pleasure, and comfort I could before it did.

His arms snaked around me and held me tight. It was all I wanted, all I needed in that moment. I let my eyelids drift closed and knew nothing more than the scent of rosemary, sage, and midnight woods.

***

I woke, gasping Troy's name, unable to find him in my head.

"Here, my love," he said.

He was stretched out on his side, watching me with his head propped on his hand, the exact way he had been after our first night together, with sleepy eyes and the same sad smile. I suspected this time he'd been thinking about the tie to Neith and the inevitability of the coming fight, but he didn't say anything about it.

The slant of the light coming through the blinds over the bed told me it was early afternoon, and the breeze drifting through the cracked window had a bite to it that said the weather would turn soon. Somehow it felt threatening in a way it hadn't before. Like an ending.

I edged closer to him, reaching out to trace my fingers over the lines of his body simply because he liked it when I did. "How long have you been awake?"

Troy shivered at my touch. "Long enough to know that Alli doesn't have an answer on the soul poisoning and that Roman reconfirmed his commitment to submit Blood Moon to Red Dawn. The weres have Sergei chained in silver and are rushing the handover ceremony to ensure we have clear leadership before the Wild Hunt starts."

"Thank fuck." It was nice to wake up to fewer problems for once. "Anything from Raleigh PD?"

"No. I think you scared them." His lips quirked in one of his more self-deprecating smiles. "You scared me, exposing yourself like that. If they're smart, the mundanes are evaluating what happened and making some kind of plan. One that doesn't involve trying to take you prisoner."

"When are they ever smart?" I flopped onto my back and watched the dust motes, making them dance faster with an idle curl of Air.

My annoyed musings were interrupted by Troy leaning over and kissing me. I pulled him closer and deepened it, wanting more of him before shit hit the fan.

"Mmph." He braced himself against the bed, pulled away, and gave me a stern look. "Arden."

"Fiiine." I let him go. "Let's see about this soul poisoning then marshal the troops." I might not have had any fucking clue what a portal opening to the gods' plane would look like, but I had a feeling it'd be a major disturbance. It'd take all of us—vampires, elves, weres, witches, elementals, and fae—to deal with it. Speaking of the fae... "Has Zanna checked in?"

"Yes. She said she's raising magic. Not sure what it means, but it sounded serious. She gave me strict orders to remind you that the lords and ladies want the gem."

"They can have it when I give it to them." Annoyed with the fae all over again, I gave Troy a last kiss and got out of bed, enjoying the way he watched me make my naked way to the bathroom to wash up before getting dressed.

Breakfast was on the table when I was ready, an omelet with chopped ham and fresh herbs. Troy's compromise for my preference not to eat breakfast with the fact that I really did need the protein if I was going to avoid the return of power hangovers.

"Darius first," I said when we were headed out the door. "Then the fae. We get this shit wrapped up today. Anyone not formally allied with us is declared outside House Solari's protection and mine. I have zero tolerance for any more foot-dragging for any reason at this point." I snagged a few figs from the tree he'd planted and headed for the passenger side of his car, content for once to let him drive like he preferred.

I had him back. We just had to get through the Wild Hunt to see the rest of forever.

"Yes, my queen." Troy sounded happy and satisfied as he slid behind the wheel, which meant he was intentionally letting me hear it in the absence of the bond. He waited for Etain and Haroun to pile into the back seat. Then off we went.

I put on my sunglasses and cap, slouched in my seat, and rested a hand on his thigh, thoughts racing as I munched on figs and we made our way to the outskirts of Chapel Hill. The fae gem made a lump in Troy's left pocket, one that made me uneasy. Fortunately, the Saturday morning traffic was relatively light, and we made good time.

I frowned when he parked in front of a Carrboro storefront in the process of being renovated. "Here? Really?"

"The Lunas set a soundproofing spell. Like the one used when they came for you at Chapel Hill PD. You could brew an entire hurricane in there, and nobody would hear it."

"Huh." I shuddered at the reminder of my kidnapping, tugged my cap lower, and got out. The shop door swung open as Troy and I approached, and I grinned at Iago. "Good to see you again."

"And you, my queen." His soft voice carried more than a little emotion, and his eyes shone. "We feared the worst when we heard about the events at Jordan Lake."

I wasn't much of a hugger, but a few people brought it out in me. Iago stiffened as I embraced him then relaxed when I said, "You've always been a friend. Thank you."

When I let him go, his tan face was flushed, and he avoided everyone's eye. "My queen is too kind. If you'll both follow me?"

Troy, looking amused as hell, fell into step beside him then clapped him on the shoulder and leaned in to murmur, "You'll get used to it."

"If you say so, my king."

I just grinned. At least if the world was ending, I was doing my part to leave it better than I'd found it, as far as I was concerned.

My smile faded into a scowl as we entered what would have been the stockroom, had the shop been active. Darius was bound to a chair, head hanging. The scent of blood filled the space. He looked even more grey and drawn than before, like whatever was consuming him from the inside out had accelerated.

His head snapped up before I could ask for an update. The feverish, disoriented look in his eyes was worse too. "The Eternal Huntress graces us with her presence at last."

I stopped a good ten feet away from him, disturbed by seeing my Captain of the Ebon Guard in the face of an enemy. "You called me that before. Eternal huntress. When you made me forget myself and soul poisoned me." I snarled, unable to help the anger simmering in me. "You tore away my bonded Hunter. What the fuck was that?"

"What I was bid."

When I glanced at the elves who'd been guarding him, they looked frustrated as hell. My guess was that they'd tried interrogating him, only to get nothing.

I took a step closer and crossed my arms. "Talk to me about the soul poisoning."

"Orion wished it done. That's all that matters."

Pursing my lips, I considered my options. Not many, even if we had the time. "Fine. Unfortunately for you, Neith had a different opinion."

As Darius frowned, I lashed out with Chaos in the move that would sever him from Aether, had I still been joined to Troy and one of the djinn.

Darius cried out and flinched.

"That was a warning." I hated the fact that he was Allegra's twin and that, at this point, I honestly didn't think he was doing this willingly. But I trusted Allegra and Troy would have tried, or ordered tried, a proper recovery. It wasn't their fault that a celestial's handiwork was beyond them—nor was it mine. Not when the world was at stake. "Do I need to call my djinn friends?"

"Call them," Darius sneered. "The djinn can't touch me."

That was interesting. He feared me. Or Chaos. But not the elves and not the djinn.

Only the blending of the two.

I took another step closer, throwing up a hand to quiet Troy when I heard him take a breath.

Darius's expression tightened. He was definitely afraid of me.

I tilted my head to study him. I was no Monteague or Luna to read the shape of a mind or an aura. But I alone could sense the gods' handiwork. I let go, slipping out of the senses of my body, opening myself to my third eye and the oscillations of Chaos.

"Oh. Duh." The pulsing energy was obvious when I bothered to look for it, a violent crimson-plum wreathing Darius's head. I squinted, trying to read the shape of it. It hooked into his mind like elven Aether did into mine but more cunning and intricate. Six months ago, even three, I wouldn't have been able to do anything. A month ago I would have been, but I would have doubted myself.

Now? There was too much at stake for that.

"Get back." I meant to say it loud, but it came out as a distracted whisper.

Auratic signatures drew away, all but one.

I drew on Chaos. It spun into me like two crossing air patterns until I forced my memory of a calm oscillation onto it and, if not tamed it, then at least made it manageable.

In the white tunnel my vision had narrowed to, Darius panted, jerking violently, fighting his bonds. Somewhere close but distant, there was shouting. I ignored it, harnessed Chaos, and with a delicate weaving, slipped a chord through the gaps left by whoever had laid this net on him.

With a subsonic boom that knocked everyone and everything in the room to the floor, the net shattered. I let myself lay where I'd fallen as my ears rang and I remembered how to breathe.

In the heavy silence, Darius gasped. "Where am I?"

Troy and Iago were both looking down at me when I blinked my eyes open, as were Duke and Iaret.

Iaret's fire-opal gaze sparked. "Were you *trying* to do the gods' work and unravel the world, or was that just a spectacular bit of incompetence?"

"Fuck off," I muttered. "Unless you know how to unweave a Chaos net."

That set them all aback long enough that I was able to push myself up to a sitting position. Two elves, one with the light coloration of a Sequoyah, one with the darker features of a Luna, leaned over Darius. The scent of burnt marshmallow redoubled in the enclosed space as they chanted under Darius's panting cries.

"I said, *where am I?* Why am I tied up? Who the fuck are you?"

302

I shook my head, trying to clear the last of the tinnitus. "Call Allegra," I said to whoever could hear me. "Let her know Orion's hold on her brother is broken and we have a new situation."

"Yes, my queen." Haroun pulled out his phone and retreated to make the call.

I hauled myself to my feet, letting Troy support me with a hand under my elbow when I wobbled. I'd never tried to manage that much Chaos alone or that delicately. It seemed especially draining without Troy or a djinni to lean on.

Duke was staring at me with a slightly incredulous look.

"What?" I snapped.

"In the millennia I've been walking this earth, I've never experienced magic like that. We felt it in the ethereal realm."

I frowned. "Do you think it reached the Summerlands?"

"We should be so lucky. I'd be more worried about the gods if I were you."

"I can't get any more worried about them than I already am." Exasperated, I moved away from him and crouched near Darius. He'd stopped hollering and looked a little dreamy as the scent of burnt marshmallow faded. "How is he?"

The healers both gave me a fist-to-heart salute.

The Sequoyah said, "Severely malnourished, my queen. Like the compulsion that was set on him pushed him so hard that he could barely stop to tend to himself."

The Luna nodded. "His aura's a mess. Not your fault, my queen," he added hastily when I grimaced. "Whatever you dispelled from him, it had been anchored for a long time. At least a year. Maybe two."

I studied Allegra's twin. "Another sleeper agent," I murmured, thinking of Dominique Bordeaux and hoping Darius was the last one. "Can he bear questioning?"

The two elves exchanged a glance then tilted their heads side to side. I got the feeling these two worked together more often than just today and wondered which Monteague had been their third and where they were.

Turning, I found Troy behind me. "He's your blood. Your call."

Troy's face went grim. "Blood or not, the Veil thins in twenty-four hours. We need to know what he knows."

"What about Omar?"

"I'll deal with Omar and Allegra."

I nodded, glad we were on the same page even if I didn't like the book we were reading from. "As you say. Let's get started."

Chapter 33

With solemn expressions, the healer pair moved away to give Troy and me privacy.

Troy squeezed Darius's shoulder. "Darius. Dari, wake up."

"Troy? Brother?" Darius said. "I'm home?"

"It's me and yes." Troy's bitter smile tugged at my heart and made Darius swallow.

"What'd I do?" His eyes darted to me. "Who's she?"

"My queen and the new High Queen in the territory. You soul poisoned her. I need to know how."

"New High Queen? What happened to Keithia? Wait, soul poisoned? I—no, I wouldn't have done that, I don't even—"

"Easy, Dari. Be easy. Do you remember Callista? Orion?"

Darius had a quiet panic, suggesting that he did and that he was shit-scared of them. This was awful. There would still have to be consequences, even if I forgave the damage done to me…which would set a bad precedent. The next elf would just have his friends addle him before coming for me.

Troy shifted and pulled the gem out of his pocket. "Do you remember this?"

Darius's reaction was visceral and strong. He jerked upright and tried to scramble away, thwarted by Troy. "Where did you get that? Get it away from me!"

This was going to get us nowhere.

"Troy," I said softly. "Give us a minute, 'kay?"

When he'd paced off, out of Darius's line of sight but not out of Troy's hearing range, I said, "Hey. Can I ask you a few questions?"

He studied me. "You're a queen? You don't smell elven. But that's a helluva power signature."

I smiled. "I'm an elemental. A primordial."

Emotions rippled over his face—fear, confusion, and oddly, wonder. "You're her. The one Callista was so afraid of. The one the Ebon Guard was hoping for."

"That's me. She's dead now, at my hand."

Darius shuddered. "Thank the goddess. She did something to me."

"I know. And she or Orion had you do something to me. Something to do with that gem and a sword that severed me from Troy."

"Severed you?"

"Long story, but there's a prophecy involved. Please, Darius, is there anything you can remember about the soul poisoning?"

He studied me with a gaze the same honey-brown shade as Allegra's. "The gem is part of it." Squeezing his eyes shut, he gasped. "That hurts to talk about."

I didn't say anything. I didn't want him to hurt. But I didn't want the world to end either.

Hissing in a breath, Darius continued. "I think I could undo it if you have a djinni you trust. It was a djinni who helped me curse the gem the first time."

"A djinni curse on a fae gem that negates elemental magic." I shook my head. "That sounds like Callista making a backup plan."

He shrugged, looking dejected. "I don't know why I went along with her. I must have caused some pain. I'm sorry."

I gave him as much of a smile as I could muster before hollering for Duke and Iaret.

"Long time no see, Darius." Duke tilted his head. "Looking a little worse for the wear."

Darius frowned. "How do you know me?"

"Grimm."

Panic flashed back into Darius's face at the mention of my and Duke's cousin. "No, no no no. Is she here?"

I caught the man and steadied him. "No. Troy killed her."

Duke's face soured at that, but he held his tongue.

Darius slumped. "Okay. Okay. She's the one who laid the soul poisoning spell on the gem. I fixed it with a trigger."

Iaret hissed. "What? That was one of us?"

Darius swallowed hard in the face of her obvious anger but nodded.

"I thought the signature tasted familiar," Duke said. "And it wouldn't be the first or only time Grimm broke the Détente fucking around with soul magic and stolen artifacts. Fine. Iaret? With Grimm dead, you've had the most recent experience with elf-flavored soul magic."

For a minute, I thought Iaret would refuse to work with an elf. Then her gaze fell on me.

"Very well," she said. "Tell me what you can remember of Grimm's curse. I want to make sure there aren't any twists in it."

We waited, increasingly anxious, for the next forty-five minutes as Iaret questioned him and teased pieces out. I suspect Troy and I were both thinking it'd be faster to use one of the Monteague's interrogation methods, but I wasn't going to ask anyone to do that and Darius was already on the edge as it was. Breaking him wouldn't help anybody.

Troy sent a few elves on a perimeter sweep to make sure my burst of Chaos hadn't triggered any local sensitives into doing something foolish. I just stood there, arms crossed, trying not to count each passing second as a loss, wondering how many different ways Duke's prophecy had meant for me to need the fallen shadow and the risen flame.

"Arden," Iaret called finally. "Little king."

Blowing out a breath, I jogged back over to where they sat. The two healers were hovering, looking like they wanted to stop us and not daring. All of us were being pushed to lines we didn't want to cross but would always wonder if it would've made the difference if we didn't.

The djinni held out her hand. "The gem."

Warily, Troy dropped it into her waiting palm when I nodded.

Iaret half-shifted to her true form, staying just corporeal enough to hold the gem. Her eyes flashed, and fire flickered over her as she whispered in a language I didn't recognize. When she was done, she passed it to Darius. "The same trigger you laid last time but reverse it."

I frowned, unfocusing to try watching with my third eye. I caught the gist of it, if not the defined shape. It looked difficult as hell, and Darius was noticeably more drained when he finished.

"It's done." He swayed and caught himself against the floor.

The Sequoyah twitched. "My queen—"

"I know," I said. "Do what you can while we see if this works."

Iaret held out the gem. "An elf will need to trigger it. Soul poisonings don't usually require both halves of Aether, but I suspect this one wouldn't have worked on you if the curse hadn't blended them in an object."

I glanced at Troy. He nodded and accepted the gem.

"The usual invocation word," Iaret said. "Then place it on…hm."

My heart jumped into my throat. We couldn't afford to fuck this up. "Hm what?"

"Normally I'd say to place it on your third eye. But that's not where the damage is, is it?"

I shook my head. "It's where the bond was severed. It feels like an abscessed dry socket in the aura at the back of my head. Something was torn out and is rotting."

Troy shuddered. "Goddess. I'm sorry, Arden. I'll heal the poisoning, but we don't have to restore the bond."

I shook my head and laid a hand on his cheek. We were well past the events that'd led to us having a bond. "I want it back if you do. I didn't want it to begin with, but we made the best of something shitty and did a lot of good. I'd do it if it meant saving the world alone."

I remembered what it felt like to *know*, without doubt, that I was loved, because the feeling was being fed straight into my mind as Troy thought of me while doing things around the house. Putting away groceries he'd gotten because I'd forgotten to shop for enough protein again. Cooking us a meal. Working with Laurel to grow poison ivy and oak at the edges of my property to discourage trespassers and spies then planting me a fig tree to balance defensiveness with simple pleasure.

Choking back a wave of emotion, I smiled at him. "It's not just about saving the world though. Call me selfish, but it's about claiming something good for myself too. I want you back. All of you."

Tears shimmered in his eyes as well, and he nodded. "I'd be honored to be your something good then."

Clutching the gem in one hand against the base of my skull, he cupped my face with the other and rested his forehead against mine. Took a breath as the scent of burnt marshmallow rose, comforting instead of threatening after all this time. Whispered a word of elvish.

I clutched his arms as blended Aether snaked over me from my skull inward, twining through each auratic point.

"Stay there," I hissed as Troy started to pull back in alarm. "Please."

Trembling took hold of me as a burning sensation roared under my skin. I panted, eyes tight shut, as the spell scorched through one auratic point after another, following the trail it had traced through me to start. I was glad I didn't remember the poisoning being done to me because undoing it hurt like hell.

"I'm here," Troy whispered. "Breathe, my love."

I gasped a breath in. A cool breeze washed over and through me, easing the burning sensation. Or balancing it, maybe. The spell went on long enough that I wondered if it would ever end.

And then it did.

I let myself fall forward against Troy's chest as he embraced me.

"That was freaky as hell," Iaret said. When I turned in Troy's arms, she was studying us with her head tilted. "Your auras blended. Well. His blended into hers. Never seen that before. Didn't even know it was possible."

Duke was giving us an evaluating look. "Side effect of the previous auratic bond?"

"Maybe." Iaret shrugged. "Whatever it is, I suspect it's unique to them. Either way, let's see if it worked."

I gave myself a moment to breathe then extended my hand.

Iaret held my wrist firm then swiped a claw over my palm and licked the blood. "Good as new. Better than, maybe. There's still an echo of the gods, probably from that knife, and there's a hint of your king as well. But it's safe to try an auratic bond now."

My heart thudded. Moment of truth.

Troy's hands slipped from me, and I grabbed one. "Come on. We're going back to where it started."

Magic was weird like that, and so were prophecies. Everything we'd done in trying to undo the damage had echoes of what had originally been done. We were in Carrboro. We might as well go back to the alley where Troy had first put the tracking tag on me.

Troy left instructions with the Guard for what to do with Darius, and we walked over with Etain and Haroun trailing behind. I pulled my cap down low, as much to ward off the light drizzle that'd started as to hide my face.

"How'd you know I was following you that night anyway?" I asked. "You broke pattern when you crossed the tracks past Weaver Street Market."

"I didn't know." Troy laced his fingers in mine. "Or at least not that it was you. Leith had just killed the second of the other members of my mission triad. I figured someone would be coming after me. When it was you, I saw my chance to get close to Leith and complete the mission. I took it." His thumb rubbed against my hand. "That's all there was back then. The mission. I was desperate. Too desperate. We'd lost too many teams to Leith. Omar was pushing hard to shut it down before Leith went for another princess. I was his best student, his protégé, so he sent me."

"When'd you put the tag on me?"

"As you were leaving. You were distracted. Rattled but trying to pretend otherwise. I'd already stung you once to drive you off when you cornered me at the Harris Teeter. Tracking tags are even lighter." He snorted, glancing at me as his face fell. "Or they should be, at least. I keep asking myself what I could have done differently then feeling guilty at how it all worked out."

"Stop." I tugged his hand to drag him to a halt, stepping in front of him when he avoided my eyes. "Hey. You made a series of shitty choices. Then you did what you had to do to pay for them, and in the process, you gave me something nobody else ever did: everything. Including your life. You *died* after I got you away from Keithia, Troy."

311

He shuddered. "Yeah. I saw that when I— Never mind. Let's get this done."

There was an eagerness under the guilt in his voice. I smiled and pulled him into a walk again. At least I wasn't alone in being selfish for wanting to steal some happiness and companionship for myself, and this time, I was sure it was something I wanted— not something I'd been forced to do or fallen into.

Both of us rocked to a halt when we found the alley.

It was less terrifying in the day, but I still shivered at the memory of following an elf into a trap on a moonlit January night. The vines on the trellis at the other end still sported a little green, honeysuckle, maybe. The waste bins were at slightly different angles, and I shifted them as we passed.

This time, when Troy swung me against the gritty brick wall, there was no anger and only a little fear as I prayed we could get this right. And this time when his fist tightened in my hoodie and his other hand cupped the base of my skull, it was followed not by a knife under the chin but by a kiss that stole my breath.

"Let it be done in love this time," he said when he released me. I stared at him until he jerked his head in an indication for me to start walking.

"In love," I repeated, dropping all my shields and letting the feeling fill my heart.

Just like before, I didn't feel the tag settle on my mind. But as Troy caught up to me and took my hand again, an explosion of sensation burst through me. We both went to our knees as my inborn Chaos, immeasurably stronger than it had been in January, twisted the link and raced through it to Troy. He panted as his own newly strengthened power responded. A polar wind scented with midnight woods whipped through me. My auratic pathways itched and burned as the thorns of Aether sunk in them and into my mind.

Etain's voice broke through. "Did it work?"

I shook my head to clear the haze and blinked up at my nervous-looking bodyguard. Haroun was very carefully minding his own business, which was watching the mouth of the alley for concerned mundanes.

Etain looked between us. "You both dropped. Is that good or bad?"

I looked at Troy then looked *for* him. He was there in the back of my head, a knot of love and protectiveness that was stronger than ever.

When he smiled, I laughed and launched myself at him in a hug before kissing him.

I had what I'd wanted, and I poured as much love as I could through to him so he'd know I'd been telling the truth about how I felt.

Now it was time to kick the ass of anyone who thought they were gonna steal happiness or anything else from me.

Chapter 34

It seemed impossible to believe that, after spending the last three seasons trying to get an alliance together, navigating my new role, securing my place in Otherside, and growing into my power, we were done. Or nearly here.

I had my alliance.

I'd rebuilt my father's House and breathed life into my mother's vision.

Otherside was united—at least here in the Triangle—and we had a chance to hold off the Wild Hunt.

We had a chance to steal back our right to shape our world in *our* way, not to take the easy way out and drown it in a Great Flood. A chance to exist openly in a world where mundanes knew us for who and what we were. For all of us to live fuller, better lives.

I'd been born to change the world. Just not in the way everyone had thought. I was done with their boxes and their narrow, fearful perceptions. From here on out, *I* was in charge of my destiny and my power.

When I told Zanna I had the gem, she got a message to her people. Everyone else was exhausted by the events of the last few days, so we reluctantly agreed to take a night to rest and convene a pre-dawn war council the next morning. I insisted that everyone come with ideas, on edge about losing time. I also had

Troy and Iaret join me for a short but heavy practice session, testing the limits of how our magic blended. We all went to bed even more tired, but at least we had some confidence in what we were doing.

With Troy and I fully reunited and in control of House Solari, the weres secure, the djinn feeling important, the elementals safe from rogue elves again, Maria mollified by an apology, the witches temporarily safe, and the mundane police temporarily off my ass, that left one more faction: the fae. I couldn't wait to see if they'd come round.

Our war council started without them, as soon as reps from every other faction were crowded into my kitchen and living room.

We'd nailed down the broad strokes of a plan when a knock came at the sliding glass door at the back. I waved for everyone to keep planning and opened the blinds. A small man stood there, Zanna's height, with skin the rich red-brown of cherry wood and an abundance of black, curly hair. Had to be one of the fae.

I slid the door open.

"Arbiter Solari," he said in respectful tones, with a little bow. "I am sent by the nobles of the fae Chamber of Lords. You may call me—"

"Ewean!" Zanna's excited shout came from behind me. "It is good to see you, old friend."

The new fae grinned mischievously. "It was me or one of the peri."

Zanna grimaced. "A disaster with the djinn here."

"They concurred. The others were afraid to leave the Summerlands." Ewean turned eyes like black moonstones on me, smiling slightly. "It's also in my nature to assist hunters. A gesture of goodwill on the part of the lords and ladies."

I inclined my head. "In that case, be welcome in my home. My table is yours, my hearth is yours, and my roof is yours, while you are here."

I stepped aside from the doorway.

Ewean bowed again and entered. "I honor my hostess. While your home is mine, my strength and that of the aziza is yours."

After exchanging greetings with Troy, Allegra, Noah, Janae, Val, Laurel, Iaret, Duke, Vikki, and a wide-eyed Doc Mike, Ewean laid out the fae's demand for the soul gem in exchange for partnership with the alliance.

That stirred more than a few reactions around the table.

"That's all they want?" Noah sounded utterly disgusted. "A rock? All this stalling over a rock? What, so they can swoop in at the eleventh hour and play hero?"

Ewean's gaze weighed heavy on him. "Not just some rock. The hereditary property of the fae king, stolen from us some generations back by parties unknown and most recently held by Evangeline Monteague to ensure our cooperation. Without it, our leadership is fractured."

Troy nodded. "The other reason for the delay."

"Just so." Ewean glanced at him then back at me. "Though you didn't hear that from me. My lords and ladies don't make an empty demand. In addition to their support tomorrow and going forward as full members of the alliance, they offer a mated pair of gytrash to serve as personal guardians to the Arbiter, now and forever, as a gesture of support and goodwill."

Troy's brows shot up. For him, it was as much a gesture of surprise as someone else yelling, "Holy shit," and jumping out of their chair. "An honorable offer. The black dogs of the fae are not traded lightly."

Ewean nodded solemnly.

I remembered the way my magic had melted around whoever held the gem. "While I appreciate this offer, the gem has certain properties that are concerning to me." I didn't bother to hide the grim note in my voice, and Troy nodded. "Were those always a part of it? Or were they added along with the soul poisoning curse?"

A small smile quirked Ewean's lips. "Always part of it. The elven queens weren't the only ones who feared the power of the original elementals. Our king of old sought a...call it a way to keep the balance. But they anticipated your concern. Hence the offer of the gytrash for protection."

I nodded. I fucking hated the idea of that gem in anyone else's hands. But I'd bullied, cajoled, and killed people to get this alliance to where it was now. We were less than twenty hours from sunset on Samhain, when the Veil would be at its thinnest and the gods could ride through.

Sighing, I shook my head. I hated not having a choice. "What makes this binding?"

"The gem in my hands this morning. The Veil is thin enough now that I can cross to the Summerlands immediately. Or as soon as I'm out of the bounds of your wards." Ewean gave Zanna an appraising look, and she puffed up proudly.

"Give it to him," I said to Troy.

Troy gave me a look long enough to register his protest but not long enough for me to call him on it, pulled the gem out of his pocket, and set it firmly in Ewean's hand. "I'll escort you to the boundary."

Ewean inclined his head. "The Arbiter's own consort. An honor."

From the flickering and suppressed reactions, everyone present had to have caught the hint of mockery in his tone, but Troy ignored it and made a sweeping bow. Whether it was respectful or mocking depended on the tone of the recipient, and Ewean's eyes sparkled as though he admired the artistry.

As the elf and the fae headed out the door, a rumble of thunder sounded. I frowned as everyone looked at me.

"Not me." I headed out back, leapt down the deck stairs and raised my face to the wind.

Something about it was unnatural. When I called a storm, I built it out of what was already present in the atmosphere, however small.

This? This was something ethereal. Leakage from another plane, impacting this one.

My skin crawled, and my discomfort rebounded back to me through the renewed bond with Troy as he realized I wasn't the source of the storm. It wasn't focused here either. It was somewhere over Durham.

"The gods," I whispered.

They—or Orion—had made their play in Raleigh and failed. In thwarting that plan, I'd shown myself to be both their greatest asset and their biggest threat. I ran back indoors.

"Get to the bar. Alert your people. The Wild Hunt is starting."

***

By the time all of us made it to Durham, an unceasing, gritty wind had started. It swirled over the city, the clouds an eerie indigo shade that matched the fae soul gem. The mundane weather stations were baffled. I was annoyed to hell and back because nothing I did could control or ameliorate the weather without significant and draining effort on my part—effort I couldn't afford to spend on a storm.

It was obvious that something was happening now, so we didn't bother hiding anymore—especially not with the epicenter over downtown Durham. The bar became our new planning headquarters. The Ebon Guard set up a command post with typical elven efficiency, and before long, we had computers projecting a different location of the Triangle on the bar's TVs, each showing spikes in paranormal activity. Scouts from every faction were given orders and sent to key points to keep the maps updated. Whiteboards ringed the space. The news blared from the screen of the last TV.

For my part, I stayed behind the bar and out of the way unless someone needed me. Etain had said that's what I was good at: being queen while letting other people do their jobs. My job would come when the gods did. Until then, I could let Vikki, Allegra, Troy, Noah, Iaret, and Janae manage the bulk of the action. Doc Mike had headed back to Raleigh to set up the medical corps at a safe distance from the storm in Durham, and Zanna was doing something with the wards outside.

The valkyrie I'd seen around the bar off and on in the last few months drifted in and studied the makeshift war council. When she wasn't driven out, she left and returned with more of her kind. I sent Troy a little nudge in the bond, and he sent one back acknowledging. Valkyries gathered in groups when they sensed carnage. It was generally considered a bad sign. For a full thirteen to be in the area was really fucking bad.

I approached them and addressed the one I remembered sipping ale over the summer. "Greetings to you and yours. How can I help?"

She inclined her head. "It is we who seek to help, in our way. I am Mist. We would ride with you, Huntress."

I started before I could catch myself. "You know what I am?"

Eyes the same icy blue shade as Leith Sequoyah's flickered like the sun on a frozen lake. "Thou art the Eternal Huntress. Odin whispers to us in our dreams. Calls us to the slaughter. The time is nigh." She raised her hand when I stiffened. "But do not fear. My sisters and I have watched these last months. Odin wishes to fill his halls once more, but thou...thou wisht only for all to have a choice in whose halls they sit. Thou art valorous. We honor thee."

Mouth dry, I inclined my head, extended a hand, and scrambled for something I hoped would satisfy them. "I am honored to ride with you in the Wild Hunt."

With a faintly amused smile, Mist clasped my forearm and inclined her head in turn. I barely bit back a small cry as the grave's chill froze me to the shoulder. In the corner of my eye, Troy whipped around, seeking the threat.

Mist caught the movement. "So it's true," she said as she released me. "The elf king is bound to thee, body and soul."

"He is," I said grimly.

The valkyrie exchanged a saucy look with her sisters. "Then we shall defend him as we do thee. Sister."

I steeled myself as Mist leaned in to brush the faintest kiss on my cheek and barely had the presence of mind to return it as the grave whispered through me.

"Sister," I breathed back, teeth chattering.

With a last mischievous grin, Mist led the valkyries out. Thunder rumbled again as they hit the parking lot, and I blinked as ghostly horses reared and whinnied in a flash of lightning, disappearing when the light did.

Troy had stayed put but was firmly focused on me. I nodded and sent a confirmation through the bond. We had more resources. He nodded back and refocused on the war council.

In the lull that followed, I called all my mundane contacts. Detectives Rice and Chan needed to be clued in. I gave them both the same advice: get people to safety. Get the governor to declare a state of emergency and an evacuation order. Anything to minimize casualties. Chan was confused but still agreeable with the effects of the elves' mindmaze. Rice called me a liar and then cussed me out so long I put the phone down on him. He'd protect his people, or he wouldn't. My job was to take care of mine.

A thundering rumble made every glass in the bar shake.

"Arden?" Troy called.

"Still not me." I closed my eyes and extended my senses as much as I could. "Interplanar crossing. Not gods. Not djinn either."

"What then?" Vikki snapped.

I shook my head. "I can't tell."

Then a rush of half-familiar magic reached me. Magic I'd felt twice before: from the knife Nils the tomtar had made for me and from the wards Zanna had set on my house.

"Fae," I amended. "Strong ones."

"About damn time," Noah muttered.

I suppressed an agreeing smirk and found my serious big girl face by the time a tall, lanky fae strode through the door.

He was pale-skinned and dark-haired, with flashing violet eyes. I had no idea what his species was, but I had a feeling it was one of those that ate people, just from the general malice leaking from him. The gem I'd given Ewean glinted on his brow in a crown that had to be platinum, and two black dogs the size of ponies trailed in after him.

"Arbiter Arden Finch Solari?" the fae said.

I nodded, and his eyes shifted over my shoulder.

"Which makes you Troy Solari."

"I am," Troy said from behind me. He'd snagged one of the snack platters Sarah had put together and a pint of beer on his way over and offered them with a small incline of his head, one royal to another.

The fae king smiled grimly and accepted the beer with a similar nod, taking a sip and eating a slice of roast beef before responding. "You may call me Rí. They are Bás and Marú." He indicated the gytrash flanking him. "We are honored to join your alliance."

"We're honored to have you," I said gravely as Troy offered the gytrash each a slice of meat. A whiff of sulfur came as they swallowed it whole. "Be welcome in our council. As we come in peace with one another, so may we leave."

"I accept your welcome and pledge to come and go in peace." Rí smiled as though that was somehow amusing, and I reminded myself that the fae were even further from human than those of us who lived permanently on this plane. They'd never quite had to adapt to human morals or laws to survive. They'd simply retreated to the Summerlands.

Rí gestured to the gytrash. "Bás and Marú are the promised pair. Their loyalty, once given, can only be broken by your betrayal, so no need to worry about them reporting to me or anyone else. They can shift to man-shape if required but best not to require it too often. It makes them cranky."

With another odd little smile, he joined the others around the four tables we'd pushed together to make one big one.

"Noted." I studied them. "How would you two like to help? Scouts? Guards?"

They tossed their heads and yipped at guards.

"Awesome. You can join Etain and Haroun—elves—in keeping an eye on the bar's perimeter. Frighten humans off. No blood. If there's an Othersider who doesn't smell like the gods, send them in."

They tilted their heads.

"Hang on." I jogged to the bar, where I'd stashed the godblade in its lead box. I really did not want to be anywhere near it, but it was the only way I was going to be able to defend myself against a celestial. Double-edged blade, indeed.

Careful not to touch the damn thing, I popped open the box. The gytrash leaned in and immediately recoiled, whuffing to clear their noses.

"Yeah." I snapped the box shut again as the knife seemed to sing to me of wildness and ruin, louder than ever. "Good?"

They bowed and let themselves out.

"That's going to take some getting used to," Troy murmured.

"If it means you come to bed and actually sleep rather than keeping watch all night, it's worth it."

He glanced at me, trying to look grouchy, but the bond echoed with his pleasure that I cared.

I nodded back to the planning table. "Go on. I'll focus on figuring out where they're likely to come through."

My money was somewhere under the big spiral of dark magic in the sky, but I'd been wrong before. I couldn't afford to get cocky now.

Chapter 35

For better or worse, I'd been right. Of course, it was a few hours later, as the sun was creeping toward the western horizon, when I'd finally given myself a break from staring at the sky and was halfway through a burger.

Magic crawled down my spine. Big magic.

I nearly choked on my bite of food, swallowing it down in a hard lump.

"Arden?" Troy called intently from the table. The room went silent.

I closed my eyes and dug into all the ties I'd made with the land, water, and sky. Reached hard enough with Chaos that somebody muttered about creepy. Shuddered as a heavy presence reached back.

I scrambled from my stool and hustled for the door, opening my third eye as I reached it. With my second sight, I could see red the shade of blood tingeing the violent clouds overhead. Red that had nothing to do with the setting sun and everything to do with an interplanar disturbance.

"Incoming!" I said.

The room exploded into activity. Troy, feeling grim and deadly in the back of my mind, came to stand at my shoulder and peer at the sky. "Looks the same to me. Not that I doubt you, just glad you can tell the difference."

I shivered. "We need to get people out of Durham. Now. How far are we on the plan to hack the emergency alert system?"

"Done in Chapel Hill. Close in Raleigh. Closer in Durham."

"Get it done. We're out of time. I give it less than an hour before something comes through. The gods are sending us a pre-game."

Troy pulled his phone out and called someone, speaking in elvish with military-sharp efficiency then brutal insistence.

Ximena approached on my other side and glared at the sky. "I thought it was supposed to be sundown? We've got a few hours still."

I shook my head. "That's when the Veil is thinnest and all the gods can cross at once, in their full entities. Nobody said other things can't cross in the meantime."

Paling, Ximena turned and snarled something at Terrence in Spanish. He rattled a reply back, and Ximena turned back to me. "We'll start getting locals out. We have community ties with some of the mundanes. Then we follow the plan and hold the invaders here."

I nodded and squeezed her shoulder. "Thank you. Good luck."

She flowed out the door with Terrence on her heels, both of them moving a little too fast and a little too fluidly to pass as human to anyone paying attention. Not that they'd have to worry. Down the road, a few people were standing on the patio of another brewery, hands over their mouth and nose and pointing at the sky as black-and-orange decorations fluttered in the wind.

I shook my head. Humans had no sense of self-preservation. Nothing about this sky looked natural. I'd be getting my ass outta town if it wasn't my job to stop all this.

Gritting my teeth against the scouring feeling of magic, I stepped outside. The air stank of blood and bowels—of death.

Everything about the environment was off in a way that made me completely uneasy. It felt like someone was trying to reclaim my land by bleeding on it, but there was nothing physical to scrub away. Only magic.

My stomach sank as I realized how deep in the shit we were going to be.

As I spun to head back inside, my phone buzzed with the insistent pulse of an emergency alert. I ignored it.

Troy fell in beside me. "It's done. Durham, Wake, and Orange Counties. General evacuation order. Environmental contamination."

I snorted. "That's definitely one way of putting it. Give my praise to the teams who got it done. That's solid work on a short timeframe."

"You just did." Troy tapped the wireless earbud I hadn't noticed.

Nodding, I searched for Iaret, finding her in a tense discussion with Rí.

"All good?" I asked as I approached.

"Simply discussing that lovely bauble," Iaret said, gesturing to the gem in his crown.

"Great. If I can intrude?"

Rí nodded. "I'll marshal the fae. We'll be doing what we can to close any smaller portals between the planes or fight what comes through. The gods aren't the only ones who'll be riding with a tear this size."

"Appreciated. Iaret?"

She followed me back over to the bar. I grabbed Troy on the way. I said, "Now that I see how the magic is working, I have an idea. One that doesn't involve all of us throwing ourselves at the gods on an individual basis."

"Oh?" Iaret's eyes sparked.

I shrugged. "Collapse the portal. Primordial energy cancels out the unreality that creates them. With both of you stabilizing the two halves of Aether, I can wield enough Chaos to close whatever the gods come through, but we have to give the mundanes time to get out. There's always a metaphysical and physical backlash when I collapse a portal."

This time, Iaret's eyes flared. "Idiot. Handling that much Chaos could kill you and warp reality on our side of the Veil. Do you have a death wish? Do you need to die? Do you want all of *us* to die?"

Her question echoed what I'd asked Troy a week and a half ago. I couldn't help my flinch as I avoided his eye, and my heart thundered as I considered the implications. "Absolutely fucking not. But how the hell else are we gonna stop all of them before they overwhelm me with Neith's magic and turn me against y'all?"

Iaret glanced at the box holding the godblade on the counter. Started to say something then shook her head. "Fine. Kill yourself then."

I did look at Troy then as defiance stabbed me through the bond. "I will do my damned best not to."

A rumble that shook the bar stopped him from replying.

I dashed back outside, somewhat relieved to see cars laden with boxes, suitcases, and families heading out of the city, even as my stomach sank to see the red in the sky spread into the visible spectrum.

The rumbles increased in frequency as the sun lowered. I sat in the bar's parking lot, feeling utterly useless but unable to bring myself to go back inside. I didn't know the first thing about planning for war or evacuation. But I could read the environment, and I could scan for portals.

Speaking of…

I shot to my feet as one opened.

A massive snake like a python with a flint-grey head started spilling through. Its coils seemed endless, striped on the back with black that was as dark as the space of the In-Between. It was easily as big around as a city bus, maybe bigger, and several times as long. A building toppled as its front part crashed into it.

"Troy!" I shouted. "Iaret! We've got entities!"

Iaret shimmered into place beside me, not even bothering to hide what she was anymore.

"Apep." Her voice was heavy with fear and loathing.

"What the fuck is an Apep?"

"Not a what. A who." She glanced at me then at Troy when he skidded to a stop beside me and scowled as he finished belting the sword Darius had carried around his waist. "Neith's child, born of her spittle into the primordial waters. It has been some time since I've seen him. We thought he was dead, finally slain by Ra. Apparently not."

My head spun. "Fuck. The Wild Hunt isn't just the gods riding against the earthly plane. It's them and all the fucking apocalyptic entities as well. *That's* why it's wild."

"Seems so."

I gritted my teeth as more of Apep poured through. "Guess that means it's time to kick some ass." I spun back for the bar.

"Now where are you going?" Iaret called.

"Something tells me I'm gonna need Neith's gift to kill her child."

A spike of fear from Troy froze me in my tracks, but when I looked back he just pressed his lips shut.

"I have to." My heart broke at the look on his face—accepting but resigned. We'd already been through so fucking much. *Just one more day.*

Apep crashing through another building sent me running in and back out as soon as I had the blade. The song of its power was worse now, but that's why I had Troy and Iaret.

The two gytrash fell in beside us. Haroun, Etain, and Duke brought up the rear. I debated closing the portal and cutting Apep in half, but that would tip my hand if the gods were watching, exhaust me too early, and destroy parts of the city before more people had a chance to flee. We'd have to do this the hard way.

As we drew nearer to the massive snake, I spotted some humans with AR-15s in a hodge-podge of mismatched army surplus armor running toward it. "Fucking idiots. This isn't a video game."

"Let them play hero," Iaret sneered. "Their deaths will get the rest of the mundanes out faster."

I didn't bother to argue with her. The time for hiding Otherside was gone to hell and come straight back. When we got to the garden of the now-abandoned brewery, I said, "Hold here."

Apep had come through fully, his portal closing behind him. For the moment, he was occupied with swallowing the military LARPers and their guns whole. Bullets were having no effect. Curved white teeth the length of a man made short work of the mundanes.

"Bás, Marú, I need you two to hold a perimeter. Don't let anyone within the bounds of this garden. Etain and Haroun, you stay close and take anything that makes it past them. Duke, you're on portal watch." As they all took their places, I extended my hands to Iaret and Troy. "I need y'all to play battery."

We'd learned last night that I didn't need to be touching them for it to work, only to be wearing my callstone and bonded to Troy. Touch added control though, which I'd need to avoid blasting pieces of the city.

Their hands slipped into mine. Their power flooded me as we all opened to each other. Fire and ice shot through me, the pain exquisite.

When I found the balance, I said, "Iaret, how was Apep supposed to have been defeated in the myths?"

"Beheading. The Great Tom Cat chopped off his head. Apep brought thunder so I wouldn't try lightning, but taking a knife and burning with fire were the last steps in the Book of Overthrowing."

"Fire it is." I wished Val was here, but she'd elected to help the mundanes in her capacity as a first responder.

Closing my eyes, I used my metaphysical senses to guide me as humans screamed and died, sirens wailed, thunder rolled, and the earth shuddered under the coils of the giant snake.

Troy grunted, and they both tightened their grips painfully on my hands as I used them as a power source to fuel and buffer my own magic. With what I was about to do, I couldn't afford to have contact burns.

In a burst of heat that warmed my face, I set Fire loose on that reptilian bastard.

Something exploded. A gas main, maybe. But Apep screamed, an unearthly howl of rage and pain.

"Incoming!" Troy hollered.

I held my ground, glaring at the burning snake crashing toward us. Transferred their hands to my shoulders. Held mine out in front of me and screamed back at the serpent as I threw a stream of pure Fire the diameter of a car at the creature.

Time slowed.

Spittle dripped from its fangs to burn the ground as it reared up to swallow us—and sizzled to noxious steam as my jet of flame went straight down its throat.

Apep dropped like a lead chain and writhed, its whipping body bringing down the brewery, knocking the corner off a parking garage, and hurling cars off the road.

I'm sorry. I'm so sorry.

Those mundanes were dead because of me, but more would have been dead if I hadn't stopped Apep.

Drawing Neith's gift, I dashed toward the snake before Troy could stop me.

I was the Mistress of the Hunt, the Eternal Huntress, and this kill was mine.

I approached from the side. Its eye swirled with primordial darkness, nearly as big as I was tall. It snapped at me weakly. Not many things could survive swallowing a burst of elemental Fire. Its broad scales burned like heated metal under my hands as I used them as ledges and Neith's gift as a climbing pick. It nearly threw me off as I reached the top of its head, but I dropped and squeezed my thighs like I was riding a horse. I cut a scale free and plunged the godblade into its spinal column, opening a wound into which I poured more Fire.

This time it did throw me free. I landed hard in the dirt as it writhed, snapped, and finally died, its head separating from its body in a stream of black sludge.

I groaned. Troy knelt over me and wiped ichor and acid from me with the cloth he kept to clean his blade then threw it from him as it disintegrated. He and Iaret rested hands on my chest, forcing back the rising tide of red from the blade until I could sheathe it.

I felt like shit, and this was just the opening salvo.

As the sun set, Othersiders fought demons and demi-gods in the streets.

A bunch of Terrence's wereleopards were ex-military, and they held up a hell of a lot better than the mundanes had. Ximena's werejaguars protected the witches serving as medics, patching up humans and Othersiders alike and getting them out of the streets. Vikki, the Red Dawn werewolves, and the Blood Moon Den Sentinels called in from Asheville ran wild with a rainbow of fae, gleeful and painted in blood as they repelled invaders and shut portals. With communications clogged by emergency calls, Duke was our messenger coordinating between Durham, Raleigh, and Chapel Hill. Maria's people and the Ebon Guard were getting mundanes out in case we couldn't stop the gods. The valkyrie rode in a wide perimeter as my honor guard, accompanied by Troy, Iaret, Etain, Haroun, and the gytrash.

For once, everyone was working together.

We had to knock out a few humans who couldn't tell which of us were on their side, but a few got the hint that the assholes dropping out of portals were not here for a drink. They watched us, wide-eyed, as we all caught our breaths between battles but had the sense not to fight us.

Finally, we reached the beginning of the liminal hour.

"Almost time," I whispered.

Magic was rising again, stronger than when Apep had come through.

The gods, and the Wild Hunt, were here.

Chapter 36

The plan had been to get me to the gods' portal and collapse it before they could come through. We made it to the epicenter of the storm downtown. Unfortunately, we didn't manage to close the burgeoning portal when we arrived, thanks to fucking Orion.

"Going somewhere?"

Troy and I whirled. Iaret hovered as a swirling cloud of smoke and flame.

We faced a giant of a man bearing a short sword on one hip, a quiver on the other, and a bow racked on his back atop a surprisingly modern-looking cargo pants and T-shirt ensemble. Curly, brown hair fell over a face that could have been carved from ivory, and angry brown eyes seemed to try skewering us where we stood. Behind him, a scorpion the size of an eighteen-wheeler minced forward on dagger-sharp feet, its barbed tail curled menacingly over its body.

I shuddered. That would give me nightmares for the rest of my life.

"You motherfucker," I spat as I looked again at the quiver and recognized the fletchings of the arrows. "You're the one who shot me at Jordan Lake."

Orion smirked. "I needed to give Darius room to work. Not sure how you reversed the soul poisoning, but fuck you all."

I sneered back at him. "You're a demi-god, and you need all those weapons?"

"Not a demi-god. Never was." Power rose. A familiar power, one that felt like mine and was almost as strong as mine. More than enough to kill Troy and bind Iaret.

Orion was a primordial elemental.

"Get clear!" I drew on my own magic.

Iaret spun away in a buzzing cloud and, to my relief, Troy obeyed too. He might argue with me when we were safe, but in battle, I was the boss bitch.

The ground under me heaved, but I used my newer affinity with Earth to keep my footing. "You were an oread?"

"That's why they trapped me next to Taurus." He glanced at the statue of Major the Bull then lifted the bricks of the square and sent them and a stream of superheated earth—nearly lava—at me.

I shifted an abandoned car with Air to block it. Molten chunks splattered over a restaurant's windows, etching the glass as they dripped down.

"Why are you doing this, Orion?" I threw a lightning bolt that he deflected with a manhole cover, sending the last remaining traffic light haywire. "We want the same fucking thing. We could be allies! Why fight me?"

"I don't need allies. I can't trust allies. I can't trust anyone. Artemis taught me that." He made the earth under my feet buckle. "You'll be my tool, as Darius was, or you'll die and I'll risk using Neith's gift to kill Artemis myself."

We warred in the streets of Durham. The asphalt cracked and exploded. Water mains burst, sending showers of water skyward as we sought to blast each other. Lightning fell in the streets around us as that fucking scorpion circled, clinging to the sides of crumbling buildings.

As Orion and I faced each other, evaluating, I caught a shadow stalking it from the corner of my eye.

Troy.

He'd obeyed me and gotten away, but he wouldn't leave an enemy at my back. The distant feeling of an icy forest grew as he drew nearer to his prey.

I couldn't help my smile then or my fierce pride. I'd started this year utterly alone. Isolated. Used. Hunted. Fearful. The world might be ending now, but I had people who would fight to the death alongside me to save it—and me, if it came to it.

That thought made me reckless.

I pushed forward, mind racing as I threw elemental attacks at Orion. He'd been an oread. Had mentioned being trapped next to Taurus. Opposite Taurus on the wheel of the sky was...Scorpio?

Aha—the scorpion Troy was stalking.

Earth and Water were complimentary for Orion. Fire and Air were not. He'd already used Fire to some extent in throwing the lava at me. So just as my weak element was Water, his was Air.

This fucker was shit outta luck.

I let go of all the other elements and pulled deeply on the one I'd been born to. A tempest built with me at its eye, stripping signage off the storefronts and bending trees.

Orion threw up a wall of earth and shattered asphalt.

I blew through it like the goddamn hurricane I was, sending him staggering back against the Bull statue. The iconic Durham mascot was made of bronze, and Orion's magic faltered as I threw him against it then readied a fortified chord of Air that would bind him to it.

He abandoned the elements and drew his sword.

Off to the side, almost in front of the coworking space that'd once hosted the office of my private investigation firm, a new portal opened. The biggest one yet, mimicking the hole in the sky, stretching further through space and time than any of the others that had opened today.

The gods.

They weren't here yet, but they were coming. Imminently.

In my distraction, the ground under my feet erupted and tried to swallow them. I stumbled and lost the chord as I countered it, even as in the back of my mind, Troy struck and lopped the stinger from the scorpion before melting away from its attention.

I shoved another burst of Air at Orion to send him staggering, but he slid in between me and the portal, raising his sword and slashing to disrupt me as I started to blend the elements into a ball of primordial power.

"Dammit, Orion, let me close that portal!"

"Oh no. I want them to come through. I want that bitch Artemis to see that she might be an epic shot but her arrow didn't kill me. She left me for dead on a cursed beach. Now I'll make sure she is."

"The people of this plane will die! Don't let your vengeance become their destruction. They didn't do shit to deserve this." When he stood unmoved, I added, "Come on. Once upon a time, you were their Master of the Hunt. You had the same choice I do now: to let these mundanes keep living their lives or to ride with them and end the world." I swallowed hard at the gamble I was about to take. "What did you choose?"

For a second, Orion hesitated. Then his features hardened in wrath. "I didn't get to choose. Artemis was my patroness. She chose me. She loved me. And then she shot me as I swam in the ocean and thought throwing my dying body into the stars would be enough to make up for her *accident.*"

"That was so long ago people think you're a damn myth!"

Power rose in the portal, and I edged closer again, only to have Orion draw his bow and nock an arrow. Its tip glinted brightly in the fires fueled by the trees dying from our battle: bronze. That was why my thigh had taken longer than usual to heal.

"I don't care." His eyes glinted as the arrow stayed steady on my chest. "I've waited millennia and more for this. You and your coalition won't take it from me."

Neither of us looked away from each other as Troy borrowed a little power from me and killed the scorpion. I tried to hide the anguish that the feeling of acid blood spraying along his right hand and arm sent echoing along my own, but Orion must have sensed it because he let his arrow fly.

Stripping Air out of the primordial ball, I threw up a wall in time to trap it. Then, in the same heartbeat, I whipped the arrow around and sent it back at him.

Shock registered in his eyes as it sank into his chest, even as the same shock bloomed in my own. I hadn't quite expected that to work. All the same, I released the elements and darted forward, drawing Neith's gift despite the risk.

I crashed into Orion. Rode him to the ground. Pressed a hand into his throat to pin him down.

"Kill me," he said when I hesitated. "Because I swear by the Goddess, I will kill you if you don't."

That was a promise I couldn't risk being false. I brought the knife down and drowned it in Orion's heartsblood so smoothly I don't think either of us had realized it'd happened until he was dying and his blood coated my hands.

Even as it did, power roared into me, and red filmed my vision.

I was losing myself to the gods. Again, and this time I was alone. I fought it and failed.

Blinking, I shook my head to clear it. The scene in front of me was unearthly. Trees and buildings burned. The air was black with smoke. Broken glass glittered, reflecting flames burning in the same unreal colors I remembered from the lich's lair: purples, greens, crimson. It smelled like someone had poured gasoline on a hog roast. Fire alarms blended with human cries, screeching in warning and pain. Grit bit at me in a hot wind, and I directed it away from my eyes with a small mental shift.

Power crawled over my skin. Nothing earthly. Not the fae. Not the djinn. Not even a demon or even anything like Apep.

The gods had come, and it wasn't a Rapture.

It was a Hunt. Slaughter.

They'd come together, from different times and places, to claim their due.

Orion's blood and the gods' arrival called my primordial power to staggering new heights. I bowed my head, power drunk, gritting my teeth and wrestling the elements, trying to remember why I was fighting to save any of this as whispers of doubt burrowed through my brain on the red tendrils of godly power.

Otherside had continually used and betrayed me. The humans had learned what we were and rejected us. Not all of them but enough that Otherside stood alone against the Wild Hunt.

That *I* stood alone. But the gods would be my vengeance. I could take my due, finally have what I was owed.

"Arden." Troy's voice.

Not quite alone, maybe. But close enough.

"Arden, come back."

I rose from the body sprawled under me and looked at Troy. Iaret hovered beside him, uncertainty sparking in her opalescent gaze. My Hunter staggered under the force of my regard, turning it into a smooth motion to kneel.

"Please. You're not alone." His voice was raspy with smoke and exhaustion. He favored his right arm. When I sniffed, it smelled like a chemical burn.

A shattered building lost a piece of itself with a sharp crack as concrete and rebar failed under the heat. It might have withstood a normal fire, but elemental fire? Nah. Humans lay like broken dolls where they'd fallen and died, too slow to escape the fight.

I glanced at the southern horizon. That was important. Why?

Oh. Allies were supposed to hold a rear guard of vampire warriors and werebeasts defending the ground route to Raleigh, behind which the witches tended the wounded. The fae were meant to be closing as many portals as they could to the west to prevent the spread to Chapel Hill.

I snarled. They were thwarting the gods' will. They'd be punished. Soon.

You're not alone.

I pressed my hands to my head. The hilt of the godblade rubbed against my forehead. I needed it. But I also wanted nothing to do with it or its song of blood and glory.

"Arden—"

"Get up." I didn't recognize my own voice.

Troy rose with a slowness that I'd think was injury if I didn't sense the pure fear in the bond. He swallowed hard enough that a rock might have gone down his gullet.

"Why should I save any of this? Any of them?" I whispered, echoing the knife's whispers, still crawling through my brain, and throwing my hand out to indicate the apocalyptic destruction around us.

"Because that's the greater good," he said. "That's why we're here to begin with." Naked fear blended, somehow, with a love and compassion so deep that I shuddered down to my soul.

The whispers grew louder, and the red filming my vision deepened, giving me an order.

I threaded my fingers through his hair and wrenched his head back, pressing the godblade to his throat. His chest heaved, but his limbs went slack in acceptance even as the knot of emotion in the back of my head went deathly still.

Iaret buzzed around us. "Arden, no!"

I hesitated but not because of her. "You'd let me kill you to make a point?"

"If it had a chance of bringing you back to yourself? Yes. I promised you anything and everything. I love you."

Back to myself. He loves me.

My hands sprung away of their own accord, and I was three steps back, hunched in on myself and shaking, before I realized what was going on.

What the hell was I doing?

Suddenly I saw it—the twining root of the gods' influence in my mind. Pushing. Amplifying. Undermining. Working to dislodge the thorns of Aether Troy had implanted to bring my memories back. It wasn't me thinking those things.

I *knew* Troy had sided with me for the right reasons. He'd chosen me. I'd chosen him.

Iaret had seen something worthy in that and chose to set aside her long, justified enmity with the elves to fight with both of us. The alliance had set aside thousands of years of precedent to come together and fight with me.

The gods didn't want that. It took me out of their control.

Panting, I closed my eyes. Drew on Chaos. Fought it. Dug at it.

The roots dug deeper.

"No," I snarled, following them down into the depths of my psyche.

My knees hurt as I fell to them. I wouldn't do this.

I loved my home. I loved my people, and most of all, I loved Troy. I clung to that, fighting doubt with love.

"Use me," he said, close enough to my ear that I could distinguish the heat of his breath from the apocalyptic winds still whipping around us.

"Use *us*." Iaret became corporeal enough to touch both Troy and me.

I did.

Iaret hissed, and Troy grunted in pain as I pulled on their strength as well as mine. The Monteagues knew minds better than anyone, could manipulate them so subtly that the target would never know the difference. I had that talent at my disposal—even if Troy now claimed my House as his own.

A sharp pain blossomed as I used Troy's instinctive understanding of minds in general and his familiarity with mine in particular to grab the deepening root of the gods' influence. Pull. And rip it free.

When I managed to stop screaming, Troy was looking down at me.

Tears made gleaming trails down soot-darkened cheeks, his hand tight around mine. I took a shuddering breath, pulled myself together, and forced myself to stand. This wasn't the time to give in to pain.

"You'll pay for that, princeling."

We both stiffened as Mixcoatl stepped through the portal that had finally matured.

"That wasn't your given purpose," the god said. Galaxies spun faster than ever in his eyes, and the red lines striping him held the dark sheen of fresh blood.

I eyed his lightning bow warily, remembering the bite of its arrows, and pushed in front of Troy and Iaret to stand between them and Mixcoatl. "If you hurt them, if you *touch* them, I'll find a way to destroy the Veil," I rasped. "I fucking swear it. You will *never* see this plane or gain tribute from it again."

The god tilted his head. Pursed his lips. "You might," he said. "You just might. You love him enough and are happy to include the djinni in the deal."

I jutted my chin at the corpse beside us. "Orion sought Artemis's death. Take his life for theirs."

"Fine," the god said after a lengthy pause. "You may have your Hunter and your friend, untouched. But you will ride with us. This city is taken. It is time."

Chapter 37

The words echoed through my head.

This was wrong. This wasn't my will. This wasn't what I'd fought and sacrificed for. I'd be damned if I became a puppet for anyone again after living as Callista's. I dug deep, looking for the root of the gods' power in me. The knife was part of it. I couldn't let that go just yet. I needed to clear the gods from this plane first and close it to them.

Better still, I could stop them all coming through to begin with. I could siphon energy from Troy at a distance. Iaret could connect to him via the callstone and use him as a channel.

I tugged the stone from around my neck and put it in his hands then pushed a focused thought at him, willing him to understand. I knew Iaret could hear. *Get everyone to safety. Then put this on so Iaret can feed me magic through you. Go.*

He tensed and inhaled sharply. *Arden?*

I need you to go. Get everyone clear. I'm collapsing the portal.

Mixcoatl narrowed his eyes as Troy reluctantly backed away, slipped the callstone around his neck, and ran. Eyes wide, Iaret vanished.

"Where are your friends going?" Mixcoatl said. "Neith said you were to have Riders."

I smiled, as though I was looking forward to what was coming. In a way, I was. "I sent them for the valkyrie. They're my Riders."

"Good. This pleases us."

I bowed my head, trying to figure out how to stall them long enough for Troy to get clear as Odin's ravens flew through in a burst of blue-black feathers, followed by Odin himself on the back of a massive eight-legged horse. Pressure built with each new god, giving me a headache. A chariot pulled by four huge silver stags rolled through with Artemis at the reins. Her blood-moon eyes landed on Orion, and her anticipatory smile twisted.

"What have you done?" she hissed. Fury lit her eyes, and her face contorted in rage and grief.

I gripped Neith's gift and edged closer. "Orion wanted you dead, my lady."

I kept my head bowed but watched the portal from the corner of my eye. *Come on Troy, hurry!*

"You lie!"

"I'm sorry, my lady. With respect, he said something about you leaving him for dead. He shot at me with bronze." Remembering the story I'd spun on their plane, I added, "It was he who wished to thwart your Hunt."

Odin cleared his throat, sounding like rocks clattering down a fjord. "Leave it, Artemis. You fucked up with the boy, and we had to wait another six thousand years for this one. Don't kill her before she has a chance to serve."

With a murderous glare at both of us, Artemis jumped down from her chariot and knelt beside Orion.

As she did, Neith rode through on a midnight black horse with a mane and tail of smoky flame and smiled at what she saw. "You got started without us. I trust my gift helped?"

I thought of stabbing it into Apep's skull and swallowed. "It did. Thank you, my lady."

"Good." She frowned. "You have no mount. You cannot ride a hunt without a mount. We must summon one for you."

"Wait. Please." I had to gain a little more time. "What is it exactly I'm supposed to do on the Hunt?"

Neith tilted her head. "You are a primordial elemental. We know our presence on this plane has increased your power, even as it has unleashed more creatures from other planes." She waved a hand at the city. "We hunt the creatures that have come through ahead of us. Then we level the city. You return it to a pristine state, wiped clean of these ugly structures. A fresh start for all."

"Oh." It was the only word I could summon.

Fortunately, a burst of power came to me through the open bond. Troy had gotten clear. As I locked my knees to stop myself from swaying, more flooded into me as Iaret connected to us both via the callstone.

Artemis frowned at me suspiciously. "Something just happened."

I shoved aside my fear and smiled. "Yeah. It did."

The gods hadn't been fully corporeal on this plane in tens of thousands of years. It made them more powerful—but as with anything given a physical form, it also made them vulnerable to elemental magic.

As more forms shimmered at the threshold of the portal, I let power flood through me.

"What is she doing?" Artemis snapped.

Neith slapped me. "We didn't order you to take hold of your power yet. Wait for the rest of us."

"No." I snarled and summoned lightning, striking Odin's ravens from the sky.

They screeched and tumbled, ebony feathers bursting into flame, as Odin roared in fury and drew his sword.

I held up my completely inadequate godblade in a guard and called a whirlwind, setting it swirling around the square as a barrier. "The Wild Hunt starts, and ends, now. *You* are the prey this time."

Eyes widening, Neith swung her *was* staff at me.

I blocked it with a wall of Air then overloaded the thread of Fire in the lightning arrow Mixcoatl shot next. It burst, sending errant firebolts shooting everywhere and making the gods howl.

Another flicker at the portal showed Ogun preparing to ride through. I was out of time.

Praying that I wouldn't burn Troy and Iaret out, I drew even deeper on the bond with them and used Air to corral the gods. They had magic weapons and frightening powers, but they couldn't use the weapons if they couldn't get to me, and my magic beat everything else on this plane.

That was why Callista had been so damn afraid of me, why she'd been so desperate to control me.

"Enough!" Neith's shout was the howl of a sandstorm.

I ignored it.

She narrowed her eyes at me then clenched a fist.

The godblade grew warm in my hand as red started filming my vision. Grunting, I dropped to my knees. My whirlwind faltered.

Pressure in the back of my mind resolved into a garbled mental whisper from Iaret, passed through Troy. *Arden. Like this.*

She yanked my attention to the godblade.

I nearly lost myself as the shift in focus allowed Neith's power to seep deeper, but then I saw it: how the djinn used objects to harness magic...and how the harness worked both ways.

Scrambling, I wrenched the control of the power flooding through the knife from Neith to me. My eyes snapped open at her cry of surprise. Light shone from me, even as shadows wreathed me from sight, the evidence of both my heritages.

With a roar of determination, I contained all the gods. Forced them, their mounts, their chariots and weapons, backward through the portal. Held them back with a wall of Air.

Another portal started opening alongside the first.

"No. Not. To-fucking-day." I coaxed Fire to join Air, embraced Earth, and then surrendered to Water. The light and shadow pouring from me flared as a blindingly bright ball of primordial power grew between my hands. I poured more into it. More. Then more still, until power burned along my skin to make it smell like burning.

Too much. I was drawing too much. But I had to be sure.

As darkness crept into the edge of my vision, I dropped the wall of Air and sent my primordial ball through the portal.

For a moment, nothing happened.

I dropped to my knees, disbelieving.

Then everything happened at once. A blast of power threw me across the square. My bones cracked, and pain roared through me as I hit the side of a building and dropped to the ground. Reality warped like it had after the first time I'd fought Neith, only on a grander scale: the twisted Bull statue and broken cars floated and spun, trees grew at right angles, the purple-and-red sky inverted to orange and green. The water spurting from a busted main raced in a horizontal stream above the streets. A subsonic boom rumbled through the ground and sent glass spinning through the air to hover in a crystalline sparkle.

The portal collapsed, and the pressure of the gods disappeared.

My power died, snuffed out from drawing from beyond what I could wield on my own, having borrowed from Troy and Iaret and stolen from the gods—and took my aura with it.

I'd always thought I couldn't burn myself out. I'd been wrong. Partly. It wasn't that my power could burn out. It was that my aura could, leaving me with nothing to protect and anchor my soul in my body.

It took me a minute to realize that I was on the edge of dying from power overdraw. Not gone yet. But my aura was gone. There was nothing to hold my soul.

I started drifting.

Fuck. Fuck no! I wanted everything I'd fought and now just about given my life for. Not an endless nothingness as a constellation or as a spirit wandering the Crossroads.

A life. Full of contentment, and friends, and love.

Uneven footsteps staggered over the broken ground. "Arden!"

Troy. I wasn't dead yet, or he'd have been knocked unconscious, the way elves were when severed from whoever held their bonds or their oaths.

"She was thrown over here somewhere. The last thing she was looking at was—there! Arden!"

Dirt and glass crunched to my side just as my body decided we weren't gonna keep living without a soul.

No! I scrabbled for the thin, fraying thread still anchoring me to my body. I was *not* going out like this.

I felt a strange ripple as Troy tried CPR. Didn't work beyond convincing blood to move through my veins a little, although the spark gave Sarah something to coax with her witch magic and gave a Sequoyah a chance to mend my broken body.

Troy could read auras well enough to see that mine was gone. That didn't stop his increasingly frantic efforts.

I wavered half on my plane and half in the Crossroads, desperately trying to stay anchored, watching as Troy fought to save my body.

Iaret and Duke hovered. The gytrash trotted up and howled, a sound that would have wrenched my soul if it'd still been in my body. Jaguars, leopards, and wolves joined them, screaming their rage and pain to the broken city.

Eshu-Elegba appeared at my shoulder. "So many would mourn your passing."

I glanced at the orisha of the Crossroads from the corner of my eye, the only way I could ever see him clearly.

"Seems so." I couldn't keep the bitterness out of my voice. They'd fought me, argued, tried to maneuver and claim favor. But they did care for me. I'd built my own little family in the end.

"Seems a shame."

"Yeah. It does." I was frustrated then, for all I'd done. All I'd sacrificed had come to this? No. Fuck no. I clenched my immaterial fists, scowling, and watched my friends try to revive me. A combination of the physical and the magical made my spirit stutter again.

"Come on," I whispered.

Troy tried something then, I couldn't tell what given I wasn't in my body. But the thin thread keeping me here strengthened, and he whooped. "That worked!"

Hope flickered in my soul.

Duke swirled closer. "What did you just do?"

"She can share my aura, remember? I pushed some of it into her auratic points."

"Holy shit." I flashed back to when Troy had cleared the soul poisoning. Something in the magic had curled into each of my points. Was it still there? Could he rekindle it? Kneeling beside him, I said, "Come on, Troy. Come on. I love you. You can do this. Bring me back. I want our chance at forever."

Elegba sighed. "Seeing as your elf has found a shortcut, let's skip to the interesting part, shall we?"

His palm slammed between my ghostly shoulder blades.

With a disorienting snap, I found my spirit back in my body. The next round of CPR brought me back with a gasp so hard it hurt as Elegba's voice echoed in my ringing ears: "Don't assume we're finished with you simply because the gods of the hunt had their turn."

I couldn't answer. I was too busy choking on air as my body remembered living.

"Arden!"

My gaze met Troy's. The relief—the love—in his eyes made me smile.

"Troy. Hey." The hand I tried to raise just flopped. I was back, but I was weak and tired as fuck.

He gathered me to him, pulling my whole body into his lap to envelop me. "Don't you ever fucking do that again. Do you hear me? Never again!"

Hot, silent tears dampened his shirt where my face pressed into it.

I'd come so close to giving everything.

But unlike I'd thought when I was under the gods' influence, I wasn't alone. I had people who cared about me. Allies to fight alongside me. A community. A man who loved me the way I demanded I be loved.

All mine.

The square echoed with the sounds of their celebration, jarring against the signs that we'd barely managed to avert the end of the world.

Durham was trashed, but we could rebuild.

When we did, I'd be damn sure that room was made for *all* of us. Otherside was out of hiding, and we were never going back to the shadows again.

Epilogue

Three months later

"Hey. Sparky."

Troy's new nickname for me pulled me out of the report I'd been reviewing. I would have been annoyed, but he only used it between us and rarely. That, and he said it was equal parts the whole fire and lightning thing and the fact that our magic still sparked when we came back together after some time apart. I'd warmed to it. In a way, it brought us even closer as I let down another wall keeping people from being too familiar with me.

I dragged myself out of my thoughts. "Sorry, what?"

"I brought wood in. You going to light the fire? I'll mull some wine. We can take a break. Talk about what to do for your first-ever birthday party."

I started to decline. The emergency bill to grant Othersiders full and equal rights in the state of North Carolina was coming up on a hard-fought conclusion. For all we'd done to save the damn world, the victory was still uncertain. The mundanes were split on the issue of the damage to Durham, despite the fact that I'd undone all the reality warping that'd occurred when I trapped the gods of the hunt on their plane and promised I wouldn't do it again as long as everyone left me alone. I thought Otherside would win in the end, but I'd been pulling long days and longer nights politicking the hell out of it with Maria.

Which was exactly why Troy was prompting me to take a break. I'd grown too powerful not to, and overwork or exhaustion made my temper shorter and my control sloppier. Channeling an elf, a djinni, and the gods' power on top of my own seemed to have stretched my magic well beyond any limit Troy and Iago had been able to uncover in their research, which was great as a deterrent for anyone looking to fuck with the territory but had also resulted in a few training accidents.

I grimaced then scrubbed a hand over my face to clear the expression before shutting my laptop. "Sounds perfect."

Relief washed through the bond, and Troy kissed my forehead as we passed each other, him headed for the kitchen and me for the fireplace. The January cold snap meant my insistence on keeping the windows cracked for air flow was chilling the house to about Troy's tolerance level.

He was getting better at speaking up. I was getting better at adjusting away from my solitary patterns. We met in the middle and were both healthier and happier for it.

I gently coaxed the wood in the fireplace to a cheerful burn, trusting that Troy had cleared the flue, then threw myself on the couch and tilted my head back. He could have lit it himself. I could have lit it from the table. But the point was this—me getting up and away from my work. Resting my eyes. Taking a well-earned break as I allowed myself to marvel yet again at how much my life had changed in a year.

Last January, an elf had walked into the office of a weak sylph and dragged her into a conspiracy.

I wasn't that fearful young woman anymore. I was the powerful High Queen and Arbiter of an expanding territory, known to Othersiders and mundanes alike. More Othersiders were pouring into the area, seeing it as a safe haven as mundanes protested and rioted worldwide.

Mindboggling. But satisfying in a way the old Arden had never dared to dream was possible. The new Arden might have given up immortality as the Eternal Huntress but maybe not. I was healing faster than I used to and matched Troy in physical strength now despite my much smaller frame. I was pretty sure my senses matched his as well. I hadn't tried going back to the Crossroads—even the thought of it made me nauseous—but I suspected I'd find it easier to travel the Veil than I had.

I'd finally grown into my potential, everything Callista had tried to steal from me. I'd fought off everyone who wanted to use me. Now, I'd focus on using my gifts and the resources I'd claimed to be a force for what *I* wanted the world to be. Somewhere better, where we could all thrive.

The scent of warm wine and spices swirled through the house.

I forced my brain to quiet, focusing on the small noises of Troy making a snack to go along with the wine, a cheese and charcuterie plate from the smell of it.

As I relaxed, he grew content. It swirled through to me in the bond, creating a pleasant feedback loop that I allowed to keep running. The man might be an ex-Darkwatch assassin commando, king of my House, and my personal bodyguard, but he got real pleasure out of shit like personally taking care of me.

No formality in my House or my home. Just love. Just as I liked it.

Speaking of love…

"How's things with Allegra and Maria?" I asked. "Maria looks like the cat who got the cream every time I see her. Well-fed and smug as fuck."

Troy snorted a laugh. "Alli is still pretending she isn't head over heels. I don't know what possessed you to make her the general ambassador for the alliance and special envoy of House Solari to the Mistress of Raleigh, but it was inspired. Not to mention probably the only thing that would have made Maria forgive you that perceived overstep. Everybody gets to feel important."

I grinned, feeling a bit like that cat myself.

Playing matchmaker was not exactly what I'd intended. But Allegra had needed more responsibility than Captain of the Ebon Guard and something to distract her from Darius's self-imposed, guilt-ridden exile. I'd promoted Allegra to princess and put Etain in charge of the Guard in her place, another knife-sharp point to the rest of Otherside that we did things differently in the Triangle.

Everyone who'd earned it was, for the time being, better off—and those who'd earned a punishment had been dealt with fairly. Now we just needed the mundanes to come around.

I opened my eyes when I sensed Troy coming.

The meats and cheeses were artfully arranged on the platter he set down, and he handed me a steaming mug with a warm smile. I smiled back, loving him and our life together. Content. My earlier frustration with the reports and the mundane lawmakers had melted away.

"Thanks," I said.

"Always a pleasure, my love."

I took a sip, appreciating the warmth of the spices layering over the rich sting of the wine. I didn't know how Troy managed to make mulled wine with all of the spice yet losing none of the alcohol, nor did I know why he risked it when he knew I was a maenad, but this was perfect. I tilted my head back and savored it, rolling the liquid over my tongue despite the near-burn before swallowing it.

"Good?" he asked after settling on the couch next to me and sipping his own drink.

"Better than good." I rested my head on his shoulder.

Taking a moment to just be in a way I hadn't been able to for most of my life.

We watched the fire together and dreamed of the future we'd fought so hard to claim. One that was now entirely in our grasp.

Want more?

This might be the end of the series, but that doesn't mean you have to suffer a book hangover just yet.

You can get more Shadows of Otherside content in a few different ways:

- Get a red-hot, free bonus epilogue with more Arden and Troy: whwrites.com/soo-spice
- Go back to the beginning and read a key scene in *Elemental* from Troy's point of view (for free!): whwrites.com/soo-difficult-decisions
- Join Whitney on social media:
  - Twitter: twitter.com/write_wherever
  - Instagram: instagram.com/write_wherever
  - Facebook: facebook.com/WhitneyHillWrites
- Subscribe to Whitney's Patreon for bonus chapters from multiple points of view: whwrites.com/patreon

Also, stay tuned for a new paranormal romance/urban fantasy spin-off series set in the world of Otherside with two new protagonists (and a few cameos from familiar faces).

Sign up to the Write Wherever newsletter for updates: whwrites.com/newsletter.

Lastly, if you enjoyed this book, **please consider posting a review**, recommending it on Goodreads or BookBub, or telling a friend who might also enjoy it. As always, thank you for reading, and for your support!

Acknowledgments

It's hard to believe that the Shadows of Otherside series is complete... for now. When I started planning the series in 2016, I only envisioned five books for it. The world has grown so much since then, and the reception has been better than I had dared to hope when I decided to self-publish *Elemental.* Now there's a spin-off trilogy planned and maybe, just maybe, more to come for Arden and friends in a new cycle (after I work on some other projects).

Writing and publishing three books every year is a huge undertaking, and the ongoing support of family, friends, and readers was sometimes the only thing that carried me through— that, and knowing how much people wanted to see the next book. I'm so grateful to my parents, sister, and RSL. My mom always told me to speak my truth, however it needed to be spoken, and gave me the courage to write all this. My dad's pride in me and my work uplifted me. My sister's commitment to living her life her way and shining bright inspired me. And RSL has always had my back.

This book in particular was a labor of love, drafted through the tail end of extreme burnout. But through it all, I had this story, and I had you, dear readers. So thank you for being there. Thank you for your enthusiasm, your reviews, and your social media posts. Thank you to those who told me my stories kept them up past their bedtime, distracted at work, or had them forgetting to pick up their kids. Thank you for investing your time, money, and attention in a Black indie author with a dream. Thank you for sharing my books with your friends, family, and colleagues.

My beta reader for the series, Stephanie, played a big role in letting me know whether I was on track. Good beta readers are invaluable, and I'm grateful I found one!

Again, thanks also go to the book blogging community. Their work is so vital to what authors and publishers do, and especially to indie authors who rely on word of mouth to drive early discovery when ad budgets are tight.

Last but not least, thank you to editor Jeni Chappelle for shepherding me and especially this last book, giving much-needed perspective and, when needed, a pep talk. I still remember sitting in a taco restaurant when Jeni, then a stranger but already someone whose work I admired, encouraged me to take the plunge and participate in #RevPit. And that, my friends, is probably why you had this whole series—so never doubt your ability to impact one person and make a ripple.

I hope you all enjoyed this bookish journey…and will join me on those to come.

Also by Whitney Hill

The Shadows of Otherside series

Elemental
Eldritch Sparks
Ethereal Secrets
Ebon Rebellion
Eternal Huntress

The Otherside Heat series

Secrets and Truths

The Flesh and Blood series (as Remy Harmon)

Bluebloods

About the Author

 Whitney Hill is an author and speaker. The bestselling first book in her Shadows of Otherside series, *Elemental*, was the grand prize winner of the 8th Annual Writer's Digest Self-Published E-Book Awards and a Finalist in the Next Generation Indie Book Awards.

When she's not writing, Whitney enjoys hiking in North Carolina's beautiful state parks and playing video games.

Learn more or get in touch: whitneyhillwrites.com
More books by Whitney: whitneyhillwrites.com/original-fiction
Sign up to receive email updates: whwrites.com/newsletter

Join her on social media:
- Twitter: twitter.com/write_wherever
- Instagram: instagram.com/write_wherever
- Facebook: facebook.com/WhitneyHillWrites

Get bonus content on Patreon: patreon.com/writewherever

CPSIA information can be obtained
at www.ICGtesting.com
Printed in the USA
LVHW010307250222
711939LV00004B/112